MR. ALBERT

Mr. Albert

The story of an ex-person.

A.F. WINTER

TKOIC Publishing

TKOIC Publishing
P.O. Box 114
Summerville, S.C. 29484
www.afwinter2011.com

Publisher's Note: This is a work of fiction. Names, characters, places, and incidents are a product of the author's imagination. Locales and Public names are sometimes used for atmospheric purposes. Any resemblance to actual people, living or dead, or to businesses, companies, events, institutions, or locales is completely coincidental.

Mr. Albert/ A.F. Winter
ISBN 978-1-7367793-1-6
First Printing, 2023

I dedicate this book to all the people I have hurt in my life.
I ask for forgiveness even though I know I will not be forgiven.
One still must ask.
One still must pray.
One still must hope.

Introduction

This book is a plavel, which is somewhere between a novel and a play. I have toyed with the term navay, but plavel seems more distasteful. And many people have found the form unpleasant. If you are one of these people, please refer to the dedication for my apology.

I have created this new literary form for this work because I do not want to change it to fit into the accepted structures. Mr. Albert, both book and character, seems perfectly suited for this unorthodox format. It has more dialogue and less narration than your average novel, and it is way too long and has too much narration for your standard play. So, a plavel it is.

And being that it is a whole new literary form, I ask for it to be read in a new way. Of course, it can be read in the old way, or in any manner that gives you pleasure, but here is my suggestion. Instead of a book club, where every member has already read the work and then come together to discuss its merits, I suggest that participants come together to read it aloud and discuss it chapter by chapter, similar to a play reading during the first week of a rehearsal process. Each participant reads a character, and one person reads what little narration there is.

However, you choose to experience this book; I hope you enjoy it.

Lives Lost

Lives lost in the memory of time.
She whispers wisps of stolen kisses
Behind a curtain,
Where sunken souls
Share no joy
In dream clouded halls.
Spirits pass like strangers
On business no longer vital,
For crypted customers
Whose eyes will remain forever closed
Lives are lost when all is forgotten.
All who would mourn are gone as well.
And we, the souls of the departed
Are apparitions forever moving
To the moaning and the groaning of the bells.

~ 1 ~

Another Beginning.
In an examination room.
The present-day.

"I'm sorry to say, Mr. Albert, that you are dead."
"Dead?"
"Dead."
"Dead?"
"Yes, Mr. Albert, you're dead."
"How could that be?"
"Well, you have no brain function, and you have no heartbeat, so you are dead."
"But doctor, how can I speak without a brain?"
"Well, son, it seems to me a lot of people do that nowadays."
The doctor chuckled.
"If I'm dead, is this heaven?"
"I hope not."
"Is this hell?"
"Only if you don't like New Jersey."
After some thought.
"Am I a ghost?"
"You mean some disembodied spirit who remains on this temporal plain?"
"Yes."
The doctor slapped Mr. Albert across his face.

"Owww! That hurt!"

"Well, you are not disembodied."

"You knew I wasn't disembodied."

"I was just making sure. You never know."

"You just wanted to slap me."

"That could be true."

Mr. Albert mumbled to himself about the injustices of life. A thought occurred to him.

"Well, am I a zombie?"

"Do you feel like you want to eat my brain now? With Fava beans and a little Chianti?"

"No, not really, but I never liked organ meats as far as I can remember."

"I guess the whole zombie thing is not applicable then."

A slight pause.

"Yes, this is a mystery."

"How about a god? Am I a god?"

The doctor spent a moment in contemplation, pondering the notion that he might be having a conversation with a higher being. He filled a plastic cup with water and placed it beside Mr. Albert.

"Turn the water into wine."

"What?"

"A Cannonau, from Sardinia. I heard that was the healthiest wine around."

"You want me to change this water into a cup of wine?"

"Yes. A Cannonau from Sardinia, if you please."

Mr. Albert squinted and made an uncomfortable face. The water remained as it was. The doctor seemed disappointed.

"Then I guess you are not a god."

"Well, what do I do now?"

"I would suggest that you go about and do the same things that you usually do. Eventually, your body will give out on you, and you'll actually be dead instead of this kind of dead."

"Oh."

"Or you can stay in the hospital and be tested."

"Tested?"

"You know, the whole autopsy thing."

"But I'm not dead!"

"Clinically, you are."

"No, I'm not."

"Yes, Mr. Albert, you are. I don't believe I have ever come across a case like this."

"I think I'd rather go out into the world."

"Probably a good idea before some government agency gets wind of this."

"You won't tell?"

"Believe me; I'm going to have a hard enough time trying to bill you."

~ 2 ~

10 minutes later.
On the street in front of Mother of Mercy Hospital.

The cold breeze blew down the nearly deserted streets of Wildwinds, New Jersey. This small seaside town, overshadowed by the bigger attractions in the area, never quite got going. Local politicians always had lofty ideas but shallow pockets. A small amusement park, a half-dozen bars, a greasy spoon, three fast-food restaurants, a few mid-range hotels, and a boardwalk in need of so much repair that it was dangerous to walk on it in bare feet was all the town had to its name. It was a good place to disappear in. Maybe that is why Mr. Albert was here.

The winds picked up. He started walking, but he could not figure out where to go. After his examination, his mind was a little cloudy. Where did he live? Did he have a family? Was anyone missing him? Worried about him? He didn't know.

He stopped walking. He looked up from the sidewalk. Before him was the Wiener King, Wildwinds most famous wienery. They boiled their hot dogs in beer and cooked their French Fries in oil that has not been changed since the Department of Health was incorporated into the Department of Animal Control several years ago.

"Ah, wieners!" Mr. Albert exclaimed joyfully as he entered. "Two, please, with the works."

The man behind the counter looked like he had seen better days. Maybe he was an alcoholic trying to get his life together. Maybe he was just released from the big house. Mr. Albert didn't know the man's story, but it didn't matter as long as he could throw a couple of hot dogs on a couple of buns and smatter them with sauerkraut, mustard, and ketchup.

Mr. Albert took his dogs and sat by the window on a small two-top table. The table rocked when he put his hot dogs on it. His chair rocked when he sat down. He got up and tried the other chair. It rocked less. He decided on the second chair, but the view was not as good as from the other side of the table. Mr. Albert stood up and shot the wiener man a disgruntled look. The wiener man did not care. Mr. Albert moved the good chair, or the less bad chair, to the more bad chair's side of the table and the more bad chair to the less bad chair's side of the table. He sat down.

The people that stay in a seaside town during the off-season are a strange group of birds, disappearing when the paying customers approach, thought Mr. Albert. *They hated the tourists but needed them to survive because they were not brave enough to stand on their own.*

Mr. Albert sensed he was very angry. He wondered if he was just as mad when he was alive or if this was a part of his death. Are all dead people angry? If there was a God, and Mr. Albert was not entirely sure there was one, being in his present situation should certainly lead one to thoughts on the subject. And God made Heaven and Hell; wouldn't the spirits be disgusted at the people still around because they are wasting their lives?

He didn't know how to feel about being dead. This didn't seem like the normal turn of events. Why was he so special?

He looked at the wiener man. "Do you believe in the afterlife?"

The man behind the counter dropped his head and shook it back and forth. After a moment, he looked at his customer and shrugged. "I don't know."

Mr. Albert turned to the man. "You don't know, or you haven't thought about it?"

"Oh, I've thought about it, but we won't know until we die."

"But what if we are dead and still don't know?"

"That would be very cruel of God."

"Yes, it would." Mr. Albert turned away from the man and took another bite of his hot dog. "But how could a God who created such a marvelous thing as this hot dog also be so cruel?"

"Are you going to stay here long because we are closing at six?"

Mr. Albert looked at the wall clock behind the counter. The time was 5:15. Mr. Albert got the hint. He finished up his meal and went back into the cold wind.

IN THE FORGOTTEN PAST - 01

The first meeting.
Savannah 1955.

Benny Benton bought two hot dogs from Anton's Deli and looked for a nice, quiet bench to enjoy his lunch. He stopped when he heard a soft, lyrical voice floating in the air.

As I went down in the river to pray
Studying about that good ol' way
And who shall wear the starry crown?
Good Lord, show me the way!

He looked around but did not see anyone who could be responsible for such beauty. He walked down the quiet, tree-lined streets in search of the voice.

O sisters let's go down
Let's go down, come on down
O sisters let's go down
Down in the river to pray

Then he saw her, across the street, in a corner house behind an iron fence, under a big, beautiful tree with Spanish Moss. He stood there, transfixed. His feet unable to move. He reached into his paper bag and pulled out a hot dog. Benny consumed it as if it was a spiritual act. He finished the second one soon after.

As I went down in the river to pray
Studying about that good ol' way
And who shall wear the robe and crown?
Good Lord, show me the way
O sinners, let's go down
Let's go down, come on down
O sinners, let's go down

The girl was the most beautiful angel he had ever seen in this world. And if he had ever visited another world, he was sure she would be more beautiful than any alien angel as well. He was so caught up with what an alien would look like that he didn't notice she was singing directly to him.

As I went down in the river to pray
Studying about that good ol' way
And who shall wear the robe and crown?
Good Lord, show me the way.

On her last note, he returned to the present and saw her beautiful eyes. She smiled, and he dropped the wiener-less Anton's deli bag. The untouched pickle, still inside, rolled onto the sidewalk. He picked up the bag with one hand and the pickle with the other. Trying to look casual, he took a bite out of the pickle before realizing it had been on the pavement. He didn't want to spit the gherkin out in front of the girl, so he swallowed it. He bowed to her deeply from the waist and then popped up like one of those toy bobbing birds. He half-cringed, half-smiled, and ran off in the direction from which he came.

And that was the first time Benny saw Genevieve.

~ 3 ~

Five hours later.
Pirate's Cove Amusement Park.

Mr. Albert had been walking for hours. He knew he had a wallet and could easily take it out. He could find out where he lived. He could look for pictures of a wife and family. But he didn't have the desire. If he had a family, they probably thought he was dead. Then he would show up and say, *"Hi honey, I'm back!"* Then he would have to explain to them that he was really dead. Then they would be upset again. He knew he would have to tell them someday, but not today.

He stood in front of a Tilt-A-Whirl, which during the summer, would throw small children into the other occupants of their car and give them mild cases of whiplash in the name of fun. There was a rollercoaster on his left and a Ferris wheel serving as a background for this small amusement park. It had a pirate theme, so there were fiberglass statues of parrots, alligators, and one-legged buccaneers scattered about in odd places.

"What are you doing here?" the security guard barked.

Mr. Albert did not stir. What was the guy going to do, arrest him? He was dead. What does a night in the slammer matter?

"Excuse me. The park is closed for the winter." The guard's tone softened as he realized the intruder was not a drunk teenager going to do some damage on a dare.

Mr. Albert turned to him and smiled. He was just doing his job. After all, it wasn't the rent-a-cop's fault he was an ex-person.

"The park is closed. You'll have to go," the guard insisted.

"I was out walking, and the park looked so beautiful in its emptiness. The gate was open in the back."

"Employee's entrance."

"I'm sorry."

"Honest mistake. Most of the other guards think this place is creepy, but I agree with you. It is beautiful in its despair."

"Despair," Mr. Albert said, thinking of his situation.

"Follow me." The guard motioned for Mr. Albert to follow.

On this cold November night, the patrolman seemed glad to have someone to talk to for a while. They walked over to the merry-go-round. Carved faces of clowns adorned the top of the children's ride, smiling and laughing, but also trying a bit too hard to appear happy. The men walked around it, looking at each carving.

"That's Bobo and Happy, and Curley, and Groucho, and Tiny, and Sebastian. I'm Shelton, by the way." The guard said, pointing at the faces and then ended with his own.

"Hello, Shelton. I'm Derrick," Mr. Albert said, purposely giving a fictitious name.

"You look more like a Carson."

"I have been told that before."

"Really?" said Shelton, quite pleased with himself.

"No, who in their right mind would name their kid Carson?"

"I think Carson is a cool name."

"It isn't. And those faces are creepy," Mr. Albert grumbled.

"Are they?" said Shelton. "I think they represent the false faces we wear in public. Revealing to the viewer that they are too afraid to let people in. Too afraid that their heart will be broken again."

Shelton remained fixated on Sebastian, his body leaning slightly to the left.

"You got that from this clown here?" Mr. Albert pointed to a particularly disturbing face.

"Fiberglass figures whose faces are frozen in happiness, like an old woman who had too many facelifts," the guard said, staring at the figure.

"From that, you got that?" Mr. Albert realized that if he was alive, he probably would be afraid of his new friend. But he was dead, so what the hell did he care? "Well, I am dead," he said to stir the pot.

"We have all been dead from the moment we were born. Walking the world as a sleepwalker. Unaware. Unaware. Terrified to be woken from our slumbers."

"Are you high?"

"A little."

"Are you drunk?"

"A little."

"How the hell are you going to stop marauding hordes of vandals?"

"We usually don't get too many troublemakers on a school night. I'm hungry. Are you hungry?"

"I could eat."

The night watchman walked off, leaving the trespasser. After a moment, Mr. Albert followed. Shelton played with the set of keys attached to his belt with a retractable cord. Pulling on them and then releasing them repeatedly as if he had a nervous tick. He opened the concession stand. Mr. Albert tried to follow him, but Shelton raised his hand as a warning.

"Only employees of The Pirate Cove Amusement Park L.L.C. can enter the concession stand."

"It's cold."

"Is anyone watching you?"

"Only the clowns and the one-legged pirates?"

"Horace?" Shelton asked suspiciously.

"I'm Derrick."

"No, is Horace the one-legged buccaneer watching you?"

"No," said Mr. Albert, not knowing exactly which statue was Horace. None of them looked like a Horace.

"Good," Shelton said, signaling Mr. Albert to enter. "I think Horace told the boss I was smoking dope the other day. Hate that bastard."

Shelton reached into the refrigerator, which had been unplugged for the off-season. He pulled out a package of hot dogs.

"How many do you want?"

"When did the season end?"

"Like, Labor Day."

"So, they have been sitting in an unplugged refrigerator for two months?"

"Yeah, so?"

"Aren't you worried about death?" asked Mr. Albert.

"Nah, I have them all the time. The boiling water kills off the bacteria."

Mr. Albert thought that if the dogs didn't kill Shelton, what harm could it do him?

"I'll have two then."

Shelton fired up the cooker, and the two went outside waiting for the ptomaine to die. They sat under the stars. The crescent moon gave them light and reflected off the abandoned rides.

"Any other deep thoughts?"

Shelton did not need to be asked twice. He looked at the Ferris wheel and spouted, "Steely skeletons clutching empty baskets like a spider having just finished sucking the lifeblood from her victim. Dead carcasses caught in her tangled web."

"I liked the clown one better."

"I know. I know." Shelton rubbed his fingers through his hair. He had the soul of a tortured poet.

"It is pretty good though," Mr. Albert said, not wishing to hurt his feelings.

Shelton sat up smiling, ready to face the world and his demons again.

"You said that you are dead?"

"Yes."

"No."

"Yes."

"Prove it."

"Take my pulse," Mr. Albert said, extending his hand.

Shelton felt Mr. Albert's pulse. "I don't feel anything."

"See."

Shelton tried to take his own pulse. After a minute, he said, "I don't feel anything either. Could I be dead as well?"

"Keep eating those expired wienies, and you will be soon enough."

"Oh, the dogs," Shelton said, jumping up to get dinner.

He returned with two plates, handing one to Mr. Albert before sitting down.

"So, you are dead?"

"I am."

"Crazy.... How did that happen?"

"I don't know, Shelton."

"Why aren't you pushing up daisies?"

"I don't know, Shelton."

"Maybe God has given you another chance."

"Another chance at what?"

"I don't know. To enjoy yourself."

Mr. Albert could not remember if he ever enjoyed himself. But he could not remember any details of his past.

"I don't know if I ever enjoyed myself."

"Don't you think it is time to start?"

"There must have been a time. Everyone has moments of happiness. I just can't remember. Happiness," Mr. Albert pondered, deep in thought.

"Well, don't you think you deserve it?"

"I don't know."

"That's stupid. Everyone deserves happiness," Shelton said, finishing his first dog.

"Does everyone deserve happiness? And if they do, does that mean they will get it?"

"I hope."

"You are young."

They sat in silence for a moment.

"These dogs are good," Shelton smiled because he had already forgotten about hope and happiness.

"Yes, Shelton, they are. Not as good as the Wiener King's, but they are good enough for right now."

"I could eat these dogs, like forever."

"I'd give you another two months," Mr. Albert mumbled.

They finished their wieners in satisfied silence. Mr. Albert thought of something.

"Shelton, could you do me a favor? Will you look at my wallet for pictures of a wife and kids? I can't remember if I was married before I died."

"Sure," Shelton looked through Mr. Albert's wallet. "Nope, no wives or kids."

"That's a relief."

"Why?"

"No one to go home to. No one to explain this to. What else do I have in there?"

"Couple of credit cards. Driver's license, fifty bucks."

He took the wallet back and looked at his license.

"Albert Albert. That's a stupid name," Mr. Albert said, disappointed.

"I thought you said your name was Derrick."

"Did I? I must have forgotten. It says I live at 9200 Atlantic Ave."

"That's about three blocks down."

"Which way?"

"That way," Shelton said, pointing to the left and then, thinking about it, pointed to the right. "Come on. I'll take you."

"Don't you have to watch for vandals?"

"I told you, a school night."

Shelton rolled his bloodshot eyes.

"What about Horace?"

"Fuck him!" Shelton shouted. And then he thought better of his outburst. "I know a back way out."

So, Mr. Albert followed Shelton two blocks to the right and then five blocks to the left before arriving at his home. Before them stood Lucy, the Elephant, a six-story novelty structure that now offers accommodations.

"You live there? You are the coolest dead person I have ever met."

"It looks like it's closed for renovation," said Mr. Albert, saddened.

"You probably just used the address to get a license."

"Possibly."

"It is still pretty cool."

"Yes, it is, Shelton. Yes, it is."

~ 4 ~

Two weeks later.
Two thirty on a Wednesday afternoon.
McKenna's bar.

McKenna's is a seedy place on a back street of Wildwinds that miraculously avoided demolition in the early days of gentrification due to its quirky history. The boom has long been over, and the trendy twenty-year-olds who filled the bars years ago because of its "authenticity" have gone on to other trendy spots. Now the dark bar has been reclaimed by the local alcoholics, like weeds in an abandoned mental hospital.

The owner, Mac, a retired policeman, arrested most of his bar's regular clientele at one time or another, but now both ex-officer and ex-cons have settled into a comfortable retirement flowing with cheap booze and forgiveness.

Mr. Albert was talking to Walter, who had been in the bar for a couple of hours before Mr. Albert arrived. He told Walter of his particular situation, and Walter readily accepted the story as if Mr. Albert had told him of an annoying bunion.

"Did you ever know someone whose life was a string of mishaps?" asked Walter, thinking of his own life.

"What do you mean?" asked Mr. Albert.

"I mean a never-ending shitstorm. Where every day is a disaster waiting to happen, and it usually does."

"I think everyone has their ups and downs, Walter."

"Bert, you're dead. Where's the upside?"

"It could be worse."

"How?"

"What?"

"How could it be worse?"

"I don't know," Mr. Albert fumbled for an answer. "But the thing about life is that it could always get worse. You could be sitting in a pile of shit with woodpeckers pecking at your eyes on a hot summer's day, and you say, *my God, this is it; I'm rock bottom. You don't think it could get any worse, but then it does, and you think, oh geez, that time before, that wasn't so bad. What I wouldn't give to go back to sitting happily on my pile of shit! That time, now that time was a good time.*"

"But you're dead."

"I don't think it matters. It never has before."

"You think this could get worse?"

"I think there is a little room for waning," Mr. Albert smiled.

"Waning? What the hell is that, Bert?"

"It is the opposite of improving."

"Waning, my ass. You are an idiot," Walter grumbled, draining his glass.

"So, you don't want me to buy you another round, Walter?"

"Maybe just one more."

Mr. Albert signaled Mac to fill up their drinks.

Savannah 1955.

"What are you going to do? Just stand here for the rest of your life? Or are you gonna come over and talk to me?" Genevieve appeared behind Benny, tapping her foot. Although she was twenty-three, she stood with her weight thrown to her left side in the manner of a much younger girl.

"I don't know. Maybe just stand here and listen to you sing your music."

"Well, that's stupid when you can talk to me."

"I am talking to you."

"And isn't it better?"

"Yes. It is. I think."

Genevieve laughed at his awkwardness.

"It's warm today, isn't it?" she asked in an attempt to make him less uncomfortable.

"Yes, it is." He took off his pork-pie hat and waved it in front of his face. Then thinking he was being rude, he waved it in front of her as well.

"Would you like something to drink?"

"I think so," Benny said, as he stared into her eyes that were so blue, they looked like a cloudless sky on a spring day.

She grabbed his hand and pulled him across the street. She slammed the gate behind them after they entered her yard.

"Momma, I got him, and he's thirsty!" She yelled.

He turned to the front door, then to Genevieve, and then to the gate. He looked as if he was trapped in a cage. Even though the latch was at waist level, he couldn't figure out how to escape. But he wasn't sure if he wanted to.

Mrs. Margaret Pierpont appeared almost immediately with a tray of lemonade and pecan shortbread cookies as if she had been expecting company. She brought it over to the lime green metal patio furniture on the other side of the walk from the big tree where Genevieve sang her songs. Genevieve sat her new friend on the right side, and she sat on the left. Mrs. Pierpont presided over the ceremony from the center.

"So, what is this charming young man's name?"

"I don't know, Momma; he hasn't told me."

"Benny, ma'am."

"Well, Benjamin, you've been watching our Genevieve for a month."

"I'm sorry, ma'am. I know it was rude, but she was so pretty, and her voice was so pretty that I couldn't come over."

"Why not," Genevieve pouted.

"You were like a dream, and I didn't want to wake up."

Genevieve turned to her mother as if to say; *I can handle this.* "Thank you, Momma. You can go now because I know you have something in the oven."

"No, dear, it could wait."

"No, it couldn't, Mother," Genevieve insisted.

Mrs. Pierpont smiled at her daughter and then turned to Benny.

"Genevieve is right again. I have something in the oven."

With that, she went back into the house and only peeked through the window when things got too quiet. And things got very quiet because Benny did not say much, a yes here and a no there, but that was all right. Genevieve could talk enough for the both of them.

~ 5 ~

A week later.
On the pier.

Mr. Albert had fallen asleep on the pier. There was something in the cold, salty air that made him sleepy. He could not be sure, but he thought he used to enjoy some fresh air. That always made him feel alive. Alive! What a thought! To be alive again instead of dead and just pretending to be alive. He certainly didn't try to deceive anyone. He existed. What is the point of deception? He also wasn't trying to impress anyone, which is why he fell asleep on the pier.

It was dark when he woke up. The streetlights were off, so he figured it was after two in the morning. The light of the full moon and the scattered lights from the hotels on the beach cast enough glow on the pier that there would be no danger of falling into the water. *That would be a rough one*, thought Mr. Albert.

They always seemed to fish out a couple of drowners every winter. Someone would get too drunk and stumble down to the pier after the bars closed. Either accidentally or on purpose, they'd fall into the cold water below. Sometimes they were naked. Those were the ones that wanted to end it all, leaving a note on neatly folded clothes. "I'm sorry, world, blah, blah, blah."

They were the lucky ones. They made a decision, and they followed through. What would he do if he wanted to die? Mr. Albert had as much say over his life as he had over his death. It's all blah, blah, blah.

He looked up to the end of the pier and saw a figure standing on a bench looking over the ocean. Mr. Albert stood up, wobbling. Getting up in the night was not a favorite thing for him to do. Plus, he had to pee. Why do dead people have to pee? Doesn't seem quite fair.

"Oi," he shouted, slowly approaching the jumper.

The man turned around. "Stay back," he threatened. "I'll jump."

"Go ahead."

"What?"

"Go ahead, jump. I don't know you."

"You want to watch?"

"Might be interesting."

"I'd die!" the man cried.

"I know."

"You wouldn't want to stop me?"

"What good would that do?"

"Probably not much."

"Then why should we both be miserable?" Mr. Albert blah, blah, blahhed. "You with your sad story and me trying to help someone who won't listen."

"Do you know me?"

"I don't think so."

"Then how do you know I have a sad story?" The man objected to the stranger's premise.

"You are about to jump off the pier into the water, in November, in the middle of the night. If you don't have a sad story, I don't know what it could be. Is this a dare?"

"No, it is not a dare. How stupid do you think I am?"

"You are about to jump off the pier into the water, in November, in the middle of the night. How smart can you be?" Mr. Albert taunted the jumper.

"You are not a very nice person."

"True, but I don't see anyone else around now. So why don't you tell me about it?" Mr. Albert sat down on the next bench over.

"Do you really want to know?"

"I have to pee."

The man sat down, relaxing slightly. "This woman I am seeing, had been seeing for five years, left me for another guy."

"Okay, I've got to go," Mr. Albert said, losing patience.

"Wait."

"I told you I have to pee."

"Don't you care?"

"Were you married?"

"No."

"Did you have kids?"

"No."

"So, what are you worried about?" Mr. Albert barked. "She left you. Good riddance."

"But I loved her."

"Love? You were having sex. At least, I hope you were having sex. You liked it, and she didn't—end of story. Move on or not, but don't think yours was the greatest tragic love story ever written. That was Romeo and Juliet, and their story was just as stupid. Teen-age hormones. Love," Mr. Albert harrumphed.

"You are one to talk." The man said, rising from the bench and stomping his feet as he paced. "What, are you homeless? Who broke your heart? You are in no better place than I am, but you don't have the guts to end it all. At least I have a job, a good one. Got a ton of money in the bank, a nice car, a three-bedroom apartment, ocean view. What do you have?"

"Less than you," Mr. Albert responded, squeezing his thighs together in agony.

"See!" the man sneered. "Telling me."

"You got stuff."

"I have stuff."

"You have a good life," Mr. Albert said, waving his hand in a circular manner, hoping to hurry the man up.

"I have a good life."

"Then why do you want to jump?"

The jumper sank onto his bench.

"I just thought it was real this time."

"Wasn't it?"

"I guess not."

"Wasn't it real for you?"

"Yes."

"She gave you five years of her life," Mr. Albert comforted him.

"Yes."

"Maybe that was all she could give you."

"Maybe."

"So, I would be happy with that."

"Would you?"

"Seems like I would be ungrateful if I weren't," Mr. Albert said, trying to decide if he would be.

"I have a decent job."

"Yes, you do."

"And a nice car, a Tesla."

"How many miles does that get?"

"300 miles on a charge," the jumper marveled at the engineering.

"Nice. And you have a three-bedroom apartment."

"Ocean view."

"Ocean view. You seem like a fortunate man."

"I guess I am. I think you may have just saved my life. My name is Santo Murphy. What is your name?"

"Mr. Albert."

"Thank you, Mr. Albert. Are you a religious man?" Santo said after a moment. "I am. I'm a Catholic. I was about to kill myself and be damned forever to hell because of a woman. What was I thinking? But I think God sent you to stop me. You are an angel, Mr. Albert. And I promise to help you. I don't know why you are on the streets, but I give my word to you. What is that smell? It smells like urine. I will help you. Mr. Albert?"

Santo walked over to his angel, who was silent. He tapped his savior, who fell to the wooden slats of the pier. Santo felt Mr. Albert's pulse but felt nothing. He turned to heaven as the sun broke through the horizon. *Ay Dio Mio* escaped from his lips.

~ 6 ~

Several hours later.
Mother of Mercy Hospital.
In the Morgue.

"Aw, fuck," Mr. Albert moaned, realizing where he was.

It was pitch black. He was in a bag. The cold metal tray he was lying on slid back and forth when he pushed against the constricting walls of the refrigeration unit.

"Well, this is great. Nothing to do but wait. Wait until they come to perform the autopsy. That will be quite a shock, quite a shock indeed. Hold on there; I'm not quite dead. Well, I am dead, but not really. I don't know what I am. Hard to define. Hard to figure out. Anyway, it's not for you to figure out. You're the coroner. I would think I need a philosopher. What is life? What is living? Is life worth living? Is living life? Or is life more than just breathing, moving, and eliminating?

I hope it is not some old guy. Probably give him a heart attack, and he'll drop dead right in front of me. Should I move when he slides my tray out to give him a warning? He would probably slam me back in, lock it, and then quit and never return. Good for him. Good for him.

I should probably wait until I am on the table and then open my eyes and say, Nothing like a nice nap! Probably still give him a heart attack or else he'll stab me with a knife or cut me with one of

29

those fancy saws. Either way, not something to look forward to. It is either going to work out badly for him or me."

Mr. Albert heard a noise from outside his refrigerated box. The metal conducted sound very well, only slightly muffling the voices.

"The body came in this morning. He just collapsed. An autopsy is scheduled for tomorrow."

"Very well. Do you think I could have a moment alone with the body?"

"It's not for anything weird, is it?"

"No, no. I examined him a couple of weeks ago. A strange case, very strange."

"All right, you have five minutes."

The door slammed, and a moment later, the slab's latch opened, and Mr. Albert's drawer slid out. The bag was unzipped.

"Hello, Mr. Albert," Dr. Johnson smiled warmly.

"Hello, Doctor, I'm glad it was you. Didn't know how a stranger would react to me."

"I'm not quite sure how I should react to you."

"Fair enough. What now?"

"We have to get you out of the morgue."

"How will we do that?"

"What do you mean how will we do that? Are you dead?"

"Technically, yes."

"Do you look dead?"

"Well, not when I'm talking."

"Let's go with that. Peterson?"

The autopsy technician appeared at the door and froze when he saw Mr. Albert sitting on his tray. Dr. Johnson waved the frightened man over.

"There seems to be some misunderstanding," Dr. Johnson smiled. "Mr. Albert was not fully dead, only mostly dead. I need to get him to the third floor to give him a full examination. Can you get me a wheelchair and a hospital robe?"

"Yes, doctor," Peterson stammered. He turned to leave.

"And Peterson, could you bring the patient's possessions?"

"Yes, sir," he said, disappearing through the morgue door.

"Well, that solves that," the doctor smiled at his patient.

"How did you know I was here?"

"When you left me the last time, I didn't think you had long to live, so I put the word out that when a Mr. Albert Albert was brought in, I should be alerted."

"Now, what?"

"I don't know. I can't keep pulling you out of the morgue. People are bound to become suspicious."

Savannah 1955.

After Genevieve took Benny's hand and invited him to tea, he became a fixture in the Pierpont home. Genevieve and her mother had grown accustomed to the sweet, strange young man and often invited him to dinner. Mrs. Pierpont noticed Genevieve had taken a romantic interest in Benny, and so a deeper conversation was needed.

They had just finished dinner. Genevieve cleared the table. When she was in the kitchen, Mrs. Pierpont started the interrogation.

"Benjamin," Mrs. Pierpont said.

"Yes, ma'am."

"You have been a guest in our home for several months."

"Yes, ma'am."

"But we know so little about you. You are always so quiet."

"What would you like to know about me?"

"He is an exceptionally good listener, Mother," Genevieve interrupted. "Most men won't shut up about themselves."

"Please excuse my daughter's vulgarity. But there are questions that a caring mother must ask a suitor."

Benny and Genevieve giggled. Mrs. Pierpont continued without missing a beat.

"Do you have a job, Benjamin?"

"No, ma'am, I don't."

"You don't have a job?" She said, biting her lower lip.

"Is that important?"

"Yes, Benjamin, it is. It gives one a sense of purpose. How will you take care of your wife when the time comes?"

"A wife? Who'd want to be my wife?"

"If you had a job, I think someone would be interested."

Mrs. Pierpont nodded at Genevieve. Genevieve cringed. Benny looked at Genevieve.

"I didn't even know you were my girl. Are you?"

"What do you think we've been doing all this time? Really, Benjamin," Genevieve stormed into the kitchen. "I need another Coke!"

Mrs. Pierpont continued, "How will you be a productive member of society if you are asking people for handouts?"

"If you think it is important, I'll get a job tomorrow. If you think Genevieve would want that."

"She would, dear," After a moment, Mrs. Pierpont asked another question. "What do you do for money?"

"Mr. Thatcher from a bank in Chicago sends me money every month."

"And why does Mr. Thatcher do such a thing?"

"I think it is because I have no mother or father."

"You are an orphan? I'm so sorry." Mrs. Pierpont gently touched Benny's shoulder.

Benny shrugged. "I don't know. I just don't remember them."

"And this Mr. Thatcher from Chicago sends you enough to live on?"

"I think so. If I run out of money, I ask for more."

Genevieve stood in the doorway. The Pierpont women looked at each other in astonishment. They had never heard of such a ridiculous thing.

"And how much does this generous banker from Chicago send you? If you don't mind me asking."

"One thousand a month."

Mrs. Pierpont sat down. "That is what Mr. Pierpont would make in three months. Genevieve, bring your mother a Coke."

"Yes, Mother," she said as she disappeared into the kitchen again.

"In a glass, please, with some ice."

"Yes, mother."

"And honey, bring me the Bacardi as well."

Genevieve returned with the drink, and her mother poured an equal amount of rum into her glass. From that point forward, there was no talk of Benjamin collecting handouts, getting a job, or being a productive member of society.

~ 7 ~

Half an hour later.

Mother of Mercy Hospital.

On the third floor.

Doctor Johnson invited a colleague, Doctor Joseph Mancha, into the examination room for a consultation.

"Mr. Albert, this is Dr. Mancha. He is a neurosurgeon. Dr. Mancha, this is the patient I was telling you about."

Doctor Mancha studied Mr. Albert closely, "You're dead?"

Mr. Albert narrowed his eyes and studied Mancha just as closely, "Yes."

"How can that be?" Mancha asked, taking out a rubber hammer and hitting Mr. Albert's knee. It showed no reflex.

"I have no brain functions," Mr. Albert replied, taking the hammer and smacking himself several times on his head.

"Life is the condition that distinguishes animals and plants from inorganic matter,

including the capacity for growth, reproduction, functional activity, and continual

change preceding death," Mancha lectured the dead man.

"The capacity for growth, reproduction, functional activity. Capacity?" Mr. Albert asked.

"Yes," Doctor Mancha replied.

"So, I do not actually have to perform any of those functions to be alive? I just have to have the capacity."

"Yes."

"So, if I don't do any of those things, I can still be alive?"

"In theory," Mancha said, enjoying the conversation.

"But a dead person doesn't do any of those things," Mr. Albert continued.

"Correct, but a dead person doesn't have the capacity to do them either."

"What if he had the capacity?"

"Then he wouldn't be dead."

"So, if I function in society, I must be alive?"

"You must be alive," agreed the doctor.

"I'm alive!" Mr. Albert screamed happily, holding his hands up to heaven.

"You are alive," Doctor Mancha said, not as cheerfully. "Although I do have a concern with your metabolism."

"My metabolism?"

"The chemical processes occurring within a living cell or organism that are necessary for maintaining life. In metabolic reactions, some substances are broken down to yield energy for vital processes, while other substances, necessary for life, are synthesized."

"And what are your concerns concerning my metabolism?" Mr. Albert challenged the

doctor.

Doctor Johnson chimed in, "You have none."

"So even though I can function in society, and I have the capacity to do things, I have no chemical processes going on within me."

"Yes," Doctor Mancha said, studying Mr. Albert's reaction.

"So, I'm alive on the outside and dead on the inside."

"Yes, very much like my first wife, emotionally, not metabolically. Although I'm not

sure. Never understood that woman."

"So, what am I?" Mr. Albert asked.

"Not sure," Doctor Mancha concluded.

Doctors Johnson and Mancha looked at each other and shrugged.

"Told you that this was a quandary," Doctor Johnson announced.

"So, life is what happens before death?" Mr. Albert pondered.

Doctor Mancha answered, "Yes."

"And death is what happens after life?"

"Yes."

"Seems pretty circular to me," Mr. Albert concluded.

"What?" said Mancha.

"It's just that if life is before death and death is after life, then we don't know what either is. It's a circular definition that doesn't make it comprehensible to anyone. It's like saying a golfer is someone who golfs. What is golf? It is something that a golfer does. Yes, but what does a golfer do? He golfs."

Mr. Albert was particularly proud of the golf analogy because he did not golf. The doctors, however, were not all that impressed.

"I'm famished. Want to grab some lunch?" Dr. Johnson looked at his peer.

"Yum Yums?" Dr. Mancha replied.

"I love their buffet!" Dr. Johnson smiled.

And so ended Mr. Albert's consultation with Doctors Johnson and Mancha.

~ 8 ~

One hour later.
McKenna's Bar.

After Mr. Albert left the doctors, he went to McKenna's bar. He found his friend, Walter.
"Hello, Walter. Haven't moved from that seat for two days?"
"Fuck you."
"Can I buy you a drink?"
"Sit down, Berty boy!" Walter gushed. "Where have you been?"
"The morgue."
"Somebody die?"
"Me, Walter. I'm dead."
"You're not dead."
"I am. I told you all this last time."
"I just met you."
"I sat with you at this very bar two days ago. That's when I told you that I'm dead."
"Stop messing with him," Mac said, bringing Mr. Albert his drink and refilling Walter's glass. "You are a good customer but making fun of poor Walter is just cruel."
"I'm not making fun of him."
"You're not dead," Mac said, beginning to lose patience.
"But I am."
"How could that be?"
"It is a pickle."

Mac grabbed Mr. Albert's wrist to feel his pulse. He was competent at looking for a pulse from his time on the force. Mr. Albert's hand was clammy and cold. Mac could not detect the slightest pulse. He recoiled from his loyal customer in horror.

"Impossible!"

"And yet it is."

"Some things are indisputable," Walter said, after taking a drink.

"My very existence disputes it. Like what?"

"The sky is blue," Walter finished his drink.

"Is it?"

"The Earth is round," Mac argued.

"Is it?" Mr. Albert could do this all day.

"Two and two equals four," Mac said, proving his point and slamming his hand on the bar, waking up Toby, another regular who had fallen asleep.

"Not always," Mr. Albert contended.

"Always. Math never changes," Mac decided to argue with Mr. Albert on this one.

"But sometimes it is different," Mr. Albert accepted the challenge.

"Give me an example."

Mr. Albert thought for a moment.

"Could two plus two equal eleven?"

"Never," boasted the bartender.

"Never?"

"That's what I said."

"What about in base three?"

"Base three?"

"It only uses three numbers: zero, one, and two," Mr. Albert countered. "If I were counting, it would go zero, one, two, ten, eleven. Four in base ten is eleven in base three."

"What the hell are you talking about?" Mac pushed away from the bar in anger.

"I am just saying, if we use a different valid system, we get a different valid result. Maybe you should look at me in base three."

"So, you're alive in base three?"

"Base three, base eleven, who knows, base thirty-seven? Maybe the only base I am dead in is base ten."

"So, could I be dead in base three?"

Mac leaned into Mr. Albert to make him uncomfortable. Mr. Albert smacked him. Mac cried out in pain.

"No, you seem to be alive," Mr. Albert smiled.

"So, if we are in base three," Mac rolled his eyes so that Mr. Albert could see. "Then what is the definition of life?"

"I don't know."

"You don't know?"

"No. I haven't thought about it."

"How could you not think about it?"

"I just haven't," Mr. Albert said, quickly losing interest in the subject.

"Don't you want an explanation?"

"Why?"

"To make things clearer."

"Why is clarity important? I am here. I am annoying you. That is all that matters."

"But what if I wasn't here?"

"Then, most probably, I would be annoying someone else."

"I can see that," Mac agreed.

"Humans are the only creatures on the planet that we know of, who need to find meaning. We build all these artificial religious and philosophical systems to give us hope and purpose. But in the end, we die without meaning, hope, or purpose." Mr. Albert finished his beer.

"You haven't died," Mac argued.

"Not yet."

"If you are not living or dead in base ten, then you must have a purpose. What are you trying to tell us?" Mac demanded.

"Damned if I know."

"You don't think you have a purpose?"

"No."

"You don't think your life-in-death is meaningful?" Mac said, demanding an answer.

"Only if you give it meaning. I saw a puppy the other day while walking in the park."

"Yes?"

"It came up to me, wagged its tail, and licked me."

Mr. Albert pointed to his empty glass to indicate he would never finish his story unless his glass was filled. Mac brought him over another drink.

"Right," Mr. Albert toasted the barman. "The puppy didn't care if I were white, black, Christian, Muslim, alive or dead. It just did what it always does. It was being a puppy. Would it help the puppy if it thought it had a higher purpose? Is it sad because it doesn't?"

"It protects its master," Mac argued. "Isn't that a higher purpose?"

"It will protect any master. It will protect anyone who feeds it."

"So, people should be like dogs?"

"Wouldn't that be nice?" Mr. Albert leaned back and savored his beverage. "Treat everyone kindly. Be happy in the moment, and if you are stuck in a house where the person who feeds you dies, eat them."

"That's what you are bringing to humanity? Be kind. Be in the moment. Eat dead people who have treated you kindly?"

"Well, I guess that's a start," Mr. Albert concluded triumphantly.

Mac's head fell to his chest while shaking it. Walter and Mr. Albert clinked their shot glasses and nodded in agreement, downing their drinks immediately. Walter let out an enormous belch and smiled. Mr. Albert saw that as a challenge and knocked back his beer chaser. He produced a burp not half as impressive as Walter's but still considered himself the winner because Walter had fallen off his chair and lay unconscious on the floor.

Savannah 1957.

"Momma, Momma, we're back!" Genevieve burst through the front door.

Mrs. Pierpont entered the dining room from the kitchen carrying a tray of lemonade and pecan shortbread cookies.

"There you are, Sweetpea; I was expecting you ages ago," she said, putting the refreshments down on the dining room table.

"Well, you know Benny, he's afraid of driving. Hardly got behind the wheel the whole time."

"Really dear, I don't know why he bought such a fancy car."

"For me, Momma, of course," Genevieve burst out laughing and hugged her mother as if they had not seen each other in years.

"Where is our conquering hero?" Mrs. Pierpont said, wiping the joyful tears from her eyes. She had missed the newlyweds. The house was so lonely without them, and for the first time in many years, she missed Mr. Pierpont.

Mr. Pierpont had worked as an assistant manager at the Liberty National Bank. He looked after his wife and two daughters in life and provided for them after the lung cancer took him. He was a good man, and all Mrs. Pierpont ever wanted. She never thought of marrying again after he passed, but her love softened to fondness over the years, and eventually, she hardly thought of him at all. She still had their children to look after and the home to manage. When the house was empty, she thought of her husband with sadness.

Now that the children had returned, all would be gay again, she thought.

"He's getting the luggage from the back," Genevieve cooed, moving towards the window. She parted the sheer curtains and smiled at her husband and her four-wheeled wedding present, a 1957 Studebaker Silver Hawk. Her mother joined her and laughed as Benny fumbled with the bags. She opened the door. He smiled at his mother-in-law, then tripped on the front step, nearly dropping his cargo.

"Oh, be careful, dear!"

"Hello, Mrs. Pierpont," he said, with a great smile.

"Uh, uh, uh," she said, wagging her finger to correct him.

"Sorry, Mother," he rolled his eyes and waggled his head before kissing her on the cheek.

As soon as the required kiss was complete, he noticed the lemonade. He dropped everything and made a beeline for the table.

"Lemonade *and* pecan cookies! I'm the luckiest guy in the whole wide world."

The women burst out in laughter and picked up the bags before joining Benny.

"All these bags, you'd think you were traveling to the moon!"

"Really, Mother. Maybe we should have gone to Savannah Beach or into a bomb shelter like the Mininsons!"

"Stop being so dramatic."

"I would have taken you anywhere," Benny chimed in, eating another cookie.

"I know you would have," Genevieve said, giving her husband a quick kiss and wiping the crumbs from his jacket.

"I did like the mermaids. Weeki Wachee, what a name!"

"Yes, dear, why don't you tell me all about it," Mrs. Pierpont said, humoring him but looking at her daughter.

"Well, Mrs. Pierpont, I mean Mother, there were these beautiful women in one-piece swimsuits. I mean, not as beautiful as Genevieve, but still nothing to shake a stick at."

"Or to sneeze at," Genevieve giggled.

"Right, no shaking or sneezing. Anyway, they did a ballet and ate bananas, all underwater!"

"Oh, goodness!" Mrs. Pierpont said, covering her mouth to hide her amusement.

The women enjoyed Benny's enthusiasm. And they loved this man who looked at life through the eyes of a child.

"Genevieve, what was the song that they sang?" Benny asked, finishing his third cookie.

"They sang a song underwater?"

"Of course, Mother, while eating a banana," Genevieve gushed.

"Genevieve, sing your mother the song."

She smiled at her adorable man, "Yes, dear."

We're not like other women,

We don't have to clean an oven

And we never will grow old,

We've got the world by the tail!

~ 9 ~

Two hours later.
On the pier.

Santo Murphy sat on the pier for several hours after the paramedic pronounced Mr. Albert dead. He was stunned that his guardian angel was gone. In his mind, that only proved that Mr. Albert was a true angel, sent from above to prevent Santo from doing the unthinkable and suffering eternal damnation.

At noon he went to the convenience store at the corner of Beach and Main. He bought some candles, three plastic flowers at the checkout counter, a cup of coffee, and a package of Yankee Doodles. His father always thought they were the best pastry ever created; a chocolate cupcake filled with vanilla cream. "How did they do that?" he often wondered out loud.

The taste of the Doodle was bittersweet. He had lost his father ten years ago and his guardian angel today. The new loss brought up unresolved feelings from his previous loss. Loss is loss. The mind doesn't separate, and the heart doesn't forget.

He sat the rest of the day on the boardwalk, leaning against the rails that less than twelve hours before he was about to jump over. People passed him, looking through the corners of their eyes, trying to figure out if he was dangerous.

By five in the afternoon, the sun fell behind the boardwalk hotels, throwing long shadows on the beach. The streetlights came on. Santo felt the cold ocean breeze. He was hungry and had to go to the bathroom. But all those physical discomforts could not get him to move. He was not done remembering Mr. Albert or his father.

Yankee Doodles and Yankee games and walking on the boardwalk in Coney Island. His father would light a smoke and lean over the rails, a bottle of Schlitz in his hand, a picture postcard looking off into the distance, dreaming of adventure. Then his left hand would rise slowly to his mouth, his lips embracing the burning cigarette. His whole body would inhale, the cigarette's tip coming alive in bright orange. Then his hand would fall, and his father would stop again. After a minute or two, in the young boy's mind, the fumes from deep within his father's lungs slowly escaped, engulfing him in a blanket of smoke. Then his right hand would rise, and his old man would drink from the bottle. After another minute, a huge burp would explode, shaking his whole body, followed by a sly smile as he looked around to see how many people he offended. His old man did not care for anyone except his wife, Maria, his beautiful Mexican bride. His Irish Catholic parents just about disowned him for bringing that wetback to their home. He didn't care. Begrudgingly, they accepted her; at least she was Catholic, they thought.

That acceptance only lasted until the cigarettes took his father, and then the family shunned her and the half-breeds she conceived. So much for the Christian belief about accepting the stranger and loving all people. His mother forgave them and bore her isolation bravely, but Santo knew how much pain his grandparents caused her. He was not as forgiving as his mother.

He looked up from his memories and saw Mr. Albert. Santo screamed and put up both hands to keep the ghost away that had come to haunt him.

"Please, please, Mr. Albert, I am sorry I was thinking hateful thoughts about my grandparents. I have not let go of my anger toward them. I have not turned the other cheek. Please, forgive me."

"Sure," said Mr. Albert casually.

"What?"

"You want me to forgive you? I forgive you."

"Bless you, my guardian angel. You have shown me the way. You have shown me what forgiveness means and how to practice it."

"What are you going on about?"

"Forgiveness is easy with a loving heart. From this moment forward, I will live with an open, loving heart."

"Do what you want; it doesn't matter to me," Mr. Albert grunted.

"Let things go. Yes, live in the moment. I dedicate my life to your teachings."

"You are an idiot. I came here to see if you jumped. Thinking about it now, I wish you had. Save the world from all this blah, blah, blah."

"You are not here to save my soul?"

"What do I care about your soul?"

"But God has sent you from Heaven to protect me!"

"The only thing you need protecting from is you! Who wanted to kill you? You did! And what is this nonsense about not forgiving people? That's you as well! You keep getting in your own way. Get out of the way and let you through!"

Mr. Albert turned to walk away.

"No, wait, Mr. Albert."

"What?"

"I know that you are my guardian angel. And you have come back from the dead because your job is not done yet."

"I am not your guardian angel, and I did not come back from the dead."

"But you were dead. The paramedic said!"

"Yes. I was dead."

"And now you're back."

"I am back, but I am still dead. And I was dead when I talked to you last night."

"Metaphorically?"

"I was dead then, and I'm still dead."

"Ay Dios Mío! It's a miracle!" Santo proclaimed.

"It's not a miracle. It's an anomaly."

"Aren't all anomalies miracles?"

"No. I think an anomaly is something people haven't figured out yet. A miracle can be explained with only one explanation."

"And what is the explanation?"

"Ay Dios Mío." Mr. Albert said, pointing up to heaven.

"But how can you be dead?"

"I don't know."

"How long have you been dead?"

"I don't know. I woke up one day, and I was dead."

"Why would you wake up if you were dead?"

"It's a mystery."

"It is not a mystery. I can tell you why you woke up!" Santo cried with religious fervor.

"You have a great purpose to accomplish in this world that has not been realized. You have a mission."

"I have no mission."

"You have a mission, and I will help you fulfill it! You have saved me from the murky waters, an icy death to help you achieve God's purpose here on this earth."

"One, I have no purpose, and two, you are an idiot. Go back to your fancy car and your fancy job and your three-bedroom ocean-view apartment."

"I cannot!"

"You will!"

"I won't!"

Mr. Albert realized he was getting nowhere. He tried a different tact.

"Okay, if you are going to help me discover my mission, you have to listen to me."

"Of course."

"Then go home and leave me alone!"

"That, I cannot do."

"But you just said you would listen to me."

"How can I help you with your purpose if I am not around? I will listen to everything you tell me as long as I agree with you," Santo beamed.

"You are giving me a headache."

"Can dead people get headaches?"

"No."

"Then you don't have a headache."

"I guess I don't."

"See how helpful I can be?"

Mr. Albert looked at Santo with exhaustion.

"Yes, you can be helpful. Come to think of it; I could use a man like you."

"Anything."

"Sometimes I go away."

"Go away......like before?"

"Yes, and I wake up in the morgue, and soon, some people might take an interest in me."

"People," Santo said, looking around.

"People," Mr. Albert said, mimicking his gaze. "And I don't want to arouse suspicion. It might interfere with me fulfilling God's purpose and all."

"What can I do?"

"Well, when I go away, I want you to put me somewhere safe until I come back. I need to avoid hospitals."

"And police stations."

"Police stations, good thinking."

"Anywhere else?"

"Applebee's. I don't like Applebee's."

~ 10 ~

Two weeks later.

At the Oceancrest Diner.

The small diner tucked in a strip mall had seen better days. The employees were frequently told that the restaurant would not make it to the next summer season. They would shrug, too apathetic to care. The diner looked remarkably similar to McKenna's bar, complete with dirty bathrooms, dirty booths, and poor lighting. It was open twenty-four hours, so when McKenna's closed for the night, the drunks could stumble to the Oceancrest for pancakes or the breakfast special at three in the morning.

Mr. Albert and Santo had each finished their early morning breakfast of three pancakes, two sausages, two strips of bacon, and two scrambled eggs when Mr. Albert could contain himself no longer. He was tired of being hounded by the man sitting across from him at the table.

"What are you doing?" Mr. Albert demanded.

"What do you mean?" Santo said, looking down at his empty plate.

"Following me."

"I thought we talked about this before. I am taking care of you when you are dead, dead until you are only dead, so you do not arouse suspicion."

"But why? Why are you doing that for me?"

"Why? You saved my life. I am your servant until I repay my debt to you," Santo vowed.

"How long will that be?"

"I don't know. It could be a long time."

"Months?"

"Could be."

"Years?"

"Quite probably."

"Decades?"

"Not beyond the realm of possibility," Santo acknowledged that fulfilling God's purpose on this earth might take a long time.

"Look, Santo. I appreciate your enthusiasm, but I have always been a loner. I don't know if I can deal with you that long. Can we put a time limit on this?"

"If that is your desire."

"A month."

"No."

"Why not?"

"How can I repay you for saving my life in only one month?"

"I thought I was being generous."

"Being generous? Is my life only worth a month? Mr. Albert, how can you insult me in this way? Ten years."

"Your life is only worth ten years?"

"It is better than a month!"

"I was thinking a year, tops," Mr. Albert countered.

"A year, Ay Dios Mío! A year? Seven!"

"Five."

"Six."

"Five and a half."

"Done," Santo grabbed Mr. Albert's hand and shook it gratefully.

"Five and a half years," Mr. Albert said, thinking of the large amount of time he would be sharing with this stranger.

"Five and a half years," Santo repeated, wondering if it was enough time.

"And what is this, Ay Dios Mío?" Mr. Albert needed to complain about something.

"It means 'Oh my God' in Spanish."

"Do you speak Spanish? Because that is the only Spanish phrase I have heard you say."

"My mother did not want Spanish to be spoken in the house. She thought it would upset my Irish father. My Abuelita constantly mumbled in Spanish when she was in our house but would shout in her fragile voice, Ay Dios Mío whenever we did anything improper."

"Improper?"

"Just about anything."

"God. help me!" Mr. Albert said, looking up to heaven.

"Ay Dios Mío," Santo responded.

"But why?"

"Why what?"

"Why are you doing this?"

"I thought we just talked about that," Santo said, having another sip of his coffee.

"We did, but we didn't. You are repaying your debt, but I am not demanding repayment. We have not signed a contract. I am not holding an I.O.U."

Santo looked into Mr. Albert's eyes and grew quiet. He fiddled with the napkin in his hands. Mr. Albert thought that this moment would be an appropriate time to die die, so he wouldn't have to wait for Santo to say what he was going to say.

"My life had no meaning," Santo said. "I was on that pier because I had nothing, but I had everything. I was successful in almost every category, wealth, possessions, respect."

"You didn't have a girl," Mr. Albert chimed in.

"That was a momentary inconvenience. What I didn't have was a purpose, and when I lost my girl, everything fell apart, You gave me meaning."

"How?"

"By saving me."

"How does that give you meaning? It just allows you to hide behind another person, another thing," Mr. Albert said, trying to get Santo to see the illogic of his argument.

"But that is just it. You are not another person, another thing. You are dead. You are nothing, but you are the possibility of everything."

"What are you yapping about?" Mr. Albert said, wishing he never started this conversation.

"I am yapping because there is a reason for you. There must be a reason why I am talking to you. You are truth."

"What truth?"

"I don't know. I am not that wise."

"So, you will hang around until I reveal my truth?"

"Yes."

"What if there is no truth, no hidden meaning to the universe? What if this is just a fluke? What if I am some random freak of nature, one in a trillion chance, that just hit the lottery and is incapable of dying?"

"We will have to see."

"You know how many people have lived in this world since the beginning of time?"

"No."

"One hundred and fifteen billion."

"Exactly?" Santo said, amused at the specificity of the number.

"Estimate."

"Because that would seem like a very exact number."

"About a hundred and fifteen billion," Mr. Albert said, his patience wearing thin.

"Better. What is your point?"

"Don't you think that in all those billions of people, there might be one person with some quirk in his chromosomes that allows him to live after his death?"

"No."

"No? A hundred and fifteen billion!"

"We will have to see."

"But I don't want to see."

"We will see about that as well."

Santo smiled. Mr. Albert started pulling at his hair. Nothing came out. The waitress refilled their coffees.

"What if, worse than that, you find some meaning in all of this, and then realize that you are wrong once again? Are you going to hold me responsible?"

"Would you care?"

"Not really. But I wouldn't want you following me around for years for nothing. What if there is no meaning?"

"There must be meaning," Santo said, with determination.

"Why?"

"I don't know."

"How can you not know?"

"Because I don't know."

"Are you going to play the stupid card constantly?" Mr. Albert growled.

"I don't know," Santo grinned.

Savannah 1958.
Lot 26, Greenwich Cemetery.

Benny held on to Genevieve. She seemed unable to support herself. The rest of the family had left an hour ago, but Genevieve still could not move.

"You won't ever leave me, will you, Benny?"

Everyone else in her life had.

"No, Genevieve, I will never leave you," Benny said without any expression. His wife was so dependent upon her mother that whatever he said would seem hollow and insincere. "Are you hungry? You haven't eaten all day. You must be hungry."

"No, I am fine. I just wish she was here."

Benny did not know what to do that would comfort his wife. But he remembered one of Mrs. Pierpont's favorite songs. He changed a word or two to make it fit the situation. He sang it barely above a whisper so that only his wife could hear it.

"From Savannah, they say you are goin'
We will miss your bright eyes and sweet smile
For they say you are takin' the sunshine
That has brightened our pathway the while."

Genevieve looked at Benny. He said very little but always managed to say what was needed. She continued, also changing a few words.

"Do you think of the city you're leavin'
Oh, how lonely and dreary it will be
Do you think of the fond heart you're breakin'
And the sadness you've cast over me."

"For a long time, mama, I've been waiting
For the words that I wish you could say
But alas, my poor heart, you are breakin'
For I know that you have gone away."

Benny kissed his wife and led her to a nearby bench under a flowering dogwood, its pink petals in full bloom. He finished the song.

"Come and sit by my side if you love me
Know that I'll never bid you adieu
And remember that I'll always love you
With a love that will always be true."

She sat beside him. He put his arm around her. They sat there until the sun began to set and a coolness filled the air. Genevieve thought that even when a person is in mourning, another person will one day mourn for them. This continuum somehow comforted her. And that was enough for the moment.

She stood up and held out her hand to Benny. She knew that he would be there for her. He was the foundation and reason for every future event. He stood up and took her hand. They walked back to the car, knowing that everything would be all right.

"I am a little hungry," she said, squeezing him so that he would warm her.

"Anton's?"

"You're not going to get a hot dog, are you?"

"The first time I saw you, I was eating a hot dog, and I have been craving one ever since."

"I love you, Benjamin."

"I love you, Genevieve."

~ 11 ~

One week later.
McKenna's Bar.

After their agreement was sealed, Santo spent several days following his savior around. He grew impatient because Mr. Albert did nothing but wake up, go to McKenna's, followed by the Oceancrest, and then pass out. Santo thought if Winnie the Pooh were an alcoholic, he would look very much like Mr. Albert, who might just as well be stuffed with fluff.

"Aren't you tired of drinking, Mr. Albert?"

"I don't think so."

"Since I have been with you, all we do is go to bars."

"Your point is?"

"How will you find your purpose if you never try?"

"Why do I need a purpose?" Mr. Albert snarled. "Walter, do you have a purpose?"

Walter turned to Mr. Albert, "What?"

"Do you have a purpose?"

"Porpoise, I don't have a porpoise!"

"Purpose not porpoise, Walter." Santo tried to get the drunk on his side. "What is your purpose?"

"When I leave here, I'm gonna go home and make a baby!"

"You have a wife, Walter?" Mr. Albert laughed.

"I did when I left."

"There you have it, Mr. Albert!" Santo exclaimed. "Even Walter has a purpose!"

"Hey," Walter objected.

"He is going to pass out in this bar and then wake up, go home, and make a baby!"

"Yes, sir!" Walter grinned and banged the bar for emphasis.

"So, if I would make a baby, you would leave me alone?" Mr. Albert proposed.

"Of course not."

"Why not?"

"Because that is Walter's purpose, not your purpose."

"I'm going to make a baby," Walter chuckled.

"Why can't both of us make a baby?" Mr. Albert argued.

"Now listen here, you will not touch Evelyn," jealousy rose in Walter's voice.

"Who is Evelyn?" Mr. Albert sat back in his chair to give a little distance.

"My wife!" Walter said, rising from his chair but finding it hard to keep his balance.

"Walter, Walter, calm down. I'm not going to have a baby with your wife. I can find my own woman."

Mr. Albert and Santo re-seated Walter.

"I won't stand for that sort of thing," Walter spluttered.

"That's good," Santo tried to soothe the jealous man.

"Nobody wants Evelyn," Mr. Albert added.

"Not good enough for you?" Walter said, standing up again.

"She is plenty good," comforted Santo. "She is just off the market."

Walter sat down. Mr. Albert ordered another round. The men sat quietly. Mac brought the bottle of Jack and filled the glasses.

"My Evelyn, my Evelyn," Walter cried quietly.

"What is it now?" Mr. Albert said. "No one will touch Evelyn."

"She died," Walter groaned.

"When?" Santo said.

"Eight years ago."

"Sorry," said Santo.

"Sorry," echoed Mr. Albert.

"No matter."

They drank their whiskey.

"It would be kind of hard to go home and make a baby then, wouldn't it?" Santo muttered softly, so Walter could not hear him.

"I guess we can cross off Walter's purpose from the list." Mr. Albert said, triumphantly.

"It doesn't matter if one will ever accomplish the purpose. It only matters that he has one. *It does not matter if the hopes you started out with are dashed, hope must be maintained.*"

"Did you say that?" Mr. Albert was impressed.

"Someone did," Santo shrugged.

"That is very helpful."

"The point is that we all need hope. We all need a purpose."

"Do we?" Mr. Albert countered. "Is Walter's life better because when he is drunk enough, he imagines that his wife is still alive? Walter, are you happy?"

"Fuck off."

"See, Santo, fuck off. I think he is probably more miserable because of this imagined purpose. If he would accept the reality of his loss and move on, he might have a chance, but he will never see the desperateness of his life. He willingly condemns himself to this fairy tale prison of his own making until he dies of alcohol poisoning in some back alley somewhere. Isn't that right, Walter?"

"Fuck you."

"And fuck you too." Mr. Albert toasted his friend.

"What is the difference?" Santo asked.

"Between what?"

"Between you and him? You are both sitting here drinking your lives away."

"I'm drinking my death away. A better afterlife I cannot imagine."

"Still, you spend your time in dimly lit bars, talking about nothing, doing nothing. Don't you think you would be happier if there were something to be done?" Santo asked.

"No."

"How did you feel when you saved me? When you talked me down from the railing, how did you feel?"

"I didn't feel anything."

"Then why did you come back looking for me?"

The point hit its mark. Santo was right. Mr. Albert shook off the truth.

"What does that prove?" Mr. Albert snarled.

"It proves that for that one little moment, you cared for another person."

"And look what it got me. Instead of paying for two drinks, I have to pay for three."

"Do you really mind?"

"Not really."

"Imagine, Mr. Albert, if every day you could look forward to not really minding this existence. Wouldn't that be nice?"

"Not convincing."

"Wouldn't it be less tedious?"

"You think this is tedious?"

"Yes, I do, Mr. Albert."

"I will let you have that point."

"Can we look for a purpose?"

"Is that important?"

"Yes, it is."

"All right, Santo, let's look for a purpose."

"Thank you, Mr. Albert. Tomorrow we will go to the library."

"What in God's name would we go there for?"

"Research, my friend, research."

Mr. Albert did not like the sound of that. But now he was stuck. He turned to Walter.

"Walter, Walter."

"Fuck off."

"Me and Santo here are going to a terrible place called a library. Don't know when we will see you again. All right?"

"All right, see you tomorrow."

"See you tomorrow, Walter."

~ 12 ~

One day later.
The Ruthie Kranshaw Memorial Library.

Santo and Mr. Albert sat in the empty library. Why a town would build a library a couple of blocks from the beach seemed ridiculous to Mr. Albert when it could make a perfectly acceptable drinking establishment. Nobody goes to the beach to read. Pretending to read at the beach is only a ruse to disguise the fact that you are checking out the glistening, tanned, unattainable bodies.

Santo convinced Mr. Albert to spend an hour or two in the library, researching his peculiar condition before visiting McKenna's. They sat in a quiet corner in the back. Santo piled stacks of books on the table. Mr. Albert tapped his pencil. Santo seemed remarkably focused on his work. Mr. Albert wanted to draw pornographic pictures in the top right corners of the books, so if you flipped through the pages quickly, you would get a real treat. But he knew Santo would disapprove.

Mr. Albert rose slowly as if he was suddenly enlightened.

"Santo, Santo, I understand now. I understand it all, my purpose. It is all so simple."

"How did you find out? What happened?" Santo said, rising, his book falling to the floor.

They jumped up and down together, grasping each other's hands, and laughing.

"It was something you said the other day," Mr. Albert continued. "How could I have been so blind?"

"What? What? Please tell me!"

"It was just this......."

Mr. Albert's eyes went glassy. He stepped towards his friend and collapsed into Santo's arms before sliding to the ground. Mr. Albert was dead dead.

At first, Santo thought it was a joke. He tapped Mr. Albert with his foot but received no response from the prone man. He kicked a little harder, and then he kicked him so hard that Mr. Albert's pelvis rose in the air and gradually settled to the ground like a balloon with a slow leak.

Mr. Albert was dead, dead. What should Santo do? He panicked and paced in ever-increasing ovals, constantly looking for suspicious librarians, who are always on the prowl to discover loud talkers, shush them into submission, and return order to the chaotic universe.

He lifted Mr. Albert off the floor and sat him on a chair. The dead, dead man slumped. He almost looked like he was asleep. A thought crossed Santo's mind that he should just leave Mr. Albert until he woke up. This was a library, after all, nobody comes in here. But then, a sense of responsibility washed over him. He made a commitment to Mr. Albert. If he wanted to be his friend, he must do what any friend would do, hide the body until he recovered.

He looked around to see how he could make an unnoticed exit. Every door was alarmed. He would have to get out through the front door. With Mr. Albert solidly sitting, Santo walked to the librarian behind the front desk, whose sour expression and poofy hairdo made him even more uncomfortable. He took a deep breath and strode up to the woman.

"Excuse me, ma'am," Santo cowered.

"Yes? How can I help you?"

"I'm not sure, but I was in the back corner over there," he said, pointing to the corner of the library furthest away from where he had left Mr. Albert. "It smells like urine."

"Oh dear, it must be the homeschoolers. They always come in here acting like they are doing a school project." She raised her hands to put air quotes around *school project.* "Who knows what they have been up to?" She headed off to find the smell.

Santo sensed his chance. He walked quickly back to the dead man and tried to sling him over his shoulders, but Mr. Albert slipped from his grip, and they both tumbled to the floor. He put Mr. Albert back on the chair and tried to hoist him up by crossing the dead man's arms on his chest. This also resulted in both men landing on the ground. Finally, Santo locked his hands across Mr. Albert's chest and dragged him out of the library. He stuffed him into his car and strapped his friend in. He'd done it! He got the dead man out of the library without anyone noticing! Now he just had to stash the corpse somewhere until he woke up.

Santo drove slowly to avoid suspicion. He stopped at an intersection even though the light was yellow. He was not going to take any chances. A couple of women pulled up beside him in a convertible and honked.

"Like your car," said the pretty blonde driver.

"Thanks," Santo said, turning his body to hide Mr. Albert.

"Where are you going?" asked the brunette passenger.

Santo did well with his Tesla. It was not only electric but stylish, and the ladies loved it!

"Just looking for a cheap hotel room." He inadvertently leaned back, revealing his passenger, who was now oozing fluid from his nose and mouth.

The women's expressions went from interest to disgust almost in tandem. They sped away when the light turned green.

Santo turned to Mr. Albert, "You are cramping my style, man."

Savannah 1959.

Hurricane Gracie hit the South Carolina coast fifty miles north of Savannah. The category four hurricane knocked down trees and power lines, leaving much of the city without power. Water filled the streets, making it difficult for emergency crews to rescue the sick and helpless.

Benny tried to be the strong man that Genevieve needed, closing the storm windows and taking in the furniture and other objects from the yard that might blow away. But once all the hatches were battened down, there was nothing to do but wait out the storm.

They sat on the couch and held each other. A quilt that Mrs. Pierpont had made lay across their laps. The moment would have been pleasant if it wasn't for the hurricane blowing wildly outside. A clap of thunder sounded close to the house.

"What was that!" Benny gasped.

"Don't worry, darling; it will pass soon," Genevieve comforted her husband.

"I know, but I still don't like it."

"Haven't you ever been in a hurricane?"

"I don't think so. I don't think they have them in Chicago."

"Would you like a drink?" Genevieve suggested.

"You know I am not a fan of the drink."

"I know, sweetheart, but it might calm you down."

"All right."

"We'll have a rum and coke because that is what Momma would drink, and I know she is looking out for us."

Genevieve went off to the kitchen, leaving Benny all alone. A burst of lightning lit the inside of the house even though the storm shutters were closed. Benny's head jerked from left to right, look-ing for salvation. The thunder followed directly after, and Benny put his head down on his knees and closed his eyes.

Genevieve returned and could not help laughing at her brave knight, although, at this moment, he looked more like an ostrich burying his head in the sand. Benny looked up when he heard her and smiled. She went over to him with the two drinks. He drank half of his in one go, almost gagging. The glass slammed down on the coffee table.

"How could you drink that poison?" he coughed.

"You get used to it," Genevieve said with a sad smile.

She put down her drink and kissed him.

"You see, this isn't so bad."

"I guess not," he said, wanting to be kissed again.

But then a bolt of lightning struck a transformer down the street, creating a large explosion. The power in the house went out.

"I was wrong. I was very wrong. This is bad, very bad," Benny said, pacing the room.

"Not to worry, Benny. Help me get some candles."

She jumped up and ran to the kitchen. Benny followed close behind. In a few minutes, the room was lit with the romantic golden glow of candles. This did nothing to change his mood.

"I don't feel well."

"Maybe you should lie down. Too much excitement."

"Too much excitement and too much Bacardi's."

"You might very well be right," she laughed. "Would you like some company?"

"Only if you get under the covers with me," he smiled.

Genevieve nodded in agreement. She was not comfortable with the terrible storm either but knew she had to be brave for Benny. After all, one of them had to be brave. She finished what was left of the two drinks and followed her husband into the bedroom.

~ 13 ~

Two days later.
The Bushwhacker Motel.

For two days, Mr. Albert lay dead in the motel room. Santo thought that maybe he was dead for real this time. This time seemed longer than his normal near-death experiences. Mr. Albert returned to the pier less than a day after he saved Santo. And that was with him spending several hours in the morgue and McKenna's.

He tried to keep his mind occupied. He thought that he would lose all hope if Mr. Albert was truly dead. What purpose would he have without his friend? And what message did Mr. Albert try to tell him before he died? He searched his memory for anything that he'd said, but everything seemed unimportant. Maybe that was it! Everything is unimportant, which would mean the opposite as well, that everything is important, and all our experiences can lead to enlightenment. But maybe that wasn't what he was saying at all.

He forced himself to think about other things until the meaning of Mr. Albert's last words revealed itself. Maybe he should sell his car to buy something a little less flashy. He couldn't have pretty girls flirting with him as he drove around a dead, dead Mr. Albert. Who knows, maybe some women would find that exciting? But where could he find those women?

He thought about why this motel ten miles from the Jersey shore would be named *The Bushwhacker.* Maybe the owner came from

Australia. Who knows? Some things are inexplicable. He looked at the dead body on the motel bed. Yes, some things are inexplicable.

On the third day, Mr. Albert sat up. Santo was asleep in the one chair by the window that always seemed to be in motel rooms. The TV was on. The volume barely above the level of white noise so as not to disturb the dead man. The Andy Griffith show was playing. Oh, dear. Andy was trying to solve another predicament that Barney got into. Poor Barney, bless his heart.

Santo opened his eyes slowly. A smile came over him like the sun rising over the ocean.

"Mr. Albert, you are dead. I'm so happy to see you."

"I can't say I am happy to see you, but I am glad you are here."

"I didn't know if you were really dead this time. How long do you think I should wait before I bury you?"

"How long was I gone?"

"Two days."

"Then you should wait longer than two days," Mr. Albert instructed.

"But how will I know when you are really gone?"

"I don't know. Maybe when I start smelling."

"You are always smelling."

"That's true. Maybe if I begin to bloat as well."

"That's good, bloating and smelling," Santo said, taking mental notes. "Anything else?"

"Let's just keep it at that for the moment."

"Very good. Shall we get something to eat?"

"I am hungry."

"So am I. I have eaten nothing for two days but saltine crackers and peanut butter."

"We have crackers?"

"Not anymore."

"Then we probably should get you a beer to wash it down with."

"But wait, Mr. Albert. Before you died, died, you said you understood your purpose. You said, I said something that made it all clear to you. Me, Santo said something that solved this mystery! What was it?"

"Yeah," Mr. Albert hesitated. "I felt like I was about to die, die, and I thought, wouldn't it be funny if I pretended I had figured out this whole mess? And that I was about to tell you, but I died like in the movies, and the killer is.... Urghh. It was funny, wasn't it? You were probably sitting here, eating your crackers, saying, *if he'd only told me, I could be happy now, happy!*"

"You are a very mean person."

"Sometimes, that is all I have. Forgive me."

"You are forgiven, but as soon as you start to bloat, I am putting you in a woodchipper."

"That's fair. Let me buy you a beer."

"Are you sure you should be drinking?"

"Santo, what kind of question is that?"

"You know, recovering from being dead dead and all," Santo worried.

"That is all the more reason to get drunk. Celebrate our blessings."

"I don't think you know what a blessing is. This is not a blessing."

"Then you can explain it all to me over a beer."

Santo helped Mr. Albert to his feet.

"Feeling okay?" Santo said, checking to see if Mr. Albert could stand on his own.

"I'm good, although your head looks exceptionally big right now."

And the two friends left their seedy motel room to get plastered.

~ 14 ~

One hour later.

The Almost There, Bar and Grill.

They had already consumed their third drink before Mr. Albert spoke.

"Santo."

"Yes, Mr. Albert?"

"I have been thinking."

"Yes?"

"There might be a time, if I fulfill my purpose, that I might actually die."

"But you are dead."

"Yes, I know that."

"But you don't mean that?" Santo said, understanding where the conversation was going.

"Correct."

"And you don't mean that you are dead, dead?"

"No."

"That you are actually no more."

"Yes," Mr. Albert smiled.

Santo sat in silence.

"What should we call that?" Santo worried. "Cause dead, dead, dead seems a little long."

"And redundant."

"What about dead cubed?"

"Interesting. We could just go with cubed."

"Cubed?" Santo said. "You're cubed. No, I don't like it. Sounds like I have cut you up

into little pieces."

"If I was cubed, you could cut me up, and it wouldn't matter."

"Ay Dios Mio! Why would you say that? I am your friend."

"Well, let's keep it open for a while until we find something more suitable."

"I won't use it," Santo held his ground.

"What if I die, die, died right now, if only God were merciful!"

"You won't."

"Who knows?" Mr. Albert said hopefully.

"You haven't found your purpose."

"I haven't found my purpose! What if I have found my purpose and already fulfilled it?"

"I don't think you have found your purpose," Santo disagreed.

"You don't know."

"It is just my feeling on the subject."

"I'm glad you are so sure."

"I'm not sure, but I do have a feeling."

"Regardless," Mr. Albert snapped. "When the time comes, and hopefully that time is

soon because I don't know how much more of this I can take. You are driving me nuts."

"Thank you, Mr. Albert. And Merry Christmas to you."

"Is it Christmas?"

"Yes."

Mr. Albert shrugged his shoulders and continued.

"When the time comes, you will have to bury me in a place where no one can find me."

"Why would you ask me to do that on Christmas?"

"I didn't ask you because I was waiting around, and it was like, *what should I get Santo for Christmas? Oh wait, I'll tell him to throw me in a ditch somewhere. That would be nice. He'll like that. No, I said that* because I just woke up from being dead, dead, and I never had someone I could ask to bury me, so I asked you."

"Really, no one?" Santo said, his eyes filling with tears of happiness.

"No, Santo. I have never had a friend like you." Mr. Albert flattered Santo.

"Well, if that is what you want, I would be honored."

"That is what I want."

Savannah 1959.

The next day, Genevieve woke up beside Benny. She hugged him as wonderful as a morning hug should be. He didn't respond, so she moved her hand from his chest to a lower area of his body. That usually stimulated the desired response, but today, Benny did not react. She noticed that he seemed colder than usual.

"Cold hands, warm heart," she smiled. It was an expression that her mother used to say.

She shook him from his sleep. He lay there, cold, silent. She sat up, worried.

"Benny! Benny, honey, wake up! Wake up!" she screamed as she jumped from the bed.

She paced around the room, mumbling, "No, no, no."

She thought of her mother leaving her and her father. Benny couldn't do the same. He promised her a long life together. He promised her!

She ran to the phone to call the police. There was no dial tone. The phone lines must be down. The electricity was still off. She put on a robe and ran to the front door. Limbs from the tree blocked her way. She went out through the kitchen door and made her way to the street. The street was submerged in a foot of water, making an attempt to get help dangerous. She went back into her house and waited.

Two hours later, she tried again to get help. Standing on her front porch, she looked for any rescue workers. She saw a man from the next street over wading through the water. He was not a nice man, and her mother warned her to stay away from him. The man saw her and waved.

"Genevieve, are you all right?"

"Yes, yes, I'm fine. My husband is right inside. Go and call on some other people. Mrs. Bryant, right on your street, probably needs to be checked up on."

"I'll do that right now and let you know."

"That's okay. We will go over to my sister's house until things get back to normal."

Genevieve did not know what condition her sister's house was in. Maybe it was swept away in the storm. Maybe the roof collapsed. They could all be dead. There was no way of knowing. But she did not want the man to come back.

Genevieve and her sister hadn't been the best of friends since Benny arrived. Jacqueline made it clear that she never liked him, even if he did have money. She never trusted him.

Her mother just waved off all that nonsense. "Your sister is just jealous," she would say. "She married an accountant who spends more time at the office than at home with her. Benny follows you around like a lovesick puppy, wagging his tail whenever you smile."

"Well, stay safe."

"You, too."

Genevieve went into her house and locked the door. *Her husband was dead*, she thought. *Dangerous people are roaming the streets. I've no one to protect me. No one cares.*

She made a big stiff drink, sat on the couch, and cried until sleep overtook her.

~ 15 ~

Two weeks later.
On the Boardwalk.

After they recovered from the dead, dead incident, Mr. Albert
spent less time at the bar and more time in the library. They didn't
cut out drinking entirely, but they only went four times a week
instead of seven. On their days off, they walked on the boardwalk
and often visited the place where Santo almost took his life.

Mr. Albert and Santo enjoyed their day by the beach. They
had stopped at the Wiener King before hitting the boardwalk. Mr.
Albert finished his hot dogs quickly and was now drinking a beer as
he watched the ocean. Santo thought Mr. Albert could be his father
if he had a cigarette in his other hand. Santo's hot dog dripped
mustard, ketchup, and sauerkraut with every bite, forcing him to
step back to avoid getting it on his clothing. It dripped on his hand.
He switched hands and then licked his condiment-covered palm.
Mr. Albert looked on disgusted.

"What?" Santo looked uncomfortable from the gaze of his friend.

"That stuff will kill you."

Santo smiled, "You just ate two before I could even finish one."

"I'm already dead."

Mr. Albert's gaze returned to the calming ocean. Santo continued to lick his fingers.

"Well, hello there!"

Mr. Albert turned and saw his friend, Dr. Johnson.

"Hello, Dr. Johnson. Nice to see you when I'm not in the morgue," Mr. Albert smiled.

"It was such a lovely day that I decided to stroll down to the ocean. It is so rare that I get a few minutes for myself. So, Mr. Albert, are you still dead?"

"Yes, I am still dead."

"Wouldn't want you suddenly to be alive again," the doctor said, chuckling.

"You wouldn't?"

"You would certainly be less interesting. Who is your friend?" he said.

"I'm sorry. Dr. Johnson, this is my......associate, Santo Murphy. Santo, Dr. Johnson."

"Associate?" said Santo annoyed.

"Associate," Dr. Johnson winked knowingly. He looked around secretly and then whispered, "Are you the devil?"

"No, Ay Dios Mío!" Santo exclaimed. "I am a God-fearing man!"

"Pity," said the doctor, losing interest. "That would have explained a lot. Well, Mr. Albert, I haven't seen you in a while. What is going on?"

"You haven't seen me because of my friend here," he looked to Santo for approval.

"Better," replied Santo, shrugging his shoulders.

"Santo squirrels me away when I go to my quiet place, so no one is the wiser. When I wake, he has a cup of hot cocoa waiting for me."

"I don't always bring him hot cocoa."

"And what do you get out of the deal?" Dr. Johnson inquired, his eyes narrowing.

"He saved my life."

"Was going to jump off the pier. Right over there," Mr. Albert chimed in.

"Why did you do that?" The doctor asked Mr. Albert.

"I had to pee."

"That explains almost nothing. When did this happen?"

"After I saved him, I died again, so you saw me later that day."

"That is right. I have not seen you since. Excellent job, Santo."

"Dr. Johnson, may I ask you a question?" Santo requested.

"Do you have pain or a growth somewhere? You'll have to come down to the hospital."

"No, it is about Mr. Albert."

"You may proceed."

"Any ideas to explain his condition?"

"Haven't the foggiest. Anything else?"

"Yes, doctor. Why didn't you turn him in, report him to the F.B.I. or the C.D.C.?"

"Too much trouble. I'm five years from retirement. Have a little place in the mountains with a lake and everything. Why would I want to stir up a hornet's nest? I kept thinking he would keel over soon enough. After all, he has no brain. He can't last too long without a brain."

"No brain function," Mr. Albert corrected.

"Yeah, yeah, whatever. Now that you are here, I expect you to keep him away from the hospital. Dr. Mancha is not as close to retirement as I am. He is quite suspicious. Well, I must go back to the hospital. Keep up the good work, Mr. Murphy."

"I will, doctor."

~ 16 ~

One week later.

The Ruthie Kranshaw Memorial Library.

Santo did not speak to Mr. Albert for almost an hour because he was so focused on his studies. Finally, Santo put down the book he was reading and looked to heaven. A light shone from within him as if he had just received enlightenment.

"What about Lazarus?" Santo beamed.

"What about Lazarus?"

"Why do you always do that?" Santo was no longer enlightened, just irritated.

"What?"

"When I say something to you, you act like you weren't listening."

"I wasn't listening."

"That is rude."

"No, you are rude, and you won't leave me alone! Dragging me to the library every day."

The two men glared at each other with various levels of disgust.

"So, what about Lazarus?" Mr. Albert said when he felt he was losing the game.

"Jesus raised Lazarus."

"From a little boy?"

"Resurrected," Santo growled.

"I know the story. What about it?"

"Did he ever die again?"

"Why shouldn't he?"

"If God brings you back to life, maybe a little bit of God sticks around, and you become immortal," Santo said, explaining his epiphany.

"So, you are saying I am Lazarus?" Mr. Albert mocked his epiphanous friend.

"Possibly."

"No, I don't buy it."

"Why not?"

"I'm not that old?" Mr. Albert struggled for a reason not to accept Santo's premise.

"That's your argument?"

"For the time being."

"Let me ask you a question," Santo approached this from another angle.

"Can I prevent it?"

"No, you cannot."

"Proceed," Mr. Albert surrendered.

"What is the first thing you remember?"

"Ever?"

"Yes."

"I remember getting drunk with Walter."

"That was yesterday."

"Yes," Mr. Albert smiled. "Good times."

"You must remember before that. What town are we in?"

Mr. Albert shrugged his shoulder absentmindedly.

"How did we meet?"

Mr. Albert shrugged as he opened and closed his mouth, making a bubbling noise. Making ridiculous noises was fun.

"I was about to commit suicide."

Mr. Albert shrugged his shoulders, rocking his head back and forth as if he was in the deepest level of Hell.

"I don't know. I don't knows, I tells ya! I have no brain function!"

"How long am I going to stay with you?"

"Five and a half years!"

"Ah ha! You remember some things," Santo said, with a triumphant grin.

"I seem to be able to remember annoying things. Little things, bits and pieces, but nothing like my parents leaving me in a department store when I was five years old."

"That is oddly specific."

"It is, but I generally live in the present and don't worry about the past."

"How will you have a purpose if you don't understand your past?" Santo chastised him.

"I don't want a purpose. You want me to have a purpose. I would be perfectly happy drinking with Walter every day until he dies of sclerosis of the liver, and then someone else would sit in his chair, and I would be just as happy with the new guy."

"That is so sad."

"Only if you think about it."

"Shouldn't you think about it?"

"What good would it do?"

"Mr. Albert, you could do so much good," Santo pleaded. "If anyone could change the world and see the effects of the change, it would be you."

"You have a point," Mr. Albert conceded, although he was not that motivated.

"Thank you."

"So, tell me more about this Lazarus fellow," Mr. Albert feigned interest.

"Jesus raised him after he was dead for four days."

"He must have stank."

"There is no mention of how he smelled. Everyone was glad to see him."

"Well, if they weren't, and Jesus was still hanging around, they would seem ungrateful."

"This is what you are thinking about? Our savior performs the miracle of resurrection, and all you think about is if soiling took place?" Santo appealed to heaven for strength.

"I guess Jesus could have taken care of the whole-body odor thing." Mr. Albert was satisfied that he had solved this great religious mystery. He sniffed his armpits.

"You are unbelievable!"

"In many ways. Did he raise anybody else?"

"Here, look at this book," Santo tossed a small book to Mr. Albert.

"*People Raised from the Dead.* Cheery title. *The promise of Christianity is that all believers will someday be raised from the dead. God the Father demonstrated his power to bring the perished back to life, and these ten accounts from the Bible prove it.* All by Jesus?"

"No," said Santo. "Elijah, Elisha, Jesus, Peter, and Paul all raised the dead."

"Seemed like a popular hobby in the olden days. I guess I don't have to be Lazarus."

"No, you don't," Santo said, sensing Mr. Albert had come over to his side. "Who would you be?"

"Could I be Jesus?"

"No, you could not be Jesus."

"Why not? Why can't I be Jesus?" Mr. Albert pouted.

"You just can't."

"Who says you get to be boss about who I am?"

"I found the book," Santo said, grabbing the book back from Mr. Albert. "Here, you can be the Israelite. *After Elisha, the prophet, died, he was buried in a cave. Moabite raiders attacked Israel every spring, one time interrupting a funeral. Fearing for their own lives, the burial party quickly threw the body into the first convenient place, Elisha's tomb. As soon as the body touched Elisha's bones, the dead man came back to life and stood up on his feet.* There! You could be him!"

"Doesn't seem like a good one. Nobody even wanted him resurrected. That is a resurrection by accident."

"A resurrection is still a resurrection."

"So, you are saying because I touched a few bones by accident, I'm immortal?"

"Possibly," Santo wavered from Mr. Albert's impeccable arguments.

"What about the others? Are they still alive, too?"

"Possibly!" Santo said louder to dispute the master debater.

Mr. Albert grabbed the book back and skimmed the stories.

"What about Tabitha? What kind of name is Tabitha? Who would name their kid Tabitha?"

"Tabitha is a nice name."

"For a cat, maybe. So, all the resurrected people are just roaming around, and nobody knows about them."

"Initially, people knew about them, but then they forget."

"Forget about somebody coming back to life?"

"Yes."

"What about the other resurrected people? Wouldn't they try to find and hang out with the other people who came back?"

"Kind of like a club?" The idea intrigued Santo. "So, all the resurrected people are hanging out together playing poker?"

"Possibly."

"But maybe they are not just sitting around," Santo's imagination ran wild. "Maybe they are secretly influencing governments to do their bidding. Maybe they have taken over the banking systems, news outlets, and the entertainment industry!"

"By Jiminy!" Mr. Albert interrupted. "The alt-right is wrong! It's not the Jews! It's the people who were resurrected! I do like pizza, but am I a pedophile?"

"If you fancied anyone younger than a thousand, you would be a pedophile."

"What?"

Santo explained, "I think social etiquette is that you could date someone half your age plus seven. So, if you were Lazarus, and he was about as old as Jesus, you can date someone one thousand and eighteen years old without too much talk at the bridge club."

"That would make the pool of prospects rather small."

Both men pondered the dating prospects for poor Mr. Albert.

"Why am I not in the club anymore?" Mr. Albert said after a moment of thought.

"What?"

"Why am I not in the club anymore?" Mr. Albert muttered.

"I don't know. Maybe they kicked you out."

"Why would they kick me out? What could I have possibly done to be kicked out of the Resurrection Society?"

"Resurrection Society. I like it," Santo said. He was never very good at thinking up catchy names for things.

"I was originally thinking of the Resurrection Secret Society, but it was too long."

"You also don't want a secret society with the word secret in the title. Gives it away."

"Agreed. The Resurrection Society is the name. But why would they kick me out?"

"You rub people the wrong way."

"Really? I saved your life, but I rub people the wrong way. Very nice."

"Maybe they wanted to do something evil, and you tried to prevent them," Santo offered.

"What did they want to do?"

"They turned evil and wanted to take over the world. You stood up for truth and justice."

"That doesn't sound very much like me." Mr. Albert said thoughtfully. After a moment, he continued. "Although, why not? Did they kick me out?"

"No, they tried to get rid of you, and you escaped. Now they are hunting you down, and they might have succeeded without the help of your trusted friend, Santo Murphy."

"Had to put yourself in there, didn't you?"

"I think it rounds out the plot. You need someone to bounce your ideas off of."

"I'll tell you what I'd like to bounce off of you."

They thought for a moment about their new roles as saviors of the world.

"Make a good story, though," Santo said, smiling.

"Better than this one. Wah, wah, wah, you need a purpose. I don't wanna have a purpose. Well, you need one! Eat your vegetables!"

"I would kick you out of my club."

"Thank you, Santo."

Savannah 1959.

The next day was just as bad as the previous one. Benny was dead, and there was no one around to help Genevieve. The waters had receded, but power and phone service had not been restored. Around midday, she decided that she could wait no longer. She put on a pair of slacks and her rain boots to protect against the vermin scurrying in the streets. The temperature was in the high seventies, but she wore a light jacket to protect herself from flying creatures.

She walked for blocks without seeing another living soul. Finally, she saw the flashing lights of a police car stopped in the middle of the street.

"Officer, I need your help."

"Please stand back, ma'am," The officer approached her menacingly.

A fallen tree had snapped an electrical cable, and the live wire danced in the street twenty yards in front of the patrol car. Genevieve stopped and waited for the officer to come to her.

"What is it? Is it an emergency?"

"Yes, my husband died during the storm. He is in my house."

"Is everyone else in your house safe?"

"Yes, officer. It was just me and my husband."

He wrote down her address and put some notes underneath it. Then he sent her home.

"But what about my husband?"

"I don't mean to be indelicate," the officer explained. "But we are in the middle of an emergency here. We are still trying to save people in dangerous situations, and by coming out of your home, you've put yourself in jeopardy. I will send an ambulance to your house when it is time to collect the body. That is all I can do. I'm sorry."

She turned and walked away. *The world gets crueler with every passing moment*, she thought. Savannah didn't even feel like home anymore. Broken limbs from the trees created obstacles to the simple act of walking. Doors were shut, and windows shuttered, warning any visitors to stay away. The streets, even though she was a few blocks from her home, seemed unfamiliar and scary. She felt like a child suddenly separated from her parents.

The air was silent. No birds sang pretty melodies. No cars beeped their horns, with anxious drivers in a hurry to get home. No happy wife who had prepared a roast and greeted her husband with a dry martini at the door. No children laughing and running through the home because they were excited to see their father. The mother appeals to her husband for help, and their father collects the little ones around his easy chair, telling them that they should always listen to their mother because she is the greatest woman in the world. The children run to hug their mother and apologize before washing their hands for dinner.

Genevieve stood in front of her home. The wonderful tree that she danced around when she was a child being playfully chased by her mother looked wounded. Many of its beautiful branches lay broken on the ground. Only death and loneliness remained here. Genevieve walked around to the kitchen steps and entered her house. She resigned herself to an eternity of solitude.

~ 17 ~

Three days later.

At Marzetti Motors, a used car dealership in Wildwinds, N.J.

"Hi, my name is Sal. Can I help you, gentlemen?" The sleazy car salesman with an unrecognizable ethnic accent and a tub of pomade in his hair said.

"Sure, you want to do this, Santo?" Mr. Albert asked.

He had no problem driving around town in the Tesla, regardless of what level of dead he was. But Santo disagreed.

"It must be done," Santo said, his voice dropping to a whisper.

Santo shook the salesman's hand, which had remnants of his most recent comb-through.

"I want to trade this in for something a little less conspicuous."

"Inconspicuous, huh? Well, you have come to the right place. Here at Marzetti Motors, we only sell inconspicuous automobiles."

"That's why we came here," Mr. Albert said. "Whenever we see an inconspicuous car in town, it is always from Marzetti Motors."

"We do our best," the salesman said, unaware Mr. Albert was not being complimentary. "Will you be trading in this car?"

"Yes, I will," said Santo with a forlorn look.

"And what will you be looking for as a trade?"

"I've got it." Mr. Albert cried from the far side of the lot.

Sal and Santo walked over to Mr. Albert, whose arms were spread out almost as wide as the grin on his face. He stood in front of a 1985 Cadillac Deville.

"She's a beauty. Isn't she?" said Sal, not believing a word he said.

"Well, it's no Studebaker, but she will do," said Mr. Albert, still smiling.

"That is a weird thing to say," Santo looked at his friend.

"Yes, it is," Mr. Albert agreed.

Sal interrupted, "She's got 90,000 miles, which is low for the years she's been around."

"Santo, a low mileage vehicle," Mr. Albert marveled.

"Does it even run?" Santo was not convinced.

"I don't know. It has been here from before I got this job."

"How long was that?"

"About two years."

"This has been sitting on your lot for two years?"

"Over two years."

"How much is it?" Santo sneered, looking at Mr. Albert.

"Six thousand. No, fifty-nine hundred," the salesman wavered.

"Does it even run?" Santo looked again to Mr. Albert for help.

"Let me grab the keys, and we'll find out," Sal ran to the office before the suckers could change their minds.

"Why? Why would you do this to me?" Santo pleaded.

"I think I could find my purpose in this car."

"Couldn't you find your purpose in a Camry?"

"Has anyone, ever, found their purpose in a Camry?"

"Probably not."

"There you have it, then," said Mr. Albert triumphantly.

"Here are the keys." Sal had returned. "Let's go for a spin."

"Can you open the trunk?" asked Santo.

"Sure thing."

The trunk popped open. It was a mess, looking like a compost heap of old newspapers and take-out containers. Santo picked up a newspaper.

"1995. This car has not been cleaned since 1995."

"Think of all the treasures we could find in here," Mr. Albert offered.

"Yes, treasures. After you, Mr. Albert." Santo indicated that he should get into the trunk.

Mr. Albert looked at Santo. "Are you serious?"

"There might be an instance when you find yourself in the trunk. Don't you think?"

"I think there might be, but we can try that out at another time. Don't you think?" Mr. Albert growled.

"But it is better to be sure before we spend fifty-five hundred dollars."

"Fifty-nine hundred dollars," Sal chimed in.

"Fifty-seven hundred dollars," Santo hissed at Sal.

Sal raised his hands in surrender before walking away. "Fifty-seven hundred, it is."

"I see what you're doing," shouted Mr. Albert.

"And I see what you're doing," Santo growled at Mr. Albert.

"Yeah!"

"Yeah! Now get in the damn trunk."

They stared at each other for what seemed like an eternity in an old Hollywood western before the hero and bad guy drew their guns and started shooting. Mr. Albert caved and got into the trunk. Santo slammed the lid.

"Sounds solid." Mr. Albert offered a muffled compliment to appease Santo.

"Let's go for a ride," Santo barked at Sal, who sheepishly got in the passenger seat.

"Hey, I can really stretch out in here," Mr. Albert chirped. He liked the trunk. It could be his new happy place.

"Good," cried Santo.

A big smile came over Santo's face when he realized that he had Mr. Albert in the trunk. He put the key in the ignition.

"Let's crank this dreamboat up," he said.

The car backfired. A cloud of black smoke exploded from the tailpipe.

"Fuck," came a shrill scream from the back.

"Do you hear something?" Santo asked Sal.

"No, not a thing," Sal said, terrified of the man behind the wheel. And off they sped.

"I think there is an exhaust leak. I can't breathe," gagged Mr. Albert.

"Does the radio work?" Santo said, turning the radio up to its highest volume.

"Sounds pretty good," Sal said.

"Santo, I think there is a raccoon in here. Help!"

"Are they still repaving Fifth Street?" Santo asked Sal, ignoring the man in the trunk.

"Yes," Sal whimpered.

"Good. Let's check out the suspension on this baby."

Santo spent the next fifteen minutes driving over potholes, speed bumps, and testing the brakes at various speeds. Cries of fuck, shit, and piss harmonized with the bouncing struts.

After the test drive, they left Mr. Albert where he was while Santo signed the papers. Mr. Albert would have been incredibly angry for the hour and a half spent in the Caddy's trunk if Santo had not let him out in front of McKenna's. All was quickly forgiven.

~ 18 ~

Three days later.
One more day at the library.

"What about reincarnation?" Santo suggested.

"Reincarnation? Being reborn?" Mr. Albert grew tired of the theories.

"Yes," Santo continued. "The Buddhists say that thirty days after you die, you come back if you didn't get a passing grade. You can be reincarnated thousands of times."

"What book are you reading now?"

"The Tibetan Book of the Dead."

"So, they are saying there is no hell?"

"I think so."

"That's good."

"Why?"

"That way, I wouldn't have to see you in the afterlife," Mr. Albert chuckled.

"You are seeing me in your afterlife," Santo said, quite proud of himself.

Mr. Albert started to say something but realized it wasn't clever enough and stopped. Another comeback came into his non-functioning brain. It was not good enough either. Finally, he conceded the point.

"Touché," said the defeated Mr. Albert.

Santo smiled, humming a little tune while continuing his studies. Mr. Albert fumed.

"What does reincarnation have to do with me? That I'm reincarnated when I die, die?"

"I don't know. You get reincarnated if you don't pass the test. Maybe you don't even make it to the testing room. You missed the bus that takes you to the test."

"I missed the bus?"

"Yes."

"My brain is not functioning, and you are still stupider than me," Mr. Albert growled.

"Prove me wrong."

"Why do I have to prove every stupid idea you have wrong? Shouldn't the burden of proof be on you? You prove you are right."

"You have not fulfilled your purpose, so God sends you right back before they can stick you in the ground."

"God does this?"

"Yes."

"You are just using God as a placeholder because you have no idea what you are talking about. God is not science. God is not fact."

"Einstein used a placeholder."

"What?"

"He used a scientific placeholder all the time. He knew that science wasn't smart enough to prove some of his theories when he was alive, so he said it would be proven later," Santo sounded like an academic.

"Name one."

"General Relativity," Santo said, as if quoting from a book, "which Einstein came up with in 1916, wasn't proven until 2016 when a group of scientists from the Laser Interferometer Gravitational-Wave Observatory finally observed gravitational waves from two colliding black holes."

Mr. Albert's jaw dropped open.

"How the hell did you know that?" he finally said.

"Well, Mr. Albert, unlike you, who feels the need to draw pornography in some of the greatest philosophical and scientific books of all time, I read. I learn. I evolve."

"I will give you another touché for that one."

"Wow, two touches. I'm impressive."

"Yes, you are certainly something. So, you think I am thrown back in my body because I haven't fulfilled my purpose," Mr. Albert reiterated Santo's theory.

"Yes."

"And I am stuck here until I figure it out."

"Yes."

"Don't you think it would be easier just to tell me and then let me do it?"

"Too easy."

"Is this a game?"

"Could be."

"Where no one knows the rules?"

"Possibly."

"That would be the stupidest game ever."

"That is because you don't understand God's ways," Santo said it like he did.

"You know what that sounds like? Chaos. God, your convenient philosophical placeholder, doesn't exist. Everyone is trying to figure out their existence, but no one can because there are no rules. Chaos is just chaos. There is no purpose. We exist because of a series of coincidences which are not connected to any larger purpose. Gravitational waves exist, not because Einstein predicted them, or because a group of scientists discovered them. Their discovery will not make anyone's life better or easier because we are all still frightened people in a terrible world which doesn't care or comfort the temporal creatures living there."

"Do you really believe that?"

Mr. Albert looked directly into Santo's eyes so there would be no confusion.

"I'm sorry, Santo, I do."

"And you don't believe you have any reason to exist."

"No, I don't."

"Tell me, Mr. Albert, if there is no reason to do anything, but you can do anything since the fear of death is not a concern, why do you choose to do nothing? Why spend your days drinking in a dimly lit bar with strangers who have given up on life when there is an entire world to explore? You can float across the Pacific Ocean on an inner tube. You can climb Mt. Everest in a Hawaiian shirt and Bermuda shorts. You can learn piano."

"I have given up."

"What could you have possibly given up on when you haven't figured things out? Mr. Albert, you have the gift of time. It is a resource that the rest of us do not have. You can do it if it takes a thousand years to figure out this puzzle. Think of the good you can do for humanity. You can't give up."

"I have given up."

"You didn't give up on me. You saved me when the world let me go. You would not have talked me down from the railing if you had really given up. You would have impassively watched me jump," Santo said, smiling because he was happy that Mr. Albert saved him.

"I'm still kicking myself for that."

"I know you don't mean that. You have a gift. Please use it."

"It doesn't seem like I have a choice. God won't let me into heaven."

"I wouldn't," Santo said.

"Do you really believe all this nonsense that you spew out?"

"Like reincarnation?"

"Yes."

"It would be nice to have another chance to do good," Santo said. "I'd like to come back as a cat. Sit in my owner's lap and purr. Letting her know the world can be a good place."

"Interesting. You know a cat will eat its owner the same day if the person dies and there is no available food."

"Why should the poor cat suffer? It takes a lot of energy to purr all the time."

"If I ever did come back, I'd like to come back as a tree," Mr. Albert thought out loud.

"Really. That is so nice."

"In a park, by a well-traveled path. And I would like one of my branches to grow in the shape of a hand. And I would like my middle branch to be sticking out so I can give all the little boys and girls the finger."

"We definitely have to find you a purpose."

Savannah 1959.

Genevieve woke up in their bed. She reached over to feel her husband. The bed was empty. She thought that maybe days had passed since the hurricane and the coroner had picked up the body. She wondered if it was all a bad dream.

She rolled over and saw Benny standing in the doorway.

"What? What is going on?" she screamed, sitting up and pressing herself against the headboard.

"It is all right, Genevieve. Everything is fine."

"But you were dead. I saw you dead. I touched you. You were cold."

"I know."

"Then how can you be here? Am I losing my mind?"

"No, you are as sane as you ever were."

"Then I don't understand," she wept, afraid of the spirit in front of her.

"I am dead," he said softly, trying not to upset his wife even more.

"Are you a ghost?"

"No."

Genevieve ran to the kitchen. She grabbed a knife and turned to the monster. Benny followed her but stopped at the door after he saw the blade in her hand.

"It is okay. I promise you. Anyway, what good would a knife do if I were a ghost?"

She lunged toward her husband and plunged the knife into his stomach. He stood there. Her eyes went from the knife up to his face. She recognized no pain or discomfort. She backed away from him until she touched the wall on the opposite side of the room. She sank to the floor.

"Please don't. Please don't cry," he pleaded as he approached her, the knife still protruding from his stomach.

As soon as he took a step, she recoiled in a ball, trying to protect herself. He stopped.

"I am dead, Genevieve, but I've been this way since we met."

"I've known you for over four years."

"Yes."

"And you have been dead all this time?"

"Yes."

"I don't believe you."

"Would you rather believe that I died during the hurricane?"

"Yes."

"That would make this very weird."

"This is very weird."

"Yes, I know, but it would make it weirder," he said, pulling the knife from his belly.

Benny looked at the blade. There was no sign of blood or goo on it. He wiped it off anyway. Now Benny had a knife in his hand. Genevieve looked terrified. He offered it to her but then thought better of it. He put the knife down on the counter and backed away. An uncomfortable silence followed.

"By the way, how many days was I out?"

"Three days."

"That seems about average."

"Average for what? What is happening, Benny?"

"Genevieve, I promise you I don't know."

"How could you not know?" She stood up, feeling less afraid.

"I don't know."

"How could you not tell me? I am your wife. Don't you love me?" Now she was angry.

"I love you more than anything." He stepped towards her.

"You keep away from me."

"Please."

"No, this cannot be happening. You must be a friend of the devil."

"Why couldn't I be a friend of God?"

"Because God doesn't do things like this."

"How do you know what God does? Haven't you said that God works in mysterious ways? Isn't this mysterious? How can we know God's plan?"

"That is what the devil would say to trap my soul."

"I'm not here to destroy your soul. I love you, Genevieve, with all of my soul."

"You have no soul," she screamed and ran past him to lock herself in the bedroom.

Maybe she needs some time, he thought.

He walked over to the locked bedroom door and leaned his head against the barrier that separated him from the woman he loved.

"That's all right, Genevieve. I know this is a lot to process, and I will give you that time. But understand that I will be here when you want to talk. I will always be here for you."

~ 19 ~

Three days later, 3 AM.
On Beach and 3rd.

After a full night at McKenna's, the customers were asked to leave. Mr. Albert said goodbye to his friends, hugging Walter, Mac, Joe, and Frankie. Santo was not comfortable embracing these alcoholic ex-criminals yet, preferring to wave embarrassingly. *What did Mr. Albert have to worry about?* Santo thought. *He's already dead. I'm very susceptible to germs.*

Mr. Albert loved McKenna's. Everyone knew his secret but didn't care. Walter thought his wife was still alive. Joe was a part-time flasher during tourist season, and Frankie was homeless because of his addictions. All one big, happy family.

Once outside the bar, his family scurried away like rats when the lights were turned on. Soon Mr. Albert and Santo were alone. The cool night air woke Mr. Albert up, giving him a second wind.

"I feel a little hungry. When did we eat last?" Mr. Albert said, over his grumbling tummy.

"About twelve hours ago," Santo shook his head. If he kept up this nonsense, he would be dead long before he paid off his debt to Mr. Albert.

"That explains it. Shhh," he said to quiet his digestive tract.

"Let me ask you a question."

"Go ahead."

"How can you feel hungry? You are dead. You've no bodily functions."

"It is a mystery. How about a wiener?"

"What?"

"A hotdog, you idiot," Mr. Albert rolled his eyes.

"From the Wiener King?"

"Yes."

"But you always say it will kill me."

"Who knows, maybe that is my purpose?"

"You should have let me jump," moaned Santo.

"Shoulda, woulda, coulda," Mr. Albert responded blissfully.

"So, your purpose is to eat a hotdog?"

"My purpose is whatever is in front of me now," Mr. Albert responded as the Buddha.

"Really?" Santo said with an air of disbelief.

"Maybe," he said, holding his ground.

Santo started to lose it. "The great Holy Father gave you eternal life so you can eat hotdogs? That is your purpose?"

"Who knows?"

"You know. I know. Even Walter knows. You are making a mockery of the whole God-given purpose thing!" Santo cried, jumping up and down.

"Maybe you are right." Mr. Albert relented because he had never made Santo behave like a cartoon character before. "But I think we should cross it off the list just in case."

"We will cross it off the list, and then we will go home," Santo said, putting his foot down. "I am tired and cranky. The Wiener King will probably be closed anyway."

"That would be unfortunate."

And so, the two drunk men stumbled off in search of a beer-boiled hotdog. Ten minutes later, they arrived at the darkened establishment.

"I told you, Mr. Albert, the Wiener King would not be open now."

"'Tis a pity," he said, feeling very medieval. "What time is it anyway?"

"After three."

"In the afternoon? What happened to the sun?"

"In the morning," Santo said, exhausted.

"Well, that explains some things."

"What things?"

"The transient nature of temporal beings," Mr. Albert said philosophically.

"I am sure it does," Santo agreed, giving up.

"Why am I so hungry?"

"It is spiritual hunger. You want to find a purpose in your life."

"I don't buy it," Mr. Albert grumbled. "Is the Oceancrest open now?"

"No, Mr. Albert. I think it is best if we go home."

"Maybe in a little while. Let me sit down for a little moment." He sounded shaky.

"No, Mr. Albert. I don't think that would be a good idea."

But Mr. Albert did not listen to Santo. He sat down, leaning against the door of the Wiener King and closed his eyes. The cold wind blew down the deserted street. Santo stomped his feet to keep warm. Ten minutes passed. Santo lightly kicked Mr. Albert to wake him. It had no effect, so he kicked a little harder. Mr. Albert fell over. He was dead, dead.

"Oh, shit," Santo muttered. "As if this night wasn't bad enough."

He reached down to lift the dead man.

"Why are you so heavy? Are your non-functioning organs made of lead?"

He finally managed to get Mr. Albert on his feet. He slung the dead man's arm over his shoulder to better support him.

"What is going on here?"

Santo turned around to see two police officers standing in front of him with their hands on their holsters, ready to pull their guns if necessary. Santo raised his hands, and Mr. Albert plummeted. Santo went to catch him, but the officers drew their weapons.

"Hold it right there. Get on the ground," Officer Robbins demanded.

Santo complied with the officer, lying face down on the cold pavement, his hands behind his back. Officer Davis went over to Mr. Albert. He felt his pulse and turned to his partner.

"He's dead, Jim," Officer Davis said.

Officer Robbins cuffed Santo and threw him against the front of the Wiener King. Officer Davis went to call backup in the patrol car parked down the street.

"What is your name?"

"Santo Murphy, Officer."

"What happened here, Mr. Murphy?"

"Me and my friend just closed McKenna's. He was hungry and wanted a hotdog."

"A hotdog at three in the morning," Officer Robbins said, his eyes narrowed.

"That's what I told him."

Officer Davis returned and announced, "The M.E. is on the way."

"Mr. Murphy here says he and his friend wanted a hotdog," Robbins told his partner.

"We saw you kicking him," Officer Davis challenged the suspect. "That is some way to treat your friend."

"That is easy to explain."

"Go ahead," Officer Robbins said.

Santo realized that it could not be easily explained. He lowered his head and thought about the negative consequences of meeting Mr. Albert.

"I thought so," Officer Robbins smiled. "Here's what I think. You're a junkie looking for a fix. You see this guy here and decide to rob him. You kick him around for a while. He dies. You want to drag him down an alley to clean him out. Then we appear, and you are screwed."

"Sounds about right to me," Officer Davis concurred. "Anything to add, Mr. Murphy?"

"No, Officers."

"Okay. We will wait until the body is picked up, and then, we will take you in and book you for murder," Officer Davis informed Santo.

"That seems about right."

Santo sat there quietly, not wanting to provoke the officers. He thought he had failed Mr. Albert. His one job was to keep him out of the morgue. Now Mr. Albert will probably end up in some top-secret government facility, and he will end up with a cellmate named Crusher.

Officer Robbins lifted Santo to his feet. The two officers loaded him into the patrol car as the M.E. took charge of the body.

Santo thought *all this trouble for a hotdog.* And then he thought, Mr. Albert could be right when he said, *A hotdog might be the death of him.*

The patrol car pulled away slowly.

~ 20 ~

Later that morning.

An examination room adjacent to the morgue.

Mr. Albert opened his eyes. The bright lights above his head made him squint for a moment until he became accustomed to his environment. The fact that he was not in a body bag gave him hope. He rolled on his side and sat up on the table. This certainly was not the morgue. He wasn't naked, still wearing the clothes he went to McKenna's in whenever he went to Mckenna's last. Where did Santo stash him? Then he saw a shadowy figure in a darkened corner of the room. Dr. Mancha stepped into the light.

"Good morning, Mr. Albert. Did you have a nice nap?"

"Dr. Mancha?"

"Yes. Although it is not quite a nap, is it? What can we call it?"

"I call it dead, dead."

"Not very creative," said the doctor.

"Didn't know I needed to send you the list of descriptors of my conditions for your approval. Where is Dr. Johnson?"

"The good doctor will not be joining us today."

"Why not?" Mr. Albert asked suspiciously.

"I think we will introduce you to some other interested parties."

"Like who?"

"Like whom?" Dr. Mancha said, correcting him.

"Asshole. I thought you were a doctor, not an English teacher."

"Can't I be both?"

"No, that is not allowed."

"Well, you can add government informant to the list as well. Please, excuse me."

Dr. Mancha bowed his head slightly before exiting the room.

"You mean sleaze-bag government informant," Mr. Albert yelled to the empty room.

The door flew open, and Dr. Johnson stood in the doorway. After a dramatic pause, he moved quickly into the room.

"Dr. Johnson!"

"Mr. Albert! We must move quickly. Help me move the body."

"The body?"

"I have another body in the storage room."

"I don't think this hospital is following all the rules," Mr. Albert questioned the standards of the hospital.

"I brought it in here when I heard Dr. Mancha moved you."

Mr. Albert looked disinterested and counted the ceiling tiles.

"Quickly, the men in black suits will be here soon."

"Men in black suits? Sounds exciting." Mr. Albert stopped counting.

"I'm afraid it won't be very exciting for you."

They replaced Mr. Albert with a body that had arrived two days before. They finished their work and slipped out the side door before the G-men arrived with Dr. Mancha.

"Where did he go?" Dr. Mancha asked, realizing the corpse was not Mr. Albert.

"He looks dead to me," the first G-man said, poking the body.

"That's not him."

"No?" said G-man One.

"But you just left," added G-man Two.

"Yes."

"So, the dead guy left, and another dead guy replaced him?" said the first.

"Mr. Albert. He was here, and now he is not," corrected the doctor.

"But if he is not actually dead, why shouldn't he move?" said the second G-man.

"Oh, he is dead. Dead as a doornail," insisted Mancha.

"Like this guy," said number two, pointing to the corpse.

"No, this guy is really dead."

"So, Mr. Albert is not dead?" said one.

"They are both dead, but this guy is normal dead."

"Mr. Albert is not normal dead," said two, shaking his head at one.

"Am I normal dead?" the first laughed.

"You are not normal dead because you are not dead," Dr. Mancha said, losing patience.

"All right, I think I have had enough. Dr. Mancha, filing a false report to the government is a federal offense. You need to come with us," said number one, no longer laughing.

"I can assure you, that everything I have said is true. You can ask Dr. Johnson."

"Come with us." The G-man took hold of Dr. Mancha and escorted him from the room.

A few blocks from the hospital, Dr. Johnson and Mr. Albert stopped in an alley to talk.

"Whew, that was a close one!" Mr. Albert said with false enthusiasm.

"Mr. Albert, this is serious. That stunt that we just pulled won't hold them for long. A quick check of hospital records will reveal the truth."

"What truth?"

"That you have been to the morgue at least three times."

"That might raise suspicion," Mr. Albert said, casually acknowledging the situation.

"Yes, it might. You must get out of town."

"Where do you want me to go?"

"Do you have a place to hide?"

"Why should I hide?"

"Because you have sent up some red flags."

Mr. Albert shrugged.

"Look, I have a cabin by a lake, up near Autumn Winds," the doctor suggested.

"Where?"

"Near Mt. Tammany."

"Where?"

"I'll give you directions. Where is Santo?"

"I don't know. He was with me when I died, died. Probably abandoned me. You can't get good help nowadays."

"Mr. Albert, you were brought in as a possible homicide. If Santo was with you, he might have been arrested for your murder."

"Interesting. Tell me about your cabin. Is there a pier? Can I fish?"

"Yes, you can fish."

"But I don't like fishing."

"Then you don't have to fish. Aren't you worried about Santo?"

"Well, they can't charge him with murder if the body walked off."

"Still, I think we had better find out if he's been arrested," Doctor Johnson insisted.

"If you think that is best."

They headed off to the police station in a surprisingly casual manner.

Savannah 1959.
Three hours later.

Genevieve emerged from the bedroom. She had a Bible in her right hand and read from Ephesians 6:10-18.

"Finally, be strong in the Lord and in the strength of his might. Put on the whole armor of God, that you may be able to stand against the schemes of the devil. For we do not wrestle against flesh and blood, but against the rulers, against the authorities, against the cosmic powers over this present darkness, against the spiritual forces of evil in the heavenly places. Therefore, take up the whole armor of God, that you may be able to withstand in the evil day, and having done all, to stand firm. Stand therefore, having fastened on the belt of truth, and having put on the breastplate of righteousness..."

She approached Benny, clear in her heart that Jesus would help her save her dead husband's soul. Benny retreated until he touched the wall in the dining room. It wasn't as if he feared the words she was saying because he was a demon. He did not understand them or what they had to do with him. But her tone revealed her anger, and he didn't like that. He backed himself into a corner and could not escape. Genevieve approached slowly and deliberately, continuing to shout verses from the Bible. This time from James 5:16.

"Therefore, confess your sins to one another and pray for one another, that you may be healed. The prayer of a righteous person has great power as it is working."

She raised her hand to the heavens bringing down on the demon all the power of her faith and the love of Jesus.

Genevieve screamed at the devil, "Confess!"

Benny began to fear the incredible power of the almighty working through his wife. *Maybe she was right*, he thought. Maybe he was an unclean spirit inhabiting the body of a person who died long ago. *Maybe he was a servant of the devil trying to destroy God's holy work on this mortal plane.* He closed his eyes and waited for the end.

She stood before him and prayed as if she could save the world with her passion. This time her prayers were from Luke 11:20.

"But if it is by the finger of God that I cast out demons, then the kingdom of God has come upon you."

She touched Benny with her finger, expecting a gush of wind to blast through the room as the demon departed, followed by the carcass of her husband collapsing on the dining room floor. That did not happen. Nothing happened. She poked him again. She poked him a third time. Benny opened his eyes and smiled. He had not been destroyed. Maybe he wasn't a monster.

Genevieve pounded his chest with her fist. She looked at her husband's face, only to see him smiling. Taking that as a sign that she did not have the power to battle the devil, she screamed and ran back to her room, locking the door behind her.

If she did not have the faith now, she would purge the sin from her body and try again when she was more powerful. Somehow, she thought that this was her task to accomplish alone. This was a test that God had given her, and if she succeeded, she would soon see her blessed mother in heaven. She paced the room throughout the night, hoping for divine inspiration.

~ 21 ~

Ten minutes later.
At the police station.

The police station in Wildwinds was reminiscent of those small-town police stations in T.V. shows from the fifties. The two floors had a front desk and police officer desks on the ground floor, administrative offices on the second floor, and holding cells in the basement. The walls were a dull battleship gray over a dull battleship blue, with the line dividing the north and south at the height of three feet.

Dr. Johnson led Mr. Albert to the front desk. An older officer looked through narrowed, suspicious eyes.

"Can I help you?"

"I was wondering if you arrested a Santo Murphy last night?" Dr. Johnson queried.

"And how does this concern you?"

"I believe he was arrested erroneously, if he was arrested."

The officer's eyes narrowed, and the doctor felt himself shrinking a little. Officer Santori picked up the phone.

"Can you come up front for a moment? Thanks." He hung up the phone and motioned for the two visitors to sit down. Mr. Albert began to whistle. Dr. Johnson shushed him. Mr. Albert tapped his foot impatiently.

"Really? Are you a child?"

"Aren't we all children of the heavenly father?" Mr. Albert said, striking a holy pose.

"Quiet," said the doctor, losing his patience.

"How may we help you, gentlemen?" Officer Davis said without looking at the two squabbling men.

"What the..." Officer Robbins, who was beside his partner, gasped.

"What is going on here?" Davis said, seeing the victim as well.

Dr. Johnson stood up, happy to escape the silly conversation he was having with Mr. Albert. He showed the officers his identification.

"Hello, I am Dr. Johnson. Mr. Albert, whom you recognize, was brought in last night for an autopsy to discover if his death was a homicide. As you can see, he is not dead, but he does suffer from Lazarus syndrome, which mimics death until the patient sits up...Surprise."

"But I took his pulse. He was dead," Officer Davis objected.

"Yes, that is typical for Mr. Albert's condition."

"Did you arrest Mr. Murphy?" Mr. Albert said, interrupting all the blah, blah, blah.

"Yes," stumbled Officer Robbins. "We were holding him until we got the coroner's report."

"As you can see," continued the doctor calmly. "You won't be getting one of those."

"Can you release my friend?" Mr. Albert smiled.

The police officers looked at each other. This would look bad for them if Mr. Albert or the doctor complained, not to mention the lawsuits that would be forthcoming from Mr. Murphy.

"Yes, right away," Officer Davis said quietly.

The two officers skulked off to release the suspect. Ten minutes later, Dr. Johnson, Mr. Albert, and Santo Murphy were outside the police station. The doctor gave Santo the directions to his cabin, and within an hour, the dead man and the former criminal were headed out of town.

~ 22 ~

Three hours later.

At Uncle John's Fish and Tackle General Store.

The closest place to buy beer to Dr. Johnson's cabin in the woods.

Santo and Mr. Albert were near the end of their journey. They had been driving in silence for some time. Neither talked of immortality or purpose. Santo thought of his incarceration and the convoluted directions he received from Dr. Johnson. But he was grateful to be away from the Jersey shore. Mr. Albert thought a bit of fluff was stuck in his nose. Occasionally, he would exhale through his nostrils abruptly.

"What are you doing?" Santo demanded.

"Nothing. Are we there yet?"

"Does it look like we are there?"

"No."

"So why are you asking?"

"To distract you."

"From what?"

"It worked."

"Tell me, what's with the nose noise?" Santo said.

"I think I have a bit of fluff in my nose. I was trying to get it out."

"Like that?" Santo imitated and exaggerated his companion's ridiculous exhaling.

"Would you rather I pick my nose? Because I will. I'll pick my nose right in front of you. Would you like that?"

Santo saw a general store and pulled into the parking lot.

"What are you doing?" Mr. Albert complained.

"I think we are about ten minutes from the cabin. We should pick up a few supplies."

"Sounds good. I am about dried out."

Santo shrugged and went into the store, followed by his traveling companion. The store was more of a museum than a bait and tackle shop. There were fishing rods, tackle, and a refrigerator with bait, but the walls had concert posters and memorabilia of bands from the sixties and seventies.

The middle-aged clerk sat in a tall chair behind the counter and picked a tune on a banjo. He sang the lyrics absentmindedly.

> *I ain't gonna grieve this world no more.*
> *I ain't gonna grieve this world no more.*
> *I ain't gonna grieve this world no more.*

"Welcome, strangers." The clerk smiled. His full, wild beard and psychedelic shirt reminded Santo of someone he never knew.

"How do you know we are strange?" Mr. Albert said, to be disagreeable.

"People are strange when you're a stranger," said the man, welcoming the snarkiness.

"Bathroom," Mr. Albert demanded.

"To the back on the left."

"Excuse my friend, we just arrived from the shore, and we are dead tired," Santo said.

"I'm dead," Mr. Albert interrupted jovially.

"Tired," Santo snarled at Mr. Albert.

"Dead," Mr. Albert over-emphasized the pause between that word and the next. "Tired."

Before leaving for the bathroom, he indicated to Santo that he would resolve his nostril fluff predicament with his pointing finger moving up and down about a foot in front of his face.

"Can I help you, gentlemen?"

"Need to pick up some food. We are staying at Dr. Johnson's cabin for a few days."

"Well, then, we need to know each other's names. I'm Jerry."

He extended his right hand. A chunk of his middle finger was missing. Santo took his hand, not wanting to offend the store clerk.

"Okay," Santo said, unsure why proper introductions were called for. "I'm Santo, and that was Mr. Albert."

"Mr. Albert? What is he royalty?" Jerry laughed.

"He is special."

"How is Wally? Working hard or hardly working?"

"Who?"

"Dr. Johnson. You must know him very well."

Santo smiled and grabbed a basket.

Jerry laughed to himself. "Dr. Johnson. Mr. Albert. Aren't we fancy?"

Santo filled his basket with instant coffee, milk, bread, peanut butter, and crackers. He wondered what they were doing here. What was the plan? Where do they go from here? Dr. Johnson informed Santo about the government agents. What if they came up here looking for them? Mr. Albert had value, but what use would poor Santo be? They would probably take care of him and bury his body in the woods while Mr. Albert ate peanut butter crackers.

"Do you have any alcohol?" Mr. Albert had returned. His nostrils looked quite fluffless.

"Just beer and wine in the cooler. Nearest liquor store is in Pennywhistle," Jerry offered.

"How far is that?"

"About ten miles." The clerk said, pointing down the road to the left.

"What happened to your hand?"

"Some childhood hijinks."

"What is ten miles that way?" Mr. Albert said, pointing in the opposite direction.

"Cumberland's Folly."

"What's in Cumberland's Folly?

"Cumberland's Folly," Jerry said deadpan.

"That's it?"

"There is a museum dedicated to the folly."

"Sounds exciting."

"Mr. Albert, do you want any beer?" It was Santo's turn to interrupt.

"Yes, thanks." He was happy once again.

Santo added a couple of six-packs to the groceries. They got the supplies in the car and continued to the cabin. Santo looked annoyed.

"Something the matter?" Mr. Albert smiled, thinking of the beer to be consumed when they stopped.

"Nothing."

"Because if it was the whole fluff thing. I promise I used some toilet paper."

Santo focused on the road. Five minutes passed in silence, then a single word escaped from his tightened lips, "Crackers."

Savannah 1959.

Genevieve stayed in the bedroom for two more days, beating herself with her bible and a belt to purify her spirit. Benny heard her weakening voice through the door, angrily debating the merits of each plan of action against the devil who had taken her husband away. Benny let her have the time to think through what had happened. He hoped she would eventually realize that he was not the devil's servant. But with each passing hour, he felt her slipping away and, she might never believe that his intentions were pure. He simply loved his wife.

He found himself sitting on the floor, leaning against their bedroom door at five in the morning. He knew she was awake. He heard her pacing.

"Genevieve, I am sorry. I should have told you before," he said to the uncaring air. "I should have told you that I am not like other people. But I was so afraid of losing you. Why would you love me if you knew the truth about me? Why would anyone? I don't know why I am like this."

The door suddenly opened, and Benny fell back to the floor, smacking his head.

"Ow."

He looked up, terrified, as Genevieve towered over him. She glared down at him.

"How can you not know you were dead?"

"I knew I was dead. I don't know why I'm not dead, dead."

"Dead, dead? That's the stupidest thing I have ever heard. For most people, just being dead is good enough for them."

"I agree with you one hundred percent," he said from his horizontal position.

"What are you still doing on the floor?" she growled.

Benny sprang up, happy that they were in the same room. Genevieve looked different. There wasn't any color in her cheeks. Even though she was only in the bedroom for a couple of days, she looked gaunt and unsettled. There were bags under her eyes from lack of sleep and bruises on her arms and legs from the self-flagellation inflicted to strengthen her resolve.

"Why didn't you tell me?" her voice softened.

"I didn't think you would understand."

"Well, how could I understand if you never told me anything?"

"I don't know anything about this."

"How can you not know anything? Do you remember your parents?"

"No."

"Any childhood memories?"

"No."

"What do you remember?"

"I've moved around a lot, and sometimes I woke up in a hospital or a morgue. That's how I figured out I was dead. And once my secret was found out, I had to move. That's why I couldn't tell you. I didn't want to leave."

"And what about your Mr. Thatcher?"

"I've never met him."

"Does he know your secret?"

"Yes, I think so."

"Then I want to speak to him. Maybe he could explain this."

"I will do anything you say as long as you forgive me."

"I will never forgive you. How can you contact Mr. Thatcher?"

"I have his telephone number."

"Well, isn't it convenient that the power is still off?"

And just as if it were a cue in a play, the lights came back on. Genevieve acknowledged the divine intervention and walked over to the phone on the living room end table. She picked it up and listened for the dial tone before extending the phone to Benny. He shuffled over to her like a brow-beaten boy and took the phone.

"Hello, operator. I'd like to make a long-distance call. Yes, ma'am. Chicago, please. Hemlock three five one zero eight. Yes, ma'am." He held his hand over the phone and whispered to Genevieve, "She's connecting us."

He smiled, hoping to get a smile in return. No smile was forthcoming.

"Yes, hello, Mr. Thatcher. This is Benny. Yes, I am all right. The hurricane gave us a scare for a moment there. But about that. My wife found out about my condition. Yes, I know. I know. The thing is, she wants to talk to you about it. Maybe you could explain things to her."

Benny offered Genevieve the phone. She snatched it from his hand.

"Yes, Mr. Thatcher. Hello? Hello? There's no one there."

She hung up the phone before turning angrily back to Benny.

"What exactly are you trying to pull here?"

"What do you mean?" Benny cringed.

"I didn't speak to any Mr. Thatcher because there was no one on the line. I don't believe there even is a Mr. Thatcher," she cried.

"No, there is. I spoke to him. Maybe we got disconnected. I'll try again."

"Don't bother. I want you out of my house."

"What?"

"I don't know who or what you are. And it does not matter. I do not want anything to do with you anymore!" her voice rising to a high-pitched scream.

"Let me just get something from the bedroom," he walked away from her.

He did not need anything. Benny thought, if he had a little more time, she might change her mind. Genevieve was not in a forgiving mood. She grabbed a vase and threw it at him. He ducked, and it hit her mother's cheval mirror. She screamed that another piece of her mother was gone. He was destroying her life bit by bit. She lunged for him and pushed him to the door. She grabbed a book from the end table and beat him.

"Get out. Get out of my house!"

Benny left quickly. He looked up, and there were people on the street wondering what the commotion was.

"She's a little upset. Hurricane ruined her camellias," he smiled with a perfunctory wave.

The neighbors exchanged knowing glances and went on their way. Benny sat down on the front steps. When the street was empty, he buried his head in his hands.

~ 23 ~

Two days later.
In Dr. Johnson's cabin in the woods.

Mr. Albert looked over the lake from the deck of Dr. Johnson's cabin. Steam rose from the lake, making it look like it was on fire.

Santo joined him on the deck, "I thought I would find you here."

"I love the water, Santo. Something about the gentle waves lapping the shore, the constant sound, the constant return makes me feel at peace. Everything is the same as it was. Everything is as it will be. I thought of a girl last night."

"Did you know her?"

"I thought I did, but it could have just been a dream."

"Tell me about her, please," Santo said, pulling up a chair.

"She had a sundress on, singing under a beautiful huge tree. Spanish Moss hanging like frozen rain, dwarfing her."

"This small girl, did she have a name?"

"I don't know what her name was. She could have been a compilation of many girls I have met. She could have been from an advertisement."

"What kind of advertisement?"

"I don't know, does it matter? Tequila."

"Interesting," said Santo, rubbing his chin.

"What is interesting?"

"She was selling alcohol, which makes someone lose their inhibitions. Maybe be honest. Maybe you were honest and open with this small girl. Maybe you were in love with her."

"How are you getting one thing from the other? She might be from a poster in a bar. And she wasn't small. A very big tree dwarfed her."

"So, you care more about the tree size than the woman you were in love with?"

"No! What are you talking about?"

"The tree is much larger in your memory than the girl. This isn't easy to visualize from your description. How big was the tree?"

"It was a normal-sized full-grown tree, thirty, forty feet high."

"Doesn't seem like a very big tree, average at best, maybe even a little small as trees go."

"It doesn't matter how big the tree was. It was the girl, the girl who I was thinking about!"

Mr. Albert cried, angry with Santo's stupidity.

"What was her name?"

"Genevieve. Wait. What just happened?"

"I distracted you."

"You are very crafty. I thought you were stupid," Mr. Albert said with admiration.

"I still might prove you right. Tell me about Genevieve, Mr. Albert."

"I don't know."

"Should I be stupid again? I have many more questions about that tree."

"No, thank you, Santo. I remember seeing her from across the quiet street, her soft lyrical voice dancing in my head. People walked past her, not even aware that this beautiful person existed, but I was aware."

"Did you go over to her? Did you talk to her?"

"No, some moments are too perfect to ruin."

"If you didn't speak to her, how did you know her name?"

"I guess I must have spoken to her at some point," Mr. Albert smiled. "I spoke to her."

"So, what do you think this girl has to do with you now?"

"I don't know."

"Memories are important."

"I surprisingly have very few memories."

"That makes each memory you have extra important. Maybe Miss Genevieve has something to do with your purpose."

Mr. Albert humored his friend if only to pass some time. "Do you think?"

"You give me so few hints. This seems important."

"Does it?"

"Yes, it does. We need some more information. What kind of tree was it?"

"Are we back on the tree?" Mr. Albert said, losing patience again.

"The tree can give us a location."

"Trees grow everywhere."

"Not all trees," Santo speculated.

"I would think the Spanish Moss would be more of a hint."

"I don't know Spanish Moss."

"Ay Dios Mío," Mr. Albert smiled.

"It doesn't grow in Jersey."

"No, it doesn't."

"Where does it grow?"

"In the South," Mr. Albert was surprised that he knew this.

"Have you ever been to the South?"

"I don't remember."

"How is it that you remember so little?"

"Santo, I don't have any brain functions. I think I am doing okay!"

"So, you may or may not have met a girl named Genevieve in a southern city sometimes when sundresses were in style."

"That sounds accurate," Mr. Albert's attention returned to the lake.

"Not much to go on."

"No."

"But more than we had to go on yesterday!" Santo said with a big grin.

"Maybe not. It could just be a random memory."

"You are a very stubborn person, Mr. Albert. Dreams are not random. Why should memories be?"

"I do not know why anything should be anything except random moments in a chaotic eternity."

"Things can be random and important at the same time."

"Really?"

"Yes, each random moment has a truth," Santo philosophized.

"How?"

"Does it not follow the rules of nature?"

"I would think."

"We recognize this lake because it is exhibiting lake-like characteristics," Santo started to sound like a physics teacher.

"True."

"But what is a lake?"

"A body of water smaller than an ocean," Mr. Albert suggested.

"That is one way to describe it."

"Is there another way?"

"There is probably a deeper truth behind the body of water idea."

"Okay."

"You are dead and not dead."

"Yes."

"You are both, but really neither. We just don't have a good definition of what you are."

"Go on."

"So, your truth is not obvious to anyone yet, but there is a truth behind your existence. You are following some laws of nature that no one understands."

"Like God," said Mr. Albert because he knew it would annoy his friend.

"You are not God."

"But I am a placeholder."

"A placeholder," Santo acknowledged the circular nature of many of their conversations.

"You said Einstein used a placeholder. I'm using the higher-being placeholder. God was a placeholder for primitive man to understand what was incomprehensible to them. Sun rises every day. How does that happen? It must be because there is something that is pulling the strings."

"So, God is a placeholder for anything we don't understand until we understand it?" Santo asked.

"Maybe."

"What happens when we understand things?"

"Then we don't need God."

"We don't need God?"

"Don't worry, Santo. There will always be something we don't understand. Even if it is the nature of God itself."

"That makes me feel better."

"I don't know why it should."

Savannah 1959.

Three days had passed since Genevieve threw Benny out of the house. He stayed in the yard even though it was getting colder at night. Sometimes she glanced out to see if he was still around. When she saw him, she screamed a verse from the bible and then went back to pacing behind closed curtains.

Benny, on occasion, would walk around the neighborhood helping people to clean up after the storm. He tried to do good for others, and they seemed to appreciate his efforts. Besides being homeless, everything had reverted to normal. Benny returned to his house to find Jacqueline, Genevieve's sister coming out the front door.

"Well, I guess you are not dead," she seemed a little disappointed.

"You spoke to Genevieve?"

"Of course I did. We are sisters. And I wanted to make sure she was all right"

"Is she?" Benny asked, hoping that his wife's anger was abating.

Jacqueline's tone softened. She did not like Benny but knew he cared for her sister. And her sister needed help.

"What is going on, Benjamin?"

"I don't know."

"How could you not know? You are her husband."

"I passed out during the storm."

"And she thought you died?"

He nodded, ashamed that he could not tell her the truth.

"But you woke up?"

"Yes."

"And she still thinks you are dead? Like *Invasion of the Body Snatchers?*"

"I think more like demonic possession."

"She has not been the same since Momma died."

"She has been very sad."

"What are you going to do, Benjamin?"

"I will wait around until she forgives me."

"Forgives you for what?"

"We have all done terrible things, Jacqueline. I'm not innocent."

"Well, let me know if I can do anything. Lord knows you two are perfect for each other."

At that moment, Genevieve burst through the door.

"Jackie, stay away from him," she screamed.

"We were just talking."

"He is a demon. He will steal your soul and drag you down to Hell!"

A few neighbors looked in their direction. Old Mrs. Mulvaney went inside to call the police. She was fed up with the racket that Genevieve had caused in the neighborhood for the last few days. "Enough is enough," she mumbled as she went back into the house.

"Please, darling," Benny protested.

Genevieve ran inside and came out with anything she could get her hands on. She threw the objects at her devil husband.

"Keep away from my sister."

A plate crashed on the sidewalk. Benny managed to sidestep the projectile.

"And get away from my house."

An atomic starburst wall clock flew past his head. Jacqueline made her way behind the tree for protection. She was horrified and amused at the same time. All those years as Momma's favorite had come to this, an embarrassment to the neighborhood and a broken marriage.

"But I love you. You are my wife," pleaded the distraught Benny.

"Not anymore. I've called my lawyer. He will take care of this."

"Please, Genevieve."

A police car pulled up, and two officers got out. A plate crashed at Officer Moray's feet. He reached for his gun but didn't unholster it. It was just a domestic dispute, and the woman seemed to be handling her own. Officer Simmons opened the gate and stepped into the yard.

"Ma'am, please calm down. What is the problem here?"

"You want to know the problem? He's dead. That's the problem."

"He doesn't look dead."

"He is, and I reported it over a week ago, but no one came to pick up the body."

"I'm sorry, ma'am, but we were trying to keep the peace."

"And then he woke up, and I thought he was the devil, and I stabbed him."

"You stabbed him?" Officer Simmons asked. The situation seemed to be escalating.

"With a kitchen knife. I stabbed him in the stomach with a kitchen knife."

"Sir," he turned to Benny. "Did she stab you?"

Benny remained silent. He did not know what to say or how to say it in a way that the officers would understand.

"Unbutton your shirt, please," the officer requested.

Benny complied. There was no wound. He smiled sheepishly at the officers.

"No!" Genevieve ran into the house.

She immediately returned with the kitchen knife. "I'll show you! I'll show you!" she howled as she charged her husband.

The police officers intercepted and disarmed her.

"He's dead. He's dead. You can't kill him. Give me your gun, and I'll prove it."

The officers handcuffed her. They struggled to get her safely into the patrol car. Genevieve hit her head on the car door but continued to curse Benny, the policemen, and the world in general. Benny ran to the car. Officer Moray told him to keep back.

"Where are you taking her?" Benny moaned.

"We will book her for public endangerment. And they will get her mentally evaluated."

"But I won't press charges," Benny argued.

"Sir, she is dangerous. Now step away from the vehicle. Please, folks, go back to your homes. Everything has been taken care of here."

The crowd that had gathered during the disturbance slowly dissipated. Jacqueline left without saying goodbye. Benny stood in the front yard all alone. He looked at the tree where he first saw Genevieve. There were the letters BB and GP encircled by a heart carved into the tree. He picked up the remnants of the clock. They had bought it on their honeymoon because, Genevieve said, *we have all the time in the world.*

~ 24 ~

One day later.
At Uncle John's Bait and Tackle.
Three days after their first visit.

Jerry, Santo, and Mr. Albert had become great friends. Mr. Albert and Jerry sat outside the tackle shop playing checkers on a whiskey barrel. They sat on rocking chairs and would lean in when it was time to make their move. A bottle of whiskey sat next to the board. They were less interested in the outcome of the game than in the quality of the whiskey, which was quite acceptable for the time of day. Santo wandered around the store, looking at the pictures and memorabilia. There was something about Jerry.

"Checkmate!" shouted Mr. Albert, taking Jerry's final piece. He knocked back his drink, slamming the glass down for emphasis.

"You have no idea how to play Checkers do you?" Jerry questioned.

"No, but I beat you, didn't I?"

"That's because I don't know how to play either."

"Another round, then?" Mr. Albert said, already setting up the pieces.

"Why not?"

They set up the board, placing the pieces in a random manner. Santo joined them on the porch bringing a couple of beers with him.

"So, I finally realized who you remind me of," Santo said, as he passed out the beers.

Jerry smiled. "On the count of three, then. One. Two. Three.... Jerry Garcia."

Santo said it at the same time. Santo and Jerry laughed. Mr. Albert was too interested in the correct setup of their nonsensical game to be amused.

"How did you know?" Santo asked.

"I get that a lot. Well, not as much as I used to. There are fewer Dead Heads around."

"Are you Jerry Garcia?"

"Jerry Garcia is dead," Jerry said seriously.

Santo looked at Mr. Albert with concern. Mr. Albert looked at Santo with a big smile. He finally got the checkers in the correct position. There were sixteen black checkers stacked on top of each other on his side of the board and all the red pieces were crowded in a corner near Jerry's side. One could only imagine the game Mr. Albert hoped to win with this configuration. He looked at Santo's sober expression and became sober himself, which was difficult considering the amount of alcohol he had consumed that afternoon.

"Yes, he is," Santo whispered, checking to see if anyone was listening.

"But I was a Jerry Garcia impersonator for this party company." Jerry went inside.

Santo turned to Mr. Albert. "I think he is Jerry Garcia."

"He's not."

"He could be."

"You think he is like me?"

"He could be."

"You're an idiot."

"I could be. But he could still be the real Jerry Garcia!"

Jerry returned with a card. He gave it to Mr. Albert.

"*Canto's Copycat Characters. Celebrity impersonators for parties and other events.* That is the worst name for a party entertainer company I have ever heard," Mr. Albert lamented.

"How many party entertainment companies have you heard about?" Jerry asked.

"This is the first one." Mr. Albert gave the card back to Jerry.

Jerry wouldn't take it.

"No, you hold on to it. You might could use it to make a little extra money."

"I don't look like anybody famous," Mr. Albert looked at Santo for his opinion.

"Ethel Merman, maybe." Santo smiled.

"Fuck you."

Santo could take the obscenity because he zinged Mr. Albert so badly. Mr. Albert snarled at Santo and went to return the card a second time. Jerry refused.

"Really. Hold on to it."

"Why? I don't think I look like anybody.... besides Ethel Merman."

"No, you do," Jerry insisted.

"Who?"

"Pope Sylvester the Second."

"Pope Sylvester the Second?"

"Yes, Santo. Doesn't he look a little like Sylvester the Second?" Jerry asked.

Both men turned to Santo.

"A little," Santo winced.

"One, how do you know what Sylvester the Second looked like?" Mr. Albert fumed.

"I went to Catholic school."

Mr. Albert sneered at Santo before turning to Jerry.

"And two, how many five-year-olds request Pope Sylvester the Second at their birthday parties?"

"He was a very popular pope," Jerry said.

Santo nodded in agreement.

"Probably not as popular as Pope Tweety bird the fifth!" Mr. Albert bellowed.

"You are right, my friend. He was a character that one. Another game?" Jerry asked.

"No, I have gone off it." Mr. Albert rose and sat down on the front step.

"Santo?" Jerry offered the game board to him.

"Sure," Santo said. Sitting down, he stared at the board, confused. "What do I do?"

"Hell, if I know," Jerry shrugged.

"Okay," Santo moved a piece from the tower of checkers. "Let me ask you a question."

"Shoot."

"You have a lot of concert posters inside. Did you go to all of them?"

"Can't say I did. I went to some. I had a Grateful Dead Tribute band for a while, but there were a lot of those after Garcia died. That's why I joined Canto's."

"Did you ever go to the South?"

"A bunch of times."

"Mr. Albert dreamed of a girl in a sundress playing guitar under a big tree with that moss stuff hanging from it."

"Was it a big tree or a small tree?" Jerry asked.

"A small tree," Santo whispered to Jerry.

"It was a big tree, forty, fifty feet," Mr. Albert interrupted from the stoop.

"That's not a very big tree," Jerry corrected him.

"That's what I said," Santo agreed.

"Fuck you. No, fuck both of you," Mr. Albert went inside to get another beer.

"Touchy, isn't he?"

"Yes, about the size of trees especially, it seems," Santo shrugged.

"We all have our burdens to bear."

"Amen, brother."

"The Chandler Oak in Savannah, Georgia," Jerry said after a few moments of thought.

"Why would you say that?" Santo asked.

"Well, it is a very famous tree, and people used to play there before they fenced it in."

"Of all the trees in the South, the Chandler Tree springs immediately from your lips."

"It is a very nice tree. I like Savannah. If you were going to track down this Southern fairy princess, that is where I would start."

"I didn't say anything about tracking her down," Santo said.

"You didn't say you weren't thinking about tracking her down."

"Who is tracking who down?" Mr. Albert returned to the porch with another beer.

"Jerry wants us to go and find Genevieve in Savannah, Georgia."

"Genevieve. That's a pretty name," Jerry smiled wistfully.

"How does he know about Genevieve?" growled Mr. Albert.

"I told him. He thinks the tree is in Savannah."

"It doesn't look like you are in any rush to get back to the Jersey shore," Jerry said.

"Well, maybe I'm not!" Mr. Albert's voice still well above normal levels. "What the hell am I yelling about?"

"I don't know," said Jerry.

"I don't know," said Santo.

"Yahtzee!" Yelled Jerry clapping his hands after collecting Santo's pieces from the board.

Savannah 1959.

The next day, Genevieve sat before a court-appointed psychiatrist. She told the constipated-looking older man of her husband's death and resurrection. She also told him about her stress at Hurricane Gracie's approach. Finally, she admitted to the doctor that she missed her mother and sometimes cried for days.

Benny tried to visit her, but she refused his request. And the psychiatrist thought that his presence would do nothing to improve her condition.

Genevieve appeared before the hearing judge two days after her arrest. She sat with Mr. Marks, the family lawyer. Two gentlemen in dark suits sat with the prosecution.

Benny sat in the back of the courtroom unnoticed by the opposing councils. This was the first time he had seen Genevieve since her arrest. She looked pale and more fragile than when she was arrested. He worried about her, and that was not a feeling he was accustomed to. His brain wasn't good, so many parts of his life were unclear, but this feeling of dread was very real. It made it hard to breathe, concentrate, or smile. He used to smile so much with Genevieve. That's all they used to do together. Now it didn't seem like happiness was possible.

The case proceeded quickly, with the prosecution asking the court to commit Genevieve to the Georgia State Sanitarium because, in her present state, she was a danger to herself and the community.

The judge spoke to the court, "A complaint was filed on October 6th by Mr. Harrison and Mr. Catrell against the defendant. A hearing was held on October 8th, where the witnesses attested that the individual, Genevieve Benton, was a mentally ill person, and presented a substantial risk of imminent harm to herself or others and that this individual needed involuntary treatment. I agreed and signed the Order to Apprehend. The day the order was delivered to the sheriff, a call came in that Mrs. Benton was disturbing the peace. She was then taken into custody, where she has been ever since. Are the original complainants present?"

The prosecutor stood up and indicated the two men sitting at his table, "Yes, Your Honor."

The judge nodded before he continued, "Dr. Gadsden, did you have a chance to examine the defendant?"

Benny had to make this better. There had to be something that he could say or do. But what? If he agreed with his wife and admitted to being dead, wouldn't he be locked up as well? Or worse things could happen. There were times in a distant memory when he was chased out of town and forced to hide from an angry crowd. It could be a story heard in his youth, but the feelings seemed visceral, like a rope coiled around his neck, choking his breath, ending all hope.

Dr. Gadsden, the psychiatrist, stood up and answered, "I have, Your Honor."

"Please take the stand."

The doctor sat on the witness stand and raised his hand to be sworn in. The judge waved him off.

"No need for that. This is a hearing, not a trial. Please tell us your diagnosis."

"I found the patient to be very anxious to the point of hysteria and suffering from delusions. She believed her husband was resurrected by the devil after he died during the hurricane. She attacked him, stabbing him with a knife. According to Mrs. Benton, the wound miraculously healed itself, so no trace of it existed when police officers came to the house during a domestic dispute several days later."

"In your opinion, is she dangerous to herself or the community?"

"There were self-inflicted bruises on her body. I believe she would also be a danger to others, which is evident by her desire to harm her husband."

"Did you sign the 1013?"

"Here it is," the doctor handed the Request for Commitment to the judge.

"Thank you, doctor. Does the state have any questions?"

The prosecutor shook his head no. The judge turned to Mr. Marks.

"Jim?"

Genevieve's lawyer replied, "No, Your Honor."

The judge spoke to Genevieve. "Mrs. Benton, please stand."

Genevieve stood up, looking as if she was lost in a dark forest, not knowing where to go or whom to turn to. She looked around the courtroom to see if her sister was there. Jacqueline wasn't. Then she saw her husband, and her anger rose.

"Do you know why you are here?"

"Yes, sir. I am here because of the demon who has taken my husband."

"Where is this demon, Mrs. Benton?"

"He is right there," she said, pointing to Benny.

"And you say your husband is dead, and this demon has taken control of his body."

"Yes, Your Honor," she said, pleading for understanding.

The judge stifled a grin, "Mr. Benton, are you a demon, or a servant of the devil?"

Benny rose slowly from his seat, "No, Your Honor."

"Have you, at any time in the last two weeks, been possessed by either a demon, a devil, or a servant of the devil?" The judge continued, regaining his composure.

"No, Your Honor. But I do have –"

"Mr. Benton," the judge interrupted. "I understand that you love this woman, and it is natural for a husband to want to do anything to protect his wife, but the opinion of this court is that she presents a danger to herself and the community. For that reason, I agree with the State that the safest place for her would be in the sanatorium until they have cured her of her numerous delusions. Don't worry. I am sure this is only a temporary women's issue, and she will be returned to you and cooking your dinner before you know it."

"Benny, tell them the truth. Tell them that you are dead," Genevieve screamed, with a mixture of anger and desperation.

"Bailiff, please remove the defendant and secure her until the sheriff can transport her to the Milledgeville State Hospital," the judge said, banging his gavel to stop her disruption.

"Please, Benny, please," she pleaded as she was removed.

"Your Honor, wait," Benny said, raising his hand to stop this madness.

But the judge had risen from the bench and walked out the door, not responding to his appeal. The rest of the players in this travesty seemed to move in slow motion. Benny looked lost as the courtroom cleared. Mr. Marks shook his hand and said, "it is all for the best."

The prosecutor passed by him without saying a word. Mr. Harrison and Mr. Catrell looked directly at Benny and nodded as if to say that this was for his benefit. He did not know those men. Never saw them in the neighborhood, never passed them in the street, or said hello. How could they know what was best for him?

In the empty, quiet courtroom, Benny realized he had lost the only person he had ever loved. He was alone, and the feeling was strangely familiar.

~ 25 ~

Two days later.

Uncle John's Bait and Tackle.

Mr. Albert and Santo were playing Scadoodle, the made-up game from two days ago. Jerry played guitar on the front porch steps. He sang an old tune with new lyrics.

Bertie, please just go.

Bertie, please just go.

Bertie, please just go.

To Savannah, bro,

Yeah, it's time to blow.

Santo was still offering theories on Mr. Albert's condition, "Maybe you are Icarus."

"Icarus?" Mr. Albert asked. "The kid who flew too close to the sun?"

"Not him. Who is the one with the rock?"

"The rock?"

"No, the boulder," Santo remembered. "Pushing it up the mountain."

"Sisyphus?" Jerry, who was still strumming softly, joined the conversation.

"Is that a real name, or are you making it up?" Mr. Albert asked.

"He was king of Corinth," Jerry said.

"Who would name their kid Sisyphus?" Mr. Albert muttered.

Jerry avoided the question. "He cheated death twice, and his punishment was to eternally roll a boulder up a hill. When he was about to roll it over the mountain's crest and end his punishment, the rock would slip down, and he would have to start again."

"He cheated death." Santo remembered the story.

"Twice."

Santo looked at Mr. Albert. "You have cheated death."

"I have not cheated death. I am dead," Mr. Albert corrected him.

"But you cheated the concept of death by living after you died," Jerry suggested.

"I'm still dead."

"Who punished him?" Santo asked.

Jerry explained the gods' thinking, "Zeus couldn't permit other people to think that kind of thing was allowed."

"Why not?" Santo asked.

"I don't know," Jerry shrugged.

"Why not?" Mr. Albert asked.

Jerry shrugged his shoulders bigger, "I don't know that either."

The three men thought for a long time. Santo was the first to speak.

"So, Sisyphus committed a crime against the natural order of things and was punished with the eternal task of rolling the boulder up a mountain?"

"Yes, that is right."

Santo turned to Mr. Albert, "Do you think you are being punished for something?"

"I don't know."

Jerry looked at Mr. Albert as well. "I think existing as a dead man alongside the living must be terrible."

"This moment is pretty bad," Mr. Albert moaned. "Don't you ever get any other customers?"

"Not often. What is it like to be a part of something but never able to be one with it? You drink but cannot get drunk. You eat but experience no satisfaction. Can you love?"

"No."

Jerry got up and went inside his store, shaking his head. "That's terrible man, everyone should be able to love someone, something."

Santo and Mr. Albert were left alone. Santo asked his friend, "Can you hope?"

"What for?"

"Can you pray?"

"Who to?"

Santo grew afraid. "Is there no salvation for you?"

"I wouldn't think so."

The silence returned.

"What did you do? What crime could you have committed to merit this punishment?"

"I think you are rambling again."

Santo continued to push for an answer. "Do you really not know? Or are you just not telling me what you have done because your sin is too terrible?"

"I don't know."

"That seems like a greater punishment."

Mr. Albert did not understand. "A greater punishment than what?"

"Than knowing. At least then, you could repent. You could beg for forgiveness."

"It is not a punishment if I don't know I've sinned," Mr. Albert argued.

"Maybe that is part of the penance."

"When we met, you thought I was an angel from God, sent to put you on the right path, and now you think I am the evilest person that has ever existed who is being punished for a crime he can no longer remember?"

"It could go either way," Santo said, pondering the question.

Jerry came out of the store. He looked worried.

"I hate to break up the party, boys but I think we are going to have visitors, and they might be looking for you."

"How do you know?" Santo asked.

"Hidden cameras," Jerry said, pointing in both directions down the road.

"Looking for us?" Santo began to panic.

"Don't get many black Escalades in these parts, mostly F150s painted with a camouflage motif," Jerry said.

"Do we need to go?" Mr. Albert asked.

"Too late. Come with me," Jerry led them into the store and clicked a hidden button behind the fishing lures. The wall slid open, revealing a small room with a desk and a couple of chairs. "I hope you find the accommodations adequate," he said, motioning for them to go in.

"You have a hidden room?" Santo asked.

"Everyone should have one." Jerry smiled.

Mr. Albert and Santo looked at each other and shrugged before entering the room. Jerry slid the door back to its original position and walked outside. The Escalade pulled into the parking lot. Two men in dark suits and sunglasses got out.

"Afternoon," said the one who was driving the car.

"Afternoon," replied Jerry.

"My name is Agent Johnson from the F.B.I. And this is Agent Brown."

Agent Brown looked at the Cadillac Deville in the parking lot and the unfinished game of Scadoodle on the whiskey barrel.

"Is there anyone inside?" asked Agent Brown.

"No, why do you ask?"

Agent Johnson walked inside the store. Jerry strolled over to the whiskey barrel and made a move on one side of the board, and took a drink from the beer bottle. Then he walked over to the other side and made a move as if he was playing for both players. He took a swig from the other beer bottle.

"Sometimes it gets lonely up here."

Agent Brown walked over to the board. He looked at the pieces but did not recognize the game. "Have you seen this man?" He showed Jerry a picture of Mr. Albert in the morgue.

"That guy looks dead," Jerry said.

"He is."

"We don't get many dead people who want to buy bait or even tackle coming here."

"He may not appear dead."

"Is he wearing a disguise? Because even with a disguise, I would know if he was dead."

"What about this guy?" Agent Brown held up Santo's mugshot.

"Now that guy looks alive."

"He is."

"I'm two for two."

Agent Johnson came out from the store and shook his head to Brown, indicating that no one was inside. "We are investigating a matter of national interest. If you see either of these men, it is important that you contact us immediately."

"Yes, sirs. I understand."

"Here is my card. Please contact me. Thank you. Any questions?"

"Just one, Agent Johnson. How did you lose a dead guy?"

The agents returned to their car and drove off in the opposite direction from where they had come. When they were out of sight, Jerry returned to the store and released Santo and Mr. Albert from their hiding place.

"Who were they?" Santo asked.

"F.B.I. agents. They were looking for you, and they knew you were dead."

"Oh, bother," Mr. Albert said, imitating Winnie-the-Pooh.

"Shush," Santo said before turning to Jerry. "Where did they go?"

"They were going in the direction of Dr. Johnson's cabin. It is not safe to go back there."

"Well, where should we go?"

"Why don't you go south?"

"South?"

"Yes, I hear the Chandler Tree is lovely this time of year," Jerry said with a smile.

~ 26 ~

One day later.

Skeeter's Hot Dogs, Wytheville, VA.

Santo and Mr. Albert entered the small restaurant. Mr. Albert had a big smile, and his hands were wide open as if he wanted to give the place a hug.

"Now, this is what I am talking about."

"Mr. Albert, please," Santo said, trying to shush his friend.

"Welcome," said the older gentleman behind the counter. He was dressed in a white short-sleeved button-up shirt, white neatly pressed pants, and a red and white striped bowtie. The owners were trying to go for that old-time feel.

"Where can we sit?" Santo asked, trying to remain as inconspicuous as possible. He was still unnerved by the close encounter with the F.B.I. agents.

"Anywhere you like. Grab a table or sit at the counter."

Santo went to a back table. Mr. Albert sat right in front of the old man. Santo sat down before he noticed that Mr. Albert wasn't with him.

"Psst. Psst," Santo said, trying to get Mr. Albert's attention.

Mr. Albert ignored him and smiled at the man, who brought him a menu.

"Psst. Psst!" Santo pssted again.

"I think your friend wants you to sit back there."

"Him? No, I don't know him."

"OK. What can I get you, friend?" the counterman said.

Mr. Albert smiled. He had a friend. He looked at the older gentleman's name tag.

"Well, thank you, Dale. I hope you are my friend."

"Everyone I meet is my friend."

"Well then, can I borrow twenty bucks?"

"Only if you lend me thirty first."

They both laughed as if they had known each other for years. Mr. Albert waved for Santo to join them. Santo walked over slowly with drooped shoulders.

"Dale, this is my other friend, Santo, and my name is Albert."

"Nice to meet you, Santo."

"We would like two of your world-famous dogs with the works."

"Each?" asked Dale.

"Each," said Mr. Albert as if he were buying drinks for the bar. "And two beers."

"Sorry, sir. We don't serve alcohol here."

"Maybe next time."

"I don't think so." The old man left to put in the order.

"Pity that."

"Pity," echoed Santo.

"I believe, Santo," Mr. Albert pontificated. "That humanity is tied together by the sausage. Anywhere you go in the world, there is some form of hot dog, and this place is the epicenter of the wiener universe."

Dale brought over a couple of glasses of water.

"Excuse me, sir," Santo said to Dale. "Why is this place world famous?"

"A German couple came in a while back and put us on their blog. They iked our wurst."

"So, your wurst was the best?" Mr. Albert smiled.

"Exactly," laughed Dale, pretending he had never heard that one before. "Since then, we've been getting lots of tourists visiting our eatery."

"Foreigners?" Mr. Albert whispered, looking around.

"Even foreigners," said Dale in his normal voice.

"See Santo, world-famous. Everyone loves the wiener." Mr. Albert smiled.

"So, where are you gentlemen from?"

"Jersey," Mr. Albert said.

"Staying in town for a while?"

"No, just passing through. We are going to Savannah."

"That's nice. Why there?" asked Dale, genuinely interested.

Santo, who had tried to keep on the lowdown, realized that it would not be of any use to shush Mr. Albert again. He thought, *why not join in?*

"We are going to track down an old flame of Albert here, and by the way, he is dead."

Santo sat scowling with his arms folded. Dale and Mr. Albert looked at each other.

"He is a very angry man." Dale said about Santo.

"He doesn't like people generally, but I think he is hungry right now."

Dale went to check on their order.

"Well done, Santo. Call attention to our situation."

"You were going to say it if I didn't."

"True, but I like saying it."

Dale came back with their dogs. He proudly placed the plates on the counter.

"Here you are. Hope this helps."

"Thank you," said Santo, still pouting.

"Thank you," Mr. Albert said.

"I was thinking of your problem while I picked up the food," Dale admitted.

"Yes?" said Mr. Albert.

"Before I met my wife, Brenda, back there, I might have just as well been dead. No hopes, no dreams, no thoughts of anything except my own desires. I was literally born the day I met her. She gave me purpose. I lived for her, and then my family, and then my community. Do you have a purpose, Albert?"

"No, I don't, Dale."

"I thought finding a purpose for him would give my life purpose," said Santo, looking down at his hot dogs and tapping them slowly with his fork.

Dale looked at them, moping at the counter.

"You are two of the saddest damn Yankees I ever met. Get your acts together. Albert, you're not dead." Dale scoffed. "If you're living, you're not dead. Get over yourselves. Get down to Savannah and find this woman of yours...."

"Genevieve," Mr. Albert added.

"Genevieve. That's a pretty name. You go find this Genevieve, tell her you love her, and marry that girl. And once you're married, send this guy packing. He's bringing you down."

"Yes, sir," said Mr. Albert.

"And you, Santo. Get your own life. Stop looking to this moron to give you purpose."

"Yes, sir," said Santo.

"Brenda, come here for a minute."

"I'm cleaning the grill," she shouted from the kitchen. She had no time for her husband's nonsense.

"Just for a minute," he pleaded.

"I'm cleaning the grill!" Brenda yelled back.

Dale turned to Santo and Mr. Albert.

"She's cleaning the grill. She'll be out in a minute. How're the dogs?"

"Very good," Santo said.

"Very good," said Mr. Albert.

"Told you they were good. How's the water?" Dale was trying to kill some time until his wife appeared.

"Good. The water's good," Mr. Albert said, although he disliked the taste of the liquid.

Santo nodded in agreement. Brenda approached and went to her husband's side.

"Hello," she said to the customers, ignoring her husband.

"Hello, ma'am," said Santo.

"Hello," echoed Mr. Albert.

"Albert here is traveling with his friend Santo to Savannah, where he will find his long-lost love and propose to her."

Brenda, who was always a sucker for a good love story, melted to the counter and stared deeply into Mr. Albert's eyes. Mr. Albert sat back, and managed an anemic smile.

"Hello," Mr. Albert repeated.

"Love is a powerful thing," she cooed.

"Yes, ma'am, it is."

Brenda, sensing Mr. Albert was not the romantic type, stood up seductively. She looked into Dale's eyes and whacked his backside with a towel that was hanging from her shoulder.

Then she turned back to Mr. Albert, "Good luck son, you'll need it."

She sauntered back to her grill. She had a real woman's walk. Small steps so the men could soak up the view. The gentle rise and fall of her hips as she walked away. The door flung back and forth, revealing quick glimpses of paradise lost as she disappeared into the kitchen. The men stared at the closed kitchen door. Brenda had become a love goddess to Santo and Mr. Albert. A creature of mystery and hope. The thought of her and the endless possibilities filled the boys' minds. Dale smiled a smile of completeness, remembering the sting of her towel. Santo and Mr. Albert knew that they could only dream of such happiness.

"Love," said Dale.

"Love," said Mr. Albert.

"Love," said Santo.

~ 27 ~

Two days later.
The Alabaster Motel.
Great Falls, South Carolina.

Mr. Albert woke up from his dead dead slumbers. He looked around. The room seemed comfortable enough. No bugs or rodents or stains on the carpets or bed sheets.

"Santo?" he said, sitting up.

There was no answer. Once again, Mr. Albert called out to his companion. "Santo?"

Once again, only silence answered him. He walked around the room. Nothing appeared to be out of place.

"He probably wasn't abducted by G-men or extra-terrestrials. That is a good sign," he thought aloud. "But where is he?"

It was then he noticed the note taped to the door.

Dear Mr. Albert,

> *Do not worry. I have just run to the store to get peanut butter, crackers, and maybe some donuts. I feel like donuts now. Strange. Maybe a cream-filled donut with chocolate on the top. You will probably still be dead dead when I come back, and if that is so, I might use the note again. Even if I don't get donuts the next time, you will understand that I haven't left for good, and I will be right back.*

> *Santo*

"Now I want some donuts, too. I wonder when he left the note. I wonder when he will be back. I wonder how many times he left this note for me. Maybe he just left it taped to the door for days, and anytime he left, he thought that same old note would be sufficient. I think that is just lazy. At least he could have put down the date, so I would know when he left it. He could have left it days ago and gotten eaten by a bear, and then I would just be waiting here, like some stupid Samuel Beckett play, whoever he is. Should I sit here until I die cubed? I don't like that either. No, the only sensible thing to do is look for him. And maybe the donut place. Now I want donuts. Nothing fancy. Maybe a glazed donut with some sprinkles. That might be a little fancy, but I feel like sprinkles."

With that, Mr. Albert left his motel on a quest to find Santo and maybe a glazed donut, either with or without sprinkles.

~ 28 ~

Ten minutes later.
Great Falls, South Carolina.

Mr. Albert walked down the main street of Great Falls. Years ago, there were three cotton mills. Now they are gone, and the town suffered because of it. Most stores were closed.

Mr. Albert thought he was like the town, nothing going on. Maybe Santo was right; he needed a purpose. Something to get him up in the morning. Something to work on throughout the day so that when evening comes, he could lay his head down proud that he accomplished something that day.

After a moment or two of thinking that Santo was right, he came to the opposite conclusion. Santo was wrong, and he should mind his own business. The only thing he and the town had in common was that they were both dead, but the town didn't know it yet.

"Now, where is that damned donut place?" he cried out in despair.

As if to answer his prayers, the bells from a nearby church rang out. The First Missionary Emmanuel Baptist church called to Mr. Albert, and he followed his calling. The sign outside the small church read, Sunday Services 10 AM and Noon. Coffee and Donuts to follow.

Mr. Albert looked up to heaven, "Thank you for the donuts."

152

There were ten rows of seats on either side of the center aisle. Several children were on the pulpit surrounding a woman. It seemed like they were putting on a play.

"But mommy," said one of the children. "What happens if my friends don't accept Jesus as our savior?"

"Then they will burn in Hell for all time," the kindly mother said.

"Don't worry mommy," said another child. "I've accepted Christ as our Savior."

"Then Jesus loves you, Jacob."

"I hate everyone who does not accept Christ our Lord," said the third.

"Jesus loves everyone, Michael, and wants all people to accept his Holy Name."

Throughout the performance, almost every line was greeted by a chorus of hallelujah, praise God, or thank you, Jesus. When the show was over, the actors were met with thunderous applause. A tall, gaunt man with a full beard approached Mr. Albert.

"Welcome, brother. My name is Aaron. Is this your first time in our church?"

"Yes, thank you. I just came for the donuts. Are there any donuts left?"

"There are, but you will have to wait until after the service."

"Are there glazed donuts with sprinkles? Because I really wanted sprinkles."

"I believe there are. Just have a seat, please."

The usher showed Mr. Albert to a pew four rows from the back, just in front of three elderly ladies who were very enthusiastic during the performance.

"Hello, sugar, welcome to our church," said the old bitty on the left.

"Thank you," said Mr. Albert. "I was wondering if you knew if there were glazed donuts with sprinkles. Sometimes I don't feel like sprinkles, but today I do."

"Hush, now. Pastor John is about to speak," the middle biddy said as she tapped him on his shoulder.

"Will he tell us about the donuts?"

"He'll tell you about everything you need to know," said the third, sitting back and crossing her hands in her lap.

Mr. Albert settled down. He couldn't remember ever being in a church before. He must have been at some time in his life. He did look like Pope Sylvester, after all. He felt a bit strange. Maybe it was because he was in a holy place. Maybe it was because he just woke up from being dead dead. But everything looked strange.

First of all, there was a family of midgets, or dwarfs, or little people. That was not too strange. Couldn't little people believe in Jesus? Of course, they could! The next thing he noticed was the considerable number of children. It was as if every woman in the place had five or six kids, and the infants all had exceptionally large heads, even for infants. Every adult male seemed exceptionally tall and thin with a long beard like Aaron. And all the women were short and round, with kids hanging from each of their arms.

Pastor John walked with great intensity to the pulpit as if in deep communion with the Almighty. He spoke with a quiet intensity that demanded silence from his followers.

"The Bible tells us that only the people who accept Jesus as our Savior and go through baptism will be resurrected at the end of times."

Mr. Albert raised his hand. The pastor stopped and looked at Mr. Albert. He was not accustomed to being interrupted. The other parishioners looked at Mr. Albert as well.

"The First Missionary Emmanuel Baptist Church of Great Falls welcomes all who enter. Are you a Christian friend?"

"I don't believe I am. But I have a question," said Mr. Albert with an earnest expression.

"All those with a quest for truth are welcomed here. Please ask your question."

"Actually, I have two questions. One is about the donuts, which I will ask later if I may. But the first question is about resurrection."

"What is your question about the resurrection?"

"Will people be resurrected only at the end of times, or could they be resurrected now?"

"Now?" The pastor said, astonished.

The church members looked around at their loved ones, unsure of what was happening.

"Yes, now, like an hour ago?"

"What?"

"My friend Santo says that ten people in the Bible were resurrected. Could there have been more?"

"Who did you say?" Pastor John said, fearing the worst.

A woman whispered, "Did he say Satan?"

The crowd gasped.

"You see, I am dead but then there are times when I am dead dead, and then I wake up, and I'm just dead again."

"You can't be dead!" The Pastor yelled.

"Dead as a doornail. I don't get that expression. Isn't any nail as dead as any other?"

"What kind of nonsense is this?" Dr. Hill, an older gentleman in a three-piece suit, stood up. "What a lot of hogwash!"

He grabbed his bag and pulled out a stethoscope. "Interrupting a Sunday service with all this mumbo...."

Dr. Hill put the instrument to Mr. Albert's chest and listened. He moved it to another area of his chest and listened. Then he let it fall as he turned to the pastor.

"He doesn't have a heartbeat."

Chaos erupted in the small church. Several women fainted. Children ran around unsupervised, screaming. Fathers shielded their wives and daughters.

The pastor held his hands up to Heaven. "Satan be gone. Fly back to the deepest bowels of Hell from whence you came! May Jesus strike you dead!"

As if to punctuate the pastor's curse, a shot rang out. One of the men had fired his handgun. The bullet passed through Mr. Albert, missed the old biddies behind him, and hit the back wall. Two of them fainted, and the third took off as fast as her bunioned feet could take her.

"Now, that was not very hospitable," Mr. Albert lamented, looking at the bullet wound.

The gunman screamed and dropped his weapon.

"Run for your lives!" cried Dr. Hill, and the parishioners did not need to be told twice.

In less than a minute, Mr. Albert was alone. He looked around at the destruction caused by the stampeders. He turned to the pulpit.

"And my second question is, are there any glazed donuts with sprinkles?" he howled.

~ 29 ~

10 minutes later.
The Alabaster Motel.
Great Falls, South Carolina.

Santo arrived back at the motel room and noticed that Mr. Albert was not there. He immediately began to worry about his friend. This was the first time Mr. Albert came back from being dead dead when Santo wasn't there. *What if he didn't remember who he was? What if Mr. Albert didn't remember who Santo was? All sorts of terrible things could happen,* he thought. He sat down on the bed. He touched the covers. They were cold.

"This is bad, bad, bad," Santo said to the empty room.

The door flung open. Mr. Albert stood like a superhero with five boxes of donuts. He stepped into the room but hit the door jam. The donuts flew from his hands and landed on the floor. Falling to his knees, the tried to collect the pastries quickly as possible.

"Ah, Dios. Mr. Albert, where were you? Where did you get all these donuts?" Santo said, kneeling to help his friend.

"I thought you wanted donuts."

"That was two days ago. I just kept the same note."

"I knew it!" Mr. Albert screamed, crushing a donut in each hand, jelly squirting everywhere. "Couldn't you date the note? Would that have been too much to ask?"

"Mr. Albert, will you tell me what happened? What is wrong?" Santo's pitch got progressively higher to match Mr. Albert's.

"We must get out of here, out of this town, and quickly."

"Why?"

"I saw your note and thought, *hmm, I want donuts too. Maybe a glazed donut with sprinkles.* Why, oh why, am I so easily led down the path of temptation?" he cried.

"Mr. Albert," Santo said to get him back on track.

"Right. So, I went out walking. What a shithole of a town. And then I got philosophical and thought that the town was a metaphor for my life. I am a shithole! And then the church bells rang. It was a sign from Heaven. I followed the sound and went into a church."

"No!"

"Yes, the sign promised me donuts, Santo. I had no power to resist."

"Go on."

"There were all sorts of shrunken people with big heads or tall people with big beards. And they shushed me when I enquired about pastries. Then the pastor got up there, and he started talking about resurrection, so I raised my hand."

"No!"

"Yes. So, I told him about my particular situation, having just awakened from being dead dead. And I wanted to know if Jesus could have risen me. I told him that you told me all about it and that I wasn't a Christian, but maybe Jesus could help a non-believer. But when I said Santo, he thought I said Satan. And people started fainting, *Oh the vapors, the vapors.* And running, *oh help me, the devil has come to get me!* Then somebody shot me!"

"No!"

"Yes! Look!" Mr. Albert cried, showing the bullet hole.

"Ewww. Does it hurt?"

"Well, it is not a pleasant experience, but what is it going to harm?"

"True. So, then what happened?"

"After the gunshot, more people fainted. I'm *coming Elizabeth, I'm coming Elizabeth!* And running, *Ahhhhhhh,*" he said, waving his hands in the air and moving in a circle. Then Mr. Albert stopped in an overly dramatic fashion. "The place was deserted, but the donuts were still there." He picked one up from the floor and took a bite. "Want one?"

"No, thank you."

"Probably wise," he said, removing a strange hair from his teeth. Santo gagged. Mr. Albert smiled.

"It's sometimes a blessing being dead."

"But why do we have to leave immediately?" Santo said, recovering from his nausea.

"I think the parishioners probably went to get their friends and more weapons."

The color drained from Santo's face. They packed quickly. Loaded the bags, the donuts, and Mr. Albert in the trunk to avoid suspicion. Before getting in, Mr. Albert checked for raccoons.

~ 30 ~

Three hours later.
On a back country road.
Somewhere in South Carolina or Georgia.

Five miles from Great Falls, Santo let Mr. Albert out of the trunk. He was covered in jelly and powdered sugar. It is hard to eat donuts neatly in the trunk of a car. Mr. Albert squinted as if he had not seen the sunlight in days.

"So bright, so bright," he said, shielding his eyes from the sun.

"You want to get back in the trunk?" Santo snarled. He was unhappy with the speedy exit they were forced to make out of town.

"I'm good," Mr. Albert responded cheerfully.

Several minutes passed in silence.

"Are we not getting on the highway?" Mr. Albert asked.

"No."

"Why? It will get us there quicker."

"I don't care."

"Why not?"

"Because. I don't care."

"I'm sorry I dropped the donuts," Mr. Albert apologized. "They were not particularly good, really," he said as he tried to lick the delicious, powdered sugar off his lips without Santo noticing.

"Not particularly good? Well, sir, I had those donuts two days ago, and I found them quite tasty."

"A few of them only spent a couple of seconds on the floor. I put those in a special box. Do you want one of them?"

"I am not angry at you because of the donuts. I am angry..." Santo stopped to think about what he had just said. "All right, I am a little bit angry at you for the donuts, but I am much, much angrier at you because of the people who may be after us."

"Why?"

"You are immortal, but I am not. If they shoot me, I am dead. If they shoot you, it is, 'Oh, that wasn't very nice!'"

Mr. Albert was only marginally paying attention. He was looking at his wound.

"Oh, look, my booboo is almost better."

And indeed, it was. For a person with no bodily functions, he seemed to heal quickly.

"How does that happen?" Santo said, amazed.

"I don't know."

"How can someone be so stupid about so many things?"

"I don't know."

"Aren't you the slightest bit curious about your existence?"

"Should I be?"

"Yes."

"Would it change anything?"

"No."

"Then there, then."

"That is a stupid expression," Santo grumbled. "I would be curious."

"That is why you are so miserable all the time."

"Maybe you make me miserable."

"Now you are making me happy."

Mr. Albert smiled and looked out the window. Just miles and miles of pine trees on either side of the thin two-lane highway. After a few minutes, they passed a billboard with two advertisements. The top one had a picture of Donald Trump reaching out to a cheering crowd. The words, *Trump 2020*, were written in bold red.

The billboard below had a bible quote; *He will save his people from their sins. Matthew 1:21.* Underneath the quote was *First Missionary Emmanuel Baptist Church. All are welcome.*

"Maybe I will vote for Trump," Mr. Albert said.

"The election is over."

"Maybe he could rise again."

Santo snarled.

"You are dead, Mr. Albert. They don't let dead people vote."

"I'm sure they do in some places."

"I don't know," Santo said, giving up.

"Oh, look," Mr. Albert said.

They passed a roadside store that sold fireworks. To attract customers, two elephant statues were standing next to each other. They looked at least ten feet high and smiled at the customers in the deserted parking lot.

"I used to live in one of them."

Santo saw an entrance to the highway in front of him. The sign read *Savannah 62 miles.* If he could cut the trip by an hour by taking the highway, he would take it.

"Ooh, we are taking the highway," Mr. Albert said, clapping joyfully.

~ 31 ~

2 hours later.
In front of the Chandler Oak.
Savannah, Georgia.

Mr. Albert and Santo looked at the tree.
"This is a very impressive tree," Santo said.
"Yes. It is," replied Mr. Albert.
"Is it the one? Is this the tree that Genevieve played her guitar in front of?"
"No. I don't think so."
"Are you sure? It was a long time ago. It could have grown a little."
"I know."
They walked around the tree in opposite directions to see if the back of the tree looked more like the tree in Mr. Albert's dream. Santo nodded his head and smiled.
"It has the Spanish Moss of which you spoke."
"Of which you spoke? What are you, an idiot?"
Mr. Albert took his frustration out on his friend.
"No, I thought I was very poetic," Santo said, deflated.
"It wasn't poetic, and I pondered from whence it came."
"Now that is stupid."
"No stupider than your, *of which you spoke.*"
"Mr. Albert, can we get back to the question? Are you positive that this is not the tree?"

Mr. Albert took another long look at the tree.

"I am positive. It is not."

"Pity," Santo said. "Now, what should we do?"

"I don't know," Mr. Albert said, giving a half-hearted shrug.

"Seems a bit anticlimactic. I mean, we came all this way. I kind of wanted Genevieve to be standing right here, and then you would look at each other, a glint of recognition in your eyes, run to each other, and kiss, kiss, kiss, and bam! She's three months pregnant."

"That's what you wanted to see? The kiss, kiss, kiss, and then bam, she's pregnant."

"I didn't want to see the bam part."

"That's nice."

"That's your business," Santo said, trying not to be intrusive.

"I'm glad. Just because you help me out every once in a while, I don't think it entitles you to any viewing rights."

"Believe me, Mr. Albert, I do not want any viewings."

"As long as we are clear on that point."

"Very clear."

"Good."

"So now, what are we going to do?"

"Fuck if I know," Mr. Albert snapped, throwing his hands up.

They walked away from the tree. Whatever purpose they had in coming to Savannah was gone. *Maybe Santo will let things go now,* Mr. Albert hoped.

Across the street was Forsyth Park. Santo walked into the park, and Mr. Albert followed. There was a crowd of people around the fountain. The music of a trumpet player filled the air, mostly Broadway show tunes from the fifties. An old musician would play half a dozen notes and then stop. After a minute or so of adjustments to his instrument, he would start another song but stop again after a few notes. Mr. Albert grimaced every time he halted.

Santo was not bothered by the intermittent music. He was focused on the road trip. "This is terribly anti-climactic," Santo mumbled. "I blame Jerry. He told us to come here. Of course, we had to leave the cabin because the F.B.I. men were looking for us. But there could have been something with the tree. Letters carved into it, enclosed by a love heart. AA and G... I don't know what her last name was. Mr. Albert, what was Genevieve's last name?" Santo stopped.

Mr. Albert was not beside him. Santo looked around. On the other side of the fountain was Mr. Albert waving. He had stopped, not wishing to listen to any more of Santo's ramblings. Santo didn't know what annoyed him more, the waving or the stupid grin on Mr. Albert's face. He stomped over to his friend.

"That was not very nice of you."

"It wasn't. I know. Forgive me."

"I forgive you, but why?"

"You built yourself up for some romantic conclusion to this story, but there isn't any. There is no reason, no grand plan. Look at all these people. Do you think any one of them has a real purpose? Something that will help the rest of humanity? *I'm a teacher. I prepare the next generation.* The next generation isn't any better prepared because all we teach them are lies. *I'm a doctor. I save lives.* Save them for what? It is all hypocrisy, so they can get up in the morning and think their life has some value. Look at them. They are taking pictures in front of a stupid fountain. Some of them have traveled hundreds of miles to be here. For what? A pretty photo? What reason is there for this behavior? *Oh, you must go to the Forsyth Fountain, it's spectacular!* It is not spectacular. It is a fountain ordered from a mail-order catalog. The water in it is practically sewage."

"Let these people enjoy their lives the way they want to enjoy them." Santo reasoned. "Look at the children running around the fountain. Does it matter how old it is or where it came from? Look at their parents watching their little miracles. Total strangers share in the joy of the children's life, reminding them that they once were joyful and can be joyful again."

"That's it? The meaning of life?"

"Maybe it is."

"You were the one who said I should have a higher purpose."

"Yes, I did."

"You wouldn't let me sit at McKenna's and get soused with Walter."

"No, I wouldn't let you."

"But you would let these people take their selfies in front of this stupid fountain."

"Yes, I would."

"Don't you think you are being unfair?" Mr. Albert pouted.

"No, most people's purpose is as simple as procreation. A small number of people have a higher purpose. You are different from them. You are different from everyone. You must have a special purpose that doesn't have anything to do with reproduction. Besides, even if you were boinking a supermodel, I think that which would spring from your loins would be very gross."

"You are probably right, Santo," Mr. Albert said, acknowledging his purpose should have nothing to do with boinking. "So, what do we do now?"

"We passed a dive bar on the way here."

"If it were possible for a dead man to love a live man, I would love you."

"Once again, very gross."

And they walked off to the dive bar down the street to get plastered.

~ 32 ~

Ten minutes later.
The Pinkie Masters Lounge.
Savannah, Georgia.

The city was full of hustle and bustle, tourists running hither, thither, and yon, trying to see this fountain, this square, this bench, but never this tree. Never this tree. The corner tavern with the Pabst Blue Ribbon banner outside was a welcome sight for the two thirsty travelers.

The bar wrapped around the bartender on three sides and was small enough that he could refill any customer's drink in less than four steps. There were several small tables scattered around the rest of the dimly lit establishment.

Mr. Albert and Santo sat at the bar with their backs facing the front door. These seats were left for the tourists so the patrons could watch who came into their bar. The regulars glanced at the strangers, and went back to their drinks.

"What could I get you?" Jimmy, the bartender, asked.

Jimmy was six-three, with a thin mustache on his otherwise clean-shaven face. The bags under his eyes made him look as if he had just rolled out of bed from a night of drinking.

"Well, your sign outside says Pabst Blue Ribbon, so bring us a couple of them," Mr. Albert said, in breathless anticipation.

When Jimmy returned with the beers, Mr. Albert had questions.

"What is the story with the bar's name?"

"What do you mean?"

"What does Pinkie Masters mean?"

"It doesn't mean anything. The guy who originally owned the bar was called Pinkie."

"Christian name?"

"Nickname."

"That's it?"

"That's it," Jimmy said, checking on his other customers.

"Another disappointment," moaned Mr. Albert.

Santo and Mr. Albert drank their beer in silence, but only for a moment.

"See, that's the thing, Santo," Mr. Albert said, as if they were in the middle of a long conversation. "You get some idea in your head. There is this whole buildup, anticipation, and then nothing. A big letdown. We drove a thousand miles to come down here, chased by G-men, Southern Baptists, and probably aliens, for nothing."

"We met Jerry Garcia and found a good place for hot dogs."

"That we did, but we didn't find any meaning in it."

"I used to love the Dead," an older gentleman sitting to the right of Santo interrupted. He was on the first seat after the bar turned. From his seat, he could listen to what tourists had to say. This conversation sparked his interest.

"My name is Michael," said the man, extending his hand.

"My name is Santo, and this is Mr. Albert." He shook Michael's hand.

"Does your friend have a first name?"

"My name is Albert Albert. Santo calls me Mr. Albert because of our special relationship."

"And what kind of relationship is that, if you don't mind me asking?"

"He is my indentured servant." Mr. Albert smiled.

"Indentured servant. Didn't know they existed anymore. Is this a personal decision? Do you want to be his indentured servant?"

"Yes. I do," Santo beamed. "He saved my life. I am his servant until I repay my debt."

"My indentured servant," Mr. Albert said, happily.

Through his drunken haze, Michael needed a little longer to process things.

"Yes?" He asked Santo for confirmation.

"Yes."

"What is an indentured servant anyway?" Michael wanted details.

"He has to serve me for a certain amount of time, and then he is free."

"How long is that?"

"Five years."

"Five and a half," corrected Santo.

"Minus six weeks."

"You have been counting?"

"Every minute of every day." Mr. Albert finished his beer and signaled for another.

"I think that is sweet." Santo was touched.

"Right, five and a half years minus six weeks. Unless you die." Michael understood it all.

"Oh no, you see, I'm dead, and he is my servant."

"Unless I die, that goes without saying." Santo corrected his master again.

"Of course." Mr. Albert accepted the amendment.

"But are you dead?"

"Yes, I am."

"Then Santo is free to go."

"No," said Santo.

"Why not?" questioned Michael.

"Because I'm not dead dead dead. I'm just dead. And Santo made this agreement with me when I was already dead, so I would have to be dead cubed for the contract to be null and void."

"Dead cubed?" Michael thought he either had too much or too little to drink. He shook his head to get the cobwebs out. "So, you have a contract for all this?"

"An oral contract. More of an understanding," Santo clarified.

"And he's dead?"

"Yes," said Santo.

"Yes," said Mr. Albert, finishing his beer.

"Where did you people come from?"

"New Jersey," Santo replied.

"It would be nice to say that explains it, but it doesn't."

Michael took out a small notebook and started writing. Santo looked at Mr. Albert, wondering if they had made a serious mistake by telling Michael anything.

"May I enquire what you are doing?" Santo asked.

"I'm a writer, and I was just making notes," he said, continuing his jottings.

"A writer." Mr. Albert signaled to Jimmy that he could bring over another round for the three of them.

"Yes. Michael Skillen. Have you heard of me?"

"No, sorry," said Santo.

Mr. Albert shook his head, "I don't read. What have you written?"

"I wrote ten books."

"Really, how many copies have you sold?" Santo had never met a real writer.

"Three copies."

"That's disappointing." Santo frowned.

"I write because I like to write. The publishing business is an enormous sinkhole swallowing talented artists and sucking out their joy."

"Sounds like anything else in life," said Mr. Albert.

"Are you going to write about us?"

"No, not as you are anyway. No one is interested in normal people."

"I'm dead," Mr. Albert reminded Michael.

"Well, that part is interesting, but it has to be set somewhere else. During the Middle Ages, in a Viking village, or in some dystopian future. I could see you two as intergalactic garbage collectors."

"I will take that as a compliment," said Mr. Albert.

"You shouldn't." Michael grinned.

"Can I be the captain of the ship?" Santo asked, excitedly.

"I don't see you as the captain type." Michael apologized. "But we need a love angle."

"Oh, we came here looking for Mr. Albert's long-lost love. We were hoping to meet her by the Chandler tree," said Santo, knowing that would help.

"Then kiss, kiss, kiss, and bam, she's three months pregnant."

"Even if you are dead, I don't think that is how it works," Michael said.

"That's what he thought," Mr. Albert pointed at Santo.

"It was a thought," Santo said, defending himself.

"What happened?" Michael asked, his pen poised to take more notes.

"Nothing," Santo said softly.

Mr. Albert raspberried.

"Boy, that's disappointing."

"Yes, it is," Santo said.

Albert shrugged his shoulders and ordered another round.

"So now what?"

"Fuck if I know," said Mr. Albert.

"Well, why don't you hang around Savannah? There are plenty of other trees for Mr. Albert not to find his true love under."

"I don't think I can drive now anyway," Santo admitted.

"You have a place in town?"

"Not yet. First, we get plastered, and then we find a place to sleep." Mr. Albert described their routine.

"Well, at least you have your priorities straight. But you won't need to find a place tonight. You'll be coming home with me, boys. I got plenty of room."

Santo checked with Mr. Albert.

"I don't care. You're not going to murder him in his sleep, are you?" Mr. Albert queried.

"I think I am too drunk tonight. But ask me again in the morning," Michael said.

Mr. Albert and Michael leaned in and stared at Santo, making him shrivel in his seat. They both laughed, and Mr. Albert ordered more alcohol. After four more rounds, the three of them stumbled back to Michael Skillen's house.

~ 33 ~

The next morning.
Michael Skillen's home.
Savannah, Georgia.

Michael Skillen had an average-sized house with three bedrooms and three baths. The master bedroom was twice the size of the two smaller bedrooms separately, but the small rooms were fine for Mr. Albert and Santo. They had not spent a night apart since Santo was arrested. They finally had some privacy for quiet reflection in their room. That privacy went unused because they were so drunk, they passed out as soon as their heads touched their pillows.

Mr. Albert and Santo had been awake for an hour before their host joined them that morning. They found peanut butter and crackers in the cupboard and beer in the refrigerator. They were quite happy sitting at the breakfast nook.

"Who the hell are you?" The writer yelled. Michael Skillen was in a pair of boxers that had seen better days and a white undershirt. He might have been frightening if he wasn't scratching himself.

"We are your house guests," Mr. Albert replied, eating another cracker.

"Did I invite you?"

"Yes," said Santo, nervous that he would be arrested again.

"How many days have you been here?"

"You just invited us last night. We met at Pinkie Masters."

"Pinkie Masters," Skillen grumbled. "How long are you staying?"

"Hard to say. Probably until we find some purpose, or the G-men track us down." Mr. Albert ate another cracker.

"Who the hell are you people?"

"This is Mr. Albert, and I am Santo Murphy. We are from New Jersey."

"Is one of you dead?"

Santo pointed to Mr. Albert.

"I thought I was having a bad dream," Michael said.

"No bad dream. Just us." Mr. Albert smiled.

"Want some peanut butter and crackers?" Santo offered.

"Is that my beer?" Michael frowned, pointing at the multiple empty bottles on the table.

"There are still a few left." Mr. Albert smiled.

"Well, I better have some breakfast." He took a beer from the refrigerator.

"It is the most important meal of the day," Santo said, relaxing, secure in the knowledge that the police would not be called. For now.

After another hour around the table, Michael Skillen was all caught up on the saga of Mr. Albert and Santo. There were times that he was not sure that these two home invaders were not making it all up.

"Look in your little book. You took notes," Santo said, trying to be helpful.

Michael grumbled as he went into his room. He returned a minute later with the book in his hand and a pair of reading glasses on his nose. He read his notes from the previous night.

"Son of a bitch," he said after a moment. Then he got himself another beer and sat down with his new friends.

"This is a nice house," Santo said, after a long silence as Michael soaked it all in.

"It has been in my family for generations. This used to be the bad side of town."

"There's no more beer," Mr. Albert said, finishing the last one. "Let's go to Pinkie's."

"They don't open for a couple of hours at least."

"Then I best go and pick up some supplies." Mr. Albert wobbled to the front door.

"Two blocks to the left and one block over," Michael called out.

He put his head on the table. Santo joined his host for a table nap.

"What about your friend?" Michael Skillen said, not knowing how he felt about taking a table nap with someone he had just met but not wanting to raise his head off the table.

"He'll be all right, or else we will pick him up from the morgue tomorrow."

"That sounds good," Michael said, closing his eyes.

But before either could doze off, they heard Mr. Albert calling.

"Santo, Michael, come quick."

Santo sprang up but then had to sit down again. The room was spinning. He hit Michael, who sat up and then put his head down again.

"Santo, Michael," repeated the outside voice.

Michael stood up and started to walk to the front door. Then he realized he had forgotten something and went back to get Santo. The two leaned against each other for support as they stumbled toward Mr. Albert, who was staring at the house.

"What?" Michael said, upset that his mid-morning table nap had been interrupted.

"The house."

"Yes, it is my house."

"The tree."

"What about the tree?" asked Santo.

"It is the tree," Mr. Albert smiled.

"What tree?"

"The tree."

"The tree?"

"Yes, the tree."

"It doesn't look like a very big tree," Michael Skillen said. "From the story, I thought it was a big tree."

"Oh, shut up."

"Mr. Albert, you are saying that this is it?" Santo laughed, trying to hold back his joy.

"Yes."

Santo grabbed Mr. Albert's hands and jumped up and down. Michael, feeling left out of the celebration, joined in. "The tree, the tree." They shouted while jumping. Just then, a family of tourists walked by. They looked at the jumping men in an odd way.

Michael turned to the tourists and said, "This is a Savannah tradition. Whenever you see a beautiful tree, you grab each other's hands, jump up and down and yell, *the tree, the tree* or *life is like a box of chocolates!*"

Satisfied with the explanation, the tourists smiled at their kids and went on their way.

"That was fun," Michael said to his new friends.

They were no longer jumping. Mr. Albert looked at Santo, and his eyes went glassy. He swooned and fell forward. Santo caught Mr. Albert.

"What's happened?" Michael asked.

"Mr. Albert! I think he is dead dead. Let's get him back in the house."

"You're shitting me."

Santo carried Mr. Albert in as Michael held the front door open.

"If this ain't a kick in the pants," he shook his head. "Hey, he didn't get any more beer. What about my beer? Damn it."

~ 34 ~

Four days later.
Michael Skillen's home.
Savannah, Georgia.

Michael and Santo stood at the door to Mr. Albert's room, looking at the dead dead man in his bed. Santo was worried that Mr.
Albert might be gone for good. Michael thought Santo seemed to be
a lot less fun without Mr. Albert. It was a good thing Michael was
already drunk.

"The little ones are so peaceful when they're dead," Michael
said, lightening the mood.

"I don't know what is wrong. Something is wrong."

"He isn't usually dead for this long?"

"No, never."

"Well, maybe he's really dead."

"No, he can't be. He is not exhibiting the signs."

"What signs?" Michael said, perking up.

"He has to be dead dead."

"He is."

"And he has to smell."

"He does."

"Not more than usual."

"That is how he usually smells?"

"Yes."

"You have got to teach him about personal hygiene."

"I know. Finally, he has to bloat. Does he look bloated?"

"Not particularly," Michael said, a little disappointed.

"Then we should wait."

They looked at the unbloated dead man for a moment.

"Maybe he fulfilled his purpose in finding the tree, and that was it," Michael suggested.

"He was walking around the world dead for centuries to find a tree. I don't think so."

"I thought you would be happy. That would mean you have satisfied your obligation and are free to go. After you help me throw him in the garbage can, of course."

"I'm not throwing him in the garbage can!" Santo cried, horrified.

"Well, I can't get him in there myself!" Michael yelled, just as horrified.

"No. You have misunderstood me. Of course, I would help you dispose of the body. You have been a wonderful host, and I consider you a friend."

"Thank you," Michael accepted the compliment.

"But I think he is not done yet. Mr. Albert must be here for a greater purpose."

"Are you a religious man, Santo?"

"I believe I am."

"Maybe he fulfilled God's purpose. Are you privy to God's wishes?"

"No. I am not."

"So, what are you so upset about then? Just be happy that you were a part of it. I'm getting another beer and sitting on the porch. Join me?" Michael left before getting an answer.

Santo shrugged his shoulders and followed. They got themselves a drink and settled onto the two pale-blue rocking chairs. The sun was out, the air was cool, and birds were chirping. It was a perfect day to sit and watch the world go by.

"I just thought Mr. Albert's purpose had something to do with me. That I would help him carry out his grand plan."

"We always think that the world cannot go on without us. The world doesn't care. We are like an itch that you can't get to. It's terrible when it's there, but then the sensation passes, and you forget all about it."

"So, what am I in that analogy?" Santo asked, suspiciously.

"You are the itch, and the world is my butt."

"That makes it much clearer. Thank you."

"You're welcome."

After a moment.

"He saved my life."

"Then maybe that was his purpose, and you are the one who has the purpose to discover."

"But I followed him here."

"Maybe he followed you here."

"Well, maybe my purpose was to meet you, and now you have to write our story."

"It is not much of a story."

"It's a delightful story."

"Meh."

"It's got everything, love, adventure."

"You ate weenies in Wytheville. That's not adventure," the writer scoffed.

"There were G-men. He was shot."

"Ech. Not much of a love story either."

"It could have been a great love story."

"He forgot her."

"He remembered the tree."

"You got yourself a real tear-jerker here, Santo."

"So, Mr. Albert fulfilled his purpose by saving me. I fulfilled my purpose by coming down here."

"I didn't say that. I said that maybe Mr. Albert had fulfilled his purpose. I don't know what purpose you have," Michael said, looking at Santo disgusted.

"This is getting worse and worse."

"Probably."

"At least when Mr. Albert was around, I had a purpose. He was my purpose. Now I am just as lost as when I almost jumped off the pier. Are you going to help me?"

"I like watching you squirm."

"I take back the whole you are my friend thing. And I will not help you stuff him into the garbage!"

"Who are you going to stuff into a garbage?" Mr. Albert asked, opening the screen door.

"Ay Dios Mío!" Santo cried, hugging his friend.

"Still not a good story, but I'll give it to him. He sure knows how to make an entrance," Michael acknowledged.

Now that all was right with the world again, Michael's gaze returned to the street in front of his house. Down the road, a group of tourists held each other and jumped up and down. Michael thought he heard them shout, *the tree, the tree.*

~ 35 ~

Ten minutes later.
Michael Skillen's home.
Savannah, Georgia.

The three men sat on the porch drinking more beer.

"How long was I out for?" Mr. Albert asked; the fog of his nap still had not left him.

"Four days," Michael said. "And your friend here was not the best of guests. Stood at your door worrying, worrying, worrying. Couldn't leave. Had to be there when you woke. *It would be dangerous to leave him unsupervised. Somebody might shoot him.* Wouldn't go and get more beer. Wouldn't even help me take out the garbage."

Santo shot him a disagreeable look, "Mr. Albert, I was worried. I thought that was it."

"Dead cubed? That would have been nice."

"Is this really the tree?" Santo asked seriously.

"I think it is. Except the house was different. The shutters were green."

"I think they were a while ago," Michael remembered.

Mr. Albert walked over to the tree. A wood sculpture of a forest spirit was nailed to it.

"This wasn't in my dream. Did you put it up?" Mr. Albert grimaced at the ugly carving.

"Mr. Muggles? He was there before I was born."

"Can we take it down?" Mr. Albert pleaded.

"No, we cannot," Michael stepped between Mr. Albert and the tree to protect Mr. Muggles.

"Can we get back to the real issue here?" Santo cried. "Did you know Genevieve?"

Michael thought for a moment, "No. I don't think so."

"Is there anyone you could ask?" Santo questioned.

"You think I don't know my own family?" Michael snapped.

"No, he's not saying that, but maybe she was around when you were younger," Mr. Albert said, trying to soothe his host.

"How old is this woman?"

"I don't know."

"How old are you?"

"I don't know."

"You don't know how old you are?"

"I was pretty young when I was born." Mr. Albert smiled.

"Mr. Albert may have been around for centuries. If he never dies, there is no telling how long he's been living," Santo said, feeling proud that he was friends with an immortal.

"Well, why should she be singing outside my house?" Michael was not impressed.

"I don't know."

"A birthday party, maybe," Santo offered.

"Were there any kids in your dream?" Michael grunted, showing his dissatisfaction.

"No kids. No birthday hats. No cake. Do you have any cake?"

"No cake," Michael said, wondering who was the bigger idiot. "I guess we can conclude that it was not a birthday party. Pity."

"Pity," echoed Santo.

"Pastry," echoed Mr. Albert.

Santo and Michael looked at him with disdain.

"What?" Mr. Albert continued. "I haven't eaten in four days, and you don't even offer me a piece of cake. Some host you are. Some friend."

"I guess we could get something to eat."

Michael got up and headed for the fence. Mr. Albert followed closely.

"Where are we going?"

"I think you will find this place amusing. It's called Rum Runners."

"I like rum," Mr. Albert smacked his lips.

"It is not a bar. It is a pastry shop."

"I like pastry," Mr. Albert was not to be saddened on such a wonderful day.

Michael shook his head and kept walking. Santo put the bottles inside and closed the door before following his friends.

~ 36 ~

Two hours later.
The Pinkie Master's Lounge.
Savannah, Georgia.

The trio had a lovely brunch at the Rum Runner, which consisted of coffee, quiche, and an assortment of pastries. Mr. Albert wanted to taste Michael and Santo's cakes but wouldn't share his own. He did pick up the tab, so all was forgiven quickly.

After their meal, they wandered around the historic district of Savannah. Mr. Albert looked to see if he could recognize any other tree. He didn't, but they saw several groups of tourists happily jumping up and down, holding hands. They shouted, *a tree, a tree,* with boundless joy. People passing by stopped to look, laughed, and then joined the jumpers. Everyone was having a grand time. Michael was no longer amused with his little joke, after he realized that it had become a thing. He would have to put up with that nonsense for years.

They had also sobered up and felt the need for adult beverages. They headed for Pinkie Masters. Michael sat in his usual seat but offered Mr. Albert and Santo seats to his right on the regulars' side of the bar. The usual patrons looked at the newbies until Michael raised his hand.

"It's okay," he said, with a dramatic pause. "They are with me."

After a moment of indecision, they nodded their heads as a tentative sign of acceptance. Mr. Albert bought a round of drinks for the bar, and their temporary status became permanent. The regulars wanted to know who the strangers were, so Michael told the enamored crowd the whole story with many embellishments. Santo couldn't help but feel that their story was good, even if, it wasn't set in a distant galaxy. And by Michael's enthusiasm, Santo thought he did too.

"So, he met a girl right in front of your house, Michael?" Teresa, whom everyone knew as Tessie, asked, thinking it was a romantic story. And she was a sucker for romance.

"Yes," Michael bragged.

"But she's lost forever?" Tessie said, as if she had known Genevieve all her life.

"At this point, we just don't know," Santo said, shaking his head.

She shook her head along with him.

"How many years ago was this?" Teresa's husband, Brian, questioned, not believing the story even if the stranger bought the drinks or if his wife fell for that malarky.

"Who knows?" Michael laughed.

"Okay. Let's see some I.D." Jimmy, the bartender, broke in, wanting to see some proof.

Mr. Albert pulled out his license. Jimmy studied it.

"It says you are only thirty-five," he said, handing Mr. Albert back his identification.

"Well, it is not going to say he's a thousand years old, is it? He's older than most countries!" Michael cried, mortally wounded by Jimmy's suspicions.

"I've also lived in an elephant," Mr. Albert boasted. "9200 Atlantic Ave. Google it!"

Rick, who was on his phone, typed it in. "That is the address for Lucy the elephant."

"An elephant with the name of Lucy. That's where I lived," Mr. Albert waved his hand as if he were the pope.

Tessie swooned. Brian caught his wife and turned to Mr. Albert with admiration. He was convinced. Rick didn't care. He took another sip of his beer and returned to searching for Japanese porn.

"And you have no idea when this occurred?" Pete asked, looking up from his classic car magazine.

Michael, Santo, and Mr. Albert shrugged and went back to their Pabst Blue Ribbons.

Pete and Rick always sat next to each other on the opposite side of the bar. They focused on their reading materials and did not like to be disturbed, except for Jimmy coming over and asking if they wanted another round. Tessie sat between Rick and Brian, mainly because when Brian sat next to Rick, his eyes wandered to the porn on Rick's phone. Occasionally, Tessie's eyes would wander as well, and then she would act disgusted and smack him as she laughed.

"What? It's anime! No women were violated for this video, only pixels," Rick would protest, rubbing his bruised arm.

But overall, the five regulars got along well.

"What are you looking at?" Jimmy asked Pete.

"A dark green 1964 ½ Mustang Hardtop."

"That's a beauty," said Jimmy.

Pete showed the picture to Rick, who showed no interest at all.

"Well, it is not Studebaker, but it is all right," Pete reminisced.

"Why would you say that?" Santo looked at Pete and then Mr. Albert.

"My dad had one. A 1957 Silver Hawk. He took this guy up north, and the guy gave him the car to get back."

"Just gave him the car?" Jimmy asked, impressed.

"Didn't want it. It was a beauty, too. My dad loved that car."

"It's a beauty," Jimmy repeated. He realized a long time ago that he didn't have to say anything else to Pete except, *it's a beauty,* and *how about another beer?*

"Got stolen two years later. Right in front of our house. What's the world coming to?"

"What was that, like sixty years ago?" Michael needled him.

"And the world hasn't gotten any better, has it?" Pete growled. After another sip of his beer, he calmed down. "I always wanted to find him another one and give it to him."

"Did you ever do that?" Santo asked, innocently.

"He died thirty years ago. All I do is drink at this fucking bar and look at these damn magazines."

Brian glared at Santo, wondering if they should demote the newcomer.

"Thanks a lot, Santo," was all he could muster.

"Yeah, thanks a lot, Santo," Michael said.

The rest of the regulars nodded in agreement.

"Thanks a lot," Mr. Albert said, distancing himself from his traveling companion.

Santo gave him a dirty look. "Really? I didn't know," he said, appealing to the jury.

"Well, the least you could do is buy the man a drink," Mr. Albert suggested, looking at his empty glass.

"Sure," Santo begrudgingly agreed. He didn't want to cause Pete any sorrow.

"I mean, you might as well buy the rest of us a drink as well because when you insult one of us, it is like you are insulting us all," Mr. Albert smiled, his evil plan complete.

Santo looked at the rest of them. They were all nodding in agreement. He signaled for Jimmy to replenish everyone's drink. A half-hearted cheer came from the crowd. Pete was still angry but accepted the gift because he was a gentleman.

After a few sips of his beer, Pete said, "I'm still hurt."

"Do you like all old cars, or is it the Studebaker that does it for you?" Mr. Albert asked.

"Pete likes anything automotive," Michael responded.

Pete smiled into his drink and nodded.

"Santo here has a 1985 Cadillac Deville," Michael continued.

Pete perked up, "Is it a V-8?"

People always seem to ask that question, even if they don't know anything about cars.

"Of course!" Santo said, feeling like he would finally be forgiven.

"I can lay down in the trunk with a family of beavers," Mr. Albert chimed in happily.

"If I drove you somewhere, would you give it to me?" Pete negotiated.

"No!" Santo protested, feeling like he was being taken advantage of.

Mr. Albert shrugged. "I don't care."

"No," Santo repeated in an angry parental tone.

Pete gave a forlorn look into his brew.

"I'll let you drive it, though."

"I guess," Pete said, not entirely giving up the notion of getting the car.

Santo stood up and wobbled. Pete stood up and swayed. Mr. Albert stood up and immediately sat down again. He tried to stand two more times before his legs were sturdy enough to support him.

Mr. Albert paid his bill. Santo paid his bill. Jimmy turned to Pete, who motioned that Santo would also pay his bill. Santo shook his head no. Pete pouted. Santo acquiesced. Pete smiled and threw his arm over Santo's shoulder. They were best friends. Mr. Albert wobbled, and Santo frowned as they exited the bar.

~ 37 ~

Two days later.
Michael Skillen's home.

Santo and Mr. Albert were up again before their host, so they ate his peanut butter crackers and drank his beer while waiting. They enjoyed Michael's company but were no closer to finding out about the girl with the guitar than they were when Mr. Albert recognized the tree in the front yard.

They were so comfortable in the house that they did not feel the desire to save any beer for the host. Michael entered the kitchen dressed for the day. He looked as hung over as he usually did. He opened the refrigerator.

"There's no beer left if that's what you're looking for," Mr. Albert offered.

"Course not," Michael shook his head. "Probably just as well. I'm going to see my mom. It's her birthday."

"Do you think we could ask her about Genevieve?" Santo perked up.

"You could ask, but she probably won't answer."

"Why not?"

"Come and see."

Mr. Albert and Santo looked at each other and agreed.

"Good," Michael continued. "Give me your car keys."

"Why?" protested Santo.

"Because neither of you are in any condition to drive, you drunk bastards."

~ 38 ~

Twenty minutes later.
Greenwich Cemetery.

The three men stood in front of Jacqueline Skillen's grave. To her left was her husband, Michael's father, Raymond. To the right of her was a space and then his maternal grandparents, Edward and Margaret Pierpont. Michael had picked some purple flowers from his garden before they left and put them on his mother's headstone.

"They are beautiful. What are they?" Santo asked.

"Hellebore."

"Is that a great plant to bring to a cemetery?" Mr. Albert grinned.

"They symbolize serenity, tranquility, and peace. So, it is as good a flower as any."

Mr. Albert and Santo nodded that it was a good plant for the occasion.

"They also are poisonous," Michael said. "Hellebores contain three active ingredients: glycosides, which slows the heart; saponin, which acts on the nervous system causing narcosis; and helleborine, a purgative found in the roots of the plant."

"You seem to know a lot about this plant," Santo said, fearing for his safety.

"You keep finishing my beer, and you'll know about it first-hand."

Santo moved to the other side of Mr. Albert for protection.

"My mother taught me all about it. I also used it to kill off one of my characters in *The Merry-Go-Round of Death*. My third novel."

"With a title like that, I can't understand why it didn't sell more copies," Mr. Albert quipped.

"It was my mother's favorite flower. She said it reminded her of love, in that there is beauty and danger at every moment."

They looked at the headstone in silence.

"As with all matters of the heart, proceed with caution," Santo said, poetically.

Michael looked at him with admiration but sensed a challenge. "You need to fear the thing you love," he countered.

Mr. Albert, not wanting to be left out, added, "Love is blind."

Michael and Santo looked at him as if he was an idiot.

"Flowers are blind, and this flower reminded your mother of love, so why can't love be blind?"

Michael shook his head before he explained. "We were coming up with expressions which juxtaposed the beauty of the flower with the poison it contains."

"Love is patient. Love is kind?" Mr. Albert's voice sounded like a child who thought he got the correct answer but had no real idea.

Michael looked sympathetically at him, "Bless his heart."

"What does that have to do with flowers?" Santo snarled at Mr. Albert.

"Patience is a flower."

"No, it isn't."

"Yes, it is."

"No, it isn't"

Mr. Albert and Santo went back and forth for what seemed like an eternity before Michael interrupted. "Impatiens are also called patience or busy Lizzie, but I think that is a bit off-topic. So, I guess Albert is right, but not really because if you went into a store and ordered patience, they wouldn't bring you anything."

"What could I get you, sir?" Mr. Albert said, playing a role.

"Patience," Michael picked up on the performance.

"What do you want?"

"Patience."

"You don't want me to bring you anything?"

"Patience."

"I'm getting angry with you. What do you want?" Mr. Albert said, raising his voice to feign anger.

"Patience!" Michael feigned just as loudly.

They both laughed. Santo scowled at Mr. Albert.

"You always ruin everything."

"I ruin everything?"

"Well, not everything," Santo admitted.

"Patience!"

They fell into silence.

"Did your parents fight a lot?" asked Santo. "She has a morbid impression of love."

"Not that I can remember."

"Was she trying to frighten you?" Mr. Albert asked.

"I never married," Michael admitted. "It might have been her intention."

"Probably for the best if that is what you can expect," Mr. Albert offered.

"I don't know. Brian and Tessie seem happy," Michael said, looking at the graves.

"They do," said Mr. Albert.

"They do," said Santo.

The three single men fell into silence.

"Is that place for you?" Mr. Albert said, pointing at the empty space between parents and grandparents.

"I guess so. I think I want to be cremated."

"Why is that?" Mr. Albert asked.

"Cause with all the alcohol I consume, I'd probably burn for days," Michael smiled.

"When he goes," Santo said, indicating Mr. Albert, "I'm going to put him in a woodchipper."

"Sounds like fun. I hope I'm around for that." Michael started back to the car.

Santo followed as he explained the wood-chipping event. They left Mr. Albert alone.

He looked around the nearly empty cemetery. *So quiet and peaceful here*, he thought. *Is this the reward of death?* His eyes went back to the space between graves. The leaves on the dogwood tree behind him rustled in the wind. There was something about that space that made him uneasy.

$$\sim 39 \sim$$

Two days later.
Greenwich Cemetery.

Mr. Albert returned to the graveyard the next day and the day after. He stared at the space between graves. There was something here that troubled his mind. He listened to the silence and the wind through the leaves of the dogwood tree, but nothing stirred his memory.

He sat on the bench under the tree and let his mind go blank. There he remained as if frozen in time, staring at the gravestone of Mrs. Pierpont.

An older man passed between Mr. Albert and the monument. He continued for another step or two before he stopped and turned to the mourner.

"You know, they are never really gone," the old man offered.

"What?"

"They are never really gone if you keep them in your heart and memory."

"But what happens if you have no memory?"

"If you have no memory, why are you here?"

"I don't know."

The old man motioned that he wanted to share Mr. Albert's bench. Mr. Albert nodded. The two men sat in silence for a minute.

"My name is John," the old man extended his hand.

"Albert," Mr. Albert shook his hand. "Nice to meet you."

"Nice to meet you as well."

They returned to silence. There is something comforting about making a new friend in a cemetery.

"Well, I guess if they are not remembered, they are not missed," the man speculated.

"Is that a terrible thing?"

"Some people believe that it is the worst thing."

"I don't think I would mind it, lost in the shroud of time. Clouded over, forgotten," Mr. Albert mused.

"Don't you want your friends and family to remember you?"

"Very few in one department and none in the other."

"You just need a couple of true friends. I'm sure you have a few of those."

"Wanna bet?"

"They'll be there when you need them," John tapped the stranger's knee to reassure him.

"I hope. Let me ask you a question. Why would there be a space between the graves? It is a family plot."

"Some people would do that to remember someone who died but is not here."

"What do you mean?"

"They might have died in another place, like a soldier who died overseas, and the body was not recovered. Did they have a soldier in the family?"

"No, but I am not certain. Someone is definitely missing from this picture."

"Is that whom you don't recall?" John asked.

"If I knew that," Mr. Albert said, rolling his eyes.

"Well, you better remember quickly. Nobody lives forever." The old man walked away.

"I'll bet you on that one as well."

~ 40 ~

Two days later.
Pinkie Master's Lounge.

Although it was early afternoon, the regular crowd was already sitting at their usual places. Brian offered his take on Mr. Albert's situation.

"Maybe you have dementia," he postulated.

"I'm dead."

"I know that, but why can't both be true, dead, and you can't remember stuff?"

"I can remember stuff. You're Brian, married to Tess. There's Porno Rick, sitting next to Mustang Pete. Jimmy's serving me the best alcohol in Savannah. Michael here is going to write my story, and I forgot this guy," he said, indicating Santo, who responded with a raised middle finger. "See, that's pretty good. What more does an alcoholic corpse with no purpose need to remember?"

"You remember the smaller things," Brian conceded. "But not the big things. Where are your memories of love, happiness, loss, and sorrow? Those are the things that give life meaning. You have none of those. Of course, you are dead."

"Brian, you make a mean drunk."

"I'm not drunk yet."

"If that's how you are when you are sober, I wouldn't want to marry you."

"The feeling's mutual, dude. I got my soulmate here."

He leaned over and kissed his wife. Then he looked into her eyes and asked for permission to continue. Her lips tightened, but she nodded her consent.

"Tessie's dad had dementia. It got so bad that he could only remember scattered bits. If you had a conversation with him, it was like it was on a loop. He kept asking the same questions, and you had to answer the same things over and over again. He just couldn't remember."

"When my mother died," Tess continued. "We couldn't tell him because he would never have been able to process the information. He couldn't fully mourn because he could never remember what had happened. Which means every day he would have to hear the news that the woman he loved more than anything in his life was gone."

"What did you do?" Santo asked, barely above a whisper.

"We told him she went out to the store. She did, actually. She had a heart attack in the cereal aisle of the Groceteria, a box of Sugar Rice Krinkles in her hand. She was gone before the ambulance arrived. We didn't get a chance to say goodbye. Every day he asked for her, and every day we told him she went to the store. She had to pick up a few things for dinner. The last thing he said to me, in the hospital, hooked up to all those tubes, in such pain from the cancer, was, *where's your mother?*"

Tessie broke down. With her head fallen, she reached for Brian, who was there for her, as he had always been. He gently pulled her shoulders to him, and she leaned into his strength.

"Bill was a great man," Michael raised his glass. "Wonderful father and husband. Not a game or a concert that his kids were in that he missed. Sitting there as proud as a man could be."

Tessie stopped crying as she remembered her daddy. "He once brought a homeless man to the house for dinner. He met him as he walked home from work. Didn't seem like the man had bathed for weeks. Momma threw both of them out of the house. My father sat the man down on the front porch and told him to wait. He went inside and came back with two plates. He sat next to the poor man, and they ate their dinner. Then my brother went out and sat down, keeping his dad between him and the homeless man. Even though he trusted his dad, Junior couldn't be sure if he trusted the beggar. I looked at momma, and she nodded, so I joined them. Soon she was out on the porch as well. My daddy brought the stranger to the factory the next day and gave that man a job. That's how he was."

The bar fell into silence, and then, one by one, they all raised their glasses to William Harris and thought of the people in their lives that were no longer there. The alcohol tasted sweeter with the realization that life is fleeting.

Mr. Albert looked at the solemn faces. He had no memories of mothers, fathers, sons or daughters. If he never died, there must have been people who were important to him at some point in his life. Why couldn't he remember anyone? Anything? He thought of Sisyphus and finished his beer.

Three days later.
Michael Skillen's house.

Mr. Albert could not sleep. To be more precise, he could sleep. He was able to sleep, and he was able to dream. But the dreams that he had were not pleasant. He dreamt of a kick line of women in bathing suits, with alligator heads singing "We Got the Funk" while doing their high steps. An audience of Macaque monkeys in Hawaiian shirts ate bananas and cheered with wild abandon. After their performance, the lady gators bowed and slithered back into the swamp.

He got out of bed and walked around the house, trying not to wake the others. There was no need to worry. Michael and Santo had barely managed to stumble home due to the heightened level of alcohol in their systems and fell right to sleep. If the house blew down in a hurricane, they would have slept through it.

The house was different at night, in the stillness. If you opened your mind to it, you could feel the spirits. It was an old house, built in the 1870s, according to Michael. Old houses are often creaky with lots of drafts. It is easy to explain things away if that was your intention. Albert wasn't interested in explanations. Something about this house lived when no one was around.

The only light in the room seeped through the batiste curtains from the streetlight across the road. Leaves from the tree in the yard created moving shadows as if spirits danced around the room.

Mr. Albert sat in the living room and watched the shadow play. The room seemed familiar, not because he had been Michael's house guest for several weeks. He was never awake and alone at this time of the night. The familiarity was more profound.

He felt happy here, although he could not say why. But the room also had a foreboding. There were secrets there that were meant to remain hidden. Or maybe it was a truth that was praying to escape. *He was not the person to pray to*, Mr. Albert thought. He had no power to grant wishes or to heal the sick of spirit.

Something passed in front of the window. He turned to look at the movement but nothing was there. *Maybe there was something outside the house*, he thought. He opened the door. The street was empty. It must have been late. The night was cool but comfortable. He sat on the porch. There was a swing on the tree. He could not remember if it was there before. It swung erratically. One side moved in front of the other side before switching places. There was no breeze that could explain the movement. He walked over to the swing and grabbed the chain. The seat continued to sway unabated. He held the seat. It stopped. He released the swing, and it remained motionless. He walked back to the porch. As he settled back into his chair, the swing began to move again. The leaves whispered. Mr. Albert felt a cold wind pass over him. The wind chimes at the end of the porch clanged briefly before falling silent.

He always heard that when people feel ghosts, there is usually a coldness in the air. Why would a spirit make the air cold? Maybe they wanted to feel the warmth of the living. It must be cold in a grave. Mr. Albert had no warmth to give the tormented soul. His heart was also cold as the grave. He wondered if the spirit of the swing was Genevieve.

"Genevieve, Genevieve, are you there? Genevieve is a pretty name. It makes me happy when I hear myself say it. I wish you could speak to me or show yourself. I should be able to see you. We are both dead."

He had never heard a ghost story where ghosts could see other ghosts. It always seemed like a solitary experience, ghostdom. He continued his one-sided conversation.

"Aren't we a pair? Me here at last on this ground, you in mid-air. I don't think the song is about ghosts. What were we to each other? I can't help you, Genevieve, if I don't know what to do. You brought me here. Why? It is a pretty night, though.

I don't know what you want from me. And I don't know why I should care. Did we even know each other? Or is it that we are kindred spirits? We are both lost souls trapped in our private pur-gatories. The only difference between us is that you are abandoned in a dark place, never able to find the light of peace, and I am stuck in this world of lights and colors, having to deal with people who are blind to the true nature of things. They keep their eyes closed to anything they don't understand. You wander blinded in the fog. I am conscious but not capable. How can I help you? I can't help myself. What a load of shit this all is."

The swing stopped its movement. Mr. Albert thought that the ghost of Genevieve had sat on the swing to listen to him.

"I was shot, in a church, true story. God-fearing people tried to kill me because they didn't understand me. I am just a walking corpse, for goodness' sake. 'When you prick us, do we not bleed?' I don't. I guess you cannot quote Shakespeare for every occasion. I hope that there is a God who will save us both. But I have lost the capacity to pray. My pleas for mercy are painful to my heart and ears. Probably because I do not think I deserve mercy. Don't we all, even the worst of us, deserve mercy? I don't think God listens to the dead. We're both screwed."

He grew tired. It calmed him to talk to the ghost of Genevieve. She was a good listener. He closed his eyes. He wasn't sure, but as he fell asleep, he felt a gentle kiss on his cheek.

~ 42 ~

In the morning.
Michael Skillen's house.

Santo opened the screen door and saw Mr. Albert on the porch. He touched his shoulder to see if he was dead dead. Mr. Albert opened his eyes. At first, he smiled, but then he recognized Santo, and the happy thought disappeared.

"I did not see you in your room. What are you doing out here?"

"I couldn't sleep. I came out here. It was cool and peaceful. I guess I fell asleep."

Mr. Albert stood up and stretched. Then he noticed that something was wrong.

"What happened to the swing?"

"What swing?"

"There was a swing here," Mr. Albert asserted.

"I don't remember any swing."

"You're an idiot, Santo."

"You are probably right. But not about the swing."

"Ah, go to hell. Where's Michael?"

"Still asleep. That man doesn't know what the AM means."

Mr. Albert waved his hand dismissively at Santo as he stormed through the house and into Michael's room. The unconscious writer was spread out in the bed, hugging an oversized pillow. Three other pillows and the comforter had been thrown on the floor during the night.

"What happened to the swing? The swing is gone," demanded Mr. Albert.

Michael opened one eye to see which madman had destroyed the sanctity of his bedroom.

"Fuck off." Michael rolled over and scratched himself through his boxers.

Mr. Albert entered the room, picked up a pillow from the floor, and whacked Michael with it. Michael tried to bury himself further in his hugging pillow but could not escape.

"Santo," Michael called for help.

Santo arrived and grabbed another pillow from the floor. He hit Mr. Albert, hoping to prevent any further violence against Michael. As Mr. Albert turned to defend himself, Michael sprang up in his bed and counter-attacked, hitting Santo with the pillow about as much as he hit Mr. Albert. Soon they were all hitting each other regardless of previous alliances.

"What are we? A bunch of tween-aged girls at a sleepover?" Santo finally yelled to stop the madness.

Michael and Mr. Albert, heavily panting, put down their weapons.

"Where's my gun?" Michael said, snarling at Mr. Albert.

"I'm dead, remember?" Mr. Albert snarled right back at him.

"I know, but it would probably still make me feel good."

"True." Mr. Albert sat down next to Michael on the bed.

Mr. Albert looked around the room.

"What happened to the mirror over there?" He said, pointing to the wall opposite the door.

"What mirror?" Michael asked.

"It was a freestanding mirror right next to the armoire."

"Mr. Albert seems to be remembering things that weren't there. He thinks there was a swing hanging from the tree in front of your house," Santo said.

"There was when I was a child."

"Green or blue?" asked Mr. Albert.

"Yellow," said Michael.

"That's it. I told you, Santo." Mr. Albert claimed victory.

"But it hasn't been up there since we came here," Santo said, unwilling to give Mr. Albert the point.

"Not for years," Michael confirmed.

"So, there. I was right."

"There was a swing!" Mr. Albert raised his voice.

"But not since we've been here."

"It could have been a ghost," Mr. Albert claimed.

"A ghost swing?" Michael asked, hoping he was still asleep.

"Could have been."

"How can inanimate objects be ghosts?" yelled Santo.

"How can people be ghosts?" Mr. Albert yelled back.

"I don't know!" Santo bellowed.

"I don't know either!" Mr. Albert matched Santo's bellow.

They both sat down on Michael's bed.

"For fuck's sake." Michael got out of his bed. "I'm going to take a piss."

He stormed off into the master bathroom.

"I guess a swing could be a ghost," Santo said, trying to apologize.

"A mirror could be a ghost."

"Lots of mirrors are haunted in scary stories."

"Bloody Mary, that was a bad one," Mr. Albert said, shaking his head.

"Agreed. I've never heard of a haunted ottoman, though."

"True. How can you make an ottoman scary?"

"Don't know," Santo shrugged.

Michael came out of the bathroom. "What are you two imbeciles talking about now?"

"Haunted ottomans," Mr. Albert said cheerfully.

"I need a drink." Michael headed for the refrigerator.

"I'll join you if you don't mind." Mr. Albert followed.

Santo made Michael's bed before joining them.

~ 43 ~

A little later in the morning.
Michael Skillen's house.

After having a few rounds, they were all friends again. Michael was still in his boxers and undershirt. Mr. Albert was still in his pajamas. Santo was the only one who was dressed before the morning libations. Looking at the other two, he felt over-dressed.

"So, you are saying," Michael said, scratching his stubble. "There was a yellow swing behaving erratically until the ghost of Genevieve sat in it?"

"Yes," Mr. Albert said, happy that someone understood the events.

"Do ghosts get tired?" Michael sought clarification.

"What?"

"Why would she have sat in the ghost swing if she wasn't tired."

"Maybe she wasn't tired."

"Then why did she have to sit down?"

"Maybe she was listening to what I was saying."

"From what you told me, it wasn't very interesting."

Mr. Albert looked to Santo for help. Santo shrugged his shoulders to say that this conversation was not very interesting.

"Well, maybe no one had spoken to her in so long that she was just happy that anyone was talking to her," Mr. Albert speculated.

Mr. Albert looked to Santo again. Santo shrugged his shoulders again as if to say maybe the ghost of Genevieve was a little lonely.

206

"It is incredible how expressive Santo is with his shrugs," admired Michael.

Santo shrugged his shoulders a third time as if to say it wasn't that impressive.

"Hey, wait a second." Santo had a thought.

"What?" asked Mr. Albert.

"Can't we figure out when Genevieve was in this house from the ghost swing?"

"How so?" asked Michael.

"Well, we don't know when Genevieve was around, but we do know that she was around when the ghost swing was here...wait, when was the swing taken down?"

"When I was about four," Michael said.

"And when was that?" Santo was on a roll.

"1965."

"Aha! Then Genevieve was here between 1870 and 1965," Santo announced proudly.

"That narrows it down to ninety-four years," Mr. Albert said, not impressed.

"That doesn't seem like much narrowing, does it?" Santo realized.

"No, it doesn't," Mr. Albert agreed.

"What I'm interested in, is the whole armoire mirror thing. Why do you think there was an armoire in my bedroom?" Michael changed the subject.

"I just remembered it when I sat on your bed. Last night it seemed like a lot of the furniture in this house was moved around."

"A lot of this furniture is quite old and belonged to my grandparents and great-grandparents. Every once in a while, you just move the furniture around," Michael said.

"Where is the mirror?"

"Don't remember any mirror."

"A freestanding mirror. It could have been mahogany or some other reddish wood."

"Don't remember any mirror, but there is an armoire in Santo's room."

Michael got up and walked to Santo's room. Mr. Albert followed him. Santo put the empty beer bottles in the recycling bin before joining them. Mr. Albert studied the armoire.

"Well, is that it?" Michael asked, not wishing to disturb Mr. Albert's concentration.

"I think it is."

"My grandmother bought it from a place in North Carolina. It could have been a wedding present."

"When did your grandparents get married?"

"In 1929."

"That means Genevieve was around between 1929 and 1965," Santo asserted.

"How do you get that?" Michael questioned Santo's analysis.

"Well, the armoire came into this house around 1929. It was a wedding present, so it probably was in their bedroom. It was moved before you were around because you weren't aware that it was there. And the swing was taken down when you were around four."

"That narrows it down to thirty-six years," Michael said.

"Thirty-six years is better than ninety-four years," Mr. Albert said, thoughtfully. "We have done some terrific work here today. Why don't we pick this back up in a few days?"

He sat on the bed and fell silent. Until this time, their adventure was all fun and games. It didn't seem fun anymore.

"Yes, we have almost solved the mystery. No need to get ahead of ourselves," Michael said picking up on Mr. Albert's apprehension

"Don't you want to figure this thing out right here, right now?" Santo asked.

"As Michael said, no need to get ahead of ourselves. We need some time to ponder about what we learned today."

"It might be helpful, so we don't draw any erroneous conclusions," Michael said. "Maybe we should consult other people."

"Whom we trust that could give us input," Mr. Albert continued.

"And other perspectives."

"You two alcoholics just want to go to Pinkie Masters." Santo shook his head in disgust.

"Pinkie Masters? I hadn't thought about that, did you, Albert?"

"Hadn't crossed my mind, but now that you mentioned it, Santo, it might solve all of the issues you have brought up."

"Trust-worthy people," Michael said.

"Time to mull things about," Mr. Albert suggested.

"Ah, the hell with it," Santo stormed out of the room.

"Don't know what he is getting so upset about," Michael protested.

"He's the one that suggested it," Mr. Albert smacked his lips, already tasting the Pabst Blue Ribbon.

~ 44 ~

Twenty minutes later.
Pinkie Masters.

After a round or two at Pinkie Masters, the regulars were brought up to speed.

"So, the ghost swing wiggled, and there was no wind," Mustang Pete pondered.

"Exactly. And then it just stopped," answered Mr. Albert.

"Interesting," Pete said, as if he were contemplating the meaning of life.

"It's a puzzle," said Michael, his mind already in a fog.

"I think it was just that Genevieve was tired and needed a rest," Mr. Albert suggested.

"Why would ghosts need a rest?" countered Brian.

"That's what I said," Michael cried, slamming his hand on the bar.

"Ghosts are eternally wandering in purgatory. They have no rest because of the wrongs they have done," Porno Rick read from Wikipedia.

"Or the wrongs done to them," Tessie added, her head shaking slowly, "Poor Genevieve."

"I'm sure she was the one who committed the heinous crime," Brian comforted his wife.

"You think?" Tess held his hand for reassurance.

"Of course. She was probably a terrible person."

"Could go either way," Rick said, before returning to his screen.

"So, there were wrongs done, and she needed a rest." Mr. Albert tried to lead the conversation back to the issue at hand.

"There were two parts here; the rocking and the resting," Mustang Pete emphasized.

"So, which one are we going to discuss first? Who wants the rocking?" Mr. Albert asked, trying to focus the group.

Brian, Tessie, and Porno Rick raised their hands.

"And who wants to discuss the resting?"

Mustang Pete, Jimmie, and Michael raised their hands. The group looked to Santo.

"Don't look at me," he pouted, mostly to Mr. Albert. "You're the one who thought these people would be helpful."

"Santo, you have to choose." Mr. Albert put his foot down.

"All right, the resting."

"There we are. We are making progress." Mr. Albert sensed things were going to be accomplished. "Who thinks she needed to rest because she committed the terrible crime?"

Mustang Pete, Jimmie, and Michael raised their hands.

"Aw, fuck," Mr. Albert muttered. "And who thinks she needed to rest because a terrible crime was committed against her?"

Brian, Tessie, and Porno Rick raised their hands. The group once again looked to Santo.

"I hate all of you."

"I hate them too. They probably hate themselves, full of self-loathing. Why else would they be in a bar at 11 am?" Mr. Albert said, trying to hurry Santo's vote.

"Hey, I have a job," Jimmie protested.

"We all are impressed," Brian shot back.

"Santo?"

"I'll go with whatever Jimmie voted for because he is the only one with a job."

"I have a job," Porno Rick said, still staring at his screen.

"That's a job?" Brian laughed.

"I review porno anime websites."

"Let me repeat the question," Brian mocked. "That's a job?"

"Quarter of a million followers. Made seventy-five grand on advertising alone."

"Why am I usually the one to buy all the drinks?" Mr. Albert protested.

"Lucky, I guess," Rick said, not looking up from his phone.

"I change my vote. What did you vote for, Porno Rick?" Santo asked.

"Fuck if I know."

"He voted with us. He voted with us." Tessie bounced up on her chair like a contestant on *The Price is Right*.

"And what did you vote for?" Santo inquired.

"Terrible crime happened to her," Tessie looked at her husband, who agreed with her.

"Okay, to review. We have decided that Genevieve needed to rest because a terrible crime was committed against her."

"That's all we decided on in the last fifteen minutes?" Mustang Pete could not believe how long this was taking.

"The cogs of society turn very slowly," Michael said.

The barflies all nodded their heads in recognition before silence settled in.

"No! Oh my gosh! I know what it all means," Tessie squealed.

Everyone turned to her.

"It wasn't a wiggle. It was an "X.""

"An "X," her husband asked.

"Yes, the swing was making an "X" back and forth, back and forth," she said, illustrating it with her hands. "Like an X marks the spot. There is something buried there that Genevieve wants us to find. I say we find it."

"There's buried treasure in Michael's yard," Mustang Pete, who always had a thing for pirates, blurted out, then immediately looked around to see if any tourist was listening.

"But it is not even noon. Surely, we can have a few more drinks before digging up my yard," Michael groaned.

The group turned to Mr. Albert.

"Sure, what the hell. How many of you want to have a few more drinks before digging up Michael's yard?"

Everyone turned to Rick for his recommendation. He was oblivious and stared intensely at his screen.

"Okay," Mr. Albert continued. "How many of you want to go right now to dig up Michael's yard?"

Porno Rick did not vote. The group leaned toward him.

"Rick, dear," Tessie cajoled.

Rick glanced up from his screen. Everyone looked at him for his vote. He rolled his eyes.

"Sure, whatever."

They all cheered and quickly paid their tabs. Jimmie was left alone at the bar with no one but tourists. He bused the glasses and wiped down the bar.

"Seventy-five thousand for watching cartoon porn. I'm in the wrong line of work."

~ 45 ~

In Michael's yard.

Half an hour later, the treasure hunters had assembled in Michael's front yard. Michael searched through his garage and found some old and rusty garden tools. He spent very little time in his yard and hired a landscaper to do the dirty work. His grandmother was the gardener of the family, and her ancient camellias were the envy of all who saw them. His mother did not inherit the same green thumb, but she puttered about in the garden out of family tradition. His father spent more time on the putting green than in their garden.

Michael looked over his motley crew and smiled. They all had gardening tools. Brian had a pointed shovel. Tessie had a rake. Porno Rick and Mustang Pete had a pair of trowels between them, but Rick was not interested in this silliness. He sat on the porch and pulled out his phone. Santo pretended he was a bear with his three-tined cultivator, hissing at Pete, who warded him off with his trowel sword. And Mr. Albert leaned on his hoe.

Michael picked up Rick's trowel and saluted Mr. Albert, "The troops are assembled, sir."

He stepped off the porch, and Mr. Albert saddled up to the top, leaning heavily on his hoe, "Men and um, Tessie." He started off badly. "What we want to do...."

"Excuse me, general," Mustang Pete raised his trowel.

"Yes?" Mr. Albert responded in a general-like manner.

"I have to take a leak. Should I go behind the tree?"

"Who wouldn't see you pissing in the yard?"

"Well, could I go inside?"

Michael confronted him. "Why didn't you go at the bar?"

"I didn't have to go at the bar."

"This is great. Does anyone else have to go?" Michael growled.

Tessie raised her hand. Then Brian, followed by Santo and Mr. Albert.

"For fuck's sake. All right, first Pete, then Tessie, Brian, Santo, and Mr. Albert."

Brian raised his hand.

"Yes, Brian," Michael muttered.

"Could I go last? It might be a while," Brian said, embarrassed, holding up two fingers.

"Oh hell." Michael threw up his hands and sat on the bottom step.

Pete ran off to do his business. Brian and Tessie had a smoke. A couple of tourists walked by and snapped a picture of the group.

"Take a picture. It will last longer," Michael barked.

The tourists walked off quickly.

"They did," said Mr. Albert.

"What?"

"They took a picture."

"I know."

"Then why did you tell them to take a picture if they already took a picture?"

"Just to mess with them," Michael smiled.

Pete came out with a sandwich, "Tessie, your turn."

Tessie ran into the house.

"Michael, you didn't have any mustard, so I used mayonnaise. Is that okay?" Pete sat in the chair next to Porno Rick.

"No, it is not okay. And what kind of sandwich is that?"

"Turkey, I think."

"I have turkey?"

"Not anymore. That is the ugliest tree sculpture I have ever seen," Pete said, indicating Mr. Muggles.

"Oh, for fuck's sake."

"Michael, you're feeding us?" Rick looked up from his screen.

"I'm not feeding you!"

"Doesn't have any turkey." Pete gave a disparaging look to their host.

"How can you invite us to your house and not have any turkey?" Rick grumbled.

"I didn't invite you to my house. This was all Tessie's idea."

"What was my idea?" Tessie said, returning from the bathroom.

"To have us over for dinner," Brian said. "Santo, your turn."

"Thanks," Santo said, and disappeared inside.

"There's nothing to eat in there. I looked," Tessie said, confused about the dinner invitation.

"There's chips," Pete chimed in.

"Sweetie, bring us some chips," Brian whispered so Michael wouldn't hear.

She went back into the house.

"What the hell is going on here? You're a pack of locusts!" Michael bellowed.

Several more tourists walked by and stopped to look at the commotion. Mr. Albert, who had made his way to the front gate to wait in line for the bathroom, turned to the tourists.

"Michael, that guy over there, invited us over to use his bathroom and feed us dinner, but was not happy when we actually had to use the bathroom, so he threw all the turkey sandwiches in the garbage."

The tourists looked confused, so Mr. Albert continued.

"It is a longstanding tradition in the South. The whole event ends when we dig up his yard looking for hot dogs that he buried there. It's called *Where're the Weenies?* Southern tradition."

Tessie came out of the house.

"Here's the chips, dill pickle flavored. And I also found a bottle of tequila behind some books on the shelf."

"I thought you were out of liquor," Mr. Albert frowned at his host.

"I knew we should have stayed in the bar," Michael said, burying his head in his hands.

~ 46 ~

One hour later.
Michael Skillen's front yard.

Mr. Albert ordered pizza to quell the angry mob. Now everyone was full of tequila and pizza and had settled into their work. Even Porno Rick searched for the treasures Genevieve left them.

There was some discussion about which garden tool each one of them was given originally and which tool they had now. This was not resolved after several minutes of intense debate and three votes, which always ended in a tie, even though there were seven of them. Finally, it was agreed that the tied votes were because someone was always in the bathroom.

This caused Michael to curse the gods and storm into the house only to find Brian with his head in the refrigerator looking for beer, which there wasn't any because the locusts had descended and picked the cupboard clean. Another time he found Mustang Pete fast asleep on the couch. Eventually, Michael banned everyone from entering his house.

Now they stood assembled, looking towards the porch. Brian had a pointed shovel. Tessie had the hoe. Porno Rick had a rake. Mustang Pete had one trowel, and Mr. Albert had the other trowel. Santo somehow managed to retain possession of the three-tined cultivator because he remembered, at one time in the afternoon, that he was a bear.

Mr. Albert tried his speech again. He was a little better this time.

"People, Tessie believes that Genevieve has left a message or an item that is important to our investigation in this yard. The swing was just about here," he said, walking over to where he thought the swing was last night. "Or maybe here," he walked to a different spot. "Or here. Damn it. I have no fucking idea where the swing was."

"In other words, dig wherever you want," Santo said.

The group spread out and started digging. Porno Rick walked around, and whenever one of the treasure hunters found a place to dig, they would point to a spot, and Rick would rake the area for a couple of seconds. Rick did this for about five minutes until he realized he had the hardest job and returned to his porch seat.

"What's this?" Brian cried, holding up a shiny object.

The others gathered around him, staring with amazement at what he held in his hand.

"It's a quarter, you idiot," Michael said, grabbing the coin from Brian's hand.

"But is it a ghost quarter?"

"Why would it be a ghost quarter?"

"It was a ghost swing. Why couldn't it be a ghost quarter?" Brian demanded.

"It was made this year. Genevieve was around before I was born, so it is not from her, and it is certainly not a ghost quarter," Michael snarled.

"Then could I have it back?" Brian asked meekly.

Michael sneered at him and put the coin in his pocket.

"What's this?" Tessie cried.

"It's a rock," Michael moaned.

"I feel the energy emanating from it."

"What's this?" cried Mr. Albert.

"It's a piece of glass," Michael yelled, losing all patience. "Are any of you actually looking for anything, or are you just bending over and picking up whatever the hell you find, thinking it's important?"

"I think it is the second thing," Santo said. "Hey, what's this?"

Santo picked up a piece of plastic in the shape of a three. It was gold and had dirt embedded into the hollowed-out back of it. They gathered around Santo and stared at it in amazement.

"Is it a ghost?" asked Pete.

"What do you think it means?" Tessie asked.

"Why would it mean anything? It is just a piece of plastic," Mr. Albert disputed.

"Genevieve wanted you to know something about the number three," Tessie divined. "What could it represent?"

"The past, present, and future," Brian pondered.

"Good. What else?" Tessie said, looking around the group. She had now become the spiritual leader.

"All stories must have a beginning, middle, and an end," Michael, the writer, contributed.

"Yes, yes," said Tessie as if in a trance. "And all our stories will have an end as well."

"Birth, life, and death," Rick called from the porch.

"Thank you," Tessie turned to Mr. Albert. "Except some people have more than that."

The group turned to Mr. Albert as well. They stared at him as if enlightenment had descended upon them.

"Well then, a three certainly doesn't portray my existence, does it?" Mr. Albert scoffed.

"That's a good point," Michael agreed.

The group then looked from Mr. Albert to Michael to Tessie. She had no answer to this mystery. The group shook their heads, no longer enamored with her powers of divination.

"Well, I can't work under these conditions." She stormed off and lit a cigarette.

Brian followed her to get a cigarette as well.

"The Holy Trinity," Santo said, looking up to heaven.

By this time, nobody was paying attention.

"I'm going to the bar. Anyone want to join me?" Mr. Albert announced.

The ex-treasure hunters dropped their tools where they were and walked off, trying to catch Mr. Albert. Michael was left alone with a yard full of abandoned equipment.

"Son of a bitch," he grumbled, as he cleaned up.

~ 47 ~

Three days later.
Michael Skillen's home.
2 AM.

Usually, the three men were asleep by this time, but tonight, the pace of their drinking was slower. They sat on the porch, Michael and Mr. Albert in the rockers and Santo on the stoop. Santo didn't want the stoop but had lost a round of rock, paper, scissors to Mr. Albert. Michael did not play. He claimed homeownership entitled him to "sit anywhere I fuckin' well please!"

Santo stomped his foot. His leg had fallen asleep.

"You think you will see the swing tonight?" Michael asked. No one had seen the swing except for Albert, and this annoyed him because he felt that home ownership entitled him to that as well. Apparently, the netherworld did not follow his rules.

"I don't think so," said Mr. Albert. "I fall asleep, dream about dancing alligators or the like, wake up, you people are sleeping, I come out here, and whallah, ghost swing!" Mr. Albert emphasized the magic of the moment with jazz hands.

"What the hell is whallah?" Michael grumbled.

"It's like special, the completion of some challenging task made seemingly simple."

"That's not whallah. It's voilà, you idiot."

"Santo." Mr. Albert made Santo the judge.

"I don't want to play."

"Just because you always put down a rock, and I always cover you with paper?"

If looks could kill, kill dead people, then Mr. Albert would be dead, dead, dead, dead, dead, dead, dead. Santo smiled evilly. Then his smile faded.

"One, it is voilà. And two, you are both idiots. Of all the terrible things that are happening in the world, this is all you could talk about?"

"Seems about as good as anything; the bastardization of language in the hands of buffoons," Michael smiled. "What would you suggest we talk about?"

"How about the fact that Mr. Albert is dead," Santo suggested. "Doesn't that make you wonder about the true nature of the universe?"

"Why should it?" Michael shrugged. "I've seen him dead, dead. Why should I doubt it?"

"Don't you want to know why he's dead?

"Why? Will that knowledge change anything?"

"It would change your understanding of life."

"All that would mean is that my understanding of life is wrong," Michael said casually. "I could either accept that I don't know anything about all this, or I can get angry about why reality doesn't fit into my inadequate understanding. I choose to accept that my understanding will always be incomplete."

"Do you accept everything that happens?"

"How could I do otherwise?"

"Rage, rage against the dying of the light," Santo argued.

"My light dies, regardless," Michael smiled.

"You are like an alcoholic Buddha."

"Namaste," Michael said, bowing his head to Santo.

The men sat in silence. This moment was a good moment. The night was calm and clear, and the three friends were drinking beers and somewhat enjoying each other's company.

"Could I tell you something, Santo?" Michael asked.

"Go ahead. It is your porch," Santo said, feeling a little more mellow.

"I was on Tinder the other day."

Santo and Mr. Albert turned with interest to their host.

"There was a woman there who fit all my criteria," Michael continued. "Pretty eyes, nice smile, knew how to fill out a bathing suit, if you know what I mean."

"Why wouldn't I know what you mean?" Santo objected. "Do you think I was sitting here saying, what does she fill a bathing suit with?"

"Couldn't fill a bathing suit with pancakes," Mr. Albert suggested. "They would fall right through. Beer? No. Not much she could fill her bathing suit with. Spaghetti?"

Michael stared at his guests. They sat quietly smiling and probably thinking about pancakes.

Michael continued, "Her profile said she was five-seven, but she liked to wear three-inch heels, so she would only date a man who was at least five-ten. I texted her, so your three-inch pumps are more important than true love? She blocked me."

"Was that a surprise?" Santo smiled.

"I don't mind being blocked. I quite enjoy it, honestly. The point is that she had a conception of what love should be, and she wanted someone to fill that space. She wasn't interested in an actual connection. She wanted eye candy."

"Don't we all want eye candy?" Mr. Albert asked.

"You want eye candy?" Santo questioned his friend.

After a moment of contemplation, Mr. Albert said, "Question withdrawn."

"We all have these ideas of what life should be," Michael resumed. "When reality does not mesh with our fantasy conception, we get angry, sad, and suicidal. We withdraw from life, and the world stays as it has always been."

"What if we don't get angry, sad, or suicidal?" Santo asked.

"The world will remain as it is, regardless," Michael said, finishing his beer.

"So, you are saying we shouldn't do anything to improve the world?"

"What would you like to make better?"

"Homelessness," Santo said.

"I took you vagrants in, didn't I?"

"Racism."

"I treat each person I meet as an individual."

Mr. Albert rose from his rocker.

"Can anyone use another beer?"

Michael and Santo raised their empty bottles. Mr. Albert collected them and went inside.

"This is nice," Michael said, breathing deeply.

"Without Mr. Albert?" Santo asked.

Michael smiled and then looked up at the stars. Santo took the vacant chair.

"So, you've given up on the whole love thing?" Santo asked, thinking just as much about his own situation as Michael's.

Mr. Albert returned with the beers. He handed them out and sat on the steps.

Michael raised his beer and toasted the universe, "Love exists everywhere, if it exists at all."

~ 48 ~

Two days later.
Michael Skillen's house.
3 AM.

Mr. Albert dreamt of walking in a park as dark storm clouds filled the sky. It grew windy. His long raincoat acted like a sail and lifted him off the ground. He was tossed about before landing in Michael's front yard. The doors and windows opened and shut, then opened again as if they were angry at the intruder. Objects were spewed out through the openings. He managed to avoid the plates and the knives, but a Bible opened to E 611 hit him directly in the face. He fell backward, looking up. The clouds took the form of angry spirits, covering, then revealing the sullen sun. Beams from the windows shot the spirits, who fell like burned embers on their descent. They landed on him, grasping and clawing at his face and neck. Before long, he was buried. A clock flew by his face when he managed to dig himself out. According to the clock, the time was 5:16. Then there was banging from far away but coming nearer.

He opened his eyes and heard a tapping on the window. He got out of bed and walked to see what was making the noise. In the front yard, it was there again, the swing. Mr. Albert walked quietly to the front porch. He sat down on the rocking chair and watched the motionless swing. A frigid stillness filled the air, like a grave. He felt a cold breeze blow by. The wind chimes clanged and then fell silent. He knew that the restless spirit had returned.

"Genevieve. I hope you are Genevieve. I don't know why, but I would like it to be you. Do you like the mess that my friends made in the yard? Dug it up because Tessie thought you had left me a present. All we found was some change, a couple of rocks, bits of glass, and a plastic three. Some message. But I don't know if you are getting my messages either. Life is stupid. Too much making too much of everything. I don't understand any of it.

There seems to be a space between where things are and where things should be. Like when a friend's friend dies. There should be something to say to comfort him, but there isn't. Maybe, *we'll all be dead soon enough.* Might try that one the next time. That will comfort them. These mortals spend so much time forgetting that the end for all is dust. Thinking they will last forever. They forget how precious life is. Vanity, vanity, all is vanity. Words, words, words.

I wish I could remember that song. Praying by a river. Cowboys in white linen. There is a space where I know something belongs. Something, some memory, someone. Do the dead not remember, Genevieve? And if not, why shouldn't they move on? Maybe I am a ghost, not being able to move on but not knowing why I remain. Is it love, Genevieve, that is holding you here? Did I love you? Did you love me? Our love must have been strong to call me from New Jersey.

The living love. It seems like it is the only thing that gives them purpose. They spend their entire lives trying to live a great love story. Great longing leads to great copulation, leads to love, leads to comfort, leads to anxiety, leads to isolation, leads to death. Longing and desire lead to death. I don't desire anything, but the world demands commitment. You must have a purpose, Mr. Albert! If you have a purpose, then I will have a purpose. Then the world will have a purpose. We attempt to accomplish important things to achieve immortality or worse, love, which only leads to a quicker demise. What did you want, Genevieve, that you could not accomplish when you were alive? Was I a part of that desire? Did I stop you?

You and I understand, Genevieve. We want nothing, will achieve nothing, and will change nothing. What do they want that can be achieved? Mountains crumble to the sea, and people learn nothing until the grave swallows them. Then they understand that all is one. There is no need to fear the darkness."

He looked up to see the swing moving. This time in a clockwise, circular pattern. He walked over to the ghost swing. It was not hanging from the branch above, but the chains ended just over Mr. Albert's head.

"Nice trick."

He looked through the swing, which seemed to be making a bullseye on the ground.

"Is that where the treasure lies?" He said, kneeling to uncover what was hidden in the ground.

But as his fingers touched the ground, the swing cracked him in the head. For a ghost swing, it sure packed a punch. Mr. Albert's face crashed against the cool dirt. He felt his consciousness evaporate. The light faded from his eyes, and he thought he heard a voice whisper; time *will tell.*

~ 49 ~

Michael Skillen's house.
The next morning.

Santo found Mr. Albert on the ground.

"You and Genevieve were out dancing the night away," Santo laughed.

Mr. Albert did not open his eyes when Santo tapped him with his foot. He was dead, dead. Santo thought that because they were getting close to solving the mystery, he wouldn't die, die anymore. But maybe he was just getting weaker. Perhaps when the mystery is solved, Mr. Albert could go on. He dragged the dead man into his bedroom before waking Michael up.

Michael got bored with staring at the corpse, "it's like watching grass grow."

He went off to Pinkie Masters and returned three hours later with the regulars in tow. They all wanted to see what a dead, dead man looked like. Tessie was the first to approach Mr. Albert. She sat on his bed, taking his hand.

"He's very cold, Santo. I think he is gone for good. I'm sorry, but I know he is in a better place," she rose and took Santo's hand.

"He is not dead. He's just dead, dead. He will be his own miserable self in a day or two."

Mustang Pete was the next to approach Mr. Albert. He took his rolled-up magazine from his back pocket and poked the dead man. When that didn't wake him, he hit him on his head.

"What are you doing," cried Santo in horror.

"I thought he was faking. Could we draw on him with permanent markers?"

"Will you leave him alone, Pete?"

"You know, if anyone wants to have sex with him, we could make a lot of money on some sites, I know." Porno Rick sensed a business opportunity. "Tessie?"

"Hey," Brian stepped forward to protect his wife.

"Brian, you're volunteering?" Rick continued. "I am not familiar with those sites, but I'm sure we could do just as well."

"Stop it," Santo barked. "No one is having sex with Mr. Albert when he is dead, dead! I do not know if he likes anyone of you in that way. It's none of my business. But when he is like this, you will all show him the respect he deserves, or at least the respect you should show anyone else that you superficially care about. Think of all the rounds he bought you people!"

"I was just trying to honor his memory," Porno Rick grumbled.

"That's how you would honor his memory?" Santo snapped.

Porno Rick shrugged his shoulders. Michael patted Rick's back, suggesting that he also thought it was a good idea. After five minutes of showing Mr. Albert solemn respect, they went into the kitchen to look for beer and snacks. When the supplies were exhausted, they all headed back to the bar. Michael and Santo stood looking at the corpse.

"Why don't you take a walk around? It is a pretty day," Michael suggested.

"Thank you, I will," Santo turned to the door.

"And Santo, as long as you are out, why don't you pick us up some beer?"

Santo nodded. The day was bright. He felt the sun on his face. He took a deep breath of the clean, fresh air. Savannah was beautiful. Just watching the Savannahians, SCAD students, and tourists do their strange dance, where worlds collide but remain totally separate, was entertaining. He walked through Forsyth Square to see the fountain and then headed over to the Chandler Oak. He studied the tree for a moment before mumbling, *it is just a tree.* He continued to the Victorian Market.

~ 50 ~

Four days later.
Michael Skillen's house.

Mr. Albert rose on the fifth day. He was groggier than usual but was glad to see Santo asleep in the room.

"Santo," he whispered.

Santo opened his eyes and smiled at his friend's return.

"Mr. Albert, how are you feeling?"

"Not as bad as a gunshot, but still pretty rough. How long was I out?"

"Five days. Longer than usual. I thought it might really be over," he said softly.

"Boy, that would suck. What would you do for entertainment?"

"I don't know, Mr. Albert."

"I am sorry for how much boredom my death would cause you."

"I found you under Genevieve's tree. Did you see the ghost swing again?"

"Look who's come back from the dead," Michael smiled, standing in the door frame.

"I'm still dead."

"Yeah, it is very confusing. Did you tell Santo the whole wonderful story of how you ended up dead, dead in my front yard? I have neighbors, you know."

"He was right about to," Santo said eagerly.

"Great, shut up, you rotten corpse. Wait until we get to Pinkie Masters, so I don't have to listen to the boring story twice," Michael joked. "Can you walk?"

"For alcohol? I'll do my best."

Michael and Santo helped him out of bed. Mr. Albert was initially unsteady but was in full stride by the time he got to the bar.

~ 51 ~

One hour later.
Pinkie Masters.

Mr. Albert finished up his story as the barflies listened spell-bound. "And that's the whole story; dream, one-sided discussion, killer ghost swing."

"And Santo told you nothing about when you were gone," Porno Rick said guiltily.

"No. He didn't. Did something happen?"

"No, nothing as far as I can remember," Rick said, with the innocence of a child.

"Nothing except he was going to pay us to have sex with you," Mustang Pete moaned.

"Hey!" Porno Rick glared at Pete, indicating he would pay for his snitching.

"Gross," Mr. Albert said, downing the rest of his beer to get the terrible taste out of his mouth. "Nothing against you, Brian."

"No offense taken. I'm very gross."

"Yes, you are. And I like it that way," Tessie said, with a smile.

"Thank you, darling." Brian kissed his wife.

Rick, Pete, Michael, and Santo looked at the couple with disgust. They finished their beers and signaled for another round.

"So, a clock flew by in your dream?" Jimmie said, as a strange thought crossed his mind.

"Yes," Mr. Albert answered

"Was it a digital clock?"

"No."

"And what was the time on the clock?"

"Five sixteen."

"No threes?"

"No. What are you getting at?"

"Hold on there. Do you have the three?"

"I think so." Mr. Albert reached into his pocket and pulled out the piece of plastic.

Jimmie took it and walked to the shelves with the liquor. Behind the Absinthe was an old battery-powered clock. Jimmie took it down and showed it to Mr. Albert. The three on the clock and the one in Jimmie's hand looked remarkably similar.

"Looks like at some time there was a clock by the tree," Jimmie smiled, handing Mr. Albert back the number.

Mr. Albert returned the smile as Jimmie put the clock back in its special place.

"Why do you have a clock over there?" Mr. Albert asked, signaling for another round.

"It was Pinkie's."

"Why?"

"He would take out the battery and set the time to fifteen minutes before closing so everyone would order a few more drinks before they had to go home. He would also set the clock ahead to get rid of some annoying patrons."

"What time would he set for me?" Santo asked.

Jimmie went back to the clock and set it for 3:30. Santo frowned at the bartender.

"Thank you for protecting my backside, Santo," Mr. Albert confided to his friend. "Brian looks like a rough one."

"You're welcome. Can I ask you something?"

"Sure."

"You seem to be dying for longer and longer periods. Does that mean something?"

"Like what?"

"Like you might actually be dying, or whatever that would mean to you."

"Don't worry, Santo. I'll bury you." Mr. Albert laughed.

"If I go and you are still around, promise to take me back to Jersey," Santo whispered.

"If I'm still around."

They clinked their glasses to seal their contract.

"Hate to break up the tender moment," Michael said, not hating it at all. "But what do you think the circular motion of the swing means."

"Haven't the foggiest," Mr. Albert answered.

"Because all of this seems to have some meaning," He took out his notebook. "I don't know what the swing means, but the 'X' motion helped us find the clock piece, and the dream had a clock in it. That can't be a coincidence."

"Why can't it? If we live in chaos, then everything is a coincidence," Mr. Albert said.

"You were called down here by a ghost in my front yard. You found me. At some point, Albert, you will have to admit that there is a reason for all of this."

"Just because you need a reason doesn't mean there is one. You are a writer, so you think of a beginning, a middle, and an end. People need to think that they are a part of a larger story. I am unconvinced. All I see is randomness."

"Without stories, there can be no connections. I will stick to my fairy tales then. Anyone want to venture a reason for the swing going in circles before it attacked Albert?"

"We are all going in circles," said Porno Rick sadly. "Just spinning our wheels."

"Thank you. I almost forgive you for wanting to have me buggered." Mr. Albert smiled.

"I will rest easy tonight," Rick said, without looking up from his screen.

"I got it," Mustang Pete said, waving his hand.

"I'm sure you do." Santo laughed. "Let's hear it."

"What is a circle?" Pete asked his friends.

"The letter O!" Michael shouted, excitedly.

"No."

"Yes, it is."

"Yes, I know an O is a circle, but it is not what I am thinking about," Pete conceded.

"So now we have to guess what you are thinking?" Michael pouted.

"Yes."

"That's unfair."

"A steering wheel," ventured Brian.

"I like how you are thinking, but you are wrong. People get up to speed. A circle is like the sun. The sun signifies the daytime. Santo found a three, so that means three days from now. Something is going to happen in three days!"

The group looked at each other confused.

"But we dug up Michael's yard a week ago."

"What happened four days ago, then?" Pete still tried to hold on to his idea.

"Santo wouldn't let Brian have sex with Mr. Albert," murmured Porno Rick.

"That was momentous," said Brian, as he winked at Mr. Albert.

"Oh, wait, I have an idea," Tessie bounced in her chair.

"What is it, Tess?"

"Maybe the X and the O were together. Xoxoxoxox. Love and kisses. Genevieve was saying that she loves Mr. Albert."

"Really?" Mr. Albert asked.

"How many people think that something important happened four days ago?" Michael took the lead.

Mustang Pete was the only one who raised his hand.

"Thought so," Michael snickered. "How many of you think Albert has a dead girlfriend?"

The rest of them raised their hands.

"It's settled then. Alberts got a girlfriend. Alberts got a girl-friend," Michael sang.

The others joined in, except for Mr. Albert and Pete, who grumpily drank their beers.

Through the singing, Mr. Albert thought he heard someone say, *Time will tell.*

~ 52 ~

Two days later.
Another restless night.
Michael Skillen's house.

This time, Mr. Albert dreamt of weenies. They were hopping in a double line in perfect rhythm. Buns were waiting at the end of a long river of mustard, and when the hotdogs joined the buns, they became hotdog-shaped angels and sang, "Let My People Go," very badly. Everyone knows hotdogs are notoriously terrible singers, even with mustard and sauerkraut. But then, a voice like a true angel stopped the abysmal choir. The flying weenies scattered, then reassembled like a flock of crows and headed for the beautiful sound. They arrived at Michael's house, but nothing was there, and the silence was heartbreaking.

Mr. Albert sat up in bed and murmured, "All silence is heartbreaking."

He walked to the window and looked at the tree. The ghost swing was there. *The dreams are a harbinger of ghostly visions*, he thought. *It would be nice if I knew what either was about.*

He walked to the front door, not caring if he woke the other occupants of the house. When spirits were around, the uninvited mortals slept as if a spell was cast upon them. Only the chosen one would wake up and make contact. He closed the door quietly—no need to tempt fate.

He sat in one of the blue rockers and did not say a word. He liked the eerie silence. The swing was still. A cold wind blew by, and the chimes rang. He slowly rocked in his seat. The swing joined his rocking. Mr. Albert noticed that when his position was closest to the swing, the swing was closest to the rocker.

He stopped when the rocker was fully back. The swing stopped at the height of its arc. Mr. Albert held the chair there for five seconds, and the swing remained motionless as well. He relaxed, and the chair went to a neutral position. The swing eased back to rest.

"Hello, Genevieve," he said softly, as one talked to their lover in the stillness of the night. "I missed you. I don't mind the weird dreams but wieners hopping in a mustard river? Either you or I have some major emotional issues.

Tessie said that you like me. Is that what the Xs and Os are about? I like you too. At least we have something in common; neither of us belongs here. Neither of us can go to where we need to be. Do you see the light, Genevieve? I don't see the light either.

When I first saw you in my dreams, you were happy. You were singing. I hope you were happy your whole life, but I doubt it. Why would you be here then?"

The wind chimes played a melody. It was a tune he had heard long ago, in another lifetime. Mr. Albert tried to remember the song but could not. He sat there and listened. Tears slowly rolled down his cheeks. He stood up and paced on the porch. The music continued.

"Please, stop," he begged the spirit.

The chimes fell silent.

"And the sadness you've cast over me."

He walked over to the swing. Tears were streaming from his eyes. He wiped them with his palm and then his sleeves, but they would not stop. All the pain he had inside poured out.

"I'm sorry. I don't know what I've done, but I must have hurt you so badly that you can't go on. Maybe if you could leave, I would be able to leave as well. That's got to be it. You brought me here so that we could both have peace. Santo was right, that fucker. Michael was right. Jerry was right. The guy that sold wieners in Wytheville was right. And I was wrong all along. You are my purpose, Genevieve. Help me, please."

He fell to his knees and clasped his hands. He closed his eyes and prayed to whatever was out there, up there, for clarity. He opened his eyes. There was no holy angel to guide him. He felt the same as he did before his prayers. Nothing had changed.

"Fucking hell," he muttered.

He looked up at the swing. It rose from its place and rocked not forward and back but from side to side. He stood up, and the swing increased its motion. It hit the carving of the wood spirit and then hit it again. Mr. Albert thought, *how did that wimpy swing knock me out?*

"Is there something about the face that you don't like? I don't like it either."

The swing struck it three more times and then disappeared. Whatever power was behind its movement was gone. Mr. Albert felt alone again.

"What secret are you keeping from me?"

He looked at the hideous face and dug his fingers between the carving and the tree to get some leverage. He pulled, but it didn't budge. He went inside and threw open Michael's door.

"Do you have a hammer?"

"What?" Michael said, barely conscious.

"Do you have a hammer?"

"Under the sink, in the toolbox."

Mr. Albert marched to the kitchen. Michael stumbled after him.

"What's going on?" he demanded.

Santo joined them in the kitchen, "What's happening?"

"The zombie has lost his mind." He pointed at Mr. Albert.

Mr. Albert grabbed the hammer and ran out the front door. He struck the carving twice before it broke apart. He used the hammer's claw to clear the remaining pieces.

"Mr. Muggles," Michael cried.

Mr. Albert stared at what was underneath the terrible carving. Michael and Santo joined him. By the porch light, it was clear as day. About the size of a woman's hand was a love heart with GP & BB carved into the tree.

"What was your grandmother's last name again?" Mr. Albert asked, as if he were numb.

"Pierpont," Michael said almost as quietly.

"Genevieve Pierpont," Mr. Albert whispered. "Genevieve Pierpont."

He touched the initials as if he were touching his lover's lips after a slow kiss.

"Mr. Albert, I'm sorry. I don't know who that woman was," Michael put his hand on Mr. Albert's shoulder for reassurance.

"But we will, Michael," Mr. Albert smiled.

~ 53 ~

Michael Skillen's house.
Late morning.

"What do you mean you can't find her?" Mr. Albert shouted at Michael.

They had been on the computer for hours trying to find out who Genevieve Pierpont was, to no avail.

"I don't know what to say. There was a storm. The records were destroyed in a flood. What do you want me to do?"

"Didn't they digitalize the records?"

"It was before they did that sort of thing."

"We are so close to discovering the answer. Why is this so difficult?"

"I don't know. You got me up at three in the morning," Michael snapped. "You killed Mr. Muggles, and then we have been on this wild goose chase for eight hours. We are out of coffee. We are out of beer. And I'm tired."

"You want to rest?" Santo asked Michael.

"No. What I'd like is a couple of shots of Jack with a Pabst chaser."

"Pinkie Masters?" Santo smiled.

"Pinkie Masters," answered Michael. "Are you coming?" He looked at Mr. Albert.

"No, not today."

Michael and Santo were halfway out the door when Mr. Albert replied. They stopped, dumbfounded. This was not the response they expected. Michael approached Mr. Albert.

"You sure you are all right?"

"Yes. I am fine."

"Do you want me to stay with you?" Santo asked, worried about his friend.

"No. I think I want to be alone for a while."

"You sure?"

"Yes, thank you, Santo. You are a good person."

The softness of his tone worried his friends even more, but they felt the need to honor Mr. Albert's request. Michael shrugged and left. Santo watched his friend for another moment before saying, "You know where to find me. I'll wait for you there."

~ 54 ~

One hour later.
Greenwich Cemetery.

Mr. Albert went back to the gravesite. He stood looking at the space between Jacqueline Skillen and Mrs. Pierpont.

"Pierpont was Genevieve's name. Jaqueline's sister? Was this space for you? What did that old man say? Space is left for someone not there. Where are you, Genevieve? Where did you go? Why doesn't Michael know anything about you? Were you his aunt? A great aunt? Do you just want to be remembered? Is that why you contacted me? But it's like everyone wanted you erased. What did you do? What could you have possibly done?"

His meditations were disturbed by laughter to his left. A group of tourists were jumping up and down, laughing and yelling; *life is like a box of chocolates.*

"Ah, for fuck's sake, it's a graveyard, you idiots. I need a drink!"

He went to join his friends at Pinkie Masters.

~ 55 ~

A half-hour later.

At Pinkie Masters.

When Mr. Albert entered the darkened bar, the regulars cheered and surrounded him to see if he was okay. They escorted him to his chair, making sure he was comfortable. Porno Rick was the only one who did not move from his seat. He looked at Mr. Albert.

"You good?" Rick asked.

"Been better," Mr. Albert responded.

"Haven't we all?" said Rick, before resuming his work.

After Mr. Albert had consumed a beer, his friends felt it was safe to ask him some questions.

"So, Genevieve loves you?" Tessie asked, sharing a sympathetic smile.

"Not unless my initials are BB," Mr. Albert moaned.

"Could be Bert Bert," Brian offered.

"Don't think so."

"So now we have to find who BB is?" Mustang Pete threw up his hands, surrendering to the unfairness of life.

"We can't find out anything," Santo grumbled. "All the records were destroyed. Some storm dumped a foot of rain on the area and flooded the basement where they kept the records."

"What about wedding announcements?" Jimmie said.

"I said all the records were destroyed," Santo snapped.

"Not at city hall. I am talking about the newspaper. The Pierponts were pretty traditional, weren't they, Michael?"

"I believe so."

"Then there would be an announcement in the papers of both engagement and wedding."

"Got it," Rick said before Jimmie had finished his sentence. He read from the newspaper article, "*Genevieve Sarah Pierpont and Benjamin Benton were united in marriage on Saturday, June 9, 1957, at five o'clock in the evening at Christ Church in Savannah, Ga. The Reverend Dr. David Shelton officiated the ceremony.*"

"Ah, a June wedding," Tessie cooed.

Rick continued, "*A reception hosted by the bride's mother followed at Anton's Restaurant. The bride is the daughter of Edward and Margaret Pierpont. Also pictured are the bride's sister, Jacqueline Skillen, and her husband, Raymond.* There's a picture as well."

Porno Rick looked at Mr. Albert and then back at his phone.

"Damn."

He handed the phone to Mr. Albert, who stared at the picture and did not say a word. Santo looked over his shoulder.

"Mr. Albert," Santo stammered. "That looks like...."

"Me," Mr. Albert said softly.

"Yes," Santo said. "You are Benjamin Benton."

"GP and BB," Mr. Albert smiled sadly.

Mr. Albert passed the phone to Michael.

"If my mom was Genevieve's sister. That would make you, my uncle."

"Yes," said Mr. Albert.

"Damn," said Michael.

Tessie grabbed the phone next.

"Look at how beautiful Genevieve was." She could not control herself and hugged Mr. Albert, kissing him on the cheek. "Congratulations."

Tears rolled down her face. She handed the phone to Brian, who examined the photo.

"When was this taken?"

"1957," Porno Rick answered.

Brian looked from the phone to Mr. Albert. "Damn, you look good for your age!"

Brian passed the phone to Jimmie.

"Pete, look at the car they're standing in front of," he said as he passed the phone to Mustang Pete.

Pete looked at the photo and recognized the car as soon as he saw it.

"A 1957 Studebaker Silver Hawk."

"Isn't that the car some guy gave your dad?" Jimmie asked.

"Yes," Mustang Pete said, realizing the implications. "Damn."

"Damn," said Brian, looking at Mr. Albert.

"Damn," said Michael, realizing he was related to his house guest.

"Damn," Mr. Albert said, feeling the responsibility of being married to Genevieve.

"Well, damn, Rick, you did it," Jimmie said, applauding his loyal customer.

The regulars followed suit. Mustang Pete slapped Rick on his back and smiled. Rick nodded before returning to his pornography. After the house bought a round of drinks for everyone, they quieted down to drink their beers and process what had just occurred. Everything was tied up in a neat little package, but nothing was resolved. A dark cloud covered the minds of the fully intoxicated.

"But what happens now?" Mr. Albert asked his friends.

"Isn't the story done?" Michael asked. "You've solved the mystery of Genevieve."

"Yes, but to what purpose? Why did I have to come all this way to find out I was married?"

"Maybe to understand that you could be happy," Tessie offered.

"But why is that important, Tessie?"

"Mr. Albert, you are a sad person. This should give you hope you can be happy again."

"All this says is that I had a wife, and I lost her. I mean, I really lost her. I don't know where she is. Why wasn't she buried in the family plot?"

They all looked at each other for answers, but no one had anything to offer.

"She must have died between 1957 and 1961 because I never met her. I don't understand why my mother never told me about her. Doesn't that seem strange?"

"Here's the thing that I don't get," Santo interrupted.

"What don't you get?" Mr. Albert asked hopelessly.

"If you are Albert Albert now and were Benjamin Benton before, should we assume that you had the initials CC before that? Did you start off with Zachariah Zelensky?"

"I don't know," Mr. Albert answered.

Brian stared into his drink. "You know, if you kept each name for twenty years, then you would be around...like..."

"Five hundred and twenty years old," Santo said.

"Damn, you look really, really good for your age!" Brian said.

"Whatever your secret is, honey, you could make a fortune off it," Tessie laughed. "Sign me up!"

They all joined in her laughter.

"If this is some sort of weird countdown, then that would mean..."

"What would that mean, Santo?" Mr. Albert smiled.

"It would mean that you are at the end. There are no more letters."

"The end."

"The end."

"No more letters."

"No more letters."

The group grew quiet. They looked at Mr. Albert and wondered how he would react. He looked into his half-finished glass of Pabst Blue Ribbon. He felt the weight of the glass in his hand and shook it gently to swirl the liquid. He held the glass under his nose and inhaled. The sweet, malty aroma made him smile. He finished the beer, savoring the taste.

"If it is my last time around, I better buy my friends another drink."

He smiled and raised his empty glass to each of his friends as Jimmie refreshed their drinks. They raised their glasses, smiled sadly at Mr. Albert, and quietly sipped their drinks.

$$\sim 56 \sim$$

One day later.

Greenwich Cemetery.

Mr. Albert returned to Michael's family plot.

He spoke to Jacqueline Skillen. "Why didn't you tell Michael about your sister? What did she do? What dirty secrets are you hiding? Why isn't she here between you and your mom? She must have died first, or you would be next to Margaret. You must have felt guilty for what you had done. That's why you left this space so that she would be remembered."

"They won't answer you."

Mr. Albert turned around. John, the old man he met several weeks ago, was sitting on the bench under the dogwood tree. Mr. Albert smiled at his graveyard friend and joined him.

"They won't answer you. My Mary never answers my questions. And I was married to her for fifty years," John continued.

"That's too bad."

"Not really. She talked a lot when she was alive. I guess she just ran out of steam."

Mr. Albert smiled but remained deep in thought.

"Albert, why do you come back here, asking dead strangers for help?"

"It turns out they are not strangers. I was married to the person who belongs in that space."

"Where is she?"

"I don't know."

"How can you not know? Albert, you must have been a terrible husband."

"That is probably true, but I don't remember."

"When did your wife die?"

"In the early sixties."

John looked at his bench mate.

"How old are you?"

"Anywhere between forty and five hundred and twenty years."

"You are a character."

"I am."

"Why wouldn't they bury her here?"

"I don't know. Her own sister wouldn't even tell her son that he had an aunt."

"Sounds like a scandal. You're not Jewish, are you?"

"I don't think so. Is that a real question?"

"Well, nowadays, people marry whomever they want. Back then, you wouldn't marry out of your circle. I figured a Jew would be out of their circle."

"How do you figure that?"

"There's a cross on each of their headstones," John pointed to the graves. "Pity."

"Pity, what?"

"You're not a Jew."

"Why?"

"Never met one. Thought it would be nice."

"Sorry that I am not Jewish."

"That's all right, I guess."

"But what else would be a scandal around here?"

"I don't think divorce would have done it. Was she nuts?"

"What do you mean?"

"Was she committed to an asylum? That would have been scandalous back in the day."

"I don't know."

"She didn't have to be, you know, bonkers. Just an embarrassment. They committed lots of women back then if they had hysterical tendencies."

"She did hit me in the head with a swing once."

"I had a cousin who was committed to Milledgeville. Never left. They found one thing, then another, then another. Once they crack open your noggin, all the bats fly out. We got him back, but there are a thousand unmarked graves. Not a happy place to spend eternity."

"Do you believe in ghosts, John?"

"Never saw one."

"What does that mean?"

"I only believe in things I can see."

"Then why do you come here? Mary has gone on, hasn't she? You can't see her."

"I can see her grave and think about lying next to her and being at peace."

"That would be nice, John. Being at peace."

"It would be, Albert."

$$\sim 57 \sim$$

Michael Skillen's house.
One day later.

Michael slammed down the phone.
"I hate people!" He howled.
"They wouldn't tell you?" Mr. Albert asked.
"They wouldn't tell me."
"Why not?"
"Because you aren't a relative."
"I am. I'm her husband."
"Where's your marriage license?"
Mr. Albert paced the room.
"It was lost in the flood!"
"I don't think they would buy it. And second, she died, what, sixty years ago? You don't look old enough."
"Your license says you are 35," Santo added.
"Fuck both of you. What about you, Michael?"
"What about me, what?"
"You're a relative."
"Can't prove it."
"Why not?"
"Because the records were lost in the flood," Michael smiled sardonically.
"What I said about both of you just now goes double for you," Mr. Albert sneered.

"Thank you," Santo said to Mr. Albert.

"Why?"

"Because, according to you, I'm only half as fucked as Michael."

"Now you are equal again."

"I liked it better in the old days," Michael reminisced. "When you knew more about yourself than anyone else. Now there's more information about you, but you can't get it. Other people own your information."

"You would think people would be upset about that," Santo said.

"They should be, but they are too busy fighting about what asshole should be in the White House. They're all crooks, stupid," he cried to the heavens. "And we only have one party which has successfully convinced the public that there are two and that there is a difference between them. It's the party of the rich, and we are all working for them!"

"Michael, I didn't know you were so political," Santo said.

"Yeah, I get this way every time I deal with some bureaucrat on the phone."

"We could always get a lawyer."

"How long is that going to take?"

"Months."

"I don't think Savannah has enough alcohol," Mr. Albert mumbled.

"Call them back up," Santo insisted.

"Why?"

"Tell them that you are getting a lawyer. That will scare the pants off them."

"They work for the state; nothing scares them."

"Try."

"Oh, hell." Michael dialed the phone. "Yes, I just talked to you, and if you don't tell me what I want to know, I will get a lawyer. What do you think of that? Yes, yes, thank you."

"What," Mr. Albert asked.

"She said she would prefer talking to a lawyer because they would know not to bother her. We must obtain a court order to receive medical records for any deceased individual who received services at Milledgeville. We must contact the Baldwin County Probate Court. She gave me the website."

~ 58 ~

Pinkie Masters.
Two hours later.

"So, there we are, stuck," Mr. Albert finished telling his friends about the trouble they were having with the Bureau of Records.

"That's terrible. So close, yet so far," Tessie sympathized.

"I blame the system. Damn bureaucrats doing their masters' bidding!" Michael cried.

"Did you let him use the phone again?" Mustang Pete reprimanded Santo.

The rest of the barflies shared their disapproval of Santo's actions.

"What about him?" Santo tried to deflect the negativity by pointing to Mr. Albert.

"Albert is in pain," Tessie said softly.

She smiled at Mr. Albert, who smiled back meekly. He enjoyed making Santo look like the villain.

"Probably for the best," Brian pondered.

"What do you mean," Tessie asked.

"You not being able to learn anymore. Did any of you ask yourself why Mr. Albert doesn't remember this woman?"

"He has very little brain," Santo said, wanting revenge.

"He seems to have enough brain to function as well as the rest of us. Maybe he doesn't want to remember."

"Do you want to remember, darling?" Tessie looked into Mr. Albert's eyes.

"I think I do," Mr. Albert answered, unsure if that was true.

"Sometimes, the things we forget are more important than the things we remember. We remember what we need to survive. We forget the things that cause us pain. Maybe what you forgot is bad," Brian continued.

'But that the dread of something after death,

The undiscovere'd country, from whose bourn

No traveler returns, puzzles the will,

And makes us rather bear those ills we have

Then fly to others that we know not of?

Thus, conscience doth make cowards of us all,' Michael quoted.

"What the hell are you talking about?" Mr. Albert demanded.

"It's *Hamlet*. You could fear what awaits you after death, so you choose to remain here."

"I have no choice. I can't go on."

"You won't go on. But what that part of the speech is saying is that you are afraid of the unknown, so you choose to stay where you are. Brian is saying you are afraid to remember whatever happened, so you push everything down until it is forgotten. Seems like the same thing," Michael said.

The others turned to face Mr. Albert. There was pity in their eyes.

"Oh, come on. I'd like to find out. We are at a dead end," Mr. Albert argued.

They continued to look at him. Mr. Albert began to doubt himself. He stormed off to the bathroom, hoping that they would have forgotten all about this when he returned. Porno Rick was waiting outside the bathroom door when he came out.

"Do you really want to find out, or are you just saying that because, you know, we can't find out?" Porno Rick whispered.

"You could find out what happened?"

"You can find out anything if you are willing to pay for it."

"How much?"

"Fifty dollars."

"Fifty dollars?"

"Too much?"

"No, no, that sounds reasonable. I thought you were going to say something like ten thousand," Mr. Albert mused.

"No, I'm just going to have to get a new burner phone."

"Okay." Mr. Albert looked in his pocket. He pulled out twenty-three dollars and sixteen cents. He put the penny back in his pocket. "It's my lucky penny."

"You still got $26.85 to go."

Mr. Albert went back to the bar.

"I need twenty-six dollars and eighty-five cents," he demanded.

Mr. Albert looked at Santo. Santo shrugged and put ten dollars on the bar.

"$16.85."

Michael put in five dollars and twenty-five cents. Mustang Pete put in seven dollars and thirty-seven cents. Brian and Tessie put in four dollars and twenty-two cents together. Rick counted it up. Forty-nine dollars and ninety-nine cents. He turned to Mr. Albert.

"I want that magic penny!"

"It's not magic; it's lucky. And you can't have it!"

"I want it."

"You're not getting it."

"Gentlemen, gentlemen," Michael crooned. "Rick, you're making over seventy grand a year. Do you really need one crappy penny?"

"I guess not."

Michael continued, "Mr. Albert, how could you not willingly part with your non-magical penny when you know the gravity of the situation?"

"I'm sorry," Mr. Albert moped.

He offered his lucky penny to Porno Rick. Rick took it and got down to work.

"Office of Records?" Rick asked, already typing

"Bureau of Records," Michael corrected.

"Got it. Genevieve Pierpont born March 22, 1933. Married to Benjamin Benton, June 9, 1957. Committed to Georgia State Hospital October 9, 1959, for *Imaginary Female Trouble*. Divorced December 16, 1959. Died March 16, 1960."

"How did you do that?" Mr. Albert questioned.

"If I told you that, I'd have to kill you?" Porno Rick warned.

"Really?" Mr. Albert asked in disbelief.

"Nah. I got in through the backdoor."

"What is the 'backdoor' exactly?" Santo said.

"Haven't the foggiest," Rick answered. "Non-computer people accept that explanation."

Porno Rick signaled to Jimmie to refresh his drink. He pointed at Mr. Albert to indicate that he was paying. He then got up and promptly left the bar. Once outside Pinkie Masters, he dropped his phone and stomped on it. Rick picked up the broken pieces and put them in a trash can. He walked briskly down the street.

"Georgia State Hospital?" Mr. Albert continued.

"It's in Milledgeville," Tessie said.

The patrons cast worried glances at each other.

"Milledgeville?" Mr. Albert whispered. "What were *Imaginary Female Troubles*?"

"A lot of husbands used Milledgeville to get rid of their wives," Mustang Pete said. "Get a friend to sign the paper. Two witnesses and the woman is off to the funny farm. Then they'd get a divorce when the wife was out of the way."

Mr. Albert's friends turned a judgmental eye to him. Santo came to his defense.

"I've known Mr. Albert longer than any of you. He is a mean, horrible man, but he is not cruel."

His friends forgave him.

"If she died, why didn't they bury her in the family plot?"

"Going to Milledgeville was a scandal. Especially if they never returned," Tessie said.

"I guess that's why my parents never told me about her," Michael realized.

"Can we bring her home? Maybe she wants to come home?" Mr. Albert said.

"Over twenty-five thousand people died there. Most of them are in unmarked graves," Porno Rick had returned with a new phone.

"Santo, I know what we need to do."

"What?"

"Go to Milledgeville and find my wife."

"Are you sure?"

"It certainly sounds like a purpose. That's what you wanted me to find, wasn't it?"

"I guess we are going to Milledgeville."

~ 59 ~

One day later.
Late morning.
Outside Michael Skillen's house.

Michael willingly got up before noon to see his friends off on their adventure. When he went outside, the car was packed. Santo and Mr. Albert stood smiling under Genevieve's tree.

"Did you two bastards leave me any beers?"

"I left you five beers," Santo said. "But he drank four of them."

"I finished the last one when Santo was in the toilet." Mr. Albert didn't feel sorry at all.

"Thought as much. Well, have a good trip, and I hope you find what you are looking for."

"We're looking for your aunt."

"Well, I hope you find her as well."

Michael hugged Santo.

"Santo, you're a good friend to him and me. I'll miss you."

Santo returned the hug.

"This probably won't take long. We'll be back in no time."

"There are ten thousand unmarked graves. I think it will take you a long time."

Michael walked away. He turned around on the top step. "You're not going anywhere yet, are you?"

"We are going to the State Hospital," Mr. Albert said, with annoyance.

"I know that, but the gang will be over shortly. You can't leave without saying goodbye."

"Didn't I say goodbye to them yesterday?" Mr. Albert grunted.

"You said goodbye like you were going to take a piss, not like you are leaving forever."

"I'm not leaving forever."

"Are you sure?"

"No."

"Then you might be. They'll be over in a bit, and it seems like I need some alcohol. I'm going to the Victorian Market. Don't leave before I get back."

"We won't." Santo waved to the departing Michael.

Mr. Albert paced around the yard. Santo watched his friend.

"What's the matter?" Santo asked.

"Nothing."

"Nothing?"

"Nothing.

"It is definitely something."

Mr. Albert stopped pacing and snarled at Santo.

"I don't like saying goodbye."

"You say goodbye all the time."

"But I don't say forever goodbye. I say, 'I'm going to take a piss goodbye.'"

"I don't ever recall you saying goodbye before you took a piss." After a moment, Santo's tone softened, "I don't like forever goodbyes either."

"But, Santo, I have said a forever goodbye to everyone I have ever met because I outlive them all. It's like having a pet. You take them into your home, and after a while, you bury them."

"We are all just like puppies that you are going to bury?"

"Yes," Mr. Albert said quietly.

"Am I a puppy that you are going to bury?"

"Yes."

"Oh, I see."

"Nothing personal."

"I can see that this is nothing personal."

"I like you, Santo, but I know you will die."

"You will die as well."

"Not likely."

"Yes, likely. Everyone dies."

"I am dead."

"I know. I mean dead cubed."

"You are using that now?"

"I like it."

"Really?"

"Meh."

They remained silent for a moment.

"I'm sorry. About burying you," Mr. Albert said, with great sadness.

"I must be buried by someone. It might as well be you. Do you really think about that when you meet someone?"

"Yes."

"That's awful."

"Not really. If you never care, you never get hurt."

"If you never care, you'll never feel love. You'll never be loved."

"You love me, Santo, don't you?"

"I can't help it. You are such a pleasant person to be around."

"It would seem like I don't have to open myself up to feelings to be loved."

"Haven't you opened yourself up already?"

"What do you mean?"

"I think you care for me, Michael, Porno Rick, and the rest of them. They care for you and have listened to you and offered their support. You care for them."

"I care for Porno Rick?"

"Yes. You do."

"It just sounds rather gross. I don't want to let anyone get close to me."

"You did once, Genevieve."

"I know and look what happened. I sent her off to the lunatic asylum to die. I was probably responsible for what happened to her."

"You can't be sure," Santo gave him a reassuring look. "You are trying to correct whatever wrong you committed. That's good, isn't it?"

"You once thought I did something terrible. What if there is no way to make this right? What if there is no way that I can receive forgiveness?"

"Then you will have to forgive yourself."

"That doesn't seem likely."

"There's the birthday boy!" Brian said, carrying a box of pastries from Rum Runners.

Tessie had a party hat and a blowout. She blew on it, and the paper rolled out, hitting Brian on the back of the head.

"Hey!" Brian groaned, as if mortally wounded.

Tessie laughed at her mistake. She had been drinking since breakfast, as she was worried about Mr. Albert. Mustang Pete and Porno Rick had party hats on also. Pete blew on a kazoo. Rick looked at his phone.

"Well, it looks like the gang's all here," Santo said, trying to cheer Mr. Albert up.

"Where's Michael?" asked Pete.

"Went to get some beer," Santo answered.

"Then I guess I'll hold on to these," Pete held up a six-pack.

"Six beers? That wouldn't last very long, would it?" said Mr. Albert disagreeably.

"Santo is driving, so he can't have any," Pete said, just as disagreeably.

"Mr. Albert, Rick found out something about Genevieve," Tessie offered.

Rick walked over to Mr. Albert and took out the lucky penny. He returned it to him.

"You could probably use it in Milledgeville."

"Thank you." Mr. Albert said.

"I wanted you to have your coin back," Rick smiled at his friend. "Mr. Albert, you didn't sign the document to get her committed. Mr. Harrison and Mr. Catrell were the witnesses bringing the complaint. Did you know them?"

"I don't remember. How was that supposed to make me feel better?"

"You didn't do it," Tessie said, touching Mr. Albert's shoulder.

"But I didn't stop it."

"Ah, stop whining and have a beer," Michael said, as he opened the gate.

Beer and pastries were passed out, and everyone had a fine time except for Mr. Albert, who sat on the steps looking at the love heart on Genevieve's tree. No matter what his friends said, he still felt responsible. Why would her ghost have called him to this place if he wasn't?

He looked at the group laughing, his senses beginning to numb. Their laughter softened. They seem to fade like ghosts. They were ghosts already but had not realized it yet. Soon, they would be forgotten. Other people will live in this house. They will have no understanding of those who came before. Then they will die and be forgotten as well. The world will spin a million, million more times, unaware of the suffering of an egotistical race that thought the world was created for them. And soon, the world will stop spinning, and all that will be left is silence.

"Can we go now?" he asked Santo.

Santo realized that Mr. Albert would not give these people another moment of his friendship. He was somewhere beyond them, and there was no way to get him to return.

"If that is what you would like."

"Yes," Mr. Albert said softly.

Santo hugged the men and kissed Tessie on the cheek.

"We are going to have to run. It's a long way to Milledgeville."

He helped Mr. Albert into the car, who seemed too weak to open the car door himself. Santo waved, but Mr. Albert did not turn to say goodbye. All he could do was look at the road in front of them.

~ 60 ~

Later that day.
On the road to Milledgeville.

Santo had been driving in silence for over an hour. Mr. Albert had given up speaking. They still had another hour and a half in front of them. They passed small town after small town with nothing but a gas station or convenience store. There was usually a young man leaning against the storefront close to the entrance. He smoked a cigarette with his head looking at the ground. He was waiting for someone, anyone, to come and rescue him from a lifetime of obscurity. His town with a couple of churches at either end. Trailers parked next to crumbling structures that once were homes. Prisoners of their poverty. Fearing the lights of the big city with its races mixing in discos, smokey with drugs and fancy cocktails. He stood there hating his life, full of envy for people he had never met.

Santo put on the radio.

Oh yeah, life goes on...

Santo turned down the volume.

"Do you think that is right?" he asked his silent friend.

"What?" Mr. Albert answered while staring at the barren farmlands.

"That life goes on after the thrill is gone."

"I'm dead."

"You are existing."

"That wouldn't make as good a song."

"What?"

"Oh yeah, existence goes on after you're dead but refuse to move on."

"You are very clever, Mr. Albert."

"I can be at moments."

"What about the question?" Santo said, steering him back.

"I still exist, but there is no thrill in existing. And you?"

"I think life is still exciting."

"Besides the weenies in Wytheville?"

"That was the highlight of our journey." Santo grinned.

"Thought so," Mr. Albert said, with an air of surrender.

"There were other thrills."

"Thrills?"

"Entertainments, then. You died died at several inappropriate times. We met Jerry Garcia."

"Who was an impersonator."

"Nobody cuts off their middle finger to be an entertainer at children's birthday parties."

Mr. Albert tired of the conversation. The scenery blurred. He wondered if he could jump from the car to escape.

"He had a secret room."

Mr. Albert shrugged his shoulders. He was too depressed to answer.

"He had a secret room," Santo continued. "He had a missing finger, and he was a celebrity impersonator. Too many coincidences to be serendipitous."

"Serendipitous? I don't see one coincidence there. Three random things. That's all they were. No serendipity anywhere." Mr. Albert got angry enough to fully enter the conversation.

"You were shot. Wasn't that exciting?"

"I did enjoy watching the terrified parishioners. Gave them something else to pray about. All strangers are servants of the devil, ahhhhh!"

"So, there you go. Frightening religious people. Something to be proud of. You scared the crap out of me, I remember."

"I do like scaring Christians."

"Why is that?"

"They believe that God is looking after them."

Santo thought of his connection with God and smiled. It is not that difficult to have a relationship with the Lord. All you have to do is believe.

After another moment, Santo said, "Maybe you won't end up in a woodchipper."

"Thank you, Santo."

And after another moment.

"We found the tree," Santo said brightly.

"Look around, Murphy; there are trees everywhere," Mr. Albert snapped.

"Yes, but we found the tree. We found the tree. We discovered that you had love. You, Mr. Albert, the most miserable creature on the planet, had love."

"Are you forgetting that we are driving to Milledgeville to see an insane asylum where my wife died? No one believed her. No one helped her. She was alone. She was scared, and she was probably buried in an unmarked grave. Forgotten by her family."

"You were not responsible for that," Santo said, barely above a whisper.

"You believe that?"

"No."

"Thank you."

Santo became uncomfortable with the silence again. He turned on the radio again. "Love is the Answer" by England Dan & John Ford Coley was playing. He turned off the radio.

"Thank you," said Mr. Albert quietly.

Silence is preferable to some songs.

"Was all this worth it for you, Santo?"

"You mean, would I have rather you didn't save me?"

"Yes."

"I'd be dead then."

"Yes."

"So, your question is, would death be preferable to driving my best friend to see the place where his wife met a horrible death, probably caused by him?"

"Am I your best friend?"

"Is there anyone else in the car?"

"You didn't say your best friend in the car."

"You wanted me to say, would death be preferable to driving my best friend, who is in the car, to see the place where his wife met a horrible death, probably caused by him?"

"It would have made the question a little clearer."

"I thought it was clear already."

"Well, it wasn't"

"I am once again undecided about the woodchipper," Santo snarled at Mr. Albert. Then he softened, "You are my best friend, Mr. Albert."

"Thank you. Would death be preferable to driving your best friend, me, to see the place where his wife met a horrible death, probably caused by him? Me again."

"Death would not be preferable to doing anything with you."

"You haven't found your purpose because I haven't found my purpose."

"Wasn't finding Genevieve a purpose?"

"I think I was better off without that knowledge."

"Maybe you will find peace in Milledgeville because you will discover the whole truth," Santo suggested.

"And what is peace for me? There is no way to make amends for the pain I caused to someone who died. Dead people can't forgive. I will exist forever with the knowledge that I have destroyed every person I have ever encountered, whom I cared about or cared about me."

"You won't destroy me because I know you for what you are, an evil zombie servant of the devil sent to Earth to drive people insane when you reveal your true nature."

Santo paused to check to see if Mr. Albert received the jab in the way it was intended. Mr. Albert smiled at Santo even as the heaviness of life crushed all hope.

Santo continued, "You are my friend, and are in pain. That is all that matters. I don't understand why you are the way you are. That is not important. I don't have to understand the craziness of life to realize that wherever I am, whomever I am with, I can do good. The thing that separates people is the true evil in this world. And when we see nothing but differences, we bring evil into our hearts. Every good deed we do for the poor, the needy, and the stranger makes this world a better place."

"Is it that simple?"

"I think it is. It doesn't make life any easier to bear. But if you could do good knowing that evil will probably win, then you have done God's work, and God will give you peace."

"You got that from me?"

"Yes."

"Me?"

"Yes."

"ME?"

"Yes, I got that from you and terrible indigestion from all the stupid hot dogs we have consumed, and hangovers too many to remember, and about a million headaches from all the fucking nonsense you spout when you are not dead, dead!"

"I think that is accurate."

The rest of the trip to Milledgeville was less mournful.

~ 61 ~

Two hours later.
The Brick.
Milledgeville, Georgia.

Milledgeville is very interesting, Santo thought while listening to the bartender.

"It is a town that has had many different lives. Today, it is a college town," Anthony explained.

Anthony had been the bartender at this local watering hole, for ten years. He knew exactly what the tourists wanted to hear.

"Before that, the town served for a time as the state capital of Georgia. And it had the world's largest insane asylum, which is now crumbling because the state doesn't want to tear the buildings down. When they fall, it is cheaper to cart off the broken bricks and crumbling steel."

Santo was enthralled. Mr. Albert stared into his half-empty Guinness and pondered the cruelness of life. Half gone. Its joy departed, never to return, like a young man's naivete in a public toilet.

"Any ghosts?" Mr. Albert asked hopefully.

"Never seen one here," Anthony said.

"Did you see one elsewhere?"

"No."

"Any other places to visit as long as we are here?" Santo asked.

"Auntie Bellum's Attic is a good place to find some strange stuff."

"You think we are into strange stuff? Are there any other bars?" Mr. Albert asked, showing his annoyance.

"Velvet Elvis is hopping after dark."

"With college kids?" Santo asked.

"Yes."

"Pass. Santo, let's go." Mr. Albert stood up.

"Wait. Any places to get a good weenie?"

"Might have to go to Athens," Anthony said, giving Santo a knowing nod.

"I meant a hot dog," Santo corrected Anthony.

"Olde Tyme Hot Dogs," Anthony said, disappointed. "On West Montgomery."

Mr. Albert felt much better after hearing the hot dog news. They drank for several more hours until the college students descended upon downtown. Then they drove to their motel.

~ 62 ~

Half an hour later.
The Royal Inn Motel, Milledgeville.

Four hours after arriving in Milledgeville, they checked into the Royal Inn Motel. They chose this particular motel because of its proximity to the asylum. They planned to get up early, have a quick breakfast, and then wander around the hospital campus before the tourists arrived.

The motel was all on one floor, with ten rooms stretching out from either side of the office, forming a rectangular "C." The parking lot was all torn up and needed major repair. Santo drove over a pothole as he parked the car.

"Hey, watch it," Mr. Albert moaned, aroused from his drunken nap.

"We're here," Santo said, thinking the place looked like the Bates Motel.

A liquor store stood at the far end of the right-wing of motel rooms. Their room was to the left, with a great view of the alcoholic wonderland. Santo tried the key, but it did not fit properly. He went back to get another key. Mr. Albert stood by the door watching the package store anxiously. He was afraid that all the booze would be gone by the time he dropped the bags off in the room. He would have left the luggage, but the area looked sketchy. In the ten minutes that Santo spent in the office, not one patron entered the store. *You could never be too careful*, thought Mr. Albert.

Santo finally returned. He opened the door. It was easier this time, but the key stuck in the lock. He wiggled the key for a couple of seconds before the lock released it. Santo turned on the light by the door.

Mr. Albert thought he heard the pitter-patter of little feet. He didn't call Santo's attention to the scurrying sounds, but focused on all of the lovely alcohol just steps away.

The room had two lights, and one of them was out. Even in the darkness, Santo could tell that the room was filthy. The bedspreads were chestnut brown, a color chosen to hide the stains.

"Oh, no," groaned Santo.

"What's the matter? I got shotgun," Mr. Albert said, as he flopped down on the bed closest to the door. The sheets crinkled as he landed.

"What makes that shotgun?"

Mr. Albert reached under the covers and pulled out a bag of Takis.

"Umm, Fuego," Mr. Albert said, eating one.

"We have to go," groaned Santo.

"Relax. Want one?"

Mr. Albert extended the bag to Santo. Santo grimaced and walked into the bathroom, not knowing what perils he would find there.

"They didn't even flush!"

"The maid probably had to go and forgot to flush on her way out."

"I don't know if we will find Genevieve," Santo said. "But Bigfoot is definitely in the area." Santo came back into the room holding his stomach and looking green. He checked the chair by the window for roaches before sitting down.

"Oh, why so sad? Would you like me to flush the toilet?"

"Yes, please."

Mr. Albert finished the bag of chips and threw it at the garbage. He never was any good at trash-can basketball. The crumpled bag hit the rim and rolled to the ground, stopping at the foot of the bed. He didn't bother to pick it up but walked to the bathroom.

"It must have been a very big maid," he said, admiringly.

He flushed the toilet. Mr. Albert did not return.

"What are you doing in there?"

"Hold on." Mr. Albert flushed the toilet again.

After another minute.

"What is happening?" Santo asked, losing his patience.

"Hold your horses."

Mr. Albert flushed the toilet again. Finally, he returned to the room.

"The thing had a life of its own. Didn't want to die. Should I check your bed for Takis?"

"Sure," Santo said, his head buried in his hands.

Mr. Albert jumped on the bed and then rolled back and forth, spreading himself out as large as possible.

"What are you doing?"

"I'm looking for Takis. No Takis here. Now I am hungry for Takis. Do you think the packie has Takis?"

"You want to get some alcohol," Santo said.

"Hadn't thought of that before. But now that you mention it. Want anything?" Mr. Albert said, jumping off the bed and heading for the door.

"I'll go with you. I'm afraid to stay in this room alone."

"Don't be such a baby," teased Mr. Albert.

As soon as the door was closed, something rumbled, and the empty bag of Takis disappeared under the bed.

~ 63 ~

The next morning.
Olde Tyme Hot Dogs, Milledgeville.

Before going to the asylum, Mr. Albert and Santo stopped at Olde Tyme Hot Dogs for breakfast. Santo, still nauseous from the motel and unsure about the concept of hot dogs for breakfast, just ordered a cup of black coffee. Mr. Albert, who had no problem with either the motel or the breakfast, ordered two German Dogs, which was a regular hot dog with sauerkraut and spicy mustard. Six empty stools faced the big plate glass window looking out on the street. Santo sat in the second seat from the left. Mr. Albert sat on the third seat from the left.

"Why don't you sit over there?" Santo said, pointing to the first seat from the left.

"I don't want to sit there," Mr. Albert said, attempting to take a bite of his dog.

Santo interrupted him, "Why not?"

"I don't like sitting in corners."

"Why not?"

"When I was a child, my mother always sat me in a corner when I was naughty. Now I am afraid of them."

"Really?"

"Of course not. I don't remember anything about my mother, childhood, or Uncle Jeff."

"You had an Uncle Jeff?"

Mr. Albert shrugged his shoulders and took the first bite of his breakfast. A smile appeared on his face like the sunrise. Santo watched him with a mixture of disgust and admiration.

"This is good."

"How could you do that to yourself?"

"How can I do what?"

"Eat that for breakfast."

"How can I do anything? I am a miracle of nature," Mr. Albert said.

Santo needed to get down to business to forget about his nausea.

"Mr. Albert, how are we going to find Genevieve?"

"I guess we'll look around and see if anything presents itself."

"The asylum was twenty-five hundred acres."

Santo had read three of the flyers he picked up in town. Now he was an expert.

"That is a big area," Mr. Albert said, humoring him. "Should we start somewhere smaller? Build up to it? I saw a Wal-Mart a couple of miles back. I wonder how many bodies are buried there?"

"I think we need a plan."

"So, you have been thinking of a plan, and now you want to tell me the plan full well, knowing that I am not interested in your plan?"

"There are five graveyards," Santo said, ignoring him. "She has to be in one of them."

"Does she? I want to walk around the buildings, see if I could pick up any vibes."

"What kind of vibes?"

"Ghost vibes."

"That's just stupid."

"What part of this adventure isn't stupid? Since I have met you, what have we done that was intelligent?" Mr. Albert said.

"Your idea is completely ridiculous. I agree. Could we do buildings in the morning, then go and have lunch? In the afternoon, we could look around the graveyards."

"Sounds perfect," Mr. Albert agreed, so Santo would stop discussing the plan.

Finishing his last bite, he brought the plate to the counter.

"How was everything?" the kid behind the counter asked.

"I think he will never eat breakfast again. But I thought your sauerkraut was the sourest kraut I have ever tasted."

"We are proud of it. Come back and see us again."

"You know I will," Mr. Albert said as he left.

Santo was already sitting in the car.

~ 64 ~

Ten minutes later.
Georgia State Hospital campus.

Santo parked in front of the first building on the quad, the Central Chapel. They stood by the car and took it all in. The grounds of the hospital were quiet. The buildings were arranged around a big open field with a dozen huge pecan trees on the outside edge. Several faded-red benches were at the side closest to the entrance facing the mostly abandoned structures.

Mr. Albert walked over to the bench closest to the car. He sat down, stretching his arms along the top of the bench and claiming it for his own. Santo followed Mr. Albert to the bench and paced in front of Mr. Albert.

Mr. Albert looked at the Powell Building directly across the field from the bench. When Santo broke his gaze with his pacing, Mr. Albert tilted his head from the right to the left like a pendulum. This lasted for several minutes before Santo cried out in frustration, "Are you picking up any ghostly vibes?"

"No, only grumpy ones. Those weenies made me sleepy."

Santo walked off in disgust and sat on the next bench over.

"Santo, if we get separated, we should meet back here."

"Why would we get separated?"

"You know if we are in a building, and you fall through the second floor down to the basement. After you dig yourself out, I might not be around."

"I'm not going into these buildings; they are dangerous. You said we were going to *look around* the buildings. To me, that implies around the outside of the buildings. And why wouldn't you help dig me out? Why would I have to dig myself out?"

Santo looked over to Mr. Albert, but he was gone. Santo stood up. He looked to the chapel just in time to see Mr. Albert disappearing around the back. Santo sat down again and grumbled to himself.

"Good, you can go. I hope a brick falls and hits you in the head. I hope you fall through the third floor down to the basement. I won't dig you out. See how you feel."

After ten minutes, Santo ran out of steam. Mr. Albert was too stupid to remain mad at. He got up and stretched against the bench. He did a couple of jumping jacks but then thought he must look crazy. Not a good look for an abandoned insane asylum. He sat down.

"He said, if we get separated, we should meet up here. No need to get up and look for him. I might leave, and he might come back. And then he would leave, and I might come back. And then I might leave again, and he might come back...."

Fifteen minutes passed. Santo started pacing again.

"What if a brick did hit him in the head? I don't think it would affect him in the least. But what if he fell down the stairs and a wall collapsed on him? That would serve him right."

Santo called Mr. Albert on his cell phone. Mr. Albert did not answer.

"What if he is dead, dead? I made a promise. I failed him once. I won't fail him again."

He walked around the back of the chapel. He tried the doors, but they were all locked. A narrow dirt road snaked along the back of the hospital buildings. He walked over to the building closest to the chapel.

The sidewalk to the Green building was covered with thorny vines, which seemed to claw at Santo's legs. The vines climbed up the entire height of the building. Most of the windows had been smashed. Bricks that had fallen from the walls lay broken on the path in front of him. He saw a door on a landing five steps up from the sidewalk and struggled to get there.

He grabbed the cold, rusty handle of the door and pulled gently. It opened. He swallowed, then he wondered why he swallowed. People about to get killed in horror movies always swallow before the knife comes down.

"Hello," he whispered into the darkness of the building.

"Hello," came a voice behind him.

Santo's heart nearly exploded. He turned quickly. Two elderly security officers stared at him. Santo could have easily run away, but he didn't want the old guys to have a heart attack while chasing him.

"You are not supposed to go into the building," said officer one.

"That is considered trespassing," said officer two.

The officers recited this speech so often that they could say it in their sleep. Each day, dozens of college kids try to explore the buildings.

"You'll have to come with us."

"And if you take one step into that building, we will have to arrest you."

Santo walked to the officers and was escorted back to his car.

"This was your only warning," said officer one.

"Yes, sir," Santo said, looking at the gravel beneath his feet.

"Next time, it'll be the slammer," said the second officer.

Santo was about to make a rude comment about the slammer line, but as he looked up, he saw Mr. Albert waving happily from the third-story window of the Green Building.

"Yes, Officer," Santo bit his lip.

He got into his car and drove off.

~ 65 ~

Later that night.
Georgia State Hospital.

Mr. Albert strolled to the back of the Walker building. The structure seemed unlikely to last until daybreak, which would be fine with Mr. Albert. If he were buried under tons of concrete and steel, that might be his end. The other side of the coin was that he remained alive under the tons of concrete and steel, fully conscious but buried forever.

Either way. Either way, Mr. Albert thought. He found an unlocked door that had wedged itself shut by the movement of the doorframe as the building shifted over the years. He pulled on the door until it gave way, causing plaster to fall from the walls around the frame. He stepped inside and was immediately hit with the smell of feces and urine. Over time, windows cracked, and animals found their way into the building, many of them unable to find their way out.

Mr. Albert smiled, thinking Santo should take a whiff of this place if he thought I smelled terrible. He thought of Santo for another moment before forgetting him.

He looked around the vacant room. Pieces of plaster dangled from the ceiling. Some had already found a home on the floor. Strange noises filled the air when a breeze came through the broken windows. The room must have been a hundred feet long and fifty feet wide. Columns throughout the room barely supported the floors above. Back in the day, the room looked as if it could have been a meeting space where patients could socialize or hear announcements.

He didn't turn his phone flashlight on. There was enough light from the moon through the windows to illuminate the space. He was content to remain in the incomplete darkness.

He picked up an old chair from the floor and tested it before sitting down. If it broke and he fell to the floor, and no one was around, would it be as funny? He looked at the door he entered through and then turned to the far side of the room. There was another door that led further into the building. He faced his chair to that door and sat down.

He remained silent for a while and let the building do the talking. Something fell down somewhere in the room, most likely caused by a small animal. The wind created an eerie melody that lulled Mr. Albert to sleep. He closed his eyes. He opened his eyes and thought he saw a shape in his peripheral vision. He turned his head, but nothing was there. A thin band of clouds drifted across the moon, throwing shadows in the room. Mr. Albert smiled. Things were about to happen. He welcomed whatever came his way. A thicker band of clouds blocked the moonlight, and the room went dark. He felt something brush against his face. The ghostly melody seemed to chant his name.

There is no fear of death if one is already dead, he thought. *What could these spirits do? Drag me off to hell? Could that be worse than the ills I have?* He thought of Michael. Death makes one unafraid. All the pain and heartache have already gone. What is there to fear?

But Mr. Albert was not done with this mortal plain. He was tied to the people he had met. He was still connected to Genevieve. He was still riddled with guilt for the unknown things he had done. As long as he had contact with the living, he would continue to suffer.

Santo was probably worried about him. Mr. Albert left him to deal with the rent-a-cops. He did not answer the frantic phone calls Santo had placed since then. Mr. Albert just turned off his phone. He turned off the outside world. He couldn't help but think that

Santo had no purpose here. This, whatever this was, had to be done by him alone. What if he never left this place? How long would Santo wait for him?

All these questions would remain unanswered because the room was full of spirits. They moved past him, unaware of his presence. A scream to the left and spectral nurses ran to attend to a patient having a seizure on the floor. Other patients crowded around the woman, laughing and screaming. The room exploded with sound and movement. Several patients knocked another patient down, kicking and yelling, revenge against a perceived wrong. Other patients tried to make themselves disappear, turning to a vacant space on the wall or rolling themselves into balls. Clouds blocked out the light. When the moon returned, the room was empty.

Mr. Albert heard a noise from the door behind him. He turned to see three college students standing just inside the room, terrified. Mr. Albert reached his hand out to them.

The students didn't wait to find out if he was a ghost or a vagrant. They dropped their flashlights and ran back to their car. Mr. Albert walked over to the door left open by the fleeing students and picked up the discarded flashlights. He looked out the door. The students had been stopped by a patrol car. They pointed to the building. The security officers pointed their flashlights at the door. Mr. Albert retreated into the building.

An officer walked to the entrance and tried to see if anyone else was around. Mr. Albert stepped into a closet and closed the door before the light beam hit it.

"The hell with that," the officer said.

The officer returned to his partner, shaking his head, and they brought the trespassers down to the station. When Mr. Albert thought the coast was clear, he attempted to open the closet door, but it was stuck. He tried several more times before giving up. He turned on one of his new flashlights and looked around the closet. The floor was relatively free of animal droppings, and there were no beavers, raccoons, or rabid squirrels for roommates. He sat on the floor and leaned against the wall to fall asleep. He would try to get out again in the morning.

~ 66 ~

The next morning.
In the Walker Building.

Mr. Albert woke up because the sun was shining on his face. The door to his closet was open. He stood up and stretched. The large room looked different in the morning light. It looked worse. Darkness has a way of softening the shadows, taking the edge off reality. Now he could see every crack in the wall, every hole in the ceiling. He walked outside.

Fog covered most of the campus. *This place never looks normal,* he thought. Mr. Albert walked to the quad and sat on one of the benches. Leafless pecan trees lined either side of the open field, their trunks hidden by the mist. The buildings surrounding the quad looked creepy, with only their upper floors visible.

"Thirteen thousand people lived here at a time. Twenty-five thousand people died here," he said, wanting the spirits to know that he understood. "How terrible it must have been."

"Good morning, you dumb shit."

Mr. Albert looked up to see Santo. He smiled.

"Santo!"

"The hell with you. I was worried. Why didn't you pick up your phone?"

"I was too busy seeing ghosts and even more horrible things, college students."

"You could have let me know you were all right," Santo said, still angry.

"For that. I am sorry, my friend."

Mr. Albert removed his arms from the top of the bench inviting his friend to sit down. Santo forgave Mr. Albert by accepting his offer.

"You really saw ghosts?" Santo asked.

"And college students."

"Did you see Genevieve?"

"I don't think I did. I hope not. What I saw was not happy. I was in an enormous room that was full of patients. They were screaming and kicking. Anger hung in the air."

"But no, Genevieve, which was good. Maybe this place was good for her."

"I don't see how this place could have been good for anyone."

"Which building were you in?"

"That one," Mr. Albert said, pointing to the third building on the left side of the quad.

"Okay. That's good," Santo said, trying to find the silver lining. "That means we can cross off two buildings from the list. Next time I will be with you to help you look for her."

"Santo, I don't want you here, not the next time or any time."

"Why not?"

"I think I have to do this by myself."

"What am I supposed to do while you wander around spooky town every night?"

"Order room service, watch porn."

"I don't like it."

"The room service or the porn?"

"I don't like you being here alone. What if something happens to you?"

"What could happen to me? I'm dead."

"You could be dead, dead."

"That could be a problem. I'll do one building a night, and let you know which one. If I'm not sitting on this bench the next morning, you could send out the search parties."

"Which one are you going to explore tonight?"

Mr. Albert looked around as if there was some logic to his decision-making.

"That one," he said, indicating the first building on the right.

"I thought we were supposed to do this together," Santo said sadly.

"What would happen if the roof caved in? You could be hurt. I wouldn't want that."

Santo turned to Mr. Albert.

"You care about me, don't you?" Santo had a big smile on his face.

"Don't make me regret saying that."

Santo stood up, fully energized.

"You must be hungry, and you smell terrible. Let's go back to the motel room, and you can freshen up, and then we will get you a big breakfast."

"I don't know which is scarier, the Royal Inn Motel or the Walker building."

"I checked out of that dump after the police released me. We are at the Hampton Inn."

"Good choice."

"It is a very nice place, and all the pictures on the walls are of Milledgeville."

"Very interesting," Mr. Albert said, following Santo back to the car. And he meant it.

~ 67 ~

Two hours later.
The thrift store.

After Mr. Albert took a shower and a nap, they decided to go into town and look around.

An hour of rambling led them to the store that the bartender recommended, Auntie Bellum's Attic. The shop was an antiquary's dream, with lots of little spaces filled with oddities, and the owners not fully aware of the value of the items they were selling. Some things were highly overpriced. Other items were practically given away.

The first section on the right after they entered was devoted to the Georgia State Hospital. Mr. Albert found a print listing reasons why people were admitted to the asylum.

"Santo." Mr. Albert showed his discovery to his friend. "Kicked in the head by a horse. How many times have you been kicked in the head by a horse?"

"Maybe three more times before I would find that joke funny. Imaginary Female Troubles. Wasn't that what Genevieve was admitted for?"

"I think so."

"What does that even mean?"

"Haven't the faintest idea. Look, Santo," Mr. Albert said, trying to avoid the subject. "Masturbation for thirty years."

"Wouldn't want to arm wrestle with that guy."

"I could think of at least two reasons why I would agree with you."

Mr. Albert tucked the print under his arm. They ventured deeper into the store. Santo veered off when he saw an old mechanical monkey that, once wound up, would vibrate randomly while smashing miniature cymbals. Santo owned a similar creature when he was a child. It was his favorite toy. He hadn't thought of the chimp in thirty years.

"Mr. Monkey." He smiled at his discovery.

After a minute, he snapped out of his nostalgia and looked for Mr. Albert. Santo found him frozen, staring into the evil face of an antique porcelain doll. The tag read, "The Enchantment of Jumeau." The creature looked as if it was seeing something terrible approaching but could not move. Mr. Albert and the doll stared at each other in horrific fascination.

"Help me, Santo," Mr. Albert pleaded. "It has got a hold on me."

Santo shifted the doll slightly, so it gazed away from Mr. Albert. Its malevolent eyes fixed on an old Minnie Mouse doll. Santo pulled Mr. Albert to the counter. Two older women were talking. Dot was sitting behind the counter, crocheting. Jennie stood to Dot's right. She was slightly younger and still dyed her hair blonde because she was playing the field since her husband died last year. They stopped talking when they saw the two men approach.

"Well, hello, darling," Jennie cooed at Santo. "Did you find something interesting?"

Minnie Mouse crashed to the floor as if it jumped off the shelf to escape the evil porcelain doll.

"Oh, dear," Jennie said, as she headed off to pick up Minnie. "Things always seem to fall off from there."

Santo and Mr. Albert looked uneasily at each other. Jennie came back to the counter.

"Can I help you?"

Mr. Albert held up the print in his hand. "Yes, I wonder if you could tell me what 'Imaginary Female Trouble' meant?"

Jennie and Dot exchanged anxious glances.

"Many women were put in Milledgeville when their husbands got tired of them. Imaginary Female Trouble was the catch-all excuse. Most of them never left," Jennie said, never taking her eyes off Dot.

"What do you mean?" Santo asked.

"You see on that list, False Confinement?"

"Yes," Santo replied.

"Well, a bored husband would have his wife committed, but the doctors wouldn't evaluate the poor woman for a year or two because they were so understaffed. By that time, many women were changed by that terrible place. They thought they were in a happy marriage. They thought they were loved. Everything was taken away from them in the wink of an eye."

Dot looked up from her work. Her eyes were red. "They let the patients do operations on other patients. My big sister, Annie, was sent there."

"I'm sorry," Santo said.

"She died there," Dot added, before returning to her crocheting.

The two women held each other's hands for support.

"Why do you want to know? Some perverted male fantasy," Jennie said, her eyes narrowing.

"No, no, my wife. I mean, my mother died there as well," Mr. Albert said nervously.

"Well, I'm sorry for your loss," Jennie said.

"We'd like to find out where she was buried. Where should we start?" Santo asked.

"Good luck with that," Jennie sighed. "All the records were lost, and all the markers were pulled up and thrown in the woods. When did she die?"

"In 1960," Mr. Albert said with a touch of desperation.

"Well, she is probably in Cedar Lane, you think?" Jennie asked Dot for confirmation.

Dot nodded but did not look up. She needed to focus on her work to keep it together.

"Thank you," Santo said.

"It won't be much help, though," Jennie replied.

"Why not?" Mr. Albert asked.

"You'll see when you get there," Jennie smiled sadly. "You going to buy that?"

"No, it just seems a bit depressing to hang on the wall," Mr. Albert said.

"These college kids think it is one big joke. They don't care about the people who lost their freedom, lost their lives in that place."

"Can I ask you a question?" Mr. Albert said.

"Shoot," Jennie started flirting again.

"You seem like you don't like this place. Why stay here?"

"It's my home. My parents are buried here. Who would visit them? Remember them?"

"Will she be all right?" Santo asked, indicating Dot.

"She's a trooper. She gets sad, but that's life. Can't all be sunshine and lollipops, you know." Jennie thought of the loss of her husband. A year later, the weight of sorrow, still heavy, hunched her shoulders. Her hand reached out to the counter for support.

Santo noticed that the store seemed darker than when they had entered it. It was filled with death and sad memories of broken dreams. Each object here was owned by someone, loved by someone, but then abandoned. The once-precious collectibles are now ridiculed as kitsch. All things go from valuable to worthless. People also follow the same trajectory.

~ 68 ~

The Jones Building.
After sundown.

As he promised Santo, Mr. Albert explored the Jones Building on the right side of the quad. He realized that security was easy to avoid, mainly because they didn't care. If the trespassers were particularly dim-witted and made a lot of noise, or threw beer bottles, or called down to their too-frightened friends from the upper floors, then the security guards would track them down and, if they could catch them, treat the scofflaws to a night in the county jail.

No one noticed you if you kept quiet and stayed in the shadows.

There were college kids in the Jones Building. The boys tried to scare their dates, and the girls would grab onto their boys tighter with every new fright. Mr. Albert wanted to avoid them as he went deeper into the cavernous structure, but they always seemed to be a few rooms behind him. Finally, he realized that his night would be wasted if he spent the whole time steering clear of them. He lay on the floor, sprinkling fallen plaster on his head to give the impression that a chunk of the ceiling had fallen and killed him. Mr. Albert closed his eyes.

"Oh, my god. What is that?" Tyler, the leader of the group, cried.

Drew and Ethan looked at Tyler, wondering if he had set this up. Tyler was worried.

Olive, Tyler's date, laughed. She knew he was screwing with everyone. She walked over to the man on the ground and lit his face with her flashlight. He didn't look like a college student.

"Who is he, your uncle?" Olive joked.

Caroline and Coraline took a step backward. They were tired of being frightened every minute by the boys, but this looked different.

"Is he dead?" Ethan asked.

Olive joined her girlfriends, "I don't know. Tyler, you're pre-Med. See if he has a pulse."

"No way. He's probably some drunk sleeping it off."

"Kick him," Drew suggested.

Tyler tapped Mr. Albert, then quickly stepped back. The body did not move. Drew stepped up to the plate and kicked him a little harder.

"What are you doing?" Caroline objected.

"Maybe he was asleep." Drew cowered from his girlfriend's look of disgust.

Olive insisted, "Tyler, see if he has a pulse."

Tyler approached the prone person. The boys retreated and joined the girls. Tyler lifted Mr. Albert's wrist and felt for a pulse. Tyler dropped the hand, which fell limply to the ground.

Tyler turned to the group, "He's cold."

"Did he have a pulse?" Coraline asked, just above a whisper.

"No," Tyler said, expressionless. He had never touched a dead body. He did not like it and was now rethinking the whole career choice thing.

Suddenly, Mr. Albert opened his eyes and grabbed Tyler's sleeve. He cried with the raspy voice of death, "Help me!"

Tyler screamed and ran past his friends on his way out of the building. The remaining five turned to Mr. Albert, who had risen to his feet, hunched over like Quasimodo, hand extended to catch a tasty college student. "Help me," he cried out louder.

Before he could take three steps, the students disappeared as fast as their trust fund baby legs could take them. Mr. Albert was alone. Three flashlights and a college ID were all that was left of the thrill-seekers. He picked up his prizes. He looked at the ID.

"Hmm, must make sure that Coraline Martinez gets her property returned."

~ 69 ~

The Jones Building.
Twenty minutes later.

Mr. Albert walked through the building. He did not see or hear another intruder, but it took some time for the smell of the living to dissipate. The building felt empty again, lonely, and desperate. Why should ghosts put on a show for people with no desire to help? To what benefit? Mr. Albert did not need to look for proof of existence after death. He was proof.

He entered a large room. The roof was pitched, and several tall steel supports held it in place. He could see the stars through the holes in the ceiling. The world outside looked peaceful. The remains of three large tables lay broken on the floor. Mr. Albert assumed that it must have been a dining room at some point.

He needed to know how many people could eat there at a time. There was no reason for this desire, but the room's scale required validation. He paced off the room. It measured fifty feet across and one hundred feet in length. Each table was four feet by twelve. He estimated that twelve people could fit at each table. He picked up a metal scrap off the floor and walked over to the wall. *If there were ten tables in a row and four tables across*, he thought, etching the numbers into the plaster, *then four hundred and eighty people could eat there at a time.*

He walked to the middle of the hall, feeling the weight of the lost souls. He leaned against a steel beam and sank to the ground, "Four hundred and eighty people forgotten by their loved ones. Four hundred and eighty people were locked away so as not to embarrass relatives, neighbors, and strangers. Santo, you bastard, why did you force me on this journey? Wasn't I happier without this knowledge? How can I make amends or change the past? These people are still forgotten. Only now, this sacred ground is desecrated by drunken college students."

He put his head in his hands and wept.

Time didn't pass. Time doesn't pass when you are in hell. Mr. Albert looked up, and through his tear-filled eyes, he noticed movement. He wiped his eyes, angry that more trespassers desecrated this holy place.

Mr. Albert did not see mortals. He wasn't sure if he was dreaming. Disembodied figures whirled around him. They had no distinct faces or features, like chiffon blowing in the wind.

Then he saw her at the far side of the room. She was the girl whom he dreamed of under the tree outside Michael's house. She looked older and frailer.

"Genevieve? Genevieve? Is that you?"

"Benny, I can't see you," his dead wife replied.

"I am here."

Her vision became sharper. She recognized her husband and flew violently towards him, stopping only when they were face to face.

"I thought it was you. Why have you come?"

"For you, Genevieve. I have come for you."

"You will burn in Hell!" The ghost screamed.

Mr. Albert could not contain his sorrow. "I am already there."

"But why am I?" Genevieve cried like a frightened child.

"I am so sorry."

"What is your sorrow to me?" The ghost hissed. "You put me here. With all these people. Where is the peace he offered me? Offered all of us? We were good. We were innocent. Where do the innocent lay under the sycamore tree?" She screamed as if she was being burned.

"What could I do? Help me, please."

"It is too late for you and me, too, too late. Help me, Benny!"

The other spirits encircled her, spinning ever quicker as her voice faded. She screamed once more and was gone.

~ 70 ~

The next morning.
On the rescue bench.

After Genevieve's departure, Mr. Albert spent the rest of the night on the dining hall floor. He could not move. He did not want to.

The morning brought peace. His demons were gone for the day. Mr. Albert was sure they would be back at sundown. He stumbled out of the Jones Building, making his way to the bench where Santo, hopefully, would meet him. He sat down. His head was so heavy that he slumped forward. He would have fallen over if he didn't support his face with his hands. Santo arrived sometime later. Mr. Albert was not sure how long he had been sitting there.

"Mr. Albert, how are you," Santo said, sitting next to his friend and putting his hand on his shoulder.

"Santo, I can't go on," Mr. Albert apologized. "You told me if I found the girl under the tree, I would have a purpose, that love would be my purpose."

"It still could be."

"Genevieve died over 60 years ago. How could she be my purpose?"

"How can a man be alive and dead simultaneously?" Santo admitted that there were more things unknown in the universe than will ever be understood.

"I don't know, Santo."

301

"I don't know, Mr. Albert."

"Please, help me."

"I will try. What happened in the Jones Building?"

"I saw her."

"You saw Genevieve? Did she tell you where she is buried?" Santo said excitedly.

"No. She hates me."

"She doesn't hate you."

"She told me I will burn in Hell."

"She's upset."

"Upset?"

"Just a little upset. Happens all the time in healthy relationships."

"You are saying that my relationship with Genevieve is a healthy relationship?"

"You hit a rough patch."

He looked at Santo with disbelief, "I'm going to hit you with a rough patch."

Mr. Albert turned away and stared across the quad. After a moment, he said, "And I don't think you are one to give me relationship advice. The first time I saw you, you were about to kill yourself because of a girl. I suppose that was a rough patch?"

"That was definitely a rough patch." Santo thought of Mr. Albert's suffering. "You look terrible. Can we leave this awful place for a few hours?"

Mr. Albert remained fixated on the Powell Building, which sat directly across from where they were sitting. He did not respond to Santo's question.

"Come on, Mr. Albert." Santo stood before him to break his gaze. "Let's get you a shower and a nap."

"Sounds good," Mr. Albert said.

Santo helped him get to his feet and supported him as they walked to the car.

"Maybe later we can either get plastered at The Velvet Elvis or get some hot dogs."

"Can we do both?"

"We will see," Santo responded. "We will see."

~ 71 ~

Georgia State Hospital.
Twelve hours later.

After sundown, Mr. Albert found himself in front of the Boone Building. It was in a less traveled part of the hospital's campus and would not be patrolled as often. He looked at the windows. Most of them were broken. He saw a pane of glass by his feet. The moonlight reflected off it and into Mr. Albert's eyes. It was unbroken. There were shattered panes all around him, but this one remained whole. Mr. Albert picked it up. A circle, like a teardrop, was at its center. He read somewhere that glass has viscosity; it moves slowly over time like a liquid.

"Science," he marveled.

He looked through the teardrop at the building. A window at the far right on the second floor revealed a flicker of light. He put down the glass to see clearer. The light was gone.

Mr. Albert walked to the window. He stood looking up. There was nothing there. He looked at the glass in his hand and held it up to look through it. The flickering light returned. He lowered the glass, and the light disappeared.

"Not science," he said, putting the unbroken pane in his pocket. He set off to investigate.

Mr. Albert walked around the back of the building to find an open door. All of them were padlocked. He noticed some thick brush covering a section of the wall, which obscured a set of steps going down to a basement door. He tried to pull the bush away, but it was covered with thorns. After several tries to get through, his hands were dripping with blood. Even though he healed quickly, it was still a nuisance. Mr. Albert stared at the disagreeable bramble before remembering the glass in his jacket.

"Aw, what the hell." He stared through the teardrop, and the plant moved, giving him enough space to walk through. The door at the bottom of the steps opened. Before he entered the crumbling building, he looked back at the shrub. As he lowered the glass, the thorns returned to their defensive position.

"This should be fun," he mumbled to himself.

He had never been in a basement here and wondered if all four floors above him would come crashing down. He focused on what was in front of him. It looked like a laundry room. The commercial-sized washers were reddened with rust where the ceramic paint had chipped off. A table, probably used for folding clothes, had two legs missing, making it seem like a playground slide. Plaster had fallen off the walls, but for the most part, the room appeared safe.

He made his way through the space. A long hallway stood before him. Mr. Albert held the glass up and saw a dim light coming from one of the doors on the left. He kept the glass up because it seemed to know which way to go. The door on the left opened to a stairway. He climbed the stairs, avoiding the beer cans on the steps.

"College kids getting drunk and wandering around condemned buildings, and I'm the one with no brain functions," he said in the darkness.

He was not afraid of bodily injury, but it still was disconcerting walking around these buildings searching for ghosts through a magic-looking glass. He continued his monologue.

"I see Lizzie, and I see Poindexter, and I see Juju."

He reached the first floor. Mr. Albert looked down the hall through the glass. The pane clouded up, but when he turned it back to the stairs leading to the floors above, the glass cleared. It seemed to signal him to climb higher. Mr. Albert wanted to stay on this floor. He won.

"You're not the boss of me," he protested.

The hallway opened up into a large meeting room. There were many spirits sitting around, talking to each other, and staring at the walls. They didn't seem to notice him.

"Genevieve," Mr. Albert called out. "Are you there?"

No spirit responded. There was one that danced through the crowd in slow motion. She was in a powder-blue hospital gown that flowed with her delicate turns. The other ghosts did not seem to notice her. She ended her performance in front of the bathroom and took a bow. When she came up, she threw off her costume with a grand gesture and exited into the bathroom.

Mr. Albert followed her into the lavatory but did not see her anywhere until he looked up. She had hung herself and was spinning slowly. When she faced Mr. Albert, her eyes opened, and she reached out to him. Her eyes glowed with anger. "Stairs," she hissed.

Mr. Albert backed out of the room and returned to the stairs.

"Stupid hanging naked lady. Stupid, stupid pane of glass in my ass!"

He stomped on the steps leading to the upper floors. Pieces of plaster fell from the walls. He continued with less stomping.

Mr. Albert returned to his Romper Room bit, "I see Johnny picking his nose. Stop, Johnny, stop. Get that finger away from your mouth. Oh, you are a disgusting little bugger! And I see Cindy Lou Boo has found a bottle of Mommy's little helpers. They are not candy, Cindy Lou! Too bad mommy is doing Mr. Jensen from upstairs, but maybe she'll find you in time!"

Mr. Albert stood on the second-floor landing. The glass indicated this was his stop.

"Second floor, women's lingerie, and sporting equipment, all out."

He looked both ways down the long hall, which seemed to stretch for miles. Mr. Albert was never good at judging distances. The glass wanted him to turn left. He headed down the hall. A door at the far end opened with the typical creaking ghostly sound. Mr. Albert approached with a fair amount of trepidation. Light seeped into the hall, encouraging him to discover the source. He no longer needed the glass as he walked to the opening. If this were a movie, the scary music would be rising to a crescendo.

He followed the light deeper and deeper into the building. In the fourth room, he saw a figure sitting in a chair looking at a burning blood-red taper on the floor. Another chair faced him from the other side of the candle. He studied the dancing flame. "The fire of life is ephemeral."

"Walter?"

The figure turned to Mr. Albert and looked at him with sad recognition.

"Who the hell else would it be?" Walter grumbled.

"Literally, anyone else in the entire world."

"Well then...surprise!" Walter said unenthusiastically.

He stood up and extended his arms out. Mr. Albert hugged him. Walter tapped the chair.

"Two chairs. Were you expecting someone?"

"Just you."

Mr. Albert sat down and acknowledged the weirdness of the situation. "How are you here? Did McKenna's close down?"

"McKenna's didn't. I did."

"What do you mean?"

"It means, Albert, that I am dead."

"When? What happened? You were so young and healthy," Mr. Albert said.

"A couple of weeks after you and Santo left, I was sitting in McKenna's at a booth. Mac came over to me to ask if I wanted another drink, and I was gone."

"Dead?"

"Yes," Walter said bitterly.

"I'm sorry. I didn't know."

"Would it have mattered?"

"Probably not. So, you are a ghost?"

"Did you just hug me?"

"Yes."

"Did I feel like a ghost?"

"No, are you a zombie? Somehow this conversation seems strangely familiar."

"No, I am not a zombie."

"Then what are you?"

"I am a figment of your imagination."

"So, you are not really dead?"

"No, I am dead."

"But how do I know you are dead if I'm just making this up?"

"I'm dead. The subconscious mind is very good at picking up vibes from the universe."

"But how does that work?"

"Do you want to spend the whole night talking astrophysics, or do you want to talk about why I am here?"

"What does this have to do with astrophysics?" Mr. Albert questioned. "Yes, I want to know why you are here."

"Why am I here, Albert?"

"That's what I asked you."

"That's a question you have to ask yourself."

"I willed you here," Mr. Albert hypothesized.

"Possibly," Walter said, giving the impression that Mr. Albert was wrong.

"Because I wanted you to help me find Genevieve?"

"Seems like a stretch but go on."

"Because you are dead, and you might have insight into the world of dead people?"

"Bertie, you are also dead. So, you have just as much experience with dead people as I do. Probably more. Who knows how long you've been like this? But maybe that's it. You know everything you need to know. You just need a way of letting all the stuff you know, come out."

A door from the hallway slammed shut.

"What's that?"

"What's what?"

"Didn't you hear the door?"

"If you heard the door, I heard the door," Walter said, rolling his eyes.

"Did you hear the ghost?"

"There are no such things as ghosts."

"You're a ghost."

"I'm a figment of your imagination."

"Isn't a ghost a figment?"

"Depends how you define figment. Yes, what you heard is a figment of your imagination."

"So, what about naked hanging lady?"

"Naked figment."

"What about my magic mirror?"

"What magic mirror?"

Mr. Albert reached into his pocket. It was empty.

Walter continued, "The subconscious mind creates ghosts and other things that go bump in the night to solve a problem."

"What problem do I have?"

Walter gave Mr. Albert a good long look.

"You mean Genevieve?"

Walter shrugged his shoulders, looking disinterested.

"How will I solve the problem of Genevieve? I don't know where she is buried."

"Don't you?"

"No, I don't."

"I think you do, and I am you, so you think you do as well."

"But if I don't remember anything, how will all this help?"

Walter took a piece of fallen plaster from the floor and hit Mr. Albert on the head with it. It broke into several pieces.

"Hey!"

Mr. Albert took a larger piece of fallen plaster and chucked it at Walter. It sailed right through his ghostly form.

"Ha," Walter taunted.

Mr. Albert sneered at Walter before taking another piece of plaster. He closed his eyes to concentrate and chucked it at Walter. It lodged in Walter's eye.

"Ha," taunted Mr. Albert.

"You're a real idiot, aren't you, Albert?" Walter said, removing the chunk. "Now I see why you need me."

"I don't need anyone." Mr. Albert got up to walk away.

"You need everyone."

Mr. Albert returned to his seat and put his head in his hands.

"You are right. I need everyone." He rubbed his temples to get clarity. "You are saying that I conjured you up to help me remember things I have long forgotten."

"It is as good an explanation as any."

"Debatable. But why you?"

"Why not me?"

"Why didn't I summon Genevieve to tell me where she is buried?"

"She is probably mad at you for condemning her to this hellhole."

"You think she is mad at me?"

"She hit you in the head with a swing."

"True. Why don't I make her forgive me?"

"You are probably not ready to be forgiven. You are a bitter bastard."

"Why didn't I conjure Taylor Swift? She isn't mad at me, is she?"

"You could have created anyone, anything to bring you this information. The mind is a complicated organ. It puts together random objects that are connected in subtle ways."

"So, there are no ghosts, and I have nothing to fear."

"I don't know if this building will last the night," Walter chuckled. "But there aren't any boogiemen lurking in darkened corners."

"Where is Genevieve buried?"

"I don't know."

"Why did I summon you then?"

"I do not know. You either find me attractive sexually, or there is something about me that will trigger a memory."

"First of all, gross. Oh, wait, like the swing hitting the tree, which led me to the carving."

"Ok. Sure."

"What do I do now?"

"Haven't the foggiest."

They sat there looking at each other.

"Really, Cindy Lou Boo overdosing on her mother's diazepam?" Walter scoffed.

"Did I go too far?"

"The whole Mr. Jensen from upstairs bit wasn't much better."

The conversation lagged. Mr. Albert squinted his eyes in concentration.

"I'm not turning into Taylor Swift," Walter growled.

"Sorry."

"Well, this is awkward," Walter said, looking everywhere except at Mr. Albert.

A breeze blew through the building, extinguishing the candle's flame. They sat in silence and darkness.

"This is worse," Mr. Albert corrected.

Walter whistled the Tennessee Waltz. Then there was silence. Mr. Albert was alone.

$$\sim 72 \sim$$

One day later.
Cedar Lane Cemetery.

Santo convinced Mr. Albert to take a day off from exploring the buildings at night. He was worried that Mr. Albert seemed to grow weaker every day. Getting a good night's sleep might be all he needed to get back to his old cheery self. Mr. Albert did not have the energy to argue with Santo but convinced him they needed to do something to find Genevieve. They decided to visit one of the Central State Hospital's cemeteries. Jennie and Dot from the antique store suggested starting at Cedar Lane.

Cedar Lane was part cemetery and part memorial for the people who died at the hospital. The parking lot could only fit five cars, calling attention to the fact that the people interred here rarely had relatives come to visit. This place was another tourist attraction for the morbidly curious. The somber memorial had 2900 steel grave markers arranged in twenty-nine neat rows too close for actual bodies to be buried there. Years ago, the stakes were ripped from their proper places and thrown into the woods to make mowing the grass easier. No one knows where the actual bodies are buried.

"Why do the markers just have numbers and not names?" Mr. Albert asked.

Santo said, "They needed to keep the names secret for privacy reasons. If the families were ashamed of their crazy relatives, they wouldn't want the names displayed in public."

They stared at the markers—so many unwanted people. Mr. Albert's subconscious reared its ugly head. Carnival music began to play. The markers popped out of the ground and became little men in dark suits and bowler hats, like the paintings of Magritte. They stayed in the memorial area as if imprisoned but moved quickly like human bumper cars. Each time they knocked into one another, both markers would tip their hats and say, *terribly sorry old chap.* The hats were returned to their heads, and the markers would start on their meaningless journey again. The music stopped, and the markers hurried to their rows and sunk into the ground. Musical grave markers without winners, forever playing this empty game. The music started again, and the markers popped up.

Mr. Albert dropped his head and closed his eyes. Santo touched his arm, concerned.

"Are you all right?" Santo asked.

"How do you know so much about this place?" Mr. Albert asked to change the topic.

"What do you think I do when you go out at night?" Santo grumbled. "I research and ask the locals questions."

"And there I thought you were just watching porn," Mr. Albert smiled.

"There was time for both," Santo said, returning the smile. "Come with me."

Santo walked to the entrance of the memorial, where a gazebo stood to inspire reflection. Santo continued down the path that went through a grove. Several broken tombstones lay on either side of the path. The men climbed a small hill, eventually coming to a clearing. A statue of an angel stood in the center of the clearing. Her left hand reached up to heaven. Her gaze, also looking up, seemed to remind God that the lost souls buried here were his children. Mr. Albert wondered why God would need reminding. The angel's right hand was lowered to the ground.

The statue stood on two round cement disks. The upper one was half the diameter of the bottom one. On the disks were stones left by visitors to the memorial.

Mr. Albert and Santo walked to the statue. In her right hand were coins.

"Why do people leave money?" Mr. Albert asked the expert.

"Both the stones and the money have their beginnings in Jewish traditions. You left a coin or a pebble on the gravestone of a loved one to tell them that they were not forgotten."

Mr. Albert looked at Santo, impressed.

"You can learn a lot from the porno channel," Santo quipped.

Mr. Albert laughed gently, but then his smile faded. He reached into his pocket, pulled out a few coins, his lucky penny included, and placed them in the angel's hand.

"I hope that will help," he told the angel.

Santo found a couple of rounded stones. He gave one to Mr. Albert before placing his on the top level of the statue's base. Mr. Albert put his stone next to Santo's. The dead man looked at the memorial of grave markers in the distance.

"It is beautiful here. But why the angel over here and the memorial way over there?"

Santo stood by his friend. "This is the graveyard."

"Where?"

"Everywhere. From the river in front of us to the road there and there and the prison to the left. Four hundred feet in every direction."

"All I see are trees in the woods."

"Yes."

"And the graves could be anywhere in this area?"

"Yes."

Mr. Albert turned to look at the statue.

"I think we are going to need a bigger angel."

$$\sim 73 \sim$$

Brantley Building.
10 PM.

After sundown, Santo dropped Mr. Albert behind the quad chapel. It was an inconspicuous place to disembark. He walked around the back of the buildings until he came to the Brantley Building and found an unlocked door. He made it up to the third floor and looked over the quad. Countless stars lit up the night sky. The ground seemed to be bubbling as the trees rocked gently back and forth like slow-motion hula dancers.

He turned back to the large room. The roof had collapsed, and a hole in the ceiling gave a view of the heavens. Mr. Albert lay down on the floor and tried to count the sparkling stars.

He decided to invite his subconscious out to play. Clearing his mind of everything except the night sky, he took a deep breath and then another. He closed his eyes. A moment later, he opened them. The stars were brighter than they had been a moment before. Some of them seemed more intense, almost pulsating with energy.

At first, the twinkling stars pulsed individually, but soon they harmonized with each other and flickered as one. The rhythm of the heavenly lights seemed to slow down as well, at first, fading almost to nothing, then regaining strength until the intensity was blinding.

Mr. Albert closed his eyes. When he sensed the light had faded, he opened his eyes to discover that he was no longer in the Brantley Building.

He was in a graveyard, but the graves markers were pinwheels, spinning fiercely in the wind. Four penguins walked about the graves. Each took a line of the verse, *Seldom can't, Seldom don't, Never shan't, Never won't.*

He saw a woman approach. She seemed familiar, but he had no idea where he had seen her. Suddenly, he knew she was Genevieve's mother. Mrs. Pierpont, dressed in a Grecian toga, floated between the rows of pinwheels. The penguins rushed to her. They joined wings and began to rise.

"Seldom can't. Seldom don't. Never shan't. Never won't," they cried, pleading for mercy.

Mrs. Pierpont raised her hand and explained to the birds, "Twenty-four to ninety-four a path without a seven. Thirty-seven falls off to twelve; you'll never get to heaven."

She faded away. The pinwheels launched into the air, slicing the penguins into a hundred dark grey rats. They ran to Mr. Albert and encircled him. With little rat voices, they chanted, "Wee wee husband, give us some money. We have no comfits. We have no honey!"

Mr. Albert did not know how nursery rhymes were helpful. He closed his eyes, hoping that all this nonsense would be gone when he opened them again.

His plan worked. He was back in the Brantley Building. The room was smoky. Mr. Albert looked out the window, but the smoke had also taken over the outside world. He looked up to see the smoke streaming through the hole in the roof like a waterfall descending from the sky. Mr. Albert tried to find the source of the flame. Orange lights five feet tall, grew brighter then dimmer, approached him from all corners of the room. On closer inspection, the smoking objects were large cigarettes that were talking to sardines of equivalent size.

"Arp, ray, lam," cried the fish. "Arp, ray, lam!"

"Poof, poof," answered the cigarettes.

Black liquid flowed in from the broken windows and turned into roaches. The bugs covered the sardines and ate them. They tried to climb up the cigarettes but erupted into flames when they reached the burning tip, leaving a thin trail of smoke. The remaining bugs turned their attention to Mr. Albert and covered him. When they reached his face, the room grew dark.

But Mr. Albert was not consumed by the insects. He felt himself ascending, like Jesus, on the third day. As he rose, the bugs turned into onyx marbles and dropped to the floor before rolling off to some dark corner.

A guitar lay on the floor. He picked it up. It crumpled in his hand and turned into dust. The dust swirled, taking the shape of a small tornado. Within the tornado was a young girl who cried, "Where are you, Daddy? Why did you leave me?" The spinning stopped, and the dust fell to the ground.

In the far corner of the room, there was a statue. Mr. Albert approached the figure. It looked like the Venus de Milo except that it was Mrs. Pierpont. His sculpted mother-in-law spoke to him.

"Benny, you said you would take care of my baby. I trusted you. You broke your word."

"I did what I could," explained Mr. Albert.

"You betrayed me. Look at where they sent her. Look at what you've done."

The statue shattered. Mr. Albert tried to put the pieces back together, but every piece he touched cut him. His hands were soon covered in blood. He stood up to run away. Bars flew in from all corners of the room, forming a cage to imprison Mr. Albert. He looked up at the hole in the ceiling to see the stars. The opening grew smaller until the heavens were blocked out, and the room darkened. A frigid wind took hope out of the air. Mr. Albert felt his consciousness leave.

~ 74 ~

The bench in the quad.
The next day.

Santo waited on the rescue bench. Mr. Albert was later than usual. Santo worried that Mr. Albert was weaker. *Dead people shouldn't appear weak*, he thought. *Mr. Albert almost seems mortal. Maybe he was really dying, and Albert Albert was at the end of the line.*

Mr. Albert appeared at the top of the stairs which led into the quad. He stood there disoriented, with the Powell Building behind him. Santo rushed across the field to meet him. Mr. Albert needed the handrail to descend the thirteen stairs. He saw Santo approaching and sat down on the bottom step.

Mr. Albert looked like a ghost, pale and withered.

"Are you okay?" Santo sat down next to him.

"The place looks different from this side. It looks less sad."

"What makes it look sad?"

"The color blue," Mr. Albert whispered.

Santo looked to the bench on the far side. The bench was a faded red. The leafless trees were grey. He did not see any blue.

"I think I'm dying, Santo," Mr. Albert acknowledged.

"Why do you say that?"

"I feel it."

"This whole trip has been very upsetting," Santo comforted him.

"Shouldn't I be upset?"

"Of course, you should be, but you rarely are."

"Isn't that a good thing, though, not being upset?"

"Yes, but that is not what living is all about. The Buddha said all life is suffering."

"The Buddha? I thought you were on Team Jesus?"

"The Four Truths are the Four Truths."

"If this is living, I'd rather be dead."

"Life can be bearable," Santo smiled.

They sat in silence, staring at the non-blue pecan trees and grassy fields.

"Did you see Walter again?" Santo asked.

"No."

"Britney Spears?"

"Taylor Swift."

"You saw her?"

"No."

"Disappointing."

"I was attacked by cockroaches and rats, who asked me for honey."

"That seems significant."

"I don't know."

"That sounds like a very weird dream. Anything else?"

"I saw Genevieve's mom."

Santo looked at Mr. Albert, annoyed.

"Don't you think Mrs. Pierpont is a little more important than rats and cockroaches?"

"In the subconscious, everything is important," Mr. Albert shrugged.

"What did she say?"

Santo took out a little notebook and a pen which he clicked several times.

"Where did you get that?"

"At the college bookstore. Look, there's a bobcat on the cover. I'm a bobcat!"

Mr. Albert turned away and put his head in his hands. Santo grew anxious.

"I bought it so I could write down everything you say when we meet in the morning. So, you won't forget anything," Santos said, trying to soothe his despondent friend.

"Good thinking," Mr. Albert did not look up. "She spoke twice. Once to the penguins and once to me."

"Penguins, interesting," Santo said, taking down each word. "What did she say?"

"Twenty-four to ninety-four a path without a seven. Thirty-seven falls off to twelve; you'll never get to heaven."

"Interesting, interesting."

"Why is that interesting?" Mr. Albert said, getting irritated.

"It's interesting. I don't know why. What else did she say to you? Another rhyme?"

"No. She was not that cryptic. She told me that I had promised to take care of her baby. I broke my word. She trusted me. And I betrayed her. Look at where they sent her, Benny. Look at what you've done."

"That's not too bad," Santo said, studying his notes.

"No?"

"It's ambiguous. It could mean lots of things."

"You are terrible at interpreting hallucinations."

"Look, Mr. Albert. It is your subconscious that was speaking to you, and obviously, anything understandable is just you not being able to forgive yourself. But we know that already. You are a terrible person."

"Thank you."

"You are welcome, but what is important are the things that don't make sense. Those are the things we should concentrate on. Those are the clues."

Mr. Albert turned to Santo and smiled weakly.

"You think?"

"I think. Why don't we get you some rest and then something to eat? Then you can give me all the strange and wonderful details."

Mr. Albert nodded his head, and they headed back to the car.

~ 75 ~

The Hampton Inn Breakfast Bar.
Two Days Later.

Mr. Albert spent the two days after the Brantley Building in the motel room sleeping. Santo went out to pick up meals. Sometimes they ordered food to be delivered. Santo also spent time in Big Lots, which was adjacent to the Hampton Inn. He bought Mr. Albert an oversized mug that read; It's *a good day to have a good day*. Mr. Albert did not find the joke amusing, but he drank out of it anyway because Santo purchased it for him. Mr. Albert did not want to admit it, but Santo was probably the best friend he ever had. It was hard to tell, though. He had little memory of past events.

Mr. Albert did not want to go to a bar or even eat hot dogs. Santo felt something was changing. When his father died, he had plenty of warnings. Cancer slowly ate away at him over a couple of months. There was time to accept the inevitable. This felt like the same thing. Soon Santo would be alone again.

Mr. Albert was still sleeping when Santo got up. He dressed quietly and went to the breakfast bar even though he didn't feel like eating. He made himself a cup of coffee and sat at the far end of the room, away from the television and the guests. He poured the creamer into his cup and watched it swirl in the darker liquid. He thought of the ephemeral nature of life.

"Why so glum, friend?" Mr. Albert stood in front of him, smiling.

"Glum is glum," said Santo, not looking up.

"And love loves to love love," said Mr. Albert, sitting down. "I think that is Yeats."

"How are you feeling?"

"I'm tired of hanging around the room. I feel like doing something fun."

"Really?" Santo said, impressed.

"Yes, can we go to the cemetery again, Mommy?"

"Why do you want to go to the cemetery? I figured that once you were strong enough, you would want to return to the soul-sucking abandoned buildings."

"Normally, I would, but I think we came here to find Genevieve. She is not buried in a building, is she?"

"Hard to tell."

"C'mon, Jimmy, let's go see the angel."

"I guess that would be as much fun as anything else."

~ 76 ~

Cedar Lane Cemetery.
An hour later.

Mr. Albert walked through each row in the memorial, looking at the numbers.

"You can't do that, Mr. Albert. You are being sacrilegious."

"Why, there is no one buried here. Probably the only section in this whole place that is clean of corpses."

Santo let him continue his desecration. If anyone else came to the memorial, he would pretend he didn't know Mr. Albert. Santo felt better once he thought of that devious plan.

"Did you write everything down in that book of yours?" Mr. Albert asked.

"Of course," Santo said, feeling important.

"What did Mrs. Pierpont say to the penguins?"

"Twenty-four to ninety-four a path without a seven. Thirty-seven falls off to twelve; you'll never get to heaven."

"Do you see a twenty-four in here?"

"Not from where I'm standing."

"Well, look."

"At every marker?"

"Do you have something better to do? Is *Betty does the Bobcats* on the porn channel?"

For the next hour, they checked each marker for a twenty-four, a ninety-four, a seven, a thirty-seven, or a twelve. The only number they found was the ninety-four. They sat down in the gazebo to think things through.

"Well, that was a waste of time," Santo grumbled.

"I sure wish Tessie was here. She always had the best ideas," Mr. Albert joked.

"They add up to one hundred and seventy-four."

"Is that interesting?" Mr. Albert asked to mock Santo.

"I don't know. Is it interesting for you?"

"I wish I was drinking again."

"What if they are groupings instead of individual numbers?"

"You mean 2494, 737, 12?"

"Maybe," Santo said, walking over to the markers.

He stopped at the first marker in the first row, on the right. He stared at it. Mr. Albert joined him. They both looked at the marker.

"2494," Mr. Albert said.

"Okay, this is creepy," said Santo.

"But much more fun."

They searched the rows but did not find a 737. They went back to the gazebo and sat down despondent.

After five minutes in silence, Santo spoke, "So, maybe that was just a coincidence."

"A coincidence? It was the first marker. That is no coincidence."

"Maybe you just saw it the last time we were here, and you re-membered it, and your subconscious spat it back up when you saw Mrs. Pierpont and the penguins," Santo suggested.

"Possibly, but just as possible that it was important."

"Possibly, but just as possible that it wasn't."

"Possibly, but more than possible, you're an idiot."

"Now you are just being mean," Santo said.

"I'm sorry, possibly, but more than probable, you're an idiot."

"I don't think that changed anything."

"And I'm sorry about that as well."

"Are we done here? Santo asked, having his fill of defiling the memorial of the lost souls.

"For now. I want to come back tonight."

"Why would you want to do that? Don't you have enough problems with the buildings? Now you want to spend the night in a spooky graveyard?"

"At least I don't have to worry about being buried in a building collapse."

~ 77 ~

That night.
Under the angel.

Mr. Albert sat on the ground in front of the statue. She appeared to be reaching for the half-moon perfectly positioned directly above her left hand. She, however, looked beyond the moon. There was something more interesting further away. What was out there that attracted her so that she would disregard the treasure within her grasp?

Her fantasy would be fulfilled. Abby the angel, Mr. Albert, just that moment decided Abby would be the proper name for her, started to spin in a clockwise direction. The top cement cylinder of the statue's base turned counterclockwise. Abby rose like a corkscrew and then floated off to her lover as soon as she was no longer connected to the base.

"Ah, young love," Mr. Albert mocked his overly sappy hallucinations.

His mockery ended abruptly when a scroll rose from the base and floated to where Mr. Albert sat. The scroll unrolled with a flourish in front of him. The parchment glowed from within with the light of truth so that Mr. Albert could read every name.

There she was, number twelve thousand, three hundred and thirty-five. Genevieve Benton, divorced, died March 16, 1960. Next of kin, Jacqueline Skillen, do not contact.

Mr. Albert had never met Genevieve's sister, but he decided that Jacqueline was not an agreeable person. She didn't want to know anything about Genevieve's imprisonment. Maybe she felt guilty on her deathbed and asked for forgiveness. That could be the reason for the space in the family plot.

Maybe her shame would matter. But how can someone who is dead forgive you? You must ask for compassion when they are still around. Mr. Albert didn't know if he was worthy of compassion. He forgave Jacqueline. Maybe that would be worth something when it was his time. *Forgiving someone is not a difficult thing to do,* he thought; *you just have to forgive.*

He stood up and looked over the grove where the bodies were buried. The land dropped gradually to Camp Creek, which designated the end of the graveyard. The wintering trees obscured the brook. Something buzzed past Mr. Albert's ear. He instinctively went to swat it away, but whatever it was, it was gone.

The stones on the statue's top base started to roll as if there were an earthquake. Mr. Albert felt no tremors. The rocks formed a line and rolled off into the shadows of the trees. Mr. Albert followed the rolling stones.

The stones zigzagged on their mission. One stone would break off from its squadron every few feet and stop. The earth would rumble underneath the rock, and a spirit of the forgotten rose from its grave. The ghost looked surprised at its resurrection, but immediately all emotion drained from it. The spirit picked up the stone and walked away.

Mr. Albert stood there stunned. He watched as other spirits rose from their graves and carried their stones toward the river. An old Gospel song floated through the air. He couldn't tell if it was the church a few miles down the road or a ghostly choir.

That moment, whatever it was, was beautiful. Music filled the air. The moon, showing through barren branches, embraced the world beneath her. The dimmed light of the departed floated slowly downhill to the creek. And the singing.

O sinners, let's go down
Let's go down, come on down
O sinners, let's go down
Down in the river to pray
As I went down in the river to pray
Studying about that good ol' way
And who shall wear the robe and crown?
Good Lord show me the way.

The ghosts waited at the shore. They could not go in to be baptized, to be saved. These souls would never be saved. If no one remains to remember your virtuous deeds, God forgets you. Mr. Albert walked to the water's edge. He could not venture in and receive salvation either.

Black shapes blocked the moon, throwing splotches of darkness everywhere. The spirits cowered and dropped their stones before they were swooped up. Mr. Albert felt a creature's talons dig into his shoulders to carry him off. The flying demon struggled but could not hold him for long and lost its grip. Mr. Albert fell and ran into the woods. The demons had no power there. Soon all the spirits by the river had been carried off to a deeper hell than lying forgotten in an unmarked grave. The forest fell silent.

Mr. Albert made his way back up to the angel. He thought maybe she could protect him. She was at the top of the hill waiting for him. He looked at the smaller base. There were no stones left. The rocks on the lower level began to rattle. They also formed a line and headed off in a different direction from the previous line.

Mr. Albert realized these stones were messengers of evil, not harbingers of peace. They collected the souls of the departed and led them to further torments. There is no peace for the hopeless, not even after death.

"I thought you were here to protect them," Mr. Albert pleaded with the angel. "Do something!"

But idols cannot help the dead. The angel focused on the heavens, not the needy in front of her. Mr. Albert decided he would save the lost souls if no one else would. He tried to step on a stone, but it rolled just ahead of his falling foot. He jumped to the ground and caught the last stone in the line.

The rock spun in his hand like a gyroscope. Mr. Albert struggled to keep it under control. Finally, the stone gave up the ghost and surrendered. Mr. Albert put the docile rock in his pocket. He smiled, acknowledging his victory over the usually inanimate object.

He looked up, ready for his next conquest. The line of stones disappeared. Each pebble found a grave and awakened its occupant. The spirits had risen and walked towards the creek.

This moment, whatever it was, was terrible. The music filled the air. The notes, now atonal, were a death knell. The moon threw sharp shadows on the forest floor. The branches jerked menacingly as the wind picked up. The light of the departed moved to their doom.

Mr. Albert tried to save them. He ran to the water's edge and waved the spirits away.

"Please, keep away. Go back to your graves."

The spirits looked at Mr. Albert with an air of resignation. They understood that nothing could help them. They waited for the end.

Mr. Albert tried to grab one of them. There was nothing to hold on to. He walked, despairing, back into the woods as the flying demons arrived. His strength had left him. He knew he could not help any of the spirits who lingered here.

He stumbled back to the angel. The base of the statue was clear of any stones. They had all taken a spirit away.

"You were supposed to help them," he said softly. Then his recriminations turned inward. "I was supposed to save her, protect her."

He fell to his knees. His head touched the ground, and Mr. Albert fell to his side, shrinking into the fetal position. He remained there until the captured stone regained its strength and banged around in his pocket.

He stood up, and his pocket pulled him in one direction and then the other. Eventually, it managed to get out and roll on the ground. Mr. Albert found it difficult to keep up with the stone. He soon lost it. He stopped and looked up to the heavens, breathing heavily. Not even one soul? Not one? He bent over and held his knees as he recovered his breath.

The music returned to the quiet forest.

As I went down in the river to pray
Studying about that good ol' way
And who shall wear the starry crown?
Good Lord show me the way!

Mr. Albert recognized the voice. It was Genevieve's. He looked up and saw her dancing in a tattered pale blue shirt-waist dress through the trees. He followed her. Soon the forest became unfamiliar. He did not recognize this part of the cemetery. He turned around to see if he could get his bearings by finding the angel on the hill, but it was gone.

When he looked back, Genevieve had vanished as well. He was alone. A breeze blew through the branches creating a soft moan. The moan turned into sobbing, which was coming from somewhere in front of him. He slowly approached the sound. Mr. Albert found Genevieve crouched in front of a tree digging. Her fingers were bleeding from the cold earth.

She turned to Mr. Albert and pleaded, "Help me. Do I have to do everything myself?"

Before he could say a word, the ground opened up and swallowed her. He ran to her, but she was gone. He looked at the tree. It had a love heart carved into it, about the size of a woman's hand, with the initials BB & GB.

He smiled; maybe this is where she is buried. He had no time to celebrate. A hand broke through the forest floor and grabbed his foot. It pulled him into the grave. He lost all hope when the ground covered him. Mr. Albert could not move. The dirt held him firm.

He could not breathe. The earth pressed against his chest. Darkness consumed him.

~ 78 ~

The morning after.
Cedar Lane Cemetery.

Mr. Albert was awakened by a tap on his foot by a Milledgeville Police officer. There were three tourists taking pictures and posting them on their social media.

"Sir, are you all right?" The officer said politely. He didn't like being filmed by the gawkers. He didn't want any trouble, but he had to do his job.

"Yes, officer, I was waiting for my friend. I must have fallen asleep," Mr. Albert replied.

"Well, you didn't have to desecrate a memorial while doing it," he helped Mr. Albert up.

Mr. Albert saw the marker he was lying under. The number was 3712. It was one of the sets of numbers he was looking for.

"Could you wait a minute," Mr. Albert struggled to break free.

The officer did not let go. He hoisted his prisoner away and threw him into the patrol car's backseat. Mr. Albert sat silently. No use causing any more trouble.

A few minutes after the squad car drove off, Santo pulled up. The tourists were still standing around discussing the excitement. Santo got out of the car and looked around. No, Mr. Albert. He walked to the group.

"You didn't happen to notice a guy in a dark wool coat."

"He was just arrested," said Millie. She and her husband, Jeff, came to Milledgeville on their thirtieth wedding anniversary and dragged along their teenage son.

"Crap," Santo cursed under his breath. Then realizing he was not alone. "Sorry."

"Do you know him?" Jeff asked.

"I kind of take care of him," Santo said.

"Didn't do a great job of it," Jeff laughed. His son laughed along with him.

"Sometimes the little bugger just gets away."

"You want to see the arrest?" Millie asked.

"Sure."

"Leyton, show the man his friend being arrested."

Leyton rolled his eyes before walking over to Santo. Mother and son were not on the best of terms. What fifteen-year-old wants to go to a haunted place with his mother? He showed Santo the post.

"Interesting. Where was he sleeping?"

"About seven or eight rows in," Jeff said.

Santo walked up seven rows and then walked across. He studied the numbers.

"Oh, Jeez, Millie. Guess you gotta call the police on another one," Jeff chuckled.

"I'll just be a minute. My friend's mother was buried somewhere in this place. Thirty-seven twelve was her marker."

Millie and Jeff looked at each other and then down to the ground. They had no idea why Mr. Albert was there. They didn't ask. They assumed the worst and called the police. Leyton did not share his parents' guilt. He walked to the gazebo, sat down, and texted his friends.

"He did go on about the marker," Millie squeezed her husband's arm.

"We're sorry. We didn't know," Jeff apologized.

"That's all right," Santo said, standing at marker 2494 and looking through 3712 to the woods beyond. "Son of a bitch," he smiled. "He probably deserved it. He really is a horrible person."

And with that, Santo jumped in his car to bail out his friend.

Milledgeville Police Station.
One hour later.

Mr. Albert was shown to his cell at the hospital's police station. It was mainly used to scare college kids so they wouldn't sniff around the abandoned buildings. The police would hold the thrill seekers for an hour or two and then release them.

He had a cellmate, and Mr. Albert recognized him immediately. Tyler was one of the college students he met in the asylum a few nights ago. He decided to have some fun.

Mr. Albert sat down at the far end of the cell and stared blankly. Tyler paced the cell but kept shooting looks at Mr. Albert.

"Have we met?" Tyler asked.

"I don't think so," Mr. Albert said with no emotion. "Why?"

"You seem very familiar."

"People say that a lot. What are you in here for?"

"Trespassing." Tyler was quite proud of himself.

"Do you do that a lot?"

"I like to bring a date to the Jones Building and then scare them. Gets them in the mood."

"Very mature. What do you do for a second date?"

"Don't often get one. What are you in here for?"

"I fell asleep in a graveyard."

"Was it scary?"

"Why should it be?"

"I don't know. I thought it might be."

Mr. Albert held up the ID he had collected from one of Tyler's friends.

"Is this yours?"

Coraline Martinez's college ID dangled from his hand.

"Coraline is my friend. How did you get this?"

Mr. Albert stared at the young man's face.

"She dropped it," Tyler said to his untalkative cellmate.

"She did."

"Wait, she dropped it when we were in the hospital."

"Did she?"

"We found something creepy."

"Did you?"

"We found a guy."

"Was he dead?"

"Yes."

"Did he reach out to you and cry for help."

"Yes."

"And did you help him?"

"No. Wait, how could you know?"

"I saw you."

"No one was there."

"I was."

"But the only people there were my friends and the dead guy."

"Yes."

"But you are not one of my friends."

"No."

"Then you must be..."

"Want to check my pulse? You were a little nervous the first time you took it."

"No, sir," Tyler said, backing away from Mr. Albert.

Tyler turned to the cell bars and shook them like in the movies.

"Can somebody help me?" he called to the guards.

Nobody answered his cries.

Mr. Albert smiled, although scaring the student wasn't as much fun as he hoped it would be. This whole journey had changed him. He wasn't drinking. He wasn't eating hot dogs. He got no pleasure from annoying strangers. Life had lost all its joy.

"Relax," Mr. Albert said. "I'm not going to hurt you."

"But how are you..."

"Yeah, yeah, I'm dead. Not a big deal. You wanted to see a ghost. I'm a ghost."

"You're a ghost?"

"No, but I'm dead just the same."

"Are you...."

"Am I a zombie, a vampire, Frankenstein's monster? No, no, no. Haven't the foggiest idea about what I am. The world is a mystery. I might have been like this for a thousand years, but I don't remember anything further back than a few months."

"Where did you come from?"

"Jersey. Does that help?"

"No."

"Of course, it doesn't. People always want to know where I came from."

"Why are you here?" Tyler asked, losing his fear of the stranger.

"I'm looking for my wife."

"Is she dead too?"

"Yes, why is that romantic?"

"Kinda."

"What do you know of romance? You think the sign of true affection is to cop a feel after you make a girl wet herself!"

Tyler smiled. He did think that was pretty cool.

"The truth is," Mr. Albert continued. "That my wife was a patient at this mental hospital sixty years ago. She died here and is buried in one of those unmarked graves. I hope to find her and bring her home."

"That is romantic," Tyler said thoughtfully.

"A regular Romeo and Juliet."

"Was her name Juliet?"

"Genevieve."

Tyler looked confused.

"Romeo and Juliet is a play by William Shakespeare. Albert and Genevieve, I mean Benny and Genevieve is this story," Mr. Albert said, waving his hands in a circular motion to indicate the present.

"That's an excellent story."

"Not what Skillen thinks."

"What?"

"Never mind."

"So, what are you going to do now?"

"Well, when I get out of this place, I'm going to go back to the Cedar Lane Cemetery and find my wife."

"How are you going to do that?"

"I've got a plan, 2494 and 3712."

"The markers? Cool."

"Albert Albert?" The police officer at the cell door asked.

"That would be me," Mr. Albert said, rising to the occasion.

"You've made bail."

"Well, Tyler. It was nice talking to you. Don't take any wooden nickels."

Tyler looked confused.

"Georgia State College?" Mr. Albert narrowed his eyes as he estimated how much Tyler's parents were spending on his education.

"Go, Bobcats!" Tyler yelled.

"Go, Bobcats," Mr. Albert said, as he left.

Tyler sat down on the cot.

"I met a ghost. Cool."

~ 80 ~

Cedar Lane Cemetery.
One hour later.

Santo took Mr. Albert back to the Cedar Lane Cemetery. Mr. Albert sprang from the car and dashed over to marker 3712.

"This is it, Santo," Mr. Albert cried. "Here is the other number we were trying to find."

"I know."

"How do you know?

"A woman showed me where you were sleeping before you were arrested."

"That's disappointing. I wanted a big reveal, maybe have you fainting at the conclusion," Mr. Albert said.

"I wanted to surprise you with the knowledge, and you would be eternally grateful."

"Well, I'm disappointed."

"I'm disappointed as well."

"We are both disappointed."

"That's disappointing."

They looked at the ground, kicking pebbles for a while.

"Did you find out what the seven means in the rhyme?" Mr. Albert grumbled.

"Yes. Seven rows back."

"Oh. That doesn't seem like much. Hardly seems worth a line in the poem."

"It's your subconscious."

"I know. You don't have to rub it in."

"I know."

They kicked some more pebbles.

"But what does it mean?" pondered Santo.

"I don't know," Mr. Albert replied.

"It has got to mean something. The first row, the first marker has the first number. Then we skip seven rows, and we have 3712."

"Maybe she is.... I don't know."

Santo walked to marker 3712. "I don't get it. Mr. Albert, stand by 2494, please."

"Why?"

"Tell me if you can see anything."

Mr. Albert walked over to the marker. He stood there. He looked around.

"I see the markers. I see the entrance and the gazebo. Up on the left over there is Abby."

"Abby?"

"The angel."

"You named the angel Abby?"

"Yes. Why?"

"Seems like a strange name for an angel."

"Well, Abby is special."

"Do you see anything else?"

"I see you and the road. That's it."

"Oh," Santo said, disappointed.

"Wait, Santo, I see you. The first marker looks at the second marker."

"So?" Santo said, looking at Mr. Albert.

"The first marker looks at the second marker and beyond."

Mr. Albert twirled his finger to tell Santo to turn around. Santo followed the directions. He looked out into the woods, to the right and downhill from the angel.

"Genevieve is somewhere in a direct line from here," Mr. Albert said excitedly.

"That is still a lot of ground to cover," Santo said, turning back to Mr. Albert. "How will we know for sure."

"Santo, I saw where she was buried. She was under a tree. The tree had a heart carved into it, with the initials BB & GB."

"Like at Michael's house?"

"Yes, but it was GB for Genevieve Benton. Genevieve."

"Who would carve that in the tree?"

"I would. Even though we were divorced, I must have visited her after she died."

"Which means you still cared for her. Which means you didn't do this to her. Something else happened that put her here. It wasn't your fault."

"I still cared for her, but I did nothing to stop it. What kind of man am I, Santo?"

"You are imperfect, Mr. Albert, just like everyone else. Except that you are dead, you are just like everyone else."

Mr. Albert looked exhausted. Santo walked over to his friend and put his hand on his shoulder. Mr. Albert looked up. Santo smiled to encourage him.

"I know you are tired, but you are almost there. I know you can do this."

"Do what?" Mr. Albert asked hopelessly.

"We are going to find Genevieve."

~ 81 ~

Cedar Lane Cemetery.
Two hours later.

Mr. Albert and Santo searched the woods in a line from the markers to Camp Creek. Two hours had passed, and they had grown frustrated. They found no tree with the carving on it. They stood in front of the creek. Santo threw a stone across the water, hitting the shore on the other side. This was not a great challenge because it was, after all, a creek.

"I don't understand. My dream was so clear."

"Maybe you left out something," Santo said, tossing another stone.

"I didn't forget anything. Stop throwing the stones."

"Why? There are plenty of stones to go around."

Their side of the creek had thousands of rocks. The other side was bare. Santo threw another stone.

"They look like the stones on the angel's base," Santo mused. "Strange how there are no stones over on the other side."

"Each stone was a soul that was taken."

Santo dropped the remaining stones, and they clattered as they hit the ground.

"Taken?"

"By the dark spirits," Mr. Albert pointed to the sky.

"I'm sorry, Mr. Albert. Should I get them?"

Mr. Albert shook his head slowly, "I think we have to."

They walked to the water. Mr. Albert stopped.

"What is the matter?" Santo asked.

"I can't go in the river."

"Why? It is not a river. It is a creek. Look, it is not deep."

Santo stepped in the water. He walked to the middle. The water was just under his knees.

"I can't go into the river because I am dead, like the souls last night. I am unclean."

"Am I clean?"

"Your soul is pure."

"Thank you," Santo said. He was touched. "Your soul is pure as well, Mr. Albert. Try."

Mr. Albert stepped in. When his foot broke the water's surface, the creek started boiling. Mr. Albert screamed in pain and fell back on the shore. Santo looked at the water passing through his legs. It was calm and clear.

"Mr. Albert, are you all right?"

He took a step towards his friend.

"Please, Santo, get the stones."

Santo crossed over to the other side and looked for the three thrown stones. Mr. Albert took off his shoe. His foot was burned and blistered. Puss oozed from his wounds. He touched his foot and screamed.

Santo collected the stones and made his way back to Mr. Albert.

"That looks gross."

"It feels gross, Santo."

"How is this possible? You get shot, and you say, where's my donut? You step in a stream, and it melts your foot."

Mr. Albert did not have time to answer before a large turkey vulture landed on their side of the creek. The bird stood over four feet, giving it the appearance of a gargoyle on a Gothic cathedral. It flapped its wings and took a step toward them. The creature hissed at Santo, who stood between it and Mr. Albert. The thing wanted the dead man. Santo picked up a branch.

"Shoo! Get away from here," Santo warned, waving the stick.

The rotted branch snapped in half as Santo reversed his swing. Santo looked at the stump in his hand. He held it out to the bird as if it were a knife. The bird hopped towards Santo and hissed again. Another vulture and then another joined it. They all approached Mr. Albert. The smell of his boiled flesh attracted them. Five more birds landed nearby. They didn't seem to care that Santo was alive or that Mr. Albert was metaphorically living. They were hungry and demanded to be fed.

"Hey, get out of here, you stupid birds," Tyler cried, banging his shovel against a tree.

The birds scattered. Mr. Albert smiled at Tyler's fortuitous arrival. The bobcat did not come alone; he brought his friends. They all banged their shovels to scare away the birds.

Sensing their odds had changed, the vultures flew off for easier carrion.

"Tyler, what are you doing here?" Mr. Albert asked happily.

"Well, I figured you needed help, and then I figured I needed help. And then I figured it would be cool if we got wasted."

"But how did you find us?"

"2494, 3712, dude, all the way!"

"I'm Santo, Mr. Albert's friend." He reached out to shake Tyler's hand. "Thank you for saving us from being eaten by vultures.

"No problema, man," Tyler had immediate respect for a guy who was friends with a ghost. "Are you dead too?"

"No, sorry," Santo said.

"No worries," Tyler said, a little disappointed. "These are my friends, Caroline, Coraline, Drew, Olive, and Ethan. You guys remember Mr. Albert?"

They all ran to Mr. Albert to shake his hand and prod him to see if he were dead. They completely ignored Santo.

"See," Tyler proclaimed. "I told you he was the dead guy. Holy fuck! What happened to your foot?"

"I wanted to go for a swim. Do you have some bandages?"

"Got a first aid kit in the car."

"Do you also have some alcohol in the car?" Mr. Albert said hopefully.

"We just got a couple of six packs and Tito's," Tyler boasted.

"See, Santo, I told you this guy was all right."

Santo helped Mr. Albert off the ground. Mr. Albert put his arm around Tyler and Santo's shoulders. They headed back to the car as Caroline, Coraline, Drew, Olive, and Ethan sang, "We're off to see the wizard," while dancing behind them.

~ 82 ~

Cedar Lane Cemetery parking lot.
Two hours later.

Tyler bandaged Mr. Albert, and then the group sat by the gazebo drinking as Santo read the notes Mr. Albert dictated to him on his exploration of the hospital's collapsing buildings. They particularly liked Mr. Albert's encounters with the college students. Soon, they had consumed all the alcohol in Tyler's car.

This was followed by another hour of the group searching the area indicated by the markers. The students stumbled around but did not find the tree by Genevieve's grave. They eventually took their shoes off and walked into the creek but did not receive second-degree burns. Overall, it was a very disappointing hour.

They returned to the gazebo, looking rather depressed. The situation was about to get worse. A patrol car pulled up. The officer got out of his car, looked at Tyler, and frowned.

"Tyler?"

"Officer Saunders."

"Didn't we just release you three hours ago?"

"Yes, Officer," Tyler said, with a big grin.

"Twice in the same day. That's a record. Usually, we only book you a couple of times a week. What's the occasion?" Then the officer saw Mr. Albert. "Aw, hell. What, are you two having an idiot contest?"

"Good afternoon, Officer Saunders," Mr. Albert said, politely.

The police officer counted the group with his finger. "Eight of you? I don't think I could fit everyone in my car."

"That would be illegal," Tyler said. His friends laughed.

"I have a good mind to drag your daddy down to the station again. We'll see how much you'd be laughing then."

"That won't be necessary, Dan," a distinguished-looking man in a tweed sports jacket, who had just arrived, addressed the police officer like they were old friends.

"Professor Rosetti, what are you doing here?"

Professor Rosetti was the students' history professor at Georgia State College. His focus was the state hospital. He also was the head of the Milledgeville Historical Society. His class on the history of the asylum was immensely popular with the students and was responsible for most of the trespassing arrests made by the police department.

"The students are here on a project for the Historical Society."

"And what about these two," the officer said, indicating Mr. Albert and Santo. "Are they working on the project as well?"

"Yes, I am told that they have information about one of the people buried here, which, as you know, is a Society project."

"There was a report that some college kids were drinking and carrying shovels around. Was drinking a part of your project?" Officer Saunders countered.

"Tyler, were you and your friends drinking while doing your research?" the professor chastised.

Tyler hung his head, "I'm sorry, professor. Mr. Albert hurt himself and asked if we had something that would numb the pain."

Mr. Albert hiked up his pant leg revealing his bandaged foot.

"I'm sorry, Officer," Rosetti apologized. "It seems they were not following the proper protocol for historical research. There will be a three-point deduction on their project grade for this infraction."

The students, picking up on the deception, gave a collective "Aww."

"Well, as long as there are some consequences," Saunders said as he walked back to his car. "Didn't want to fill out all the paperwork anyway."

He drove off. Professor Rosetti looked at his students disdainfully.

"Tyler, are you okay to drive?"

"Yes, Professor."

"Then why don't you take your friends and get more of whatever you were drinking? Mr. Albert here looks like he is still in pain."

Tyler and his friends sulked to their car and drove off. They didn't think they were being punished, but it felt that way. Professor Rosetti looked at the two strangers.

"So, which one of you is dead? Tyler told me all about it."

Mr. Albert raised his hand sheepishly.

"And you're looking for your dead wife's grave in this cemetery," Rosetti walked over to the markers.

"Yes, sir," Mr. Albert admitted.

"When did she die?"

"In 1960."

"What were the numbers in your Scooby Doo mystery ghost story?"

Santo took out his notebook and read Professor Rosetti the rhyme.

"So, this is your 2494," Rosetti said, pointing to the first marker in the first row.

"Yes," said Mr. Albert. "And this is the 3712." He hobbled over the second marker.

"It is seven rows back," Santo chimed in.

Professor Rosetti looked unimpressed.

"It points in that direction," Mr. Albert pointed to the woods.

"Interesting," said the professor as he turned and walked to the gazebo.

Santo and Mr. Albert followed him. The professor sat down deep in thought. Santo and Mr. Albert sat down and leaned in, anticipating that the professor would solve the mystery. Rosetti leaned back and looked at the two strangers.

"So, you want to tell me what is actually going on here?"

Mr. Albert avoided the professor's stare.

"What do you mean?" Santo asked innocently.

"Well, your friend is clearly not dead."

"I'm dead."

"If you were dead, how could you be hurt? And if you were hurt, you wouldn't feel your injury. So why bandage it?"

"That is a mystery," Mr. Albert acknowledged.

"And you don't look old enough to have a wife that died sixty years ago. So, what are you here for, and why are you bothering my students?"

"We have a friend in Savannah who found out his aunt was committed here," Santo blurted out. "He never met her because his mother was ashamed that Genevieve was sent here."

"That is typical for the time period. You didn't answer the question, why are you here?"

"We told him we would help locate her grave. Michael wants to move the remains to the family plot in Savannah," Santo said.

Rosetti thought for a moment. Then he turned to Mr. Albert.

"And what is this whole nonsense about you being dead?"

Mr. Albert realized that it would be no use telling the truth.

"I was in one of the buildings at night, and Tyler and his friends found me snooping around," Mr. Albert said. "I pretended I was dead to spook them. Tyler is not particularly good at taking pulses."

Professor Rosetti grew silent. He had all the information he needed to solve this problem. All he needed was time. He sat back in the gazebo, crossing his legs at the ankles. He folded his arms and scrunched up his face, changing the scrunch each time he changed his position.

The students returned and laughed as they approached with drinks in their hands. They stopped when they saw their professor's thinking expression and the shush that came from both Mr. Albert and Santo. They stood silently waiting for an answer, although they weren't sure what the question was. Two minutes later, Professor Rosetti stood up.

"One more question, why do you think it is this cemetery?"

"I saw the grave here," Mr. Albert stood up, winching from the pain in his foot.

"If you saw the grave here, then where is it?" the professor queried.

"It might have been a hallucination. I've been seeing visions."

"Because ghosts see many visions," Rosetti chided the dead man.

"Yes, we do," Mr. Albert responded slowly.

"And how do you know it was Genevieve's grave?"

"There was a tree above it with a carving in it. A heart with the letters BB and GB."

"What was Genevieve's last name?"

"Benton."

"And who is BB?"

"Benny Benton."

"But your name is Mr. Albert?"

"Yes, Albert Albert."

"Albert Albert is Benny Benton?" Rosetti said, humoring him.

"Yes, I am," said Mr. Albert.

The professor turned to his students.

"You guys believe this?"

They looked at each other before nodding yes. Rosetti shook his head in disgust.

"Ethan," Rosetti growled.

Ethan snapped to attention, "Yes."

"What grade are you getting in my class?"

"A *D*."

"You deserve it."

He walked back to the markers. The rest of the group followed closely. He looked in the direction the two markers made and followed the path down to the creek. At the water's edge, the professor turned back to the grave hunters.

"This creek is the original boundary of the Cedar Lane Cemetery. You probably noticed no tree with a carving expounding the love between this man and his dead wife because his wife was never here!"

His students gasped. Mr. Albert felt his heart sink. Santo checked his notebook.

"He was lying to us, professor?" Ethan grumbled.

"I didn't say that."

"Then what are you saying?" Santo cried.

"If she died in 1960, she wasn't buried here. This graveyard was closed before then."

"Where is she buried?" Mr. Albert felt his hope rising.

"There is another cemetery that opened in the 1960s, and it is located about a mile in this direction," Rosetti turned around and pointed in the same direction that the markers indicated.

"Your markers were right. Your graveyard was wrong. Follow me," the professor said in an overly dramatic fashion. "My fellow investigators, we are off to Central State Hospital Cemetery #2 off Laying Farm Road!"

They walked quickly back to the car park and, after several rounds of the newly acquired alcoholic beverages, made their way to the next graveyard.

~ 83 ~

Central State Hospital Cemetery #2.
Off Laying Farm Road.
Twenty minutes later.

When the convoy arrived at the cemetery, Professor Rosetti drove to the second set of wooden fences, which marked the edges of what used to be the road through the cemetery. He got out and unrolled a map of the area on the trunk of his car. The rest of the searchers formed a semi-circle around him.

"We are standing in cemetery number two. It is inactive, which means it is no longer accepting guests. It opened for business around the time Mr. Albert's wife was buried. Plus, the markers at Cedar Lane are directly northeast of here, and they were pointing southwest, so this is "X" marks the spot. If she is anywhere, she's probably here."

"But there are no graves here," Ethan said.

"There are plenty of graves, just no markers. They got in the way of mowing the grass. The markers were tossed in the woods. No depressions or markers around. The few gravestones that were here are now well below the sod. There are at least sixty-seven rows of graves, with maybe 30 in a row. Over two thousand people could be buried here. But hopefully, we won't have to dig up everybody. Does anyone want to guess why?"

His students looked confused. Mr. Albert looked depressed. Only Santo met the professor's stare.

"Because we are looking for a tree carved with Genevieve's and Benny's initials, and this is a field without trees," Santo said.

"You would do well in my class," he smiled at Santo.

Santo smiled back.

"That means we need to walk along the edges and check out every tree," the professor instructed. "Hopefully, it is still around. If it is not, Mr. Albert will never find his true love. Two teams. The boys go from the left. Girls go from the right."

"What are we, in third grade?" Drew complained.

"It is the only way to ensure you kids are not doing it in the woods instead of looking for the tree. I need you focused. Any other questions?"

The students shook their heads sadly because they would not be doing it in the woods, at least for the moment.

"Well then, let's get to it, and if you find any markers, photograph where they were and bring them back. It will help with possible future identifications," Professor Rosetti clapped his hands, and the students went scurrying off.

"Do you mind if I go looking around?" Mr. Albert asked.

"No, try to pick up more psychic visions," Rosetti said, smiling.

"Want company?" Santo asked Mr. Albert.

"No. I want to go by myself. I appreciate your help, Professor."

Mr. Albert walked away as if a great weight was on his shoulders.

"Don't worry, Santo. I am sure he will be all right," the professor said.

Rosetti rolled up the cemetery map and put it back in the trunk. He grabbed a couple of beers and handed one to Santo. They both twisted off the top together.

"Cheers," Santo said, toasting his benefactor.

"Cin-Cin," Rosetti said, clinking Santo's bottle.

"You don't believe any of this?" Santo asked.

"No, not at all," said the professor.

"Then why are you helping us?"

"It's a beautiful day, and I got the students to buy me some beer. Don't tell the Dean."

"That's all?"

"You two intrigue me. Mr. Albert definitely belongs in a lunatic asylum, but you seem to be a reasonable man. How did you end up with Don Quixote over there?"

Mr. Albert looked like he was hopping from stone to stone in a river in the middle of the field. Occasionally, he would bend down and pick up a rock. He would shake it and bring it up to his ear. Then he would say loudly, "are you there?"

"He saved my life."

"Literally or figuratively?"

"Both."

"Go on." The professor studied Santo like a bone fragment on a paleontological dig.

"I was about to jump off a pier in New Jersey one night in the middle of November. I would have been taken out with the tide, and no one would have missed me. He was there and talked me down. I thought I owed him for that. I have been following him ever since."

"That seems excessive. How long are you going to do that for?"

"About five more years."

"I guess you are just as wacky as he is," Rosetti said.

"Probably so."

"You know it is improbable that we will find anything."

"I know."

"So, why are you doing this," Rosetti smiled because he had turned the tables on Santo.

"It's a beautiful day."

Rosetti nodded at Santo. They drank their beer with an appreciation for the life they had been given. In the distance, there was a commotion. The girl team was jumping up and down and waving their arms.

"I guess I was wrong. Get in the car," Rosetti commanded Santo.

The boys arrived first, and then Mr. Albert. Rosetti drove until the overgrown road ended. He and Santo ran the rest of the way. The others were standing in front of a tree twenty feet from the clearing. Four feet off the ground was the carved heart with the initials.

"Fuck me," said Rosetti.

The group stood in silence. Mr. Albert started swaying. Santo ran to support his friend.

"We found the tree, Mr. Albert," Santo hugged him.

"We found Genevieve," he responded.

"Let's start digging," Tyler crowed as he headed back to the car to get the tools.

"Now, hold on there, partner. This is a historical site, and things must be done correctly," Rosetti explained.

He threw his car keys to Drew.

"Get me the GP8000 from my trunk."

"The what?" Drew replied.

"The thingy-ma-bob with wheels," Rosetti sneered at his student. "Ethan, go with him. No, Olive, you go. Ethan, look for flying saucers."

"Yes, sir," said Olive.

"Yes, sir," said Ethan, studying the sky.

"The thing cost me ten thousand dollars. I am not letting Ethan near it," Rosetti whispered to Santo.

"What is it?" Santo asked.

"It is a ground penetrating radar, GPR. It will tell us if there is anything down there. Mr. Albert, in your vision, where was the grave?"

Mr. Albert walked about three feet in front of the tree.

"It was about here."

The GP8000 was set up quickly. Rosetti maneuvered it over the spot where Mr. Albert pointed.

"Damn," Rosetti said, showing Mr. Albert the screen. "There is definitely a body."

The students cheered. They felt like real archaeologists. Santo laughed with joy. Mr. Albert stood there numb.

Rosetti took several pictures with his machine. He also took snapshots of the tree to document the discovery.

"Great. Now can we dig?" Tyler pleaded.

"Sorry, Tyler, but this is a historical site, and things must be done correctly," the professor repeated himself and rolled his eyes. "We need to get permission from the state, and that will only come after we find a relative that will request to have the body exhumed. Mr. Albert, is there any way you could prove that you are Genevieve's husband? That any rational person would believe?"

"No," he shook his head and looked to the ground. He had come so far. Now he realized he would never get Genevieve home.

Professor Rosetti thought for a moment. A smile came to his face.

"Is Michael an actual person, or did you make him up," he asked Mr. Albert.

"He is real."

"What is his full name?" Rosetti asked, pulling out a small notebook from his pocket.

"Michael Skillen," Santo answered.

"The writer? Damn. Would he consent to a DNA test?"

"Yes, of course," Santo said.

"And you said that Genevieve was his aunt?"

"Yes, his mother's sister," said Santo.

"What was Genevieve's maiden name?"

"Pierpont."

Professor Rosetti put away his notebook and addressed the crowd.

"Well, between the initials on the tree, the GPR, and Mr. Skillen's consent, I believe there is enough evidence to ask for the body to be exhumed for testing. I want you all to listen to me. Ethan, stop looking for UFOs," he snapped his fingers, getting everyone's attention. "No one is to go near this grave. If it is disturbed, this becomes a crime scene. These graveyards are on the National Register of

Historic Places. Tyler, you will go to jail for a long, long time. I am not talking about hanging out with your friends in lock-up for a few hours. I am talking forever. And Mr. Albert, Genevieve's remains will be sealed up in a police evidence locker and forgotten. She will never, ever go home. Do we all understand?"

The crowd all nodded their heads sadly. The exciting part of their adventure was over.

"Bureaucracy is not much fun, but this is what I do, and I do it well. I promise, Mr. Albert, we will have her home soon. Mr. Albert?"

Mr. Albert's eyes rolled to the back of his head, and he fainted. Santo caught him and laid him down on the ground.

"Is he all right?" Rosetti asked.

"He's breathing," Santo answered.

"That's good," said the professor relieved.

"It's unusual," Santo said anxiously.

"Why don't you take him home? Make sure he is safe and comfortable. Then come down to my office, and we could start some paperwork."

"Yes, that sounds good."

"And the rest of you, not a word to anybody."

The kids drove away after helping Santo get Mr. Albert into his car. Professor Rosetti stayed behind to pack up his equipment and make further notes.

He looked at the tree's initials again and said, "Fuck me."

~ 84 ~

Three days later.
Genevieve's grave.

For two days, Mr. Albert did not leave his bed. Santo stayed by his side the whole time except for when he went down to the breakfast bar to get enough food for the rest of the day. He was tired of bananas and Lucky Charms for dinner. On the third day, Mr. Albert wanted to see Genevieve. They bought a foldup camping chair and some snacks from Big Lots. After the car was loaded, Santo drove to the gravesite.

Mr. Albert did not want company. Santo was concerned but decided to help Professor Rosetti with the paperwork. Mr. Albert promised he would not die or dig up Genevieve's body while he was gone. He just wanted to be with his wife. Santo got into the car and drove away, promising Mr. Albert he would return in a couple of hours.

Mr. Albert remained silent for a long time. It was a pretty spot to be buried. He sat down in his folding chair and closed his eyes. He envied Genevieve. Her pain had passed. His pain remained. But what was the point of his suffering? Didn't he accomplish his task? His goal? His purpose? Genevieve would be brought home. Why couldn't they both have peace?

His thoughts turned dark. She was dead. That was the only reason she was at peace. There is no peace for the living because all life is suffering. Someone important said that. He could not remember who. He understood that his subconscious created a suffering spirit so that he could torture himself. Genevieve did not care where she was buried. This relocation business would not release him from his guilt.

He stood up and walked around the tree. He circled it a second and a third time. A frigid wind blew through the trees. The sky grew dark. He felt different, younger if that was possible. He looked at his clothes but did not recognize them. His pants were new and belonged to a suit. His shoes had been recently polished. What was he dressed up for?

The grave was open. A ladder leaned against the end where Genevieve's head would rest. Dirt flew from the grave, falling neatly in a pile at the foot of the grave. A bowler hat would rise and fall with each thrust of the shovel into the cold earth.

"Three by eight and five feet down. Time to sleep. Forever bound. You will see him with the crown when covered up and five feet down," the gravedigger sang.

The shoveling stopped. The shovel dropped. Shuffling feet. The ladder moved to the other end of the grave. The shovel was picked up. The shoveling began again.

"Five feet down and eight by three. The visions you're about to see. Sleep with the Lord; you will be free. Five foot down and eight by three."

The shoveling stopped. The shovel dropped. Shuffling feet. The ladder moved to the original end of the grave. The shovel was picked up. The shoveling began again.

"Five feet down and three by eight. Heaven calls; no time to wait. Be with the Father; pain abates. Five feet down and three by eight."

The shoveling stopped. The shovel flew from the grave and landed with a twang in the fresh pile of dirt. Shuffling feet and climbing the ladder. The bowler hat was first to appear, then the rest of the gravedigger. He stood three feet tall. Black boots and pants and a dark vest over a muddied white shirt. His hat hid his face. He dusted himself off and looked into the grave.

"Hurry up, lads. The party's about to begin," the creature said, before turning his gaze to his audience.

The gravedigger looked exactly like Mr. Albert.

"Hold your horses," yelled a voice from down below.

The ladder was moved to the other side of the grave. Another shovel flew in the air and landed beside the first one. The ladder shook as another bowler hat appeared, followed by the rest of the gravedigger. After he was out, he looked into the grave.

"Move it along. The guests will be arriving soon!"

The second gravedigger looked precisely like the first. Two more shovels flew from the grave. The ladder was moved back and forth several times before a third and fourth gravedigger emerged, resembling the second. After dusting each other off, they turned to Mr. Albert.

"All ready for your big day," asked the first gravedigger.

"You must be excited," squealed the third.

"Your mother must be very proud," cried the fourth.

"No need to be nervous," gushed the second.

The tiny men surrounded Mr. Albert and nudged him towards the ladder.

"What are you waiting for? Get in," urged the first one.

Mr. Albert climbed into the grave, which seemed much deeper than five feet. Gravedigger two stepped on the top of the ladder, which pivoted the bottom up to ground level, leaving Mr. Albert stranded. The ladder was removed in a flash.

"What do I do now?" Mr. Albert asked.

"Lie down," said the third.

Mr. Albert stretched out on the floor of the grave.

"Like this?"

"Yes, yes, of course," said the fourth impatiently. "Are you comfortable?"

"He's a little cramped," grumbled the second. "I told you we should have made it wider."

"I measured it precisely," said the third gravedigger as he picked up his shovel and set it crashing down on number two's head.

Number one howled with laughter. Number two clanged his shovel on number one's head for laughing. Number one hit number four, and number four hit number three. Then they all turned and hit the gravedigger who hit them. This continued for several minutes, and with every successive clump, each gravedigger sank further into the ground until they were buried up to their waists.

"Excuse me. What do you want me to do?" asked Mr. Albert, not wishing to disturb the commotion.

"What do we want you to do?" cried the first gravedigger springing up to ground level. "We want you to die, of course!"

The rest of the creatures shoveled the dirt from around their waists into the grave.

"Wait, please. I do not belong here."

"If not here, where?" shrieked the third.

"If not now, when?" taunted the fourth.

The creatures buried Mr. Albert in the cold, silent earth. All was black.

"Hello? No? Testing, testing, hello, hello," he called to the emptiness.

"Mr. Albert, Mr. Albert, are you all right?" Santo said, shaking him.

Santo had finished his work with Professor Rosetti for the day and hurried back to Mr. Albert, fearing the worst. When he drove up, Mr. Albert seemed to be sleeping peacefully in his new chair.

Santo called his name, but Mr. Albert did not stir. He ran to him to check if he was dead, dead. His chest rose and fell. He shifted in his chair. He was alive. He was just somewhere else.

When they first arrived in Milledgeville, Mr. Albert's visions only happened when he explored the abandoned buildings at night. Then the visions came when he was alone. Now they come all the time. It seemed as if his subconscious bubbled up to the surface whenever it wanted. His subconscious and all the disjointed apparitions had taken over.

There is a medical belief that the lights a person sees at the moment of death result from the body shutting down. Santo felt that Mr. Albert was shutting down. It was hard to tell what exactly was going on in his body. This must be how a dead person dies.

Mr. Albert's eyes fluttered. He opened them slowly, at first not recognizing Santo. Then he smiled and reached out to his friend.

"Santo," he said.

"Mr. Albert, how do you feel? Did you have another vision?"

"Yes."

"But why? We found Genevieve. Did we not find Genevieve?" Santo began to worry.

"Yes. We found her, Santo."

"Then what did you see?"

"It was about me."

"What did you see," Santo repeated himself, his level of anxiety rising.

"Nothing for you to worry about, my friend."

"Did you see Genevieve?" Santo did not want to let the subject drop until he knew what Mr. Albert saw.

"No, I did not see Genevieve. She has gone away. Genevieve doesn't need me anymore."

"You saved her..."

"How did I save her? We are relocating her. The dead don't care. The dead don't care," Mr. Albert said, dropping his head to his hands.

Santo put his hand on Mr. Albert's shoulders.

"I am sure she cares. I am sure she is grateful to you. But you look tired. Let's get you back to the motel room. We could come back tomorrow."

"No," Mr. Albert implored, standing up quickly.

He lost his balance, and Santo steadied him. He brushed off Santo's hands, needing to stand by himself.

"No," Mr. Albert repeated. "I do not need to come here again, not yet. I have done what I have set out to do. I have fulfilled my purpose. See how happy I am. This is what accomplishment looks like, Santo. This is what you wanted."

He staggered away from the grave but only managed a few steps before falling to the ground. Santo came to his aid and lifted him.

"Yes, you are right, Mr. Albert. We are done here. We will go back and rest up. You will have another dream in a few days, and we will be off on a different adventure. You will see. You will see, Mr. Albert."

~ 85 ~

At the motel room.
One week later.

Mr. Albert would not visit Genevieve's grave for fear of being buried again by weird gravediggers. He wanted to be alone with Genevieve so that she would forgive him. He understood that would never happen, and going to the Georgia State Hospital, whether to the buildings or the graveyards, would only leave him open to attack by visions of his self-hatred. Deep down, he knew that he did not deserve forgiveness.

Santo would spend a couple of hours each day with Professor Rosetti, filling in paperwork, contacting state officials, and arranging for the remains, when exhumed, to be genetically tested. Mr. Albert spent that time flipping through channels on the television or sleeping. He did not have the energy or the desire to do anything else. After Santo's return, they went out for something to eat, and if Mr. Albert felt strong enough, they would sit on a bench on the college campus and watch how lovely the world was.

Santo opened the door quietly; in case Mr. Albert was sleeping. He was watching an episode of "House."

"Bet you couldn't figure out what's wrong with me," Mr. Albert mumbled bitterly.

"Mr. Albert," Santo said. "Look who has come to visit with you."

Mr. Albert turned his head to look. Michael Skillen stood in the doorway, smiling.

"Mr. Albert, you old bastard. You did it. You found Genevieve." Skillen laughed as he went to hug Mr. Albert.

"What are you doing here?" Mr. Albert asked.

"I had to formalize the request with Professor Rosetti. I also had to go to the hospital for the DNA test," Michael said.

"They are going to exhume the body tomorrow. We should have the results by the end of the week," Santo added.

"That's good," Mr. Albert said quietly.

"You don't seem all that excited."

"I am. I'm just a little tired, that's all."

"Mr. Albert is saving his energy for our next adventure," Santo covered for his friend.

Mr. Albert turned back to the television and raised the volume. Michael and Santo looked at each other. Michael did not know what to think. Mr. Albert had changed so much since the last time they saw each other. Santo nodded at Michael with sad recognition.

"Mr. Albert, do you want to show Michael where we found Genevieve," Santo suggested.

"No, I'm okay."

"But I came all this way, and I want you to show me where you found her," Michael said.

"That's okay. Santo can show you."

Michael and Santo exchanged glances again. Santo tried one more time.

"Please, Mr. Albert, for me," Santo pleaded.

"Then we will go and get something to eat. Any hot dog places in town?" Michael asked.

Mr. Albert wanted to be left alone but realized these intruders would give him no peace until all this nonsense was done.

"Sure," Mr. Albert said. "Whatever you'd like."

He struggled to sit up in bed. Santo and Michael helped him up. They got him dressed, then went off to show Michael, Genevieve's resting place.

~ 86 ~

By Genevieve's grave.

Thirty minutes later.

They stood silently in front of the tree where Genevieve lay hidden. Minutes passed. Birds sang. Leaves rustled in the wind. Small woodland creatures moved about in the fallen leaves, hiding from the visitors.

"I don't know what to say to thank you," Michael said.

"Then don't say anything."

"The silence does not seem to be enough."

"The silence is all there is," Mr. Albert said.

"He just wants to thank you, Mr. Albert," Santo explained.

"He did that."

"I know."

"Does your thanks improve upon the silence?"

"No."

"Then let the silence be enough."

Mr. Albert stared at the ground in front of the tree. The grave will soon be uncovered, and Genevieve's body removed. Mr. Albert will replace her in the earth. He looked up and thought he saw one of the gravediggers hiding behind a tree in the distance.

This grave was Genevieve's home for the last sixty years. What right did he have to move her? Her family did not want her. Why should she want to lie down next to the sister that shunned her in life? Genevieve loved her mother, though. Maybe that was enough.

"Did you carve the heart in the tree?" Michael asked.

"Yes," said Mr. Albert, still lost in thought.

"Do you remember carving it?"

"No. It could have been someone else."

"Of course, it was him," Santo interjected. "BB is Benny Benton. You loved her."

Santo looked around and saw a stone on the ground. He picked it up and put it on Genevieve's grave as a sign of respect. Michael picked up a stone as well.

"Don't do that, please," Mr. Albert's voice showed more power than he had in weeks.

"Why?" Michael asked.

"What's the matter?" asked Santo.

"I don't want the spirits to take Genevieve before we get her to safety."

He removed the stone from the grave and threw it deeper into the woods. At that moment, Mr. Albert realized there was a reason to move her.

"Best not to attract the evil eye," Mr. Albert said as he scanned the woods for spirits.

Santo and Michael exchanged glances.

"Mr. Albert is tired," Santo pointed out. "Let's get some hot dogs before they run away."

"They must be some really fresh hot dogs," Michael joked.

They helped Mr. Albert into the car. His gaze remained on the woods as they drove off.

~ 87 ~

In the motel room.
Two days later.

Mr. Albert had grown weaker. There was no reason to get out of bed. The remains in the grave were Genevieve's. She would be home soon. All was right in the world. And Mr. Albert's job was done.

Santo sat by Mr. Albert's bed and read a book, monitoring his friend while he slept. He lost interest in the book several chapters ago and only kept reading to keep himself focused. Santo was glad when Mr. Albert opened his eyes.

"How are you feeling?" Santo asked.

Mr. Albert tried to swallow, but it was difficult. Santo gave him some water. He took small tastes and, after three sips, held up his hand to indicate he had had enough. Santo put the glass back on the nightstand and smiled at Mr. Albert.

"Would you like anything else?"

Mr. Albert smiled and shook his head no.

"Thank you," Mr. Albert said softly.

"You're welcome," Santo replied. "Are you hungry? Want some Lucky Charms?"

Mr. Albert shook his head no.

"Fruit Loops?"

"Sure."

Santo opened the single-serving box and poured the cereal into a bowl.

"Want milk?"

"No, thank you," Mr. Albert's breathing slowed down.

Santo filled up the plastic spoon with the cereal.

"Just the orange ones," Mr. Albert said.

Santo emptied the cereal back into the bowl and scooped up the orange circles. He put the spoon near Mr. Albert's lips, who ate them one at a time. When they finished the orange rings, Mr. Albert requested the yellow ones. He gave up after only a few of them.

"Do you still believe in God, Santo?" Mr. Albert asked after his meal.

"Yes, Mr. Albert. Of course, I do. Why?"

"How come you don't say Ay Dios Mío anymore?"

"I don't say it because I no longer question God. I know he is here with me all the time."

"How do you know that?"

"Because he sent you to me."

Mr. Albert laughed, "I'm your proof of the existence of God?"

"Yes."

"How?"

"Because you are a miracle, Mr. Albert. There is no reason for you to exist, but you do."

"Why do I exist, Santo?"

"There are always mysteries in life, but God is constant. That is all I need to know. Because I love him."

"Do you love me, Santo?"

"Yes, I do, Mr. Albert. Why would you ask that?"

"Because I do not know if anyone ever has."

"That is silly," Santo scoffed. "Plenty of people have loved you. You have lived for thousands of years."

"I am not a very nice person."

"Everyone at Pinkie Masters loves you."

"I bought them drinks."

"Regardless. Love exists in us if we allow it to exist. It is entirely up to us."

"That is just it, Santo. What if I never allowed it in? What if I was too afraid?"

"Do you love me?"

"I don't know."

"After all the things we have been through, you still don't know?"

"You won't kiss me if I say I do?"

"No worries about that."

"I guess I do, then."

"You guess?"

"I do."

"That's more like it."

"Was it really important to say it?"

"To me, it was."

"Okay," Mr. Albert closed his eyes for a moment. He opened them again. "Can you do me a favor?"

"Of course."

"Can you bury me in Genevieve's grave?"

"Don't you want to be buried beside Genevieve back in Savannah?"

"I want to be, but I don't deserve to be."

"Of course, you deserve to be."

"My demons have not yet forgiven me."

"You just have to forgive yourself."

"I cannot. Thank you for the Fruit Loops. How slowly life moves, even in death."

Mr. Albert closed his eyes and never reopened them.

Santo stayed with him for a week, but Mr. Albert remained dead, dead, dead. Dead cubed did not seem as funny as it used to be. Santo followed Mr. Albert's wishes and buried him close to the tree with the initials BB & GB.

$$\sim 88 \sim$$

The Skillen Family Plot.
Greenwich Cemetery.
One week later.

The cemetery workers finished lowering Genevieve's remains into the ground between her sister and her mother. Michael, Santo, Tessie, Brian, Mustang Pete, Porno Rick, and Jimmie had come for the ceremony. Each took a turn tossing a few shovels full of dirt onto the plain pine casket before passing the shovel to the next mourner. The shovels made their way back to the workers, who finished the job unceremoniously in five minutes. The friends stood in silence while the workers packed up and left.

It was a while before anyone said anything.

"Welcome home, Aunt Genevieve," Michael said.

"Welcome home," the rest of them agreed.

"Pity Mr. Albert isn't around to see this," Santo said.

"Pity," the rest of them agreed in their own way.

"Why did he die?" Tessie asked.

"He couldn't live any longer," Santo said.

"What will you do now?" asked Michael. "Go back to New Jersey?"

"I don't think so," Santo said. "Professor Rosetti said he needed help identifying remains and returning them to their families. I might do that for a while."

"That would be nice of you, Santo," Tessie smiled.

"You are a good man," Michael agreed with Tessie.

"They let you bury him at the hospital?" Brian asked.

"They did not know. Tyler and some of his friends helped me in the middle of the night."

"So, was he a zombie?" asked Mustang Pete.

"No," Santo replied.

"And he wasn't a ghost?" Pete asked a follow-up question.

The rest of the group looked at him.

"No," said Santo.

"But how was he walking around? That is all I'm asking," Pete insisted.

"It's a mystery," Porno Rick responded, using Mr. Albert's words.

"Does it matter?" asked Jimmie. "We measure a man by his actions, not by medical definitions."

"And he was a man, all right, a true bastard," Michael smiled.

The group smiled. Mr. Albert was a true bastard.

Michael pulled out a flask and took a slug. Brian looked at Michael and held out his hand. Michael passed the flask.

"It would have been nice, been simple if he just told us why though," Jimmie said, pulling his flask out and having a drink.

Brian passed Michael's flask to Tessie before reaching out to Jimmie. Jimmie handed Brian his flask.

"Life is not simple; life is mysterious. Simple is for simpletons," Porno Rick pulled out a flask and had a drink.

Brian passed his flask to Michael and signaled to Rick that he was parched. Rick gave Brian his flask. Tessie passed Michael's flask to Mustang Pete.

"All I know was that he was a lovely man, and I will miss him," Tessie said, wiping a tear from her eye.

She took out her bottle and had a slug before passing it to Brian, who already had his hand out. Brian passed Porno Ricks' flask to Tessie. Mustang Pete passed his flask to Porno Rick. Michael gave his flask to Jimmie.

"It's a mystery," Mustang Pete pulled out his flask.

Mustang Pete knew the drill and, after a quick gulp, passed his flask to Brian, who passed his flask to Tessie, who passed her flask to Porno Rick, who gave his flask to Michael. Jimmie passed his flask to Mustang Pete. They continued taking a drink and then passing whatever bottle they had.

"He was a good man," Tessie threw down an empty bottle to punctuate her statement.

"He tried to do what was right," Michael threw his empty bottle down.

"He treated everyone equally," Mustang Pete said, tossing his bottle.

"He always paid his tab," Jimmie said, dropping his bottle

"He was my friend," Santo said, finishing his bottle and dropping it to the ground.

The group stood there wobbling slightly and nodding in agreement. Mr. Albert was everyone's friend. They loved him.

Brian reached into his pocket and pulled out his flask. He tilted his head back and finished off the alcohol without sharing. When he threw his empty bottle to the ground, the others were looking at him.

"What? I was thirsty!"

They shook their heads and headed back to the Pinkie Masters, leaving Brian alone. Even his wife left him. He stumbled off after Tessie.

"Okay. The first round is on me."

~ 89 ~

Sometime in the future.

Santo helped Professor Rosetti with his work. He enjoyed returning the remains of the patients to their relatives. Mr. Albert had indeed given Santo his life's purpose.

Professor Rosetti retired after three years. By that time, Santo was qualified to continue the work. By the time Santo retired, he had helped one hundred and twenty-seven families, including Dot from the consignment store, find closure.

Santo often drove to Savannah to visit his friends at Pinkie Masters. Mustang Pete died of a heart attack one day. Fell right off his seat and was dead by the time he hit the floor. Jimmie fell in love and got married. He left Pinkie Masters for a job at Amazon to support his growing family. Porno Rick moved to Japan to be closer to the anime pornography community but eventually lost interest and ended up working for a covert internet hacking group that brought down several Russian oligarchs. Brian and Tessie moved to Alabama to be closer to her family. Michael and Santo were the only ones left. Michael became interested in Rosetti's organization and wrote for the Historical Society's newsletter, and would often visit Santo in Milledgeville.

What Santo liked doing most was visiting with Mr. Albert. The cemetery was peaceful and always put him in a happy frame of mind. He and Mr. Albert had gone on a great adventure, solved a mystery, and brought Genevieve home. He had given Mr. Albert a purpose and, eventually, peace. He never discovered how Mr. Albert could live while being dead, but that didn't matter. Not all mysteries need to be solved. Not every "t" needs to be crossed. Not every "i" needs to be dotted. It is only an "i." It is only a "t." And we are only people.

~ 90 ~

Sometime further in the future.

Another peaceful day. The temperature peaked at 120 degrees, which was cool for this time of year. Trees in this area had been burnt by the wildfires that swept through two years before. It used to be a graveyard. The graves were removed by developers who wanted to put in two hundred single-family homes, but that was before the floods. Now squatters camped out here when they did not want to be disturbed.

Life goes on. Squirrels hide and then forget about their nuts. Hawks eat the squirrels, and their remains fertilize the forgotten nuts, which, after a frosty winter, break through the frozen earth, and life begins again.

A new sprout grew in the shadow of a broken tree, its tiny stem reaching for the sun. Just as you would think that the plant might have a chance to survive, the earth started rumbling. The ground began to heave up and down like a person having difficulty breathing. Suddenly, the earth cracked, and a finger broke the surface. Then two fingers. Then a hand pushed its way through the dirt and rose to the sun. Behind the hand, the broken tree stood knowingly with the charred inscription; BB loves GB.

Acknowledgements

There are many people who have helped me with this book.

My Monday night writers' group for your encouragement on the work I brought to the group. My Beta readers, Jill and David Weiner, Amber Antill, Gina Causey, Jennifer Santmeyer, Megan Stauch, and Electra Nanou from Book Breath. You have helped me look at my book from many viewpoints.

My dear writer friends, Carol Webster, Regina Williams, and Syril Kline, for the constant guidance and support of my writing.

I would also like to thank Shari Stauch, owner of Main Street Reads, creator of the Main Street Reads writer's group, and driving force behind Writers Win. My mentor and friend. The lessons she taught me about the art and the business of writing might be ignored, but will never be forgotten.

My kids, Eliza, Juliet, and Helena. Everything I write, I write for you. Hopefully, some of my words will give you a better understanding of how truly confused your father has been.

My dog, Millie, who always finds a place underneath my chair when I am writing, letting me know that when I am done creating for the day, I have to return to the real world and take her for a walk.

A.F. Winter has written books on the theatre and numerous plays, winning the South Carolina Playwright's Festival. This is his fifth published novel. He has also written several books of poetry. He lives near Charleston, SC, with his dog, Millie, and is overjoyed when one of his three exceptional daughters comes to visit.

Learn more at www.afwinter.com.

Other books by A.F. Winter

Theatre Builds Character
The Actor, the Script, and the Ox
A Walk in the Valley
I Am Vincent
Happy
Cinderella's End
Ireland in Black and White (with Sam Beckett)
Sleeping With Macbeth
In Love's Twilight
She Does It All
Man in the Pandemic

Learn more at www.afwinter.com.